On Fire's Wings

CHRISTIE GOLDEN

LUNA

www.LUNA-Books.com

LUNA

First edition July 2004

ON FIRE'S WINGS

ISBN 0-373-80208-0

Copyright © 2004 by Christie Golden

This edition published by arrangement with Harlequin Books S.A.

® and TM are trademarks of Harlequin Books S.A., used under license. Trademarks indicated with ® are registered in the United States Patent and Trademark Office, the Canadian Trade Marks Office and in other countries.

www.LUNA-Books.com

Printed in U.S.A.

This book is dedicated to every woman who has feared her own power…and embraced it anyway

ACKNOWLEDGMENTS:

I would like to gratefully acknowledge the help and inspiration provided by the following people:

Robert Amerman and Mark Anthony,
for being such terrific "wise readers"
Lucienne Diver and Mary-Theresa Hussey,
for their enthusiasm and faith in this project
Michael Georges, my deeply supportive husband
Anastacia Chittenden, Lila Tresemer, Katherine Roske
and all the women who have walked
the Path of the Ceremonial Arts,
for opening so many hearts to the Divine Feminine

…and my wonderful readers, past, present and future.

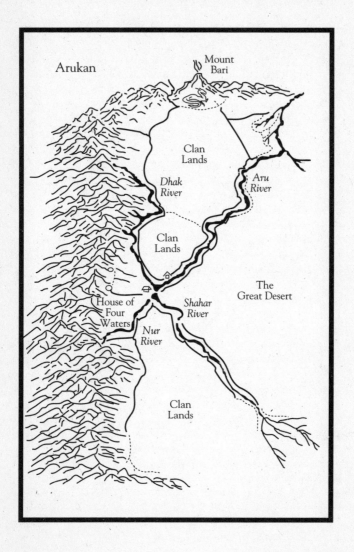

Arukan

Mount
Bari

Clan
Lands

*Dhak
River*

*Aru
River*

Clan
Lands

The
Great Desert

House of
Four
Waters

*Shahar
River*

*Nur
River*

Clan
Lands

Prologue

The wind, cold and scented with death, seized the queen's hair with cruel fingers and set it to dancing. Two weeks before, despite the queen's years and the children she had borne, that long, thick hair had been only touched with gray. Now, there was little ebony left in the mane. The white of fear and resignation had swallowed the black, as the Shadow that loomed on the horizon had swallowed everything in the world save this lone castle and the few terrified souls it still housed.

She was tall, and stood tall even now, staring not at the rolling fields and forests and streams that would have met her gaze a fortnight past but at a pulsing blackness that mocked her defiance. She leaned forward, resting her hands on the cool strength of the stones that formed the wall of the parapet's balcony. This, at least, was real, was solid— for the moment.

"It's only been two weeks," came a soft voice. The queen glanced down at the beggar boy who stood beside her, staring as raptly at the Shadow as she. There was puzzlement in the young voice, as if he, like the queen, could not truly believe that so much had happened in so brief a time. She closed her eyes, straightened, and her hands left the reassuring stone to wrap the thick embroidered cloak more closely about her frame.

"Less than that, little Lorekeeper," she replied.

He did not say anything further, but she knew what he was thinking as if he had shouted it aloud: *I didn't know in time.* Etched upon her memory, for the brief while she had left to live, was the look on the boy's grimy face as he forced his way through crowds and guards with reckless determination. He had clutched desperately at her robe, uttering the words that chilled her to the bone: *The Dancer needs help!*

But the warning from the suddenly awakened memory of the base-born Lorekeeper had come too late, the queen thought bitterly, though it was no fault of the child's. The wind stung her face, brought tears to her eyes. She blinked them back. Too late to save the Dancer, too late to salvage their own existence; too late, too late.

Following the boy, the king, accompanied by an elite group of guardsmen and his best healers, had stumbled across the body in an alleyway exactly as it had appeared to the boy in his vision. The Dancer, a youth as well-born as the Lorekeeper was base, had been robbed and murdered. His powers—probably unknown to him yet, he was terribly young—had not been sufficient to protect him. But he had rallied enough to exact revenge upon his slayer, it appeared, for the killer's body was little more than a charred skeleton. The Dancer's pouch, still filled with coins, lay a little distance away.

The king returned from his grim mission, seeming to her suddenly old, to tell his wife the story. With him was the boy, still clad in the vermin-riddled clothes of the streets, his thin body shaking and bowed with the weight of the world.

"It is not your fault, my child," the queen had soothed, fighting back her own rage and despair. "You went for help as soon as you knew. The blame for...for what will come must lie with the man who murdered the Dancer."

And who had, in that one greedy, violent act, destroyed their only hope to avert oblivion.

Not long after that, the king had ridden off to fight the Shadow, their son, still young, still unbloodied by war, at his side. The queen had kissed the hollow-eyed man who had once been passionate and proud; kissed her round-cheeked son, who was naive enough to think this a real battle, not a suicide.

And as they rode off, the queen thought with a spark of contempt: *Cowards!*

They did not have to sit and mind a castle full of terrified merchants, farmers, and beggars. They did not have to watch the death of everything creep closer by the hour. They ran to meet their doom, thus cheating it of the terror it doubtless craved.

The queen's eyes narrowed and she stuck out her sharp chin defiantly.

She was the last queen of the world. It was up to her now, how they would all die. She reached out to the Lorekeeper, slipping her arm around his shoulders. By the hitching and shuddering of those shoulders, she knew he wept.

"You alone will remember," she said softly.

The Shadow pulsed, coming nearer. It stretched upward, seething. Soon even the sky would be gone.

"I—I don't want to," the little Lorekeeper whispered. He dragged an oft-mended sleeve across his wet face.

"But you must," she continued, her voice still quiet, still calm. "You are a Lorekeeper. You remember all that has gone before—all the other times when the Dancers have come and lost, or won. You would have been drawn to that Dancer had he lived, even as you were drawn to him in his death. You would have been able to help and guide him to the others, but... This time, the Dancers have failed. Yet there were times when they succeeded, and their success has bought us a final chance."

The wind picked up. For an instant, forgetting herself, the queen reached up to smooth her tousled hair. *The knots will take Ahli hours to untangle,* came the simple, everyday thought. But Ahli tended the princess now, caring faithfully for the mad girl whose mind would not let her see the Shadow. The queen would not look upon her daughter again. That last time had been enough. She could not bear to watch the gentle, once-intelligent girl sit and babble, rubbing her swollen stomach and chirping happily of the son-to-be. The son who would, now, never be born.

Such simple problems as tangled hair were things of the past. The queen let the wind have its way with her once-raven locks.

"Your Majesty."

Her seneschal. The queen turned. "Yes?"

He stood in the doorway, clasping and unclasping his hands as he searched for the words. As it turned out, they were simple enough, if brutal. "The well...it's gone dry."

The queen closed her eyes, forcing her face to be tranquil. "Then let us open the wine cellars. I would not see my people without something to wet their throats." And perhaps the drunkenness would take away the sting. Not long, not long now.

"And light all the torches," she added. "Build fires." She

turned again, her gaze drawn to the encroaching Shadow. "Let us keep the light as long as we may."

The man bowed, retreated. They were alone again on the parapet, beggar and queen, staring out as if mesmerized at their approaching destruction.

"Twice failed," whispered the Lorekeeper in a voice that cracked with fear and an ancient grief. "Twice succeeded. Only one more chance."

"The fifth time the Dancers come," agreed the queen, "will be our final chance. Eternal salvation...or nothing at all, ever again. It may well fall to you," she said with a quiet urgency. "Do not forget."

"I won't," the boy promised. "I won't."

She folded him close, held him, as she would her own son. He was their hope. He, and the other Lorekeepers, and the Dancers who would not yet be born for another five thousand years.

The Shadow stretched, languidly.

The twin suns went out.

PART I

In the House of Four Waters

Chapter One

The day was hot, and lines at the public well in the marketplace were long. Brown faces shone with sweat, save where the dust had clung, turning bronze skin a shade paler. In the distance, false oases beckoned, their shimmering heat lines tricking the unwary into traveling just a little farther, just a little more.

People talked, among themselves, haggling with merchants, or crying their wares. Horses jangled their tack, blew and stamped impatiently. The reek of horse and dung vied with the rich fragrances of cooking meats, the tangy scents of fresh fruits, and the sweet, heady aroma of a variety of incense and spices.

This marketplace was the most elaborate in the land. Merchants came from all over Arukan to sell their goods. In one booth were fine daggers and swords, with intricately carved hilts and embroidered sheaths. In another, an artisan displayed carefully crafted jewelry to high-caste women. Unable to afford a booth, a man in his middle years had spread out a carpet in front of the jewelry seller. His pots were beautiful, but he did not appear to be selling many. By contrast, the weaver's booth across from the potter and the jeweler was crowded, and customers exclaimed over her blankets, carpets, saddle tack, and horse regalia.

By far the most popular vendor, today as every day, was the wizened, toothless little man who crafted charms. The jeweled pendant, cleverly fashioned to look like an amber eye with a slit pupil, would make the Great Dragon, guardian of the Arukani, look upon one with favor. And the necklace that was a small mirror would reflect the evil gaze of the demonic *kulis*. It also, as one woman was proving, was useful for making sure nothing was lodged in one's teeth.

Other things were for sale, too—roasting meats, fresh and preserved fruits and vegetables, breads, clothing, toys and games, and services of all varieties.

Kevla took a small sip from her waterskin. An unkind soul might have used the word "scrawny" to describe the ten-year-old, but there were muscles beneath the loose *rhia* that draped her body. Her hair, reddish in the harsh sunlight, was pulled back into a braid that fell the length of her back. Her eyes, almost too large in her small, sharp face, missed nothing. Kevla knew the visitors to the marketplace well, and if Keishla had earned no coins today, the girl knew that it was hardly her fault.

Kevla had been calling since the first vendor opened for business shortly before dawn, and her parched throat was testimony to her hard work. She could, of course, stand in line for water at the well as others did, but that would take her away from her prized spot at the intersection of the two main streets. She might miss a customer. Better the thirst than her mother's wrath.

Keishla carried herself with a quiet, regal air. She was some-times unexpectedly gentle, and when she smiled, Kevla thought her beautiful. But more often Keishla would sit silently, her thoughts far distant from the present, and if Kevla interrupted her mother at such moments she knew Keishla would turn upon her, as if Kevla were the cause of all her pain. Kevla didn't understand, but she was wise enough to recognize these moods and be quiet when they were upon Keishla.

She permitted herself another miserly sip. The bag would have to last her throughout the day, and it was only mid-morning. Kevla retied the goatskin bag around her tiny waist, dragged a hand across her sweat-dappled forehead, took a deep, dusty breath, and resumed her task.

"Hey-la, hey-lo," she cried in a singsong voice. Her feet stamped in the dust, and her little body swayed with the rhythm of the chanting. "Hey-la, hey-lo! Sweeter than wine are the lips of Keishla! Keishla the fair, Keishla the wise, Keishla who knows what a man desires! Soft are the thighs of Keishla, and the dance of pleasure played out between them is known only to the most fortunate of men!"

She was engrossed in her cry now, and spread her arms, lifting the folds of the shabby, oft-mended *rhia* to reveal the toes of her bare, dirty feet. It was as far as she dared go. If she lifted the *rhia* to reveal a glimpse of calf or even ankle, she might be accused of practicing the same skills as her mother. That would not do. Those skills could be peddled in the marketplace, yes, but the actual conduct of business needed to be done in private. And Kevla, despite her words and knowing moves, was not skilled in such matters.

So Kevla, her eyes bright and darting about for anyone, male or female, who might be a potential customer, kept the *rhia* at its proper, yet tantalizing, length.

"You there, *uhlal*," she cried, invoking the term of high respect, "you look like a man who would enjoy sampling

Keishla's charms!" She pointed a finger at him, flashing teeth that were remarkably strong and white considering her poor diet.

The man looked about, stammering, "I—I—"

"Come, sir, lay your mighty staff in the sweet honeyed nest of passion!"

The man turned crimson, and too late Kevla realized that behind him, blocked from her short-statured view, walked a woman who was undoubtedly his wife. Quickly, the girl changed her approach.

"Hey-la, *uhlala!*" she addressed the woman, making a deep obeisance. "The beautiful Keishla will gladly teach what she knows to any woman, for the right fee. Will you come with me, and learn how to keep that man by your side from straying for all time? It is a small price to pay, hey?"

It was a desperate attempt to salvage the situation, and Kevla was not surprised when the woman glared at her and reached to clutch her husband's arm, steering him away from temptation.

Kevla sighed. But when the man cast a furtive, apologetic glance over his shoulder, her spirits lifted. Perhaps tomorrow, or the day after, he might come back and sample Keishla's "wares."

In the meantime, she was not finding her mother customers, and without customers, she would not eat. Kevla cleared her throat and was about to resume her chant when a flurry of movement down the wide, hard-packed dirt road caught her attention. A few stalls down, everyone was falling to their hands and knees, heads touching the ground, heedless of the dust. That could mean only one thing. A very high-ranking *uhlal* had decided to visit the market today instead of sending his servants. It happened, from time to time, and Kevla rejoiced. Occasionally, the *uhlals,* especially a *khashim,* one of the clan leaders, felt generous and scattered coins and jewels to the lower castes. Keishla had once spoken with scorn of the practice, claiming she'd rather keep her pride than scrabble in the dust for a *khashim's* amusement.

Kevla, who had been gnawing on a dried piece of three-day-old bread at the time of Keishla's statement, had said nothing. But she thought that one single gold *kha* would have bought a week's worth of food, and a week's worth of food just might be worth scrabbling in the dust for a *khashim's* amusement.

Praying to the Great Dragon that the approaching *uhlal* was in a generous mood, the girl quickly fell to her knees. She heard the clopping sounds of the horse's hooves as it approached, and strained her young ears for the tinkling of tossed coins.

That hoped-for sound did not come. Instead, the horse stopped in front of her. She stared at its hooves. Suddenly afraid, Kevla did what tradition and the mercilessly strict caste system practiced in her country absolutely forbade her to do.

She looked up.

And met the gaze of a tall, handsome man who seemed all the taller for being perched atop one of the most splendid horses Kevla had ever seen. The beast's sand-colored coat gleamed with careful grooming, not yet dulled by the dust of the day. It mouthed its bit impatiently, revealing gold-tipped tusks. Its striped legs and face were a rich loam hue, and its tack and saddle were decorated with beads and jewels. Its rider's fine clothes and proud pose bespoke his high caste.

He was clad in the man's short *rhia,* and the powerful legs that gripped the horse were covered with snug-fitting white silk breeches. Belt and boots were of finely tooled leather, and his dark hair was protected from the harsh rays of the Arukani sun by an embroidered kerchief. His face was clean-shaven, proof of his rank, for only _khashims_ shaved their beards. Gold earrings glinted, catching the sparkle of bright eyes that were now trained intently on Kevla. Fastened to the leather belt were an expensive sword and matching dagger. At a respectful distance, mounted on their own horses, two servants waited and watched.

"You cry the services of a _halaan,_" said the _khashim_ without preamble. His voice was a rich, deep rumble, quiet and self-assured. When Kevla stared up at him, transfixed, he gentled his tone further and said, "You may answer truly, child. None will punish you for your...impertinence."

Kevla swallowed hard. If her mouth had been dry earlier, now it seemed as vast a wasteland of drought as the Arukani desert itself. She tried again.

"Most honored _uhlal,_ great _khashim,_ I do indeed." A thought occurred to her and she ventured in a hopeful voice, "Perhaps my lord is interested in Keishla's services?"

The _khashim_ smiled at that, a smile that seemed to Kevla to be somewhat sad, which made no sense to her at all.

"Not her services, child, but I am indeed interested in Keishla. Are...are you her daughter, perchance?"

Kevla nodded.

His dark eyes roamed her face. Almost, she could feel his gaze like a physical touch as it glided across her small nose, large, dark eyes, and soft mouth. For an instant, she knew fear. Perhaps the man would want her instead of her mother. Some men, she knew, liked young flesh—very young indeed. Keishla had promised her daughter that she would never be used in such a manner. But if a _khashim_ came asking, with gold and jewels to offer...?

For the first time, Kevla was grateful for her mother's stubborn sense of pride. If Keishla would not go diving in the dust for coins for a *khashim's* amusement, then surely she would never give her daughter over for one's pleasure.

"I had thought as much," said the *khashim* softly, more to himself than to Kevla. He straightened and seemed to shake off his melancholy. "Take me to her. What is your name, child?"

"Kevla, great *khashim.*"

"Kevla what?"

A blush of shame rose in Kevla's cheeks. She hesitated for a moment, then replied softly, "Kevla Bai-sha." She hated the name. It literally meant "female without father," and was as unkind an epithet as "*halaan.*" Bai could and sometimes did hold various positions in society, but never high-ranking. They were permitted marriage, but only among themselves. Few Bai knew trades; who wanted to teach them? Most begged for the food that nourished them, counting on the shame of those who had perhaps fathered such misfits.

"But I think, great *khashim,*" continued Kevla, "that you knew that before ever you asked."

Again he smiled that sad smile, and nodded. "You are right, Kevla." He deliberately did not utter her mark of illegitimacy. For that she was grateful. Bad enough she had to suffer the jeers and taunts of others daily. Somehow, she felt very strongly that she did not wish to hear this large, powerful man calling her "Bai-sha."

He turned in his saddle toward his servants and said, "Leave us."

"But, most honored lord—" one protested.

"I said, leave us. And no word to your mistress. She need know nothing about this, and as I understand, both of you have families to feed."

The meaning was clear. The two servants inclined their heads and turned their mounts back toward the marketplace.

Kevla watched them go and smothered a smile.

"Shall we go?" said the *khashim*.

Kevla nodded, stepping forward into the dusty street to lead the way when suddenly she was seized and hauled upward. She had just tightened her limbs to struggle when she was plopped down in front of the great *khashim* himself. Startled, she craned her neck to look quizzically at him.

"We will make better time mounted," he said simply, as if he was not aware that he had just granted her status inappropriate to her caste.

"Great *khashim*," breathed Kevla, truly meaning the word now, "might a humble girl inquire as to your name?"

"I am *Khashim* Tahmu-kha-Rakyn, of the Clan of Four Waters."

Kevla's heart skipped a beat. The Four Waters Clan was the most powerful clan in Arukan. Their monopoly on the land in which two of the largest rivers of the country intersected granted them that status, and from all she had heard, Tahmu-kha-Rakyn was a worthy leader. What exactly Tahmu wanted from Keishla was still uncertain, but Kevla permitted herself to hope that it might bode well.

She told him which streets to take, and then indulged herself for a moment, enjoying the feel of the horse between her thighs. Her back was pressed against the firm torso of the greatest *khashim* in the land. She felt his steady breathing move her slightly forward and then back. From time to time as they rode, Tahmu would raise an arm as if to help the girl make sure of her unfamiliar seat.

There was nothing unchaste about the gesture, only an absent concern for her safety. The horse's beads and bells clattered and jingled, and his mane under Kevla's brown fingers was silkier than any she had ever touched.

For a brief, daydreaming instant, Kevla fancied herself the daughter of the great *khashim*. The servants who attended him would hark to her offhanded commands as well, should she utter them; a horse as fine as this one awaited her in a stable that was more elegant than her home. This was a pleasant outing among the lower castes, nothing more, and soon she would return to the opulence of a great House, to the delights of a bath—a *bath*—of precious water and richly scented soap....

But all too soon, they had left behind the sounds and smells of the crowded marketplace, and were making their way along a hard-packed earth road. Those who could afford to do so lived near the few natural springs and rivers that prevented Arukan from being a total wasteland. Their clansfolk lived near the house of their *khashim,* some in brick and stone buildings, many more in elaborate tents that served as a home that could be broken down to travel with their leader on the not-uncommon raids.

The poorest of the poor, those of the lowest castes, lived on the fringes of their clan leader's lands or near the marketplaces that provided their living. They, too, had tents, but theirs were miserable things. Many times when a sandstorm rose out of the heart of the desert, it would leave behind the wreckage of the inadequate shelters—and of the people who had dwelt in the flimsy tents.

Toward such a grouping of tents rode Kevla and her unusual companions. Her dreamy smile faded, to be replaced by the carefully guarded expression she wore almost constantly. Without waiting for assistance, she slipped off the still-walking horse and approached a small tent. It would hold only two or three people, in contrast to the clanspeople's tents, which provided room for a family of ten or twelve. Its sides and roof were made of goatskin, and a faded blanket hung over the entrance. Kevla lifted the blanket and scurried into the tent.

"Mama!" she whispered excitedly. "Mama, wake up!"

Careless of Keishla's possible anger, Kevla plopped herself down on the pillows beside the sleeping *halaan*.

Keishla rolled over, rubbing at her eyes. "Kevla, you had best have someone out there for me," she warned, yawning.

"Oh, I do. And such a someone!" Kevla rocked back on her heels, hugging herself happily. "I was calling in the market, and I heard a horse, and everyone bowed down, and it was a *khashim,* and he seemed pleased when I talked about you and he's here, with his horse and his servants, except he sent them away, and he gave me a ride, and—"

"A *khashim?* Are you sure?"

Kevla stared, insulted. Could her mother really believe that Kevla wouldn't know a *khashim* when one rode right up to her? "Of course I'm—"

Kevla's mother startled her by reaching out suddenly to embrace her. The girl tensed at first—blows were more frequent within the walls of this tent than embraces—then relaxed into Keishla's arms. Keishla smelled of sweat, hers and that of her customers, but the perfume she wore managed to cover the worst of it. And her thin body was soft. Hesitantly, Kevla reached her arms up and hugged back, closing her eyes happily.

"We will eat well tonight and for many nights, my daughter," said Keishla, stroking Kevla's braid. She pulled back and began fiddling with her own raven locks, plaited with beads. "Where is my clean *rhia?* Water, girl, quick!"

A grin on her face, Kevla hastened to obey, helping her mother into the flimsy white *rhia* reserved for special customers and pouring water into a brass bowl. Keishla laved her face quickly, slapping and pinching her cheeks and biting her lips to redden them. She could not afford the small ceramic jars of paint that more expensive *halaans* used, but Kevla thought her mother prettier than any artificially decorated woman.

Now Keishla turned to her daughter, spreading her arms. "Well? How do I look?"

Tears pricked Kevla's eyes. There was a happy warmth in Keishla's voice, an animation in her movements, that Kevla hadn't seen in a long time.

"Like a goddess of desire, worthy of the highest *uhlal* in the land," she replied, using one of the phrases that was part of her repertoire.

Mockingly, Keishla slapped her with a teasing hand. There was no sting, only a brush of palm on face.

"Silly child. Here, wait…" She hastened to the pillows on the carpeted earth and positioned herself. "Now…now you can show him in."

Kevla composed her face. When she emerged, she again bowed low.

"Most honored *khashim,* the beautiful and many-talented Keishla awaits you."

When she glanced up, veiling her gaze with her lashes, she could not decipher the expression on his face. Kevla had led dozens, perhaps hundreds, of men here. None of them had looked the way Tahmu did at this moment. He did not look shy, or frightened, as the young ones did. But neither did he appear to be excited and full of anticipation. He looked wary, strained, yet hopeful.

Very strange were the *khashim* indeed.

He slipped off his horse, shaking his head when Kevla reached for the reins. "He will not leave, and no one would dare steal him."

He reached into a small pouch hanging from his belt and produced a coin.

"Most honored *khashim,* it is Keishla who should receive your payment."

"I—I will pay her at the appropriate time. This is for you."

She stared at the silver coin on his brown palm. Fear of

the great man, put aside during the pleasant ride here, now resurfaced. Keishla had told her daughter that some men had certain curious desires. Kevla had always before given her mother privacy with her customers, and truth be told Kevla had no desire to see Keishla at work, but she did not know how to refuse Tahmu.

"Great *khashim*—it is my mother who—"

Comprehension dawned on the handsome face and his dark brows drew together. Kevla shrank from the expression.

"By the Great Dragon!" Tahmu cried. "Don't tell me your mother has put you to—child, no, this is to thank you for bringing me here and to ask that you leave us for a time. That is all."

She smiled in relief, taking the coin and bowing. "Then I thank you, and I shall leave you to your pleasure."

She turned and strode off to amuse herself elsewhere. She did not look back, but her sharp ears caught the rustle of the blanket as it was lifted and fell back into place. As she walked the circumference of the tent village, Kevla's mouth began to water as she imagined the delightful food she and Keishla would enjoy together.

Keishla reclined on the cushions with her back to the *khashim*. Languidly, she stretched, revealing slim curves. Tahmu's eyes roamed over her body, relishing this moment—this moment when he saw her but she did not see him.

She rolled over, and the lascivious smile of welcome on her face vanished. She bolted upright, her eyes grew enormous, and one thin hand went to her throat. Her lips parted slightly, but no words came out.

Tahmu waited. He would let her speak first. She deserved that much. At last, Keishla found her voice.

"After ten years of whoring," she said slowly, her voice

cold as stone and bitter as poison, "Kevla brings me a *khashim*. And it is you. The Great Dragon does love a jest."

Tahmu's throat worked, but he did not answer. He walked slowly toward the *halaan* and knelt on the cushions beside her. His face was only a few inches from Keishla's. With a growl like that of a hurt beast, Keishla raised her hand and cracked it across Tahmu's face.

Tahmu only smiled. "I deserved that," he said.

Keishla began to cry, softly, and that sound pained him more than the sting of her blow.

"I used to dream of this. That one day, you would come to me. I used to know what I would say, what I would do. But now here you are and I have no words...Why did you do it? I would have crawled across the desert on my hands and knees for you, Tahmu, you know that! And now, look, look at what you have done to me, look how far I have fallen...."

Gently, Tahmu folded her into his strong arms. She clung to him, the soft sobs increasing in force, racking her bony frame. For a long time, they sat thus, then Keishla drew back, wiping at her wet face.

"You should have come to me when you knew," Tahmu said. His brown hands gripped her upper arms tightly. "I would have taken care of you. I would never have let..." He gestured, at the poor tent, at her indecent clothes. "I would never have let you fall into this."

Keishla laughed at that, bitterly. "Life as your concubine, living in the shadows, sharing you with...*her*...." She shook her head. Her beaded locks clattered with the movement. "And you could not have given me what I needed the most—a name for the girl."

"I had a responsibility to the Clan," said Tahmu, restating what they both already knew, had argued about so long ago. "Had I been third son, or even second, I might have defied my father, but I couldn't—not as the only heir. The Clan of Four Waters would have been ripped apart had I left my position for you. But I swear to you, Keishla, I did not know about the girl."

He hesitated, then claimed his responsibility. "I did not know I had a daughter."

Chapter Two

The word hung between them. Tahmu coughed, trying to regain his composure.

"There is much we need to discuss. Perhaps something to wet our throats...?"

Keishla looked down, quickly, then nodded. She rose from the pile of pillows with all the grace he remembered.

Silently, he cursed himself for yielding to impulse. He should not have come. Better to have sent Sahlik, who had put this plan into motion. But he'd wanted to see the girl, to make certain. And that first glimpse of little Kevla, with her features a heartbreaking blend of his own strong visage and the more gentle countenance of Keishla, whom he had once loved with all his heart—who could have resisted that?

You could have, Tahmu reprimanded himself. *Which fe-*

male was it, Tahmu—your daughter or your lover that drew you here?

His eyes had now had time to adjust to the dimness after the dazzling light outside, and he realized his first impression of Keishla as dwelling in squalor had been misleading. The tent was roomy enough, and surprisingly well-furnished. The rugs that covered the earth were old, but finely crafted. He reclined on soft, comfortable cushions. He noticed that there was no equipment for such womanly tasks as making butter or bread. Keishla had only herself and the girl to feed, not a large, extended family. But in the corner, there were expensive-looking ewers, bowls, cups, and all the various pieces of equipment for making the bitter, hot drink *eusho*. Tahmu raised an eyebrow at that. At one point, Keishla must have been doing quite well.

Anger cut through him like a dagger. How many men had she lain with since him? What unspeakable acts had she performed? Did she look upon them with admiration, call them *uhlal*, cry out with pleasure as they took her for a handful—nay, perhaps only one or two!—copper coins?

As abruptly as it had crested, the anger ebbed, leaving only the ache of regret in its place. Tahmu had loved—still did love, there was no point in denying it—the woman who now set about preparing a beverage for the two of them, moving with the grace of a liquid-eyed *liah*. He had loved her as he had never loved his wife Yeshi. The marriage had been arranged by Tahmu's mother, as was her right, and the union had solidified a clan on the verge of splintering. But oh, to awaken next to Keishla each morning, and to have that pretty little girl-child chirping affectionately at him, playing with Jashemi in a happy, carefree way as two siblings should....

"It will take time to prepare *eusho*," said Keishla. "We will have tea instead."

Tahmu did not need to be a *kuli,* a demon, to be able to read Keishla's mind. She did not want him to stay.

"Tea would be welcome," he replied. She nodded curtly and continued her preparation.

An awkward silence descended. Abruptly, Tahmu had had enough of the forced courtesy, the tense pauses, the sharp words.

"I will say what I have come to say, and then let this be an end to it."

Keishla paused in her busy movements and turned to face him. He pointed to the cushions. For a moment, Tahmu thought she would say something, then instead, she settled herself quietly on the pillows, her face composed. A dark nipple appeared, then disappeared, brushing against the thin white fabric like something floating to the surface of the river only to submerge again. Tahmu's breath caught in his throat. Keishla could still make him ache with desire as Yeshi never had.

If only it had been different. He felt a flicker of angry mirth. If only horses could fly.

"There was a great passion between the two of us once, Keishla. But our love was forbidden because of the gulf between our castes. We must pay the price for daring to flaunt the ways of our people. You have already paid. You brought forth a child, unasked for, unwanted. And over the last eleven years you have sold your body to keep food in your daughter's mouth. Surely, even the Great Dragon must have forgiven you by this time.

"But the child has also suffered, for a sin that she did not commit. Keishla, you ever had a temper, and there is little doubt in my heart that you have raised your hand to her more often than was needed."

He held up a commanding hand, forestalling Keishla's denial. "I would not hear you lie, so be silent. I know, once-darling of my heart, that your anger was born of pain and frustration at me, and at what the girl represented. And that is a sin for which I must atone."

Keishla's color was high, but she was not contradicting him. That was good. If she knew how tenuous his control was at the moment, how his emotions threatened to boil over and destroy his calm demeanor, he would never be able to say what he needed to.

"One of my servants noticed Kevla in the marketplace two days ago. I wished to come then, but I feared what I might do. Only today have I calmed myself so that I might speak as befits a *khashim,* and not a lovesick boy."

He permitted himself a sad smile. Tears sprang to Keishla's eyes. Her own lips tentatively curved in response. Tahmu's heart jumped, but he forced himself to remain composed.

"I knew at once that Kevla was ours, conceived in love and born in disgrace, to serve as punishment for our transgression. You have atoned, Keishla. Now, it is my turn. I would take the child back with me, to—"

"*No!*" Keishla cried. "*Kulis* take you, son of a *skuura!* You took my love, you took my life, and now you want the only piece of you I have left to cling to? You did not lie with a docile *liah,* Tahmu, when you lay with me—you lay with a *simmar!*" Indeed, Keishla seemed as wild now as one of the dangerous desert cats that were the bane of the goat- and sandcattle-herders.

Tahmu replied calmly. "Think of the child," he said softly, "not of yourself."

"A child belongs with her mother!"

"A mother who does not want her? Who beats her? Who would raise her to be a *halaan?*" Had he struck her, Keishla could not have flinched more.

Tahmu's stomach twisted, but he continued mercilessly. "Keishla, you are too proud to accept help for yourself. Accept it for her. This I swear to you—she will never want for food or a safe place to sleep. No man will dare lay a hand on her without my permission. Her work will be light, and if she desires, perhaps I will.even have her educated."

For a long moment Keishla was silent. Her breasts heaved with anger, but when she spoke, her voice was frighteningly calm.

"You spoke of a servant. Was it Sahlik?"

Tahmu nodded.

Keishla swore. "She hated me, Tahmu. She did everything she could to keep us apart, and she was the one who convinced you to discard me as if I were a soiled *rhia.*"

"Sahlik only voiced what we all knew to be the truth—that we could never marry."

"Was it really the truth? Caste lines have been crossed before. It was Sahlik, right from the start, who decided that I was not good enough for you—she, a lowly five-score!"

"Blame Sahlik if you must, or blame me, who deserves it more. But give me the child."

Again Keishla was silent, staring at the carpet. Tahmu let her take her time. He would, he knew, get what he had come for. He always did.

"She—you will not make her a five-score, will you, Tahmu?" she said, referring to the traditional five slashes—"scores"—made on a servant's arm.

He shook his head. Though the law entitled him to make any servant a five-score, Tahmu preferred to keep to the initial purpose of the ritual scarring. The custom originated as a way of establishing dominance over captured prisoners of war. Any man, woman or child captured in battle would be honor-bound to serve the victorious clan leader for five years. The penance could be light or it could be grueling, depending entirely on the whims of the *khashim*. Each year, the prisoner/servant would receive a slash on the arm. At the end of five years, the final slash would be made and the prisoner returned to his people. He or she would be free, but the scars would remain, telling all who saw of the shame suffered by the bearer.

Finally, Keishla raised her eyes. They were cool, calm, free of tears. Tahmu couldn't read her expression. She rose and lifted the blanket, calling for Kevla. After a moment, Tahmu heard the girl's footfalls.

"Kevla, come inside."

"Of course, Mother." There was puzzlement in the girl's voice, a puzzlement that Tahmu shared. What was Keishla doing?

When Kevla had entered the tent and was sitting cross-legged on the floor, casting furtive glances at Tahmu, Keishla spoke.

"You are a smart girl, Kevla. You have no doubt guessed that the *khashim* knew me before you led him here."

Uncertainly, Kevla nodded. Tahmu frowned slightly. Where was this leading? Was Keishla going to tell Kevla her parentage? Tahmu desperately hoped not. The fewer who knew, the better, including Kevla herself.

"Because of the pleasure I have given him in years past, Tahmu has asked to take you with him to be a servant at the House of Four Waters." Kevla gasped, but before she could say anything Keishla had turned to Tahmu and said in that unnaturally calm voice, "We must discuss payment. Kevla performs a valuable duty when she cries my services in the marketplace. I shall have to hire a new girl."

Tahmu was taken aback. Out of the corner of his eye, he saw Kevla cringe. *Must you make her suffer even more?* Tahmu had thought better of Keishla and did not attempt to keep his displeasure from his voice.

"If you love gold better than the child, you will be amply

compensated." He reached in his pouch and tossed a handful of coins at her, contemptuously watching as she hastened to pick them up.

"That will cover the cost of a new girl," said Keishla, "but what of my silence?"

"You have kept silent thus far, *halaan!*" he exclaimed, taken aback by her insult. "Why should I fear your words now?"

Her lips curled in a smile that had no warmth in it. "There is the matter of your *khashima.* I do not think she would react well to having her husband's *halaan* show up at her door."

Tahmu got to his feet. His face nearly purple with rage, he emptied his pouch. Keishla laughed as the coins showered her upturned face. The *khashim* felt physically ill, and his memories of the woman turned sour as he watched her.

Enough of the mother. Time to think of the child. "Gather your things, girl, and let us be on our way."

Unsteadily, Kevla got to her feet. Her face was drained of color and her eyes were enormous. Then, as Tahmu watched, it seemed to him that a mask suddenly covered her face, rendering it impassive.

She shrugged slightly. "I have nothing of my own," she said simply. She was now composed, revealing none of the hurt she must be feeling. Such would have to be the shield of a Bai-sha, Tahmu reflected. He would say nothing more to Keishla. She had forfeited her right to kind words and gentle looks with her greed. But when she called his name as he was about to leave, he paused.

Kevla was already outside. "Wait for me by my horse," he told her. She nodded and padded up to the patient beast.

Tahmu let the blanket fall and turned around. A hard word was on his lips, but it faded like a drop of water before the heat of the sun at the look on Keishla's face.

Gone was the sly calculation. In its place was the expression of one who had lost everything. The coins lay where they had fallen, and tears coursed down her cheeks.

"We play parts, you know, for our customers," she whispered. "That...that was my best performance yet." She swallowed hard. "It will be easier on her, to think I wanted her gone. She loves me, Dragon knows why, and would not have gone with you, no matter how hard I would have beaten her or chided her...though she never needed a beating, not really...oh, Tahmu...."

All the love he thought quelled now rushed to flood Tahmu. Silent, shaking, he went to her, tangled strong fingers in her long, beaded hair, pulled her head back and kissed her. For an instant she was stiff in his arms, and then she yielded. Her arms snaked around his neck, and she opened the sweetness of her mouth to him. Her breasts crushed against his chest, and he could feel her heart racing as fast as his own. For a long, dizzying moment, he was not a *khashim*, but merely Tahmu, a youth hotly in love with the most beautiful woman he had ever seen, who took his passion and returned it a thousandfold.

Reluctantly, he pulled away, ending the kiss. They were both breathing heavily, and trembling, and for the first time since he had arrived he saw the young woman he had loved in Keishla's face and not the angry countenance of a bitter *halaan*.

He allowed himself one last caress, running his fingers over the sharp cheekbones and stubborn jaw, brushing them softly over her lips.

"You were ever my great love," he whispered.

Tears stood in Keishla's eyes. "And you mine, Tahmu. Will—will she know who she is?"

He shook his head. "No. The fewer who know such a secret, the better. You, Sahlik and I are the only ones."

She nodded. "It is safer that way, for you and for her, too. At least, while she is little. Promise me..."

"Anything," he answered, recklessly.

"When you judge the time to be right—when she is older—tell her who she is. Tell her she was conceived in love, the daughter of a *khashim,* not the fruit of a man who paid to lie with her mother. Tell her, her mother loved her enough to let her go, that it was never her fault when I grew angry and hit her. Will you do that for me?"

Emotion choked him and he could only nod. She smiled, slipped gently from his embrace and turned her back to him. It was harder than he had expected to step back and bring his attention to the present. Somehow he managed, taking a deep breath to steady himself. He pulled back the blanket, letting sun rush into the darkened tent. He glanced back one last time, marking the thick hair, the slim back and thighs, the bared feet, then turned and left.

Kevla stood beside the horse, reaching a cautious hand to pet its soft muzzle. The other hand wiped her face quickly. She did not want him to see her tears.

"Does he have a name?" she asked.

"Of course. His full name is Swift-Over-Sand, but I call him Swift."

"Hello, Swift," Kevla said softly. The horse blew against her fingers and she jerked them back, no doubt suddenly recalling Swift's gold-tipped tusks, then giggled delightedly. Tahmu smiled. For the first time since he had laid eyes upon the precocious child, she truly looked and acted like a ten-year-old girl.

"It is a long trip to the House of Four Waters," he said, reaching to pick her up and place her astride Swift. "We had best be on our way."

It was, in truth, not *that* long of a journey, not by horse-back. But Tahmu was used to galloping, and he knew that

Kevla was unfamiliar with riding, so for the most part, he held Swift to a walk. Tahmu had expected the child to be full of questions, but the parting with her mother had clearly affected her deeply. She would not, of course, bawl like a proper caste child at the separation and the cruel words with which Keishla had sent the girl on her way. Not a Bai-sha. After the one delighted outburst at the softness of Swift's muzzle, Kevla was quiet for a long time, saying nothing even when they passed through the heart of the marketplace, when she might have been expected to gloat just a bit.

Tahmu drew rein at a stall not far from where, earlier, Kevla had been crying her mother's wares and bought her a meat pie, rich with spices and candied fruits. If the shopkeeper recognized Kevla perched atop so magnificent an animal as Swift-Over-Sand, he gave no sign as he handed Tahmu the pastry with much bowing and averting of eyes.

Kevla accepted it with a deep nod and a polite, "Thank you, *Khashim* Tahmu." Once again, she confounded him. He had expected her to gobble it down. Instead, she ate daintily, taking small, ladylike bites although she must have been famished.

Whatever else, Keishla had trained the girl well in courtesy. Tahmu was glad. It would make integrating Kevla into his household that much easier.

They left the marketplace behind, passing through wide, flat areas of land where horses, goats, and other domesticated beasts were temporarily corralled. Livestock was for sale at the marketplace, too, at this time of year. Unable to help himself, Tahmu cast a quick glance over the beasts. Sorry, sickly things, most of them. They lay panting in the hot sun, their coats blotchy with sweat. Bones were visible beneath the skin, and even from this distance Tahmu could see their eyes were running with a thick, black ooze. The horses barely had enough energy to swish their tails at the flies that swarmed about them. It was better to trade directly with the Horserider Clan or the *Sa'abah* Clan than to pick up an animal here at the market.

And, Tahmu mused sourly, *it is better to trade with those clans than to fight with them.* Unfortunately, the choice was not always his.

They followed the road toward the mountain range that jutted skyward like a mouthful of broken teeth. Tahmu finally decided that this silence from the little sparrow of a girl he had seen dancing on the street corner was not to his liking, Bai-sha or no.

"Do you not have any questions as to your duties, little one?"

She sat in front of him as she had before, and his arm was a strong support about her waist. He felt her shrug against him.

"I am certain that the great *khashim* has head servants to explain my duties once I have arrived," she said, quite properly.

Tahmu sighed a little in exasperation. Chuckling, he said, "I do not know how to handle you, little one. If you were—" His voice caught. He coughed, as if dust had tickled his throat, and continued. "If you were my child, I would know. If you were the daughter of a stranger, I would know. If you were a servant, I would know. But you are none of these, and I touch you with my words as I touch a young hawk with my fingers—gingerly, with gloves, ready to jerk my hand back or pet you on the head."

That roused a giggle from her, as he had intended. Continuing the gentle joke, Tahmu patted the sun-warmed top of her head cautiously. The giggling increased.

"How curious your hair is, Kevla. Your mother's hair is black, as is—as is nearly everyone's. Yours seems black, but in the sun, it is red. Did your mother perchance use henna on it?"

"No. It's always been like that." She twisted to look at him, her eyes revealing a sudden fear. "Is—is that wrong?"

"No, no," soothed Tahmu. "Perhaps it is because you were out so often in the sun with no head covering. When we reach the House, you will be given proper clothing, as befits the servant of a *khashim*."

She lowered her eyes at that, her face clearly showing the struggle between fear and hope. Poor, lost little girl. He hoped she would be happy living at the House, and voiced that desire to her.

"They say many things about the noble *khashim's* great House," said Kevla, seizing upon the distraction. "Are they true?"

"Well, that depends on who 'they' are and what 'they' say."

"Oh, so many things! I have heard there is water, more water than anyone could ever drink. I have heard there is even water for *bathing,* hidden in a great cavern beneath the House. I have heard the walls are of glass, and many colored, and that you have strange beasts that can cross the desert with only a cupful of water!"

She turned again to face him. Her words came faster as her enthusiasm for the tales—some of them quite fabulous—came pouring out.

"I have heard it is cool in the House in the day and warm at night. I have heard there is feasting every single evening! I have heard that the birds are trained to sing songs on command, that your hunting dogs can outrun a horse, that your wife's beauty would blind a man if he did not look upon her with proper respect, that—"

Kevla's eyes were fixed on Tahmu's face. He knew he ought to discourage such familiar behavior, but he could not. Not today, not after the cruel but ultimately kind words Keishla had said. Time enough for Kevla to learn such things along with her other duties, once they had reached the House. So instead of rebuking her, Tahmu let the girl prattle on with her "I have heard" stories, smiling down as the tales grew more and more outrageous.

So intent was Kevla on recounting the stories, turned around in the saddle with her attention fully upon Tahmu, that she did not notice when the horse passed beneath a rock outcropping and made a sudden turn.

Tahmu waited until Kevla paused for breath. "Well, now, here is your chance to see what is true and what was spun by taleweavers," he said, laughter warm in his voice. Gently, he turned the girl around.

And watched as Kevla Bai-sha gazed for the first time upon the verdant estate that belonged to the *khashim* of the Clan of Four Waters.

Chapter Three

Kevla swayed forward, tightening her grip on Swift's mane to keep from tumbling off the horse in her shock. No capering fantasy creature, no nebulous dream of wealth, nothing she had conjured inside her head over many otherwise-empty hours had prepared the girl for the stunning reality that unfolded before her.

Green. It was all so *green*. The greenness dazzled the eyes, like the sun if one risked a glance at its brilliance. She noticed for the first time on a conscious level a sound she'd been hearing for several minutes; a strange noise, reminiscent of hot soup on the boil, but not quite. Now, she beheld what had been making the sound. Twining like a pair of snakes, two greenish-brown rivers intersected, then went their separate ways. The sun glinted off the surface, making Kevla's eyes water. She blinked, annoyed at having her view of this amazing sight interrupted even for an instant.

Along those Four Waters traveled what Kevla knew to be boats, although the only ones she had ever seen had been toys. One type of boat was made of reeds tightly bound together. Sometimes this boat was flat, like a blanket spread upon the water, and other times its ends swooped up to mimic the other style of boat that meandered along the curving waterways. Kevla could not tell what this second one was made of, but it had large triangular pieces of fabric that caught the winds and propelled the boat much faster than simple poling would have.

Marvelous, both of the boats. Marvelous, the people that imagined such things, designed and knew how to direct them, to harness the wind and water as others harnessed the broad necks and shoulders of sandcattle.

She dragged her gaze away from the ships, letting it rove over the startling greenness of the crops and trees that grew parallel to the life-giving rivers. Kevla had seen trees before, but they had been withered, stunted things fighting for survival in a land of hard-baked earth, where the only water came from the fitful, unpredictable rains that were a rarer sight than a *khashim* in the marketplace. But these trees—some of their leaves were, Kevla was certain, big enough for her to lie down upon. They swayed in the wind, and Kevla caught glimpses of many-colored fruits. Moisture flooded her mouth. She could almost smell them, and imagined them sweeter infinitely than such fruits in the marketplace, where their scent competed with those of roasted meats.

At various points along the rivers, boys clad in short, loose *rhias* pumped long handles. Kevla narrowed her eyes, puzzled for a moment, then realized that the boys were bringing water from the river inland. Long troughs carried the precious fluid well into the cultivated lands. No wonder the crops did so well, hand-fed water as they were, becoming that assaulting, wonderful *green*.

As she watched, the sound of voices crying out in alarm jerked her attention back to the waters. One of the flat boats had capsized, and the water frothed violently. Kevla's heart felt squeezed, and breathing became difficult. Surely, these men knew how to swim, didn't they? What, then, was the panic about?

She opened her mouth to ask Tahmu when the churning water turned from white to red. Kevla saw, for just an instant, the torso of a man surface, his mouth open and screaming, his arms reaching out of the bloody waters imploringly to his fellows on the shores. Then he was gone.

It seemed as if the dreadful incident was over, and Kevla began to breathe again when there came a quick movement.

Something rose up from the depths. It was gray and shiny, and a crest of sharp spines adorned its monstrous head. Between its teeth it held the corpse of the man Kevla had just seen pleading for aid. The men on the shore rallied, and with many curses flung stones, sticks, anything they could upon the creature.

With a sinuousness that mimicked the river in which it dwelt, the beast submerged, taking its prize with it. This time, when the waters quieted, they remained still. Only the rapidly dissipating crimson tinge of the water and the overturned boat were left to bear testimony to the tragedy.

Now Kevla's breath returned to her, and she sobbed, just once. She clapped her hands to her mouth immediately, for she had no wish to shame herself in front of the mighty *khashim* with her weakness. To her surprise, she felt his arm go around her, gentle and steadying.

"The waters give life," said Tahmu. "They make it possible for me and my Clanspeople to live, and to live well indeed. But the waters are full of dangers as well. I would have warned you of them, but I think, now, there is little need."

Wordlessly, Kevla shook her head. Her trembling was starting to subside, which was good, and her stomach had decided not to rid itself of the meat pastry she had eaten earlier, which was better. She took a deep, steadying breath. She had seen death before, but that had been beggars stiffening on the streets, not this sudden, violent snuffing out of life.

Think of something else! she thought fiercely, trying not to see in her mind's eye the gray monster and its human victim.

"Where...but where is the great House?" she asked, her voice quivering only a little.

"Just a few more steps along the path, and you will be able to see it," said Tahmu. He squeezed Swift with his thighs, and the horse obediently moved forward.

Scarcely had Swift taken twelve paces when another set of miracles came into view. The green fields continued upward, climbing gradually up the side of the hill in a series of levels. Buildings appeared, and courtyards with trees and benches and—Kevla gasped—pools of water that seemed to have a life of their own. Streams of water leaped upward and then splashed down. Almost, it seemed the work of a *kuli,* not something man-made, but Kevla knew better than to think that a *khashim* would traffic with such evil beings, even for so beautiful a decoration.

Swift continued forward, and then Kevla saw the jewel in this agricultural crown—the House of Four Waters itself.

"Oh," she said, softly. The word was a sigh, a prayer.

Every other building Kevla had ever seen was made either of stone or mud. The colors were that of the surrounding desert landscape—yellow, red, brown, or gray. Some people occasionally covered their walls with white plaster, the better to keep out the hot sun. But the House of

Four Waters was a riot of colors. It was several houses, really. Each one was larger than any other four houses Kevla had ever seen. The background was white, but they had been painted. Geometric shapes of green, red, black, blue, yellow, orange, purple—every color Kevla had ever seen and some she had no names for. Swirls and dots, sharp angles, gentle waves caught the eye of the viewer and lured the gaze along the lines of the houses. Even the walls that penned in the domestic animals were gaily hued. Kevla admired the spirited horses, the healthy-looking goats and sandcattle, the—

"Oh!" It was a gasp this time. "What *are* they?"

She had, she hoped, managed to contain most of her shock and ignorance. But the sight of the pale brown creatures grazing in the pen had startled her more than anything she had yet beheld.

They were roughly the size of horses, but built like no horse she had ever seen. Their hind legs were massive, while their forelegs were small, with dainty appendages. As Kevla watched, one reached up toward a tree that hung over into the pen, plucked a fruit from it, and, for all the world like a human, held the food in its forepaws and nibbled at it. A huge, fluffy tail served to shade it completely. Large ears swiveled back and forth as the creature fed.

"They are *sa'abahs,*" said Tahmu. "I am not surprised that you have never seen one. Even I have only four of them. The *Sa'abah* Clan demands a high price for them, and only then if they are in the mood for conducting a trade. Most often," and there was a hint of disappointment in the *khashim's* rich voice, "they are eager to fight. It seems they value a horde of five-scores more than food for their people."

"*Sa'abahs,*" breathed Kevla, her rapt gaze still on the creatures. "I have heard of them. They can cross the desert on a cupful of water. They can eat anything. Their feet are so broad they can walk across sand without sinking. They—"

"Enough," chuckled Tahmu. "It is true, they need little water to traverse the desert, but they certainly need more than a cupful. Rare and worth their weight in water indeed they are, but they are beasts, nonetheless, not magical creatures."

"If the great *khashim* says so, then so it must be," replied Kevla, doubt creeping into her voice, "but my eyes tell me otherwise."

Tahmu laughed aloud at that, then sobered. "Kevla, turn and look at me."

The girl obeyed. Tahmu's face was serious.

"You are wise for your age, so I think you will understand. No one must know that your mother was a—did what she did. To all who ask, you must reply that you are a poor orphan I found in the streets of the marketplace."

Kevla frowned. "But great *khashim,* I have skills that a lady would value. I know how to dress hair, to apply henna. How will I explain knowing these things?"

Tahmu thought for a moment. "A good point. We will— you will say your mother was a dancer. Not a highly regarded profession, but better than a *halaan.*"

Kevla considered this. "But even a dancer has a name."

His eyes were compassionate as he spoke the words that dashed her hopes. "Then you must still be Bai-sha. I am sorry for that; I would have spared you shame where I could. But the story of a dancer is closer to the truth, and a lie that has a seed of truth in it is easier to tell."

He placed his finger under her chin and tilted her face up. "It is better to be Bai-sha in the House of Four Waters than Bai-sha on a dusty corner, is it not?"

Kevla thought of her mother's last words to her, of the

coolness with which she had sold her only daughter. An ache welled up in her heart, threatening to spill out as tears.

She blinked them back. That life was over.

"What you say is true, *khashim*," Kevla said.

"Now. The sun is hot, and I am thirsty. I am not a *sa'abah*, and I need more than a cupful of water a day. And you do, too. Enough gawking. Hang on tightly to Swift's mane, Kevla, for I am impatient to be home and in the shade!"

Kevla turned around and obeyed the instructions, lacing her fingers in the silky softness. With a sudden thrill of excitement that banished the lingering shame of Bai-sha and mitigated the pain of parting from her mother, she felt the beast gather itself.

"Hua, hua!" cried Tahmu, striking Swift-Over-Sand on the rump with his hand.

Swift-Over-Sand proved to be Swift-Over-Rocky-Path as well. Kevla couldn't suppress a squeal of delight as the animal surged forward. Swift lowered his head as his body stretched out and found its stride, shaking his head and gnawing the bit, his gold-tipped tusks catching the sunlight.

Down toward the miracle of greenness and water the horse plunged, taking the path at a confident gallop. The path twisted and turned, revealing the valley's secrets in greater detail. All at once they were on a flat path, galloping past workers in the fields, who made haste to prostrate themselves as their master passed. Then up again, a gradual incline, past many of the beautifully painted buildings, past the stone corrals that housed the magnificent horses and the unbelievable *sa'abahs*, in through a huge gate that closed behind them—

—and suddenly, there in the courtyard of the main house of the *khashim*'s estate, exultation and excitement slowed in Kevla's heart as Swift-Over-Sand's pace slowed and clattered to a halt.

Tahmu slipped off the beast. He made no move to help her down. Instead, a servant stepped forward and reached hands up to Kevla.

She ignored the friendly hands and smile of the servant, instead finding her own way off the stamping, snorting animal. She landed hard, but gave no sign of pain, rising from her hands and knees to stand straight and silent.

Tahmu nodded approvingly. "Come with me."

"Sahlik, I have a new servant for you to train."

Sahlik did not drop to her knees. Tahmu would not expect it, not with her inflamed joints. She turned slowly around from the cookfire she was tending.

"You," she said, gesturing to a girl who huddled on the floor, "get the *khashim* and his new servant some water."

The girl scurried to obey, presenting a dripping, hollowed-out gourd to her master with a deep bow. He drank, and then handed it to the child who stood beside him.

Sahlik looked at the girl as she drained the dipper. Her heart rose. She glanced from child to *khashim,* and though her lips didn't move, Sahlik had a smile of approval in her eyes for Tahmu.

He had gone, as she had urged.

Two days ago, Sahlik, on a rare visit to the market with some of the kitchen servants, had heard a long forgotten name and spotted Kevla on the corner. Few servants now remained at the House of Four Waters who had seen the young Tahmu through that heartbreaking time eleven years past. It had been Sahlik who had given the cold, but ultimately wise, advice that he had to leave Keishla. And it had been Sahlik who had held her young lord in her arms as he wept after the deed had been done.

There had been no mistaking the youthful energy of the young Tahmu in the child's vigorous dance, nor the sloe eyes of Keishla in her face. Sahlik had known the girl for what she was, and had urged her master to take pity upon her.

A good boy, Tahmu. He listened well.

But no one else must know, not even the girl herself. Sahlik turned her attention to Kevla, her eyes narrowing. Far too thin. Walking slowly over to the child, she examined the new servant the way Tahmu might examine a horse he was planning to purchase. Sahlik opened the girl's mouth and felt around her teeth and gums. Good. No teeth were loose yet, and Dragon willing, they would not come loose later. Her eyes were clear, her thin arms surprisingly strong with muscle.

"She looks well enough," Sahlik said, stepping back. "Where did you want her, my lord?"

"Put her in as one of Yeshi's attendants."

By the Great Dragon, he was courting trouble. "Are you certain, my lord? Such positions are usually given as rewards for years of service."

She was speaking, of course, what they both knew. She hoped Tahmu would sense the other, unsaid words.

"Kevla's mother was a dancer, before her untimely death," said Tahmu in a conversational tone. Only Sahlik, who knew the man better than nearly anyone, could have caught the undercurrent of tension in the everyday words. This, then, was the story Tahmu and Sahlik would spread.

"Kevla knows many useful skills—hair decorating, henna, massage—things that a woman would appreciate. If she does not work out, there is always another position for her, yes?"

"Certainly," Sahlik agreed. If Tahmu wanted an easy lot for the child of his blood, then it was not her place to disagree. Yeshi was an unobservant woman. It was possible, perhaps even likely, she would not notice the resemblance. Sahlik would leave such matters up to the discretion—or lack thereof—of the *khashim*.

She wiped at the perspiration gleaming on her forehead. Even though she wore a light *rhia* that permitted air to circulate and cool her body, Sahlik found she endured the extreme temperatures less well than she once did.

"It is hot on these old bones," she said. "I will prepare Kevla myself."

She grasped the girl's hand. Without waiting for the *khashim's* dismissal, Sahlik led Kevla away.

Kevla followed obediently, showing none of the lively, rather coarse enthusiasm she had displayed the other day in the marketplace. Sahlik was pleased. She led the girl through the kitchen storage house, back out into the bright sunlight, and into another low, ornately decorated building. This one, unlike many of the others, had a wooden door. It was only one story, and much smaller than the other buildings. Torches burned in sconces fastened to the outside walls, even though the day was wiltingly hot. Kevla turned, a question on her lips.

"Why—"

"You'll see soon enough, child. And it's not too soon to learn to speak when you are spoken to, and not before."

Kevla bowed her head meekly. Sahlik noticed that the child's hair had extremely red highlights in the sun.

"Very good," approved Sahlik. "Now, open that door, and let's be about it."

Kevla hastened to obey, pulling the door open and stepping back to allow Sahlik to enter first. The old woman reached for a torch, and stepped into the darkness.

Cool, thought Kevla. *It's cool in here!*

She realized that this building was made not of mud or brick, as the others were, but of stone. She followed the old serving woman inside.

"Close the door behind you."

Kevla obeyed. Now, the only light came from the flickering torch borne by Sahlik. Kevla kept close to the head servant, uncomfortable in this darkness. The tent in which she had spent all her life had not been able to shut out the light as this building did, and even a moonless night outside had a crowded field of bright, twinkling torch lights to keep her company.

Sahlik moved forward, her steps swift for her age, and certain. Kevla realized that there were stairs ahead that wound down even farther into the darkness.

Sahlik continued, moving steadily downward. Other torches hung on the walls, and these she lit as she passed. Wide-eyed and silent, Kevla followed.

The stairs seemed to wind downward forever. At last, a sound reached Kevla's ears. It seemed familiar, but amid the echoes she couldn't be certain. Surely, it was not the gurgle of water that it sounded like. That was to be expected from rivers such as those she had seen earlier, but not here, not at the bottom of a house.

At last the descent ended. Sahlik stepped forward, Kevla at her heels, into a large stone cavern.

Kevla gasped, softly.

It *was* water.

A spring bubbled up into a large pool of gently moving liquid. Kevla could barely see it in the dim illumination provided by Sahlik's single torch, but it took only a little light to catch the gleam of the water and reflect it back. A second, smaller pool had a large pump, and several buckets sat beside it. Sahlik sat down on a stone bench, groaning and rubbing her knees.

"It is a long walk for me, and the trip back to the surface will be even longer. But it is always worth it. What do you think, Kevla?"

Almost, there was warmth in her voice. Kevla glanced at the old woman, but in the faint light she couldn't read Sahlik's expression.

"Is—did the *khashim* make these?" she asked, turning her attention back to the pools.

Sahlik laughed. "No man can create water, child. But yes, a tunnel was dug many years ago between here and the river. It is one of the House's greatest strengths. We will never run out of water for drinking or bathing."

"B-bathing?" Kevla's voice cracked.

"Of course. Did you think I came all this way simply to give you a drink, girl? Take off that dirty *rhia*. Can't have a servant to the *khashima* running around in that mouse-chewed thing."

Hesitantly, with a sudden bout of shyness, Kevla drew off the garment. Crossing her arms over her chest, she padded over to the larger pool and glanced at Sahlik for confirmation. At the old servant's nod, Kevla sat down on the smooth stone. She took a deep breath, suddenly filled with a nameless, unreasoning fear, then swung her legs into the water.

It was cool, soft, like a gentle hand caressing her legs. A bath. She, Kevla Bai-sha, was about to take a bath, in the underground spring of the greatest *khashim* in the land.

She buried her face in her hands and began to sob. She wasn't sure why, it just seemed that now, at this moment, it was the only thing she could do.

And when suddenly Sahlik was there, her bony shoulder a curious comfort, her gnarled hands soothing Kevla's hair, Kevla did not think to ask how Sahlik had understood so readily. She merely leaned into the embrace and sobbed her young heart out, her legs, submerged to the knees, splashing the alien water gently.

Chapter Four

Sahlik was glad the girl wept. She knew it was not good to keep powerful emotions locked inside as if in a sealed jar. She herself was no stranger to tears stolen in rare moments alone, although life had been good to her in these later years. A smile curved her lips as she thought, *I am perhaps the only woman I know who is happier as an old servant than a young wife.*

The smile faded. She knew the situation in which she had found herself as a young woman was far from unique.

She held the girl as the child sobbed. When Kevla at last drew back, dragging her thin arm across her wet nose and face, Sahlik decided it was a good opportunity to begin the instruction of etiquette.

"Yeshi would have you flogged if you did that in her presence," Sahlik said gently but firmly.

Kevla's eyes widened and she froze. "Cry? I would not cry in front of a *khashima*," she said.

"I did not think you would," replied Sahlik, "but I was referring to this." She imitated Kevla's gesture, exaggerating it. Through the tears still on her face, Kevla giggled. "If perchance something made you sneeze, or your eyes water, you would beg permission to excuse yourself and bathe your face. Like this."

Seated next to Kevla beside the pool, she bent, cupped some water in her hands and delicately splashed her face. By the Dragon, it felt good. Kevla followed suit, saying with a faint trace of pride, "I have washed my face before."

Sahlik smothered her laugh. "That's good," she said. "Now, it is time to wash your whole body." She removed her own clothes and slipped off the edge into the pool. The water came to her waist. Each time, it became harder for her to climb out. She would ask Tahmu about installing some steps inside the pool.

Kevla remained seated as if she had turned to stone, staring at the dark water.

"Are you afraid?" asked Sahlik. Kevla hesitated, then nodded. "Do not be. I know how to swim and I will teach you. I will teach you many things, child. Now, slip into the water. I will be right here."

Kevla looked up, her eyes searching Sahlik's. She took a deep breath, and then, displaying what Sahlik knew to be great trust, slipped into the water. True to her word, Sahlik caught her.

"It's not too deep," she said as the child began to flail. "You can stand. Hold on to the side. That's it."

The water came to midchest on Kevla. She was breathing quickly, but remained admirably calm as she found her footing.

"Many a boy-child has panicked the first time in the

pool," Sahlik said. "Even Tahmu's son Jashemi did. Yet you are already standing. Very good. Now, let me wash your hair and body. From now on, you will be able to do this by yourself. When we are done, I will teach you how to use the brush and the oils, so that you may be presentable to the mistress of the House of Four Waters."

Kevla's body and hair were scrubbed and oiled. Skin and hair, clean and perfumed, gleamed in the torchlight. Sahlik tossed Kevla's old *rhia* into a woven basket in which other items of clothing were jumbled. From a second basket, the old woman withdrew a garment that, to Kevla, seemed impossibly white and fresh.

She reached out and touched the fabric, rubbing it between thumb and forefinger. "It is so beautiful," she breathed. "Surely you cannot mean for me to wear this? Is this not more fitting for the *khashima?*"

Sahlik chuckled. "Yeshi would be outraged if anyone suggested she wear this. You'll soon learn the quality of her clothing. This is standard for all of the young women of the household. It's a working garment. You'll be getting something better soon, once the seamstress has had a chance to take a fitting."

Kevla's lip trembled and her eyes welled with tears. She gulped and forced them back. "Of course," she said. "A servant to the *khashima* must reflect her mistress's style and wealth." She slipped the *rhia* on, but despite her attempt to sound worldly, her small brown hands kept touching the fabric.

Sahlik plaited her hair, clucking her tongue at its coarseness and shaggy length. "You will need a few days before you are ready to serve the mistress," she said. "This hair must be cut and oiled repeatedly. And these hands—you will stop biting your nails at once. Yeshi likes long, painted nails and she likes for her women to have them, too."

"Certainly," Kevla replied immediately.

Sahlik sighed. She turned Kevla around to face her. "Listen to me, Kevla. I will tell you the truth of what life here will be like. Tahmu is a great man, a kind master. We are fortunate to serve in his House. But you will not see him much. Your mistress will be his wife Yeshi. She is beautiful, and quite aware of that beauty. Her world centers on herself, and that is not a bad thing for those who serve her as long as they remember that. It pleases her to have her handmaidens be healthy, pretty, and adorned nearly as lavishly as herself. She likes them smiling and happy and enjoys giving them gifts and treats. Serve her well, put her at the center of *your* world, and your life here will be a very pleasant one."

"And...those who serve the *khashima* poorly?"

A tendril of the dark, oiled hair had escaped the braid. Gently, Sahlik tucked it back in place with a gnarled hand.

"Yeshi once had a servant that was almost as close to her as a sister. When Yeshi found her trying on her cosmetics, she ordered the woman beaten and turned out onto the streets. The last I saw of her was her back, as she walked away from the House. Blood was beginning to seep into her white *rhia*."

Kevla swallowed hard. "I will seek to please my mistress," she said firmly.

"I'm sure you'll succeed. So, this is what you wear when you are serving Yeshi. Tahmu is forward-thinking for a *khashim,* and does not demand that his women constantly wear the veil, but there are times when tradition demands it. Have you ever worn a veil?"

"No, nor did my mother."

This did not surprise Sahlik; *halaans* were hardly known for womanly modesty.

"The veil is to be worn when you venture anywhere outside the House or the healer's hut. And you must wear it to all formal functions that Yeshi asks you to attend. A simple way to remember the rule is, the men of the household may see your face, but male strangers may not."

Kevla nodded her understanding. "Veils are pretty," she said, somewhat wistfully.

"Yes, they are. Now, child. You should have something to eat. Then you will show me exactly what skills you know."

They returned to the kitchens and Sahlik sat Kevla down beside one of the large tables. The girl sat as if glued to the bench, her thin body as upright as if she had a rake handle for a spine. Her eyes followed Sahlik's every move. Sahlik assembled some food on a plate, selected a small cutting knife, and poured watered wine into a chipped ceramic goblet.

Kevla's eyes grew almost as large as the beaten metal plate. She hesitated.

"Go on, you must be hungry," Sahlik said. She was glad that this was a time when the normally bustling kitchens were quiet, although that was always a relative term.

Delicately, Kevla plucked a few grapes and popped them into her mouth. She chewed and swallowed, then looked at Sahlik for approval.

"Good, good. Keep going."

She didn't say anything as Kevla picked up a *paraah*. Kevla sniffed at it, then bit into it. She made a face, then quickly changed her expression as she tried to chew nonchalantly, as if the fruit were completely to her taste.

Sahlik chuckled. She took the *paraah* and cut it up as she spoke. "Spit that out, Kevla. No, no, into your linen. The first things you ate were grapes. This is a *paraah*. You'll need to either cut it up, like this, or peel it. Now, eat the inside, not the outside. Like this."

Kevla watched her intently, her small, freshly cleaned fingers holding a *paraah* segment daintily, then imitated Sahlik. A shy smile lit up her face as she chewed.

Such a pretty thing, Sahlik thought, and wished sadly that Kevla had been born in the right bed.

She took Kevla through holding and cutting meats, eating olives (she warned the girl ahead of time to be careful of the hard pit), sipping wine, and drinking soup. Each time, Kevla closed her eyes briefly, savoring each morsel. She ate much less than Sahlik had expected, and she told Kevla so.

The girl ducked her head, grinning sheepishly. "The great *khashim* bought me a meat pie at the marketplace," she said, as if she were imparting a secret.

Sahlik threw back her head and laughed. "And here I thought you had a dainty appetite. You've surely had enough. So, now you know how to peel a *paraah* for Yeshi. Come to my quarters and let me see what else you know."

Sahlik was pleasantly surprised. The child's hands, though small yet, were skilled in the art of massage. Although her own locks kept escaping the braid, Kevla was able to work Sahlik's graying, coarse hair into several different and attractive styles. Kevla could grind and mix henna, sing passably well (although all she knew were bawdy songs), and had a natural talent for dancing. Her little body moved with a lithe freedom and grace that Sahlik envied.

At one point, ready to see what Kevla could do with henna, Sahlik slid back the sleeve of her blue and gold *rhia* to expose her upper arm. Kevla gasped.

"What—oh. You have never seen a five-score before?"

Kevla shook her head, staring at the four old scars that rose on Sahlik's lower left arm. Gingerly, she reached to touch them, running a forefinger over their puckered, raised edges.

"There are only four," she said.

"You can count. Good! How high?"

"As high as need be," Kevla replied, still distracted by the four scars. "These are old." She looked up at Sahlik. "Your service should be over. Why are you still here?"

"It is...a long story," said Sahlik.

Kevla readied her tools and squatted beside Sahlik. As she began to scoop the ground plant paste from a bowl and apply it in a pattern to the older woman's arm, she said logically, "You must stay here for some time while I apply the henna and let it dry. There is time for quite a long story, I would think."

Sahlik laughed at that. Kevla couldn't know how much she reminded Sahlik of Tahmu when he was young.

"You are certain it won't distract you? I would not like an ugly spot on my arm to compete with my scars."

Kevla grinned and her eyes sparkled as they met Sahlik's. In a soft, pleasing voice, she said, "I will give you a beautiful pattern, *uhlala,* so that all eyes may fasten upon its exquisiteness and none will notice anything else."

"Yes, I think you will please Yeshi greatly," said Sahlik dryly. "Very well. Nearly thirty years ago, when I was but a young woman, I was one of many slaves captured in a battle by Tahmu's father, the great Rakyn."

"May his name forever be spoken," murmured Kevla. The polite phrase was always uttered when speaking of the honored dead.

"Yes, may it be so," Sahlik replied, pleased. "I served him well and loyally, and for four years on the anniversary of my capture, as is the custom, he made a score on my arm. On the fifth year, Rakyn stood to make the fifth cut, but I told him to hold."

Kevla continued to apply the henna with a steady hand, but Sahlik could almost feel how intently the girl was listening.

"'Great *khashim,*' I said, 'You have counted the years

wrong.' He stared at me as if I had been *kuli*-cursed and was gibbering with madness. 'With this last score, Sahlik, you go free,' he said. 'But great Rakyn, I will be free to do what? Free to return to my husband, who loves his wine better than me? You have scored my arm, but you have never broken my bones. So I say again, with all respect: You have counted the years wrong.'"

"And what did he say?"

"He said, as he lowered the dagger, 'The sun has dazzled my eyes. There are not four cuts on your arm, Sahlik. It seems I have counted the years wrong.' And neither he nor Tahmu has made a fifth score, and I continue to serve the House of Four Waters."

"Sahlik is a bold woman," said Kevla, finishing the design.

"Sahlik had nothing to lose," Sahlik replied.

Kevla met her eyes, and to Sahlik, they seemed much older than her ten years.

"Neither does Kevla," she said.

"My master?"

Tahmu looked up from the scroll he was perusing. Sahlik stood in the door. From the expression on her face, Tahmu knew exactly why she had come. He motioned her in. She closed the door behind her.

"How is she doing?" he asked.

"She is a most impressive youngster. There will be jealousies among the women."

Tahmu made an impatient gesture. "Quarrels among Yeshi's women are the least of my worries," he said. "Kevla will hold her own among them, then? That is well. Has anyone...?" He could not find the words. Sahlik knew what he asked.

"The servants think I am growing deaf in my old age, and speak freely when my eyes are not upon them. I have not chosen to enlighten them." Sahlik smiled fiercely. "Kevla has slept in a corner of the kitchen, seen by many. No one else has noticed the resemblance, although you and I see it strongly."

Tahmu let out the breath he hadn't realized he'd been holding. "Perhaps it is because we know the truth that we see the resemblance. Still, I would like to be present."

Sahlik shook her head firmly. "No. You are not usually present to introduce a servant. You must do nothing out of the ordinary with this girl. Finding her and bringing her here was strange enough. Draw no more attention to her, and she will take care of herself."

While Sahlik's words were full of wisdom, Tahmu had a father's heart. It had been difficult to refrain from stopping by to see Kevla. She was a pretty child, and her brave acceptance of her fate combined with her ability to continue to take delight in the world around her had already charmed him.

"I will be outside, then. If Yeshi sees her and knows...I want to be able to take care of Kevla."

Sahlik stepped forward and briefly rested a hand on Tahmu's broad shoulder. No other servant would dare attempt such familiarity, but Sahlik's bond with this man went deep.

"Your kind heart does you credit. You have given the girl a new life, a better life. Be content with that."

Tahmu's strong brown hand closed over the old woman's and squeezed it. He nodded, but she saw that his eyes were still haunted as he imagined what could have been.

Sahlik waited for the perfect opportunity. It came the day after she had spoken with Tahmu.

She had gone to see Maluuk, the healer for the Clan, in his small stone home near the great House. Maluuk was almost as old as Sahlik, and like her, was plagued with stiffness and pain in the joints. The discomfort was incentive for Maluuk to constantly work on perfecting a salve to ease such pain, and he and Sahlik often commiserated on the perils of growing old.

She sat now on a bench in his cool stone house, which was rich with the fragrance of herbs. They were everywhere—in jars on tables, hanging to dry from the ceiling, growing outside in the garden. Maluuk sorted and labeled jars while his apprentice Asha ground herbs and mixed the ointment.

"I have started adding this," he said to Sahlik, extending a jar.

She took a cautious sniff, and then began coughing. Maluuk wheezed with laughter.

"I find...nothing amusing," she managed to say, tears streaming from her burning eyes. She gulped from the waterskin he held out to her.

"I could not resist," Maluuk said, chuckling. "I add the ground pepper to the salve, and it warms the joints. Trust me, it will feel good."

Sahlik gave him a skeptical look and was about to make a sharp comment when a shrill cry interrupted her.

"Maluuk!" The voice belonged to Tiah, one of Yeshi's attendants. "Maluuk, come quickly, Ranna has been bitten!"

Faster than Sahlik would have given the old man credit for, Maluuk had leaped off his stool and raced out the door. Sahlik followed.

Tiah, a curvaceous woman about Yeshi's age, was gently leading Ranna up the steps toward the healer's house. The younger girl stumbled from time to time, as her eyes were fixed on her right hand, which swelled almost before Sahlik's eyes.

Maluuk met them halfway. His touch was always gentle, but Ranna cried out and tried to pull her hand away.

"What bit her?" he asked Tiah.

"I'm not sure," Tiah replied. "A fly, a wasp...."

"Asha!" Maluuk called to his apprentice, "Insect bite. What do I use?"

"Garlic and then a white clay mud poultice," the boy replied.

"Good. Come, Ranna, we will take care of you."

Sahlik said, "I will pick up my ointment later." Maluuk nodded, barely hearing her as he led the two distraught women into the hut.

Despite a particularly sore knee, Sahlik hastened down the steps toward the House with alacrity. The moment would pass soon, and she was determined to seize it.

Yeshi strolled in the garden alone, her long, well-manicured fingers reaching to touch a fragrant bloom now and then. Because of the House of Four Waters' claim to that most precious of fluids, she was able to enjoy growing things that would normally never be seen in the desert. There was insufficient water to grow the exotic fruits and vegetables for trade, but enough so that Yeshi's table always had something intriguing for her to nibble.

Both her women were gone, after Ranna was stupid enough to touch the flower that had the angry-looking insect hovering about it, and Yeshi was bored with no one to talk to. Ranna hadn't looked well, and she certainly hoped the girl was all right, but her first thought as Ranna's hand began to swell like a filling water bladder was that it would be some time before Ranna would give her one of her magnificent massages.

Yeshi liked the garden, as she liked all pretty things, but she had no real interest in learning much beyond which flower had which scent. Now she lounged on a long, intricately carved and padded bench in the small pavilion. The thin fabric walls billowed with a fragrant breeze, and she idly wondered what her husband planned for the evening. Her hand dropped to the beaten gold bowl beside her and she snared a lush fruit.

"Great *khashima,* forgive me for disturbing you," came Sahlik's raspy voice.

Yeshi sighed in exasperation. A frown marred her pretty countenance. "Enter. What is it, Sahlik?"

"I saw that Ranna and Tiah were with the healer, great lady," Sahlik said, stepping just inside the pavilion. "I thought you might be lonely."

"Not lonely enough to want your company, old woman."

Sahlik didn't bat an eye. "Of course not, great lady. I have brought someone more to your taste. Kevla, bow to your mistress."

A girl stepped into the pavilion. She was about ten years old and very slender. She was dressed in a green and blue *rhia* with sleeveless arms. A matching belt encircled her tiny waist, and her hair was pulled back in a single braid that fell almost to the floor as she bowed.

"Your husband went to the market on a whim, great lady, and found this pretty bird for your amusement. Her name is Kevla."

The girl remained bowing. Yeshi couldn't see her face. Intrigued, for it had been long since Tahmu had bothered to think of her when he traveled, even to the market, she propped herself up on an elbow.

"Come here, child," she commanded in a kindly voice.

The girl obeyed at once, scurrying over to the bed and dropping to her knees beside it. The deference pleased Yeshi, who reached and tilted the child's face up to hers.

"Look at me." The girl did so. Yeshi smiled at her. Somehow, the girl seemed familiar, but that was impossible. Yeshi seldom deigned to visit the marketplace, so it was unlikely she had seen the girl before. All the lower castes looked alike, she supposed.

"A pretty little bird indeed. I am bored, Kevla. What might you do to entertain me?"

"I have many skills and talents, all to be used as my mistress desires," Kevla replied promptly. Her voice was pleasant. "It is my understanding that the great *khashima* enjoys massage and adorning her lovely self with henna."

Yeshi thought of Ranna's swelling hand. It was a soothing, relaxing day and she had been counting on Ranna's massage to complete the drowsy pleasure of the afternoon. She rose and sinuously dropped her ornately embroidered *rhia* on the carpet.

"The oils are there," she said, pointing to several small jars. She lay back down on the bed on her stomach, resting her head in her arms. "Let us find out if my little market bird can ease her mistress's aches and pains."

Moving easily and confidently, the girl poured some scented oil in her hands, rubbed them together, and placed them on Yeshi's shoulders.

Such small hands to be so strong. Yeshi sighed happily, relaxing under Kevla's ministrations. She heard a rustling as Sahlik withdrew, then she closed her eyes and concentrated on what she excelled at—enjoying herself.

Tahmu stood behind a large stone statue in the gardens, careful that his shadow not fall upon the pavilion and reveal his presence. He could hear the sounds of voices, but was too far away to catch their words. There was no shout of indignation or the sound of a slap, however, so he dared to hope that all was well.

After a few moments, Sahlik emerged. Their eyes met. Sahlik smiled, almost imperceptibly, and Tahmu sagged against the statue.

Thank the Great Dragon. Yeshi, as they had counted on, was too obtuse to notice how much her new servant girl resembled her husband. He wiped his face with a hand that trembled.

Forgive me, Keishla, my love. But our child is well and safe now. Perhaps, indeed, you and I have been forgiven our transgressions.

As he returned to the duties that awaited him as *khashim* of the Clan of Four Waters, Tahmu felt that, after so many years, he had reconciled with his past.

He dared to hope the worst was over.

Chapter Five

After the massage, Yeshi and her new handmaiden retired to Yeshi's quarters.

"Here is the room you will share with Ranna, Tiah, and the other women who serve me," Yeshi pointed out as they passed a large, airy room with a small table, a basin and pitcher of water, and dozens of soft-looking cushions scattered on the floor. Kevla tried not to reveal her shock at the opulence.

"And this is the room I share with my lord," Yeshi said, as she opened the door onto a room three times as large as the handmaidens'. There were two or three lounging chairs, cushions on the floor, and glorious tapestries adorning the thick walls. Candles, lamps, and a small brazier sat ready to be lit at nightfall. The bed that Yeshi and Tahmu shared seemed to Kevla to be large enough to accommodate three or four quite easily. It was circular in shape, elevated off the floor by short, sturdy stone pillars.

"I am in need of refreshment," Yeshi said. "Go to the kitchens and ask Sahlik to prepare a plate. Make sure there is something you enjoy on it, too, Kevla."

Kevla floated down to the kitchens and repeated Yeshi's request to Sahlik. The head servant nodded, pleased.

"Don't forget to let her eat first," she said as she arranged the tray. "And don't pay any attention when she tells you to have some *paraah,* it's her favorite fruit and she'll want to eat it all herself."

Kevla nodded obediently. It was perhaps natural that Sahlik should worry, but there was no need. Kevla understood exactly how to handle someone like Yeshi.

After Kevla had lit the lamps, candles and brazier, she and the *khashima* lounged on embroidered pillows, nibbled the delicacies, and sipped a beverage that was both sweet and tangy and which made Kevla feel a bit light-headed. Yeshi was chatting and Kevla was listening as attentively as possible, giving the potency of the drink, when there came a knock on the door. Yeshi sighed.

"And we were having such a good time, just the two of us," she said. In a harder voice, she called, "Who knocks?"

"Please, my lady, it is only us," came a timid reply.

"Enter." The door opened and two young women stood in the hall. The older one, whom Kevla suspected was in her late twenties, was tall and voluptuous, her dark blue *rhia* straining across her full breasts. She started when she saw Kevla and her eyes widened, then whatever emotion was in them was quickly hooded.

The younger was only a few years older than Kevla and shorter and slimmer than her companion. The most noticeable thing about her was her hand, which was swathed in bandages. Kevla felt a pang of sympathy and wondered what had happened.

"You are late," said Yeshi.

Their eyes widened in apprehension. They exchanged glances. "Didn't Sahlik tell you?" asked the larger woman.

"About Ranna's hand? Yes, but there was no reason *you* needed to stay with her so long, Tiah." Yeshi's gaze returned to Kevla, and she smiled affectionately. She was quite lovely when she smiled, thought Kevla.

"It was lucky that Kevla is as skilled as you are, Ranna, otherwise my back would have been protesting your absence. It looks as though it will be some time before you will be able to rub my feet."

Ranna's dark face flushed. "Yes, my lady."

Tiah glanced at Ranna and said, "Maluuk said that it was lucky she did not die."

"Mmm," said Yeshi. "Well, Ranna, you have one good hand. Go down to the kitchen and get me another skin of wine."

Kevla knew she was a good observer, but even the greatest dullard would have had no trouble interpreting the looks both handmaidens shot her. She swallowed hard, and despite the strange sensation the wine was causing in her, wished she dared have another cup.

"Ranna," said Yeshi, "I did not mean tomorrow."

Ranna jumped slightly. "Of course not. Forgive me." She reached with her good hand to take the wineskin and darted out the door. Tiah moved to settle behind Yeshi on the cushions and reached to touch her hair when Yeshi ducked her head.

"No. Kevla will brush my hair. Tiah, you will bathe and massage my feet."

Kevla rose and did as she was commanded. Tiah, safely out of Yeshi's line of vision, mouthed the word *skuura,* female dog, and glared as she rose. A knot in her stomach, Kevla knelt behind Yeshi and began unbraiding the thick locks with nimble, gentle fingers.

Yeshi chatted on about nothing. Ranna returned with the wine. All three servants chimed in with appropriate noises from time to time. Tiah bathed Yeshi's feet in a ceramic bowl of water scented with flower petals, lavishing attention on them. She dried them carefully and massaged oil into them, her gaze darting up now and then to gauge her mistress's reaction.

Kevla dutifully brushed and oiled Yeshi's hair, and while pleased to hear such compliments as "Your touch is so gentle, child!" and "That feels good, Kevla," wished silently that Yeshi would spare a kind word or two for Tiah's ministrations as well.

At last it was time to ready the bed. She thought, as she gingerly touched it, that the mattress made the pillows she had sat upon feel hard as old rugs. Over it were intricately woven and embroidered blankets and silks. The sheets felt like water in her hands.

"Kevla!" The sharp voice of Tiah startled her and she jumped. "Don't touch the *khashima's* things like that!"

Kevla gulped. She had been certain that she would know how to handle Yeshi, but already, on the first day, she was going to incur the woman's famous wrath....

To her ineffable relief, Yeshi only laughed. "Poor child, you've probably never seen anything as lovely, have you?"

Not daring to speak, Kevla shook her head, keeping her eyes averted. Yeshi's long, cool fingers brushed her chin, tilting Kevla's face up.

"My lord is going to be away for a while, visiting another clan. The bed is large enough for about fifty such as you. Stay with me tonight; keep me company while I miss my husband. It will be pleasant to have someone to whisper secrets to."

Kevla dared not look at Tiah as the other young women bowed and left. Yeshi, now clad in a diaphanous garment that covered her from neck to toe, crawled into the bed and yawned. Kevla went about the room, extinguishing the oil lamps and candles, then, her heart racing, climbed into the bed. The only light came from the red glow of the brazier's coals.

She almost uttered a cry as she slipped beneath the sheets. So soft, so smooth....surely Tahmu and Yeshi slept deeply and dreamed sweet dreams.

"I imagine you are Bai-sha," said Yeshi, breaking into her reverie. Kevla went cold. "That is unimportant to me. You are a sweet girl and you handle yourself well. Did you know I have a son?"

"Of course," Kevla replied. "He is the young master, the *khashimu* Jashemi-kha-Tahmu."

"That's right," Yeshi said. "He's been away for almost a year now, learning from his uncle. That's one of our traditions, Kevla; to send the heir to live with his closest male relative. He'll leave me again for another year when he's married. I miss him. I adore my son, but I often think how sweet it would have been had I borne a daughter."

Tentatively, Kevla said, "My lady is still young and beautiful. Perhaps the Dragon will grant her a daughter soon."

Yeshi chuckled, but there was an undercurrent of sadness in her voice. "You are still a child, and there are things you don't yet understand."

In the darkness, Kevla grinned. There wasn't much about male and female coupling she didn't understand, but she wasn't about to tell Yeshi that.

"My son is a little younger than you," Yeshi went on. Kevla wondered why the *khashima* was speaking so freely. Perhaps it was the shield of darkness. Perhaps it was that Kevla was such a nobody. Yeshi turned over, and the silk sheets rustled. "I am glad Tahmu brought you to me. To-morrow will be very hot. Would you like to spend all day in the caverns?"

"It if please my lady, I would enjoy that very much."

"It will be so, then. Good night, Kevla."

"Good night, my lady. Dragon send you sweet dreams."

But Kevla did not dream at all that night. She was asleep within minutes. In the morning, she awoke before dawn and slid out as silently as possible.

She closed the door carefully, turned, and gasped. Tiah and Ranna stood in the hall. Even the slim, injured Ranna scowled, and Tiah loomed over Kevla like a *kuli*. Before Kevla could react, Tiah spat in her face.

"Bai-sha," Tiah snarled in a hoarse whisper. "You'd better watch yourself."

"I can't believe you took advantage of my injury," said Ranna, sounding more hurt than angry.

Kevla wiped the spittle from her face. "I—" she began, keeping her voice soft. But they didn't let her finish.

"You are just one of many. You may be Yeshi's favorite today, but that doesn't mean you'll stay that way," said Tiah.

"Tiah, Ranna," Kevla whispered imploringly, holding out a hand to each one of them, "Yeshi is a great lady and has many needs. Surely, she requires all of us to tend her."

"Yeshi is a spoiled *skuura*," said Ranna in a low voice, "and we were doing fine until you came along."

Kevla's eyes filled with tears. "I only—" Footsteps coming down the hall gave her an excellent excuse to duck past the two women and scurry to the kitchen.

It was an inauspicious start to a day which only got worse. Yeshi, as Kevla would soon learn, often changed her mind. By the time she had risen and been bathed and dressed, the great lady had decided not to spend the day in the caverns after all. She was going to visit the market, and Kevla was to prepare a traveling basket of food and wine and accompany her. Kevla nodded and kept her face impassive. But she could not hide her feelings from Sahlik.

As Sahlik helped Kevla prepare a basket, she said in a low voice, "It will not be as hard as you think, child. You will be wearing the veil, so no one will recognize you. Don't look anyone full in the face and all should be well."

"I don't want to go back," Kevla whispered. "I don't know why Yeshi wants me to."

"She wants you to see what change can be wrought in a day's fortune," Sahlik said. "Be quiet and grateful and in all likelihood, she will never take you back to the market again. It's not her favorite pastime." Sahlik hesitated, then said, "Do not speak to your mother if you see her."

Kevla shook her head. The lump in her throat forbade speech. Miserable and apprehensive, she covered the basket and went to join the other handmaidens.

She and Tiah dressed in clean *rhias*. Ranna would not be accompanying them; riding would take two hands and hers was far from healed. Kevla watched closely as Tiah put on her veil and did a fair job of imitating her, drawing the thin yellow fabric over her head, around the lower part of her face and tucking it in. By the contemptuous flash of Tiah's eyes, Kevla had not quite gotten it right. She hoped Yeshi would not notice.

But she could not hide her inexperience with riding when she and Tiah went into the courtyard and two sand-colored mares were brought out for them. With the help of a stable boy, Tiah climbed easily into the saddle. Kevla stared at her own mare.

"What's the matter?" Tiah challenged. "Yeshi is already in her litter waiting for us."

"I cannot ride," Kevla said, trying hard not to cry.

"Well then, too bad for you," said Tiah. "Yeshi and I will go alone to the market." She pulled her horse's head around and rode out of the courtyard to where Yeshi was waiting.

Kevla lowered her head and trudged back to the House. She was not sorry to avoid going to the market, but feared that her inexperience might count against her. Tiah and Ranna had made it plain this morning that they regarded her as competition for Yeshi's affections. Now, Tiah would have Yeshi's ear all day. It would be an excellent opportunity to turn her mistress's mind against her new handmaiden. Kevla did not think the *khashima* would make a great attempt to find the truth if malicious gossip started spreading. She had reached the top of the stairs when she heard a male voice calling her by name. Surprised, Kevla turned to see a stable boy running across the courtyard to her.

"The *khashima* has sent me for you," he said, gasping for breath. "She says if you cannot ride a horse, you will be taught, and until you learn, you may ride in the litter with her."

Yeshi's litter was, not surprisingly, a glorious thing. It was a padded armchair that could seat two people comfortably, carried by twelve powerfully built servants. There was room to stretch one's legs, and a canopy shaded the two women from the hot sun. Despite the physical comfort, Kevla knew that if Tiah knew how miserable she was, the older girl would be delighted. She would much rather be on a horse, equal to the other handmaiden, than feel the hot jealousy emanating from Tiah.

Her stomach tightened as the outskirts of the marketplace came into view. Nervously, she adjusted the veil, grateful for the anonymity it provided. She hoped Sahlik was right, that no one would recognize her. Particularly, she hoped she would not see her mother.

The *khashima's* appearance in the market created quite

a stir. Those on foot hastened to get out of the way and bow to the great lady. Kevla noticed they did not prostrate themselves, as they did for the *khashim,* nor did they avert their eyes from her face after they had shown their respect. Indeed, some of the bolder merchants went so far as to directly approach the litter, so that the great lady could better see their merchandise.

Yeshi was having a grand time. She thrived on the attention, and ordered her servant to purchase all manner of jewelry and trinkets. She generously bought drinks, honeycakes, and meat pies for Kevla and Tiah, and Kevla realized that the delicacies she had so carefully packed would be forgotten and spoil in the hot sun.

Tiah ate her cake quickly, clearly enjoying the sticky sweetness of it. Kevla found it too cloying, but knew that Yeshi wanted her to eat it. She was just about to take another bite when someone cleared his throat.

"Most honored *khashima,*" said a smooth voice. "What a pleasant surprise to encounter you here."

The speaker was a high-caste man who stood beside the litter. His clothing was almost as fine as Tahmu's and his oiled, well-trimmed beard parted to reveal white teeth. Kevla took an instant dislike to him. She thought that Tahmu would not have approved of the way this man's eyes roamed over Yeshi's face and dropped briefly to her body.

Yeshi, however, seemed pleased to see the stranger. Leaning over, she purred, "*Uhlal* Bahrim. You have been absent from our feasts lately."

"Not by my own will, great lady. My lands need supervision if they are to yield crops satisfactory to the *khashim.*"

Her smile grew and she asked, "So it is your love for my lord that keeps you from our hall?"

He leaned in closer to the litter and said, "Nothing else would keep me from the radiance of your company."

Disgusted with the exchange but careful not to show it, Kevla returned to her honeycake. Suddenly, a cry rang out.

"It is you!"

Every head turned in the direction of the shout. A poorly dressed, low-caste man was pushing his way toward the *khashima*. It was obviously a beggar, but Kevla had never seen any of the beggars who frequented the marketplace be so assertive.

Yeshi's men set the litter down as quickly and smoothly as possible. Drawing curved swords, four of them stepped protectively in front of their mistress. Others moved toward the increasingly hysterical man. Yeshi's face was impassive, but Kevla saw her painted fingers tighten on the chair arm. Bahrim took the opportunity to lay his hand on hers.

"It is you!" the man cried again, pointing directly at—

"Me?" Kevla whispered, her hand going to her throat. He must have recognized her from the market. But how? The veil hid everything but her kohl-rimmed eyes. Bahrim gaped at her.

"I've been trying to find you!" the man continued. Flecks of spittle flew from his lips and his eyes were enormous. "She and I," he said, turning to look at Tiah, "we've been waiting for you!"

Kevla looked over at Tiah, but the other woman stared back at the man. She seemed turned to stone in place atop her mare.

"You will not address my women so," said Yeshi coldly.

"They are not your women, great lady, they are ours— they belong to all of Arukan! I have dreamed of you. Had visions of you riding the Great Dragon—"

Visions? The *Dragon?* Kevla felt horror seep through her. The man was not simply an aggressive beggar. He had *visions*. He was blaspheming the Great Dragon. That could only mean one thing.

"*Kuli*-cursed!" screamed a voice from the crowd. The word seemed to jolt everyone into action. Yeshi's men sprang upon the man. He went down under a pile of muscular, sun-browned bodies, and when they got to their feet the man's face was bruised and bloody.

"Great lady, what would you have us do with him?" one of Yeshi's men asked, slightly out of breath.

Yeshi's eyes were wide and her breathing was quick, but other than that she seemed perfectly in control. "The *kulis* have seduced him. There is only one punishment for the *kuli*-cursed."

Kevla began to tremble and clenched her hands hard in her lap. Everyone in Arukan, including her, knew the punishment for being unfortunate enough to be cursed by demons.

The man cried out. "Great lady, I implore you, I am not *kuli*-cursed! My visions are true, they are sent from—"

Yeshi's men again turned on him and this time when they stopped, the man had been beaten unconscious. Kevla kept swallowing, grateful that she had only eaten a few bites of the honeycake, struggling to keep even those few bites from coming back up. Yesterday, she had watched a man being devoured by a river creature. Today, she would see another man burn to death.

Nothing in Arukan was more feared than the *kulis,* unless one considered the Great Dragon himself. But the Dragon was honored and revered, and his laws protected his people and kept them on the right path. The demons who lurked in the caves at the foot of the mountains and who haunted one's dreams had no hint of goodness about them. To attract the attention of one, to become then cursed, was a fate that made being burned alive seem like a blessing.

"It will be done, my lady," continued Yeshi's man. "Do you wish it now, or shall we wait for the morrow?"

There was only one reason for waiting. When a *kuli*-cursed was burned, it was important for as many people as possible to witness it, so that they would be reminded of how dreadful it was, and would be on their guard. Yeshi looked around at the sea of people in the marketplace.

"There are many here to witness," she said. "Do it now."

Bahrim lingered with Yeshi, offering his consolation for the traumatic encounter.

Precious as wood was in a land where trees grew only by the few nurturing waters, everyone at the marketplace was anxious that the cursed man be destroyed as quickly as possible, lest they, too, become victims of the *kulis*. The vendors offered their stools and chairs, which were broken into pieces. Dried grasses, used to feed the animals, were offered for quick kindling. Yeshi smoothed the sacrifice by tossing coins for the proffered wood. Before Kevla quite realized what was going on, a pyre had been built outside the market area and the unconscious beggar, bound hand and foot, doused with lamp oil and with a rag stuffed into his mouth, was hurled atop it.

"Death to demons!" someone shouted, and the chant was taken up: "Death to demons! Death to demons!"

Someone grabbed a torch and lit the pyre. Kevla looked away, but Yeshi's hand closed on her wrist. Kevla gazed into the hard eyes of her mistress.

"He wanted to drag you and Tiah into his madness," Yeshi said. "He could have tainted both of you, accused you, too, of being demons. Then you and Tiah would be on that pyre with him. It is well that he is punished quickly. Watch, Kevla. Watch and remember this day."

Kevla couldn't imagine that she would ever forget it. Reluctantly, she raised her head and watched as the fire consumed the body. Thick, acrid smoke, laced with the stench of burning flesh, scalded her throat and made her eyes water. She heard the shouts and cheers of the crowd as their fear was assuaged, and she was grateful that the guards had beaten the poor, deluded soul senseless before they burned him.

Please, Great Dragon, she prayed silently, *please don't let this happen to anyone in the House of Four Waters.*

Chapter Six

Yeshi and her entourage returned to the House of Four Waters subdued by the incident. The handmaidens prepared their mistress for bed, and what little conversation there was, was brief and spoken in low tones. Yeshi did not ask Kevla to stay with her again. Kevla retired to the room she shared with the other girls and prepared for sleep in silence. While she didn't expect that Tiah and Ranna would ever become her friends, the fire that had fueled enmity between the handmaidens and the newcomer seemed to have been extinguished. It was as if Tiah felt that being included in the madman's raving with Kevla made problems between them less important.

Days turned into weeks, then months. Kevla adapted to being around so many people and grew used to the unpredictability of serving Yeshi. While each day began the same way, there was no telling what direction it might take. Each morning the girls would arise with the sun, eat some bread, cheese, and fruit and drink a cup of *eusho,* then descend into the cool caverns to bathe. After that, they would go to Yeshi's wing, where they would awaken, bathe, and dress their mistress. How the day developed from there depended entirely upon what Yeshi wished to do. As the months passed, Kevla had done everything from spending all day with Yeshi in the caverns, to lounging in the gardens under the pavilion, to even traveling once or twice to another *uh-lala's* household.

She saw Sahlik often, her benefactor Tahmu infrequently, and concentrated on mastering the art of pleasing Yeshi. It was an easy life, much easier than standing on a corner crying for customers, and Kevla thrived. Now and then, she would think of her mother, and with a pang wondered how she fared. As time passed, however, even that brief thought came with less frequency.

One day, Kevla glanced in the mirror as she was tidying Yeshi's room and saw that her face had changed. Her cheeks were slightly less round, her eyes longer, her lips fuller. With a shock, she realized that more than a year had passed since she had first arrived at the House of Four Waters. She smiled at her reflection, and thanked the Dragon for her good fortune.

Kevla learned that Tahmu and several of his servants would shortly be leaving for a wonderful reason—the *khashim* of the Clan of Four Waters was going to fetch his son, the young master, and bring him home.

After Tahmu departed, Yeshi alternated between moping and anticipating her husband and son's return. A few weeks after Tahmu departed, Kevla was in Yeshi's quarters opening a window when she spotted a cloud of dust. She stared at it, frowning.

"Kevla," asked Yeshi, "what do you look at?"

"I am not sure, great lady. There is some dust in the east."

"Please the Dragon, not a dust storm," muttered Tiah, as she shouldered Kevla aside to see for herself. She gasped.

"Great lady," cried Tiah, "I am happy to report that a *sa'abah* rider comes!"

Yeshi was up from her cushions and at the window in a heartbeat. She squinted, cursing a little as the sun dazzled her eyes, and then laughed. She reached to hug Tiah, saying, "An extra glass of wine for you at the dinner tonight, sharp eyes! It is one of Tahmu's scouts! My boy is coming home!"

She rushed from the room, crying, "Sahlik! Sahlik, Tahmu's scout comes! Have wine and food ready for him!"

The three handmaidens hastened after their lady. They found her where Kevla had never seen her before—in the kitchens. Sahlik had prepared a plate of juicy fruits and light grains. There was a skin of wine at the ready, but the thirsty scout clearly preferred simple water. His dark face was white with sand and Kevla wrinkled her nose at his smell. But Yeshi had pulled up a stool right next to him.

"And my brother's wife? Is she well?" Yeshi asked.

"Yes, great lady. She has many letters for you, which will be coming in the caravan. I would have brought them myself, but the *khashim* bade me travel lightly, to make good speed."

"Yes, of course. Do not rush your meal, and when you are through, take all the time you like in the caverns."

The exhausted man's eyes lit up. "Thank you, great lady."

The House exploded into activity. The rider was only three days ahead of the caravan, and much had to be done if the *khashim* and the heir of the Clan of Four Waters were to be received with all due honor.

The kitchens, which usually were quiet for at least a few

hours in the depths of night, were bustling nonstop. Lambs, calves, and goat kids were slaughtered and prepared for the feast. Servants were sent to the marketplace for tempting tidbits to adorn the table. Cakes and pastries were prepared, stuffed with fruits both fresh and dried and drizzled with honey and crushed nuts. Barrels of wine, aging in the caverns where they were cool and protected, were uncorked and decanted.

All the rugs were taken out and beaten, the floors swept and mopped with precious, scented water. Metal plates and decorative objects were polished until one's reflection could be seen in them. Flowers from the garden were brought into every corner of the great House, so that a pleasant, fresh scent permeated the place.

Yeshi was tended to almost nonstop as well. At first Kevla was worried when Yeshi requested Tiah to do her henna.

"My lady," stammered Kevla, "are you not pleased with my designs?"

"Quite pleased, my little bird," Yeshi replied soothingly. She added, with a wink at Tiah, "but there are some parts of my body that you are too young yet to henna."

Tiah smiled, and the two older women laughed together. While there was not a single spot on her mother's body that Kevla had not, at one time or another, adorned with the green plant paste, Kevla feigned shyness, and smiled at Yeshi when she patted the girl's cheek and left arm in arm with Tiah.

"You will help me," said Sahlik, coming up behind Kevla and taking her arm. "Ranna, I know that Maluuk will need to stock up on supplies. Go see what he needs."

Sulkily, Ranna said, "He has an apprentice. Let Asha do the work."

Sahlik straightened and looked the young woman in the eye. "You obey Yeshi," she said with deceptive softness. "When Yeshi is not around, you obey me. Asha will be busy preparing salves and ointments. He will not have time to run to the market."

"Why not send Kevla?"

"Because I'm sending you. I have other duties for Kevla."

Ranna sighed. "Very well, Sahlik." She slowly moved in the direction of the door.

Kevla watched her go, unable to suppress a smirk of satisfaction. No doubt, Sahlik had something special, something fun, to offer her.

She did not.

Halfway through the task that Sahlik had assigned Kevla—that of opening and freshening the rooms of the *khashimu*—Kevla wished that she'd been the one to go to market and shop for herbs and oils for the healer.

Jashemi's rooms had been sealed up for almost two years. With no air to waft through them, they smelled stale and unwelcoming. Kevla, laden with sweet-smelling, just-washed linens, wrinkled her nose despite the opulence of the chambers.

The bed was bare. Fine dust had settled on every piece of furniture, proof that the powdery sand found a way where even fresh air did not. Kevla looked around and put the bedclothes safely down outside, in the corridor. She put her hands on her narrow hips, surveyed the enormity of the task, sighed, and went to work. It took her the better part of the afternoon, and by the time she was done, she smelled worse than the room had. But it was finished.

She had beaten the mattress and pillows to rid them of dust, and covered them with sumptuous blue and green fabrics. The pillows were embroidered with gold thread, which shone among the deeper hues. Jashemi's clothes had been removed from storage, washed, and now rested in a chest made of a light wood that smelled tangy and sharp-sweet.

Kevla wondered if the young master would have outgrown them; he had been gone for a while.

Kevla had polished the table and filled ceramic bowls with fresh fruit. Another bowl and a pitcher of water stood on a small pedestal beside the bed. She had cleaned and refilled the oil lamps, beaten the rugs, swept, and mopped the floor, and now, as Sahlik had instructed her, tucked dried whole fruits studded with cloves among the bedding and here and there.

She ached, but she was proud of her handiwork. The young master's room was ready.

As she went to the caverns to cleanse herself from the dust and sweat of the day's labor, she wondered what this boy would be like. He was not much younger than she. Would he be kind and wise, like his father? Would he be petty and spoiled, like his mother? She had strained her ears listening for any gossip that would give a hint, but no one talked about Jashemi-kha-Tahmu very much, except as his father's heir.

Kevla was putting the finishing touches on Yeshi's hair, weaving dried flowers and jewels into the glossy black locks, when a strange, wailing sound made her jump.

"Ouch!" Yeshi's manicured hand went to her head and rubbed to ease the sting that Kevla's sudden tug had caused.

"Great lady, I am sorry! But the sound—"

Ranna and Tiah laughed, looking slightly superior. "I suppose a market Bai-sha girl would not know the sounds of the *shakaal*," said Ranna, in a voice meant for Yeshi to interpret as fondly indulgent but that Kevla recognized as condescending.

Yeshi chuckled, the pain forgotten. "They are long horns. If you blow on one end, the sound you hear comes out the other. Hurry, girl! If the *shakaal* has been sounded, they are not too far away!"

Yeshi looked happier and more animated than Kevla had ever seen her. Kevla felt a warmth in her heart at Yeshi's anticipation that was almost maternal.

"You three will attend me at the dinner. Kevla, watch the others and learn. They have been to many such events and I'm sure will be happy to share their knowledge."

Kevla looked at the other women. Even now, she doubted very much they would be happy to share anything with her. "Lady," she began, "I have attended you at dinners before."

"Not like this one!" Yeshi exclaimed delightedly.

If Kevla had thought that the House had been a flurry of activity two days ago, it was nothing compared to what she saw now. Yeshi disappeared, flitting about to check on everything. Ranna and Tiah took off somewhere immediately afterward. Left on her own, Kevla tentatively wandered throughout the House, keeping out of the way but observing everything. She had a fluttering in her stomach. Ever since she had prepared Jashemi's room, she had wondered what the *khashimu* would be like. She was anxious to see him, although she knew that he would barely acknowledge her presence. Tahmu was not old, but he would not live forever. One day, the boy whose room she had cleaned would be the *khashim* of the Clan of Four Waters.

She had never ventured into the Great Hall before; she had had no need. While Yeshi and Tahmu often entertained guests, the room in which they received them hitherto was much less formal. Now, though, she peered inside, and her brown eyes grew large as eggs at what she beheld.

It was so vast, she had utterly no reference to compare it to. It seemed to her to stretch forever. A low table of dark, polished wood ran almost the full length of the hall. Dozens of pillows flanked it, and after a quick count Kevla realized that nearly fifty people would be fed here tonight. Colorful rugs, every hue of the rainbow, further cushioned the stone floor. Twenty fans made of the feathers of some huge bird were propped up against the walls. No doubt, servants would provide a cooling breeze as their master and his guests dined.

"If you've nothing better to do than gawk," came Sahlik's voice, "then go back to the kitchen and help with the feast."

Disappointed, Kevla nodded. She was there for the next three hours, basting chickens, carrying bowls, grinding herbs. So it was that at one point she was given a jug of a mint-and-vinegar beverage and thrust into the throng of servers. Unsure as to what to do, she imitated the others, kneeling to the left and pouring the drink into the ceramic cup, not the glass one or the golden one, and wiping the lip free from any drops.

She might as well have not been present, for all the attention she drew. She knelt and poured for fragrant, bejeweled, and veiled women and for bearded, bold-voiced men. She saw clothing in colors she had only seen before in dreams, and weapons of all varieties lying beside men who seemed as large to her as a horse.

Kevla had lost track of how many glasses she had poured when a hand seized her wrist. She gasped, but the fear faded when she saw that it was Tahmu. It returned full fold when she saw the mixture of anger and—was it fear?—in his eyes.

"Kevla!" he hissed. "Why are you not sitting behind Yeshi? Why are you not wearing the veil?"

Her heart sinking, Kevla glanced over at Yeshi. The *khashima* was seated opposite her husband and talking animatedly to Bahrim, the *uhlal* who had approached her litter in the marketplace so long ago. Neither Yeshi nor her handmaidens had noticed Kevla yet. While Yeshi's face was bare—she was, after all, the second highest-ranking person present—Ranna and Tiah wore the traditional veils. Sahlik's words, uttered on her first day, returned to her: *The men of the household may see your face, but male strangers may not.*

And there were many, many male strangers present.

"I am sorry—Yeshi dismissed us—Sahlik sent me to the kitchen—" She glanced around wildly. None of the serving women had veils. But she now saw what she had been too busy to observe earlier—that all of the high-caste women and their servants, kneeling obediently behind their mistresses, were veiled at this highly formal, highly public occasion.

"Great *khashim,* I meant no dishonor—" she began again. A movement caught her attention, and before she could think to avert her gaze she found herself staring at a high-caste boy who could only be Jashemi-kha-Tahmu.

He was slightly younger than she, about eleven, still slim with a child's build. His face, though, was strong and appealing, as was his father's, and he had his father's sharp eyes and curly dark hair. He was staring at her in shock, no doubt outraged at her disrespectful conduct, his mouth, with lips as full as a girl's, slightly open. Before she could look down, his dark gaze flickered to his father's face, then back to hers.

"Veil yourself and take up your position behind your mistress," said Tahmu. "Hurry, Kevla. Go now."

She nodded, biting her lip to keep the tears from spilling down her cheeks. As she turned and walked as quickly as she dared from the hall, she felt someone staring at her. The feeling was so unnerving that she had to turn around. As she did, she saw Jashemi, her young master, watching her every move.

Shame washed over Kevla, and she was grateful to make her escape before hot tears flowed down her burning cheeks.

Chapter Seven

Jashemi-kha-Tahmu was happy to be home. He was not overly fond of his mother's brother, with whom he had spent the last two years. Naram was loud and boisterous, the opposite of Tahmu, and Jashemi had had barely any chance to interact with his cousins and his aunt. Jashemi was uncertain as to what he was supposed to be "learning" during the two years. Apparently, the vast majority of what Naram had to teach was how to yell, how to drink, and how to make rude comments about females.

Naram's fondness for physical activity, though, did translate to his nephew. Jashemi had ridden more in these two years than he ever had in his life. He had also learned how to hunt, though he was always sorry to extinguish the light in the beautiful, soft brown eyes of the *liah,* and he found that he did enjoy male company, other than that of his uncle. He learned to sleep soundly on hard-packed earth beneath a sky crowded with stars, and to travel on almost as little food and water as a *sa'abah* needed.

Jashemi quickly learned to enjoy what he found pleasant, steel himself against what he disliked, and get through the time with patience. But when he saw his father's colors on the horizon, flapping in a rare breeze, Jashemi's heart was so full of happiness that he almost wept.

He had not rushed to greet his father. Such displays were for children. Instead, he prostrated himself as all did before the *khashim* of the Clan of Four Waters, but he did so without the obsequiousness that the others displayed. Tahmu bade his son rise first, in acknowledgment of Jashemi's rank as heir to this vast clan. There was a raucous party to mark Jashemi's last night, and the boy was relieved to see that despite his polite demeanor, Tahmu appeared to dislike the drunken revelry almost as much as his son did.

He rode alongside his father the entire long way home, telling Tahmu what he had learned and trying to minimize the less savory aspects of two years spent with Naram and Pela.

At one point, Tahmu asked him how Naram treated his family and his servants. Jashemi hesitated, loath to speak badly of his mother's brother.

"I am the only one who can hear you," Tahmu said, "the others are riding too far away. And I have raised you to speak the truth to me, Jashemi."

After a moment, Jashemi spoke. "There is no one like Sahlik in Naram's household," he began.

Tahmu smiled. "There is no one like Sahlik anywhere," he said. "She is unique, one of our household's true treasures."

"What I mean is, there is no servant who...." Jashemi struggled for the words. Finally, he resolved to simply speak bluntly. "There is no one there who dares question Naram, even when he is clearly wrong."

"Many believe that is how a great House should operate," said Tahmu. He was staring straight ahead, mounted atop Swift-over-Sand. He spoke mildly, and Jashemi could not determine what answer his father wanted to hear.

"But you don't," Jashemi challenged. "You want Sahlik to tell you if you are going to do something wrong, something that would hurt the Clan. I've heard you speaking to her sometimes."

Tahmu's face was inscrutable. "Go on."

Jashemi licked his lips and reached for the waterskin fastened to his saddle. He took a drink, wondering what his father was doing. Was this a test of some sort? And if so, was he giving the right answers?

He continued. "And my mother...you do not force her to veil herself if she steps outside her quarters. Nor do you deny her anything."

"Do you think I should?"

Jashemi recalled his aunt's behavior—subservient, soft, mild. He never saw his uncle strike her, but by the way she sometimes cringed when he began to yell, he suspected that Naram might reprimand Pela with more than harsh words. The servants all seemed afraid of him. They never spoke against him, of course, but they never seemed to be happy around him, either.

But Jashemi was old enough to realize that sometimes his mother took advantage of his father's indulgences. He wondered how she would seem to him now, after two years' separation.

"No," he said, at last. "I would not want my wife to be afraid of me. I would want her to love me, and respect me because I am worthy of respect, not because I enforce it. I like it that our servants smile and hasten to obey our requests with joyful steps. I would not want anyone scurrying away from me with downcast eyes. Somehow—somehow I think that is wrong."

He turned and looked at his father. "I would know your thoughts on this, Father."

Now, at last, Tahmu smiled down at his son. They rode close enough so that the *khashim* could easily reach over and squeeze Jashemi's shoulder.

"My boy is becoming a man," he said, "with a man's wisdom and perception. I agree with all that you have said, my son. I do not wish to speak ill of my wife's brother, but I do not approve of how he runs his household. I, too, saw the fear in the servants' eyes. I saw how Pela watches his every move, not out of love but out of anticipation of a blow. He cannot hold his wine and he has not earned the respect of his equals. I permitted you to go only because it is tradition. I am pleased that you learned anything at all. I thought I might have to spend the next year undoing what Naram has done."

Jashemi smiled, relieved.

"A leader commands respect because it is deserved and earned. I have spent my life striving for that goal, and I believe I have a household that would die for me if need be."

"And a wife who is happy," added Jashemi, thinking of his mother's flamboyance in comparison with Pela's mousy reticence. When his father did not answer, Jashemi glanced up at Tahmu sharply. Sorrow sat upon those elegant features.

"I have done what I could to make your mother happy," Tahmu said softly. "But I do not know that I have succeeded." He kicked Swift and cantered up to ride alongside his Second, Halid.

After the welcome-home feast, Jashemi went to his old quarters. They smelled fresh and clean, and he idly picked up a bright yellow cloved fruit tucked among the pillows and inhaled its spicy citrus scent. His servants undressed him; they seemed so pleased to do the task that he had not the heart to dismiss them as he was perfectly capable of removing his own clothing.

As he lay in bed, Jashemi's mind kept returning to that conversation. Even though they had had several more days' travel ahead of them, Tahmu had not initiated such a personal conversation again.

He thought of the girl he had glimpsed at the feast.

"I think I know why you cannot make Mother happy, Father," he said softly. With a sigh, he rolled over in the soft sheets, closed his eyes, and slept.

The next morning, the men of the household were to go hunting. Jashemi's servants woke him well before dawn, presenting him with a hot cup of *eusho,* hard-boiled eggs, and fruit to break his fast. He sipped the beverage slowly, nibbled on the sweet *paraah,* and then headed down to visit the caverns. His servants offered to come with him, to wash his hair and scrub his back, but he ordered them to stay behind. He wanted to be alone with his thoughts.

He descended the stone steps quickly, his mind elsewhere, and before he knew it he was standing in the cavern, gazing at the underground pools.

A girl shot to the surface, expelling air with a gasp. Jashemi felt heat rise to his cheeks and he turned away.

"Oh!" cried the girl. "Oh, my lord, forgive me, I shall depart at once." He heard her emerge from the pool, heard the splattering, slapping sounds of wet feet padding quickly over to the clothes basket.

"There is no need," he told her, not turning around. "I will come back later."

"No, my lord, no, you are the *khashimu.* I beg forgiveness; usually no one comes down here at this time...."

That's right, Jashemi thought. *There are set times for ser-*

vants and family. The wet feet approached him and then went silent. Curious, he turned around to see the girl huddled at his feet. Her long hair was wet and tangled. Water dripped from it to pool on the stone. Odd, it seemed to him almost red in the torchlight. His heart leaped. It was the girl from the banquet....

"Look at me," he said, his voice adopting the tone of command.

She did so, lifting her eyes to his. But apparently, she did not see in his face what he saw in hers. He smiled at her.

"What is your name?"

"Kevla, my lord."

"There is nothing to forgive, Kevla. Servants have as much a right to enjoy the bounty of the House of Four Waters as I do. I've been so long away I've forgotten who bathes when."

She gave him a tentative smile. "You are kind to say these words. May I have my lord's permission to leave?"

"Yes, Kevla. You may go."

Jashemi turned to watch her as she scurried up the steps, her white rhia turning dark where it clung to her still-wet body, her little feet leaving clear footprints on the stone. He wanted to call her back, to talk to her, but he did not know what to say.

He bathed in silence, his thoughts even heavier now than they had been when he descended.

The morning air was cool on Jashemi's face as they rode their *sa'abahs* away from the House and toward the mountains. His heart lifted a little as he saw Mount Bari far in the distance. Naram lived well south of the House of Four Waters, too far away for Jashemi to see the sacred mountain, and he had missed it. He said a quick prayer to the Dragon who lived in its heart, and asked that it would be in a forgiving mood when he spoke to his father.

There were eight of them riding out to hunt today: Jashemi and Tahmu, Tahmu's Second, Halid, and five servants. Two would ride with them and assist in the hunt, dressing the animals that their lord and his son were certain to bring down, while the other three would set up a camp and have shade, cool drinks, and meals ready for the hunters during the heat of the day.

With the exception of Sahlik—who was the exception to so many things—Jashemi had never really paid much attention to his servants. He had never been unkind to them—his father would not permit abuse of servants and besides, it was not in Jashemi's nature to be cruel—but he had never truly thought of them as people, as he and his parents and Halid were people. Now he watched them from under long lashes, trying to remember their names, if they had families.

"You are quiet today, my son," Tahmu said, bringing his mount alongside Jashemi's.

"I...do not have much to say, Father," Jashemi replied. His face burned at the lie. He had quite a bit to say, but he wanted to talk privately. "Perhaps we can speak later...just the two of us?"

Tahmu's dark, wise eyes roamed his son's face. He sighed, looking somehow older than he had a moment ago.

"Of course. When the scouts leave to flush the quarry."

Jashemi looked at Halid, who was riding not far away. Tahmu's Second was a fixture in Jashemi's life. He sat straight in the saddle, a mountain of a man, with a thick black beard and long, wavy hair that was presently covered by a white kerchief. If anything happened to Tahmu before Jashemi came of age to inherit, Halid would assume leadership of the Clan. Halid was as familiar a presence in Jashemi's life as his father, but this was not even for his ears. Jashemi would speak to Tahmu about something much more personal than leadership of the Clan.

Some time later, one of the scouts hurried back. "I have spotted a herd at the base of the mountains."

"Excellent, Dumah. Send them round." Tahmu licked a finger and lifted it in the air, testing the wind's direction. "We will fan out in case they bolt. Halid, circle around to the right. Jashemi, you and I will head south. Hua, hua!"

He kicked the *sa'abah* and the great beast lurched into action, lowering its head and flattening its ears. Its tail curled over its back, providing shade for both mount and rider. Jashemi followed his father's lead, kicking his own *sa'abah* and crouching on its long neck. Tahmu rode well out of hearing range of the others, and then brought his mount to a walk.

"Speak," said Tahmu. "We have several minutes before the *liah* are flushed."

Jashemi opened his mouth. He had been rehearsing this since last night. He would be reasonable, eloquent, calm. He would behave like an adult.

What tumbled from his lips was, "Kevla is your daughter! How could you betray Mother like this?" He clamped his mouth shut, cursing himself.

Strangely, Tahmu did not grow angry. The *khashim* sighed. "I am sorry you saw her. She ought to have been veiled."

"That doesn't matter! Why did you—?"

Tahmu's head jerked around and he glared at his son. "Did you not notice that Kevla is older than you? I have never betrayed your mother, Jashemi, never!"

"But...she is so little...."

"She is small and thin because she has been raised in poverty as the daughter of a *halaan,*" said Tahmu, bitterness creeping into the words. "I did not even know of her existence until recently. It was Sahlik who spotted her, dancing on a street corner and crying her mother's—"

He broke off and looked away, his throat working. "Let me tell you a story. It is the story of a man who was in love with a woman. He wanted nothing more than to spend the rest of his life with her. But he was a *khashim,* the leader of a great and powerful clan, and she was low-caste. His clan was quarrelsome, and on the verge of tearing itself apart. He needed to marry a high-caste woman, to pacify a powerful section of the clan that was threatening to break away. There was a choice between duty and love, and the man chose duty."

Jashemi listened intently, barely breathing.

"The man's heart was broken. He married the woman he was supposed to, and promised himself that she would want for nothing. And she does not. The woman he could not marry disappeared, until one day, the man's servant spotted a girl-child dancing in the marketplace, a girl-child who looked so much like the *khashim* that the servant could hardly believe it.

"The *khashim* realized that his love for the low-caste woman had brought forth a child, an innocent who had done no wrong who should not suffer for what her parents had done. So the *khashim* convinced the girl's mother that her daughter would be safe and well cared for all of her days, as a servant in the great House.

"And so it is that Kevla is safe. She has food, a place to sleep, and pleasant, easy duties. I can offer her a good life, and I choose to do so."

Jashemi was silent, staring at the mountain. He wondered if the Great Dragon could hear this "story." At last, he said slowly, considering every word, "It would have been wrong of you to have left Kevla to her fate, knowing what you did. But she is your daughter. My sister. Does she—does anyone know this?"

"Sahlik knows. And now, so do you."

"Kevla should know," Jashemi said.

"No. It would be too dangerous. She would be used by those who would try to hurt me through her. The fewer who know, the better."

Jashemi looked up at his father and took a deep breath. "Then you are compounding your sin by lying, Father. She has a right to be acknowledged."

"To what end, my son? To hurt your mother, whose only real crime is that she is not the woman I loved? To mark Kevla as a target for schemers and plotters? To plant false hope in her little heart? She is and always will be Bai-sha. Even if I acknowledged her, she will have no legal rights. She has a better life now than any she could have expected."

This was wisdom, and Jashemi knew it. And yet....

"You will understand when you are older, my son. For now, I will ask you to swear that you will reveal what you have discovered to no one."

"Of course. But others will notice. The resemblance is strong, Father. Especially when you or I are close to her." He took a sip from his waterskin.

"Then we must take care not to be seen close to her," Tahmu replied. "People do not notice servants, Jashemi. Yeshi has not, and she has picked Kevla as her new favorite girl."

Jashemi choked on the liquid. "You placed Kevla with Mother? You rub her nose in this?"

Again, Tahmu sighed. "I cannot love your mother, Jashemi. The Great Dragon knows that I have tried. What I can do is honor her and—"

"Honor her? By giving her your Bai-sha child?"

"Jashemi!" Tahmu's voice was sharp and hard, and the boy started. "I have been patient with you, but do not presume to judge me. Yeshi is kind to her women, and also, they are not as often seen wandering in the household. It is best for Kevla to be with Yeshi. And she is good at what she does—Yeshi is happy. How then is this wrong?"

Tears stung Jashemi's eyes and he blinked hard, not wishing to cry in front of his father. He felt a dreadful helplessness wash over him. He loved his mother, and he had assumed Tahmu loved her, too. To learn in the space of one day that he had a Bai-sha half sister and that his father had never loved his mother was almost overwhelming. He wanted to hate Tahmu, but he understood his father's reasoning. He wanted to hate Kevla, but she was unstained by this. She seemed bright and spirited, the sort of girl he would have been delighted to call "sister."

Of course, he could not call her anything.

Or could he?

His father had asked him not to reveal his secret. Jashemi would keep that promise. But Tahmu had not forbidden his son to seek out Kevla.

Had circumstances been different, they might have been true brother and sister. Kevla would have been raised with respect and honor. In the past, Tahmu had even spoken in favor of women learning to read, so Jashemi assumed that if Kevla had been legitimate, she would have been educated.

They could have been playmates.

They could still be playmates.

Hope stirred inside him, replacing that awful sense of anguish and helplessness. He could not force his father to love his mother. He could not undo what Tahmu had done years ago. But Jashemi could see to it that Kevla knew more than comfort as Yeshi's handmaiden.

"Jashemi?" Tahmu regarded his son intently. Jashemi averted his eyes, fearful that his father would be able to read his plan somehow. "What are you—?"

"Father!" Jashemi cried, pointing at a roiling cloud of dust. "They are coming!"

Father and son sprang into action. Jashemi kicked his mount, clinging to the creature as if molded to its furry, pale body. The *sa'abah* began to run, its hind legs devouring the sand in great long strides, its body stretching out to cut down resistance from the wind. It was trained as a hunting beast, and knew what to do.

Jashemi reached for the bow fastened to the saddle. In one gesture, he raised the bow and fitted an arrow to the string, holding it taut, straining with the pressure, until he had a clear shot. Then he opened his fingers and the bolt flew.

A cry of pain went up, and Jashemi, as always, shrank from the sound momentarily. *Liahs* sounded like a woman screaming when they were in pain, and although Jashemi had brought down his share of the creatures, he never got used to that cry.

His father, too, had taken aim and shot. A second scream went up. Jashemi shot again, but the arrow missed its target, landing in the sand. Halid was bringing up the rear, also shooting.

Jashemi lost track of how often he aimed and let an arrow fly. His *sa'abah* easily kept pace with the herd, maneuvering closely enough so that Jashemi could see the golden coats with the pale horizontal stripes, the rolling eyes, the long, black horns. He smelled dust and the musky stench of fear.

Finally, Tahmu cried, "Hold, hold!"

Six *liahs*, four males and two females, lay dead on the sand. Two more struggled to rise, blood streaming from their flanks. Tahmu quickly turned his mount around. He held out his bow to Halid, who rode alongside him, and exchanged the bow for a long spear. Tahmu kicked the *sa'abah* and it lunged forward.

As he came up alongside the dying creatures, Tahmu lifted the spear and plunged it deeply into the flailing *liahs*.

It was a mercy killing, and Jashemi knew it. He hated to see the lovely things suffer and was glad his father always made sure they were slain as quickly and as painlessly as possible. Naram liked to leave the wounded ones to die on their own, killing them only when it was time for the hunting party to depart. Such cruelty ruined the meat, but Naram thought it fit to give to the servants. Jashemi had watched the wounded *liahs* linger for hours, bloody froth at their mouths, their eyes rolling....

My father is not like Naram, Jashemi thought fiercely. *No matter what he has done, what mistakes he has made, Tahmu-kha-Rakyn is a good man and a wise leader.*

Even so, Jashemi would not tell Tahmu what he planned when they returned to the House of Four Waters.

Chapter Eight

When Sahlik summoned her one afternoon while Yeshi napped, shortly after the *khashimu* had returned, Kevla was curious but not concerned. She stood in the kitchens, waiting for Sahlik to acknowledge her.

Sahlik turned and took her in from head to toe. "I have a new task for you. Since Jashemi has returned, Yeshi has taken much more of an interest in the functioning of the House. She will have less need of her women."

Kevla gnawed her lower lip. If Yeshi had less need of her women, would not Ranna and Tiah quickly step in to command what time their mistress deigned to give them? And if Kevla was set another task, would not Yeshi forget about her?

But Sahlik had continued speaking and Kevla quickly returned her attention to the older woman.

"...healer," Sahlik was saying. "You will study with him several times a week. Such skills will be useful."

A lump welled up in Kevla's throat. She was going to be sent away. They had decided she was not worthy to serve Yeshi, and had come up with a way to get her out of the great House.

"As Sahlik wishes," she said thickly, bowing. She felt a gentle hand on her shoulder and looked up.

"You're not being punished, Kevla," Sahlik said. "I promise. I'll keep an eye on Ranna and Tiah for you." And she winked.

Relieved, Kevla grinned, and ran to the healer's small house. When she reached the brightly painted red door of Maluuk's hut, she yanked it open and said breathlessly, "Maluuk, I'm here to—"

The words died in her throat as the occupants of the hut looked up at her. Asha and Maluuk she expected, but not the third person. Seated on a small stool was Jashemi-kha-Tahmu.

She dropped to her knees. "Forgive me, I did not know—"

"Kevla, rise." Jashemi's voice was patient. Kevla scrambled to her feet, looking at the healer with a mute inquiry.

"Jashemi is also to be taught knowledge of healing," Maluuk said mildly. "For this time together, you are equal as my students. There is no master here." He stood up straighter and his eyes twinkled. "Except for me."

Kevla wondered if this was a trick of some sort and her gaze darted to that of the young master for confirmation. His kind smile widened into a grin at her expression.

"It is true what Maluuk says. During this time, you and I are equals." He rose, took her hand, and squeezed it reassuringly. Kevla's hand remained limp with shock in Jashemi's strong but gentle grip as he led her to a stool.

"Now," said Maluuk, clearing his throat, "we will begin with the treatment of minor injuries."

* * *

As the classes went on, Kevla learned to enjoy them. Maluuk was a good teacher and encouraged both students to ask questions. Her quick mind followed everything that Maluuk taught them, and Jashemi proved to be an intelligent young man. She accepted the situation, but what did strike her as odd was the fact that Maluuk would leave them to themselves for the second half of each "lesson," which lasted three hours in the afternoons. They were told to talk about what they had learned that day, and at first, in formal tones, that was all they discussed.

Then one afternoon, Jashemi said, "Can you play *Shamizan?*"

"What is *Shamizan?*" Jashemi's eyes lit up. For the first time since she had known him, Kevla thought that he looked like a boy her own age, not a small adult.

"Oh, it's so much fun! Let me go get my set—" He rose and ran out of the hut, returning only a few moments later, flushed and out of breath. Kevla suspected he had run the entire way. Hardly proper behavior for a future *khashim,* but it was good to see Jashemi so happy.

"It's easy to learn." He placed a carved wooden board with black and white interlocking circles painted on it on one of the small tables. The overlapping sections of the circles were gray. He motioned that Kevla should draw up a stool. She hesitated. It was one thing to sit beside the young master during class, or even when they were discussing the lesson. But he had dropped the formality and was treating her as if they were of the same caste. Uneasy, she obeyed.

From a small pouch tucked under his arm, Jashemi withdrew a handful of clear, shiny stones, cupping them in his brown palm.

Forgetting herself, Kevla exclaimed, "They are beautiful!" and added quickly, "my lord. What kind of stone are they?"

"They are only glass," Jashemi said. "There are five families of colors: reds, blues, greens, yellows, and purples. So up to five people can play. Within each family, there are three shades. You place them like so, on the areas of black, white and gray."

They might be only glass, but Kevla thought the "stones" exquisite. They caught and held the light, and the colors were so intense. She was drawn to the reds and picked one up. It was the color of flame, and for a brief moment she thought it might feel hot in her hand. But it was cool and smooth. She rubbed it on her cheek, blushing when she caught Jashemi looking at her.

The rules were easy: dark hues were placed on the black areas of the board, light hues on the white, and medium tones on the gray. There was a roll of marked ivory sticks to determine play, and the object was to eliminate the opponent's pieces.

Easy to learn, hard to stop, Kevla thought. At one point, she looked up from the board and saw Jashemi regarding her with an intent gaze. His face dissolved into delight as she ducked her head and smiled.

"You like the game, then?"

"Oh, yes, very much."

"I am so glad. I hoped you would."

Shamizan quickly became a regular feature of their "study sessions." So, too, did another unexpected development. Jashemi began to teach Kevla how to write and read. He was a patient teacher, and Kevla a quick student, so the task was a pleasant one for both. Still, Kevla felt awkward when he would touch her hand as she held a pen, correcting the placement of her fingers, or casually put a hand on her shoulder as he leaned in to observe her work. He seemed to find it very easy to forget that he was *khashimu* and she was Bai-sha.

Despite her unease, Kevla looked forward to these sessions, and missed them on the days when they did not occur. Sahlik had told her to stay quiet about the healer's teaching. It was not truly a secret, Sahlik said, but Kevla would be wise not to draw attention to herself. Kevla agreed. She had no desire for Tiah and Ranna to have something else to resent. And of course, not even Sahlik knew about the furtive sessions of reading and writing instruction and the endless rounds of *Shamizan*.

One day, after she had sent Tiah and Ranna away for her nap, Yeshi called for Kevla. "You sent for me, great lady?"

Yeshi looked wonderful. She had been much happier since Jashemi had come home, and Kevla had observed that mother and son spent much time together and enjoyed one another's company. Yeshi, as Sahlik had said, had become more involved in the running of the household, and seemed to have less need of her usual self-indulgent pleasures.

Yeshi smiled as she reclined on the bed—a true, genuine smile that made her look radiant. "Yes, Kevla. Sahlik tells me that you have been studying under Maluuk. Is this so?"

For a moment, Kevla panicked. But Yeshi didn't look upset, and she knew it would be unwise to lie.

"Yes, great lady."

"That is good news to me." She patted the bed beside her, and Kevla, growing more and more confused, obediently climbed up to sit beside her mistress.

Gently, Yeshi took Kevla's hand and placed it on her belly, below her navel. "I am pleased, because I would like you to assist Maluuk in delivering my baby."

Kevla's jaw dropped. "Your baby?"

Yeshi grinned and nodded her head excitedly. "You are my good luck charm, little Kevla. My personal blessing from the Great Dragon. After ten years I have been able to conceive!"

Kevla's eyes filled with tears. Gently, she spread her fingers on Yeshi's belly and said, "Blessings on this baby. And blessings on the House of Four Waters!"

It was two days after the festival of Kur, and Kevla and Jashemi were engaged in a particularly delightful game of *Shamizan.* As they were younger than most of the household, they had not celebrated Kur with as much vigor as the adults had.

Kevla was familiar with the wild nature of the celebratory festival. It was the one time a year when the people believed the Great Dragon turned a blind eye to indulgent pleasures. Keishla had always had more business than she could handle during the three-day celebration. The people of Arukan drank to excess, ate to excess, and did many other things to excess during Kur. There was a great feast and much flowing wine at the House of Four Waters, but compared to what Kevla was used to encountering with Keishla and her customers, it seemed rather staid to her. The next few days were astoundingly quiet, as most of the household seemed averse to noise, light or rich foods.

"Ha!" cried Jashemi triumphantly as he picked up no fewer than eight of Kevla's red pieces. "You only have six markers left, and I have over a dozen!"

They both started when they heard the unmistakable sound of the *shakaal.* Their gazes locked.

"What—" Kevla began.

The transformation in Jashemi was startling to her. In a heartbeat, he had gone from a playful, mischievous youth gloating over a board game victory to the stone-faced *khashimu* of the Clan of Four Waters.

"I'll find out. Stay here. Say nothing of our being together."

His robes rustling softly, he rose and hastened out the door. When Jashemi did not return immediately, Kevla occupied herself by finishing the ointment Maluuk had requested she make. Her ears strained for any sound.

The door banged open. Maluuk and his apprentice rushed in. Clinging to them, an arm slung around each of their shoulders, was a rider close to collapse. His face was pale with sand, and there were dark red patches on his white *rhia*.

"Kevla, water," snapped Maluuk. He made straight for the long table. With a swift motion he sent the board and the pieces clattering to the floor and lay the stranger down on the table's cool surface.

Kevla poured a cup of water and brought it to the healer. Maluuk lifted the man's head up and dribbled some of the precious liquid onto lips so dry they cracked and bled. A swollen tongue crept out and caught a few drops, then the man began to drink eagerly.

"Gently," said Maluuk, "a sip at a time. Kevla, keep giving him water, slowly. Asha, help me."

Kevla cradled the man's head in her arms and did as she was told, watching anxiously as Maluuk and Asha cut away the rider's torn, bloody *rhia*. Her eyes widened as she saw the injuries that had been inflicted upon the stranger: cuts as long as her arm, and one festering wound in the shoulder where a small length of broken arrow shaft still protruded.

"Tahmu," gasped the man. His voice sounded as dry as the desert sands he had crossed. "Messages...we were attacked...."

"Kevla, go find Tahmu." She nodded, placed the rider's head down gently on the stone table, and sped out the door.

She raced down the little hill, searching frantically for her lord. If the *shakaal* had been blown, then it was likely that the household was already alerted. Jashemi, too, would have learned what had transpired. Even as she stumbled and nearly twisted her ankle, she saw two white shapes running out of the house toward her: Jashemi and his father.

She ran toward them, her legs pumping. "Rider!" she screamed as they caught sight of her. "He's hurt! He says he was attacked! He's at the healing hut, come quickly!"

In midstride she turned and raced back the way she had come. The men overtook her and by the time she had returned to the small hut, Tahmu was at the rider's side. He clutched the stranger's hand and bent his head close to the man's mouth, straining to catch the faint words. Jashemi stood on the other side, his gaze darting from the injured man to his father.

Kevla was gasping for breath, her heart hammering so loudly that it was hard for her to hear anything over it.

"In the middle...night," the rider said, "after the...celebration of Kur...no one attacks during Kur..." He coughed, and Kevla saw to her horror that there was bloody foam on his lips. "There were many dead when Father...me to you...message in my pack...."

He hissed as Maluuk bathed his injuries. Kevla could not take her eyes off the sight. She was no expert, but she could tell he was grievously wounded.

"Keep speaking," Tahmu said.

"Father, he is badly hurt. Surely he needs rest and—"

Even though Tahmu's look was not directed at her, Kevla shrank from it. Jashemi fell silent at once.

Maluuk and Asha were now slathering on a thick, pungent ointment. Tahmu gripped the man's hand harder, pressed it to his chest.

"Keep speaking, Sammis," he urged. "Everything you can tell us is precious."

Sammis opened his mouth, but the words never came. His eyes suddenly became fixed and staring, and his body went limp. Tahmu sighed. He held the dead hand for a moment longer, then reached and gently shut the wide eyes.

"Sammis was a dead man before he arrived," Tahmu said to Jashemi. "That is why I did not let him rest. No healer could have saved him, and I had hoped he would live long enough to tell me what had happened."

"You knew him?" Kevla blurted. Everyone turned to stare and her and she blushed.

"Yes," Tahmu said. "He was my nephew. Jashemi's cousin."

Kevla turned compassionate eyes on the boy. His face was impassive, though his eyes were shiny and his lower lip quivered slightly. Their gazes locked, and an unspoken message passed between them.

"Maluuk, prepare him for the pyre. Jashemi, find his mount and fetch the messages he said he carried."

"Yes, Father." Jashemi headed for the door. Impulsively, Kevla followed. They stood outside the door, hands raised to shield their eyes from the sun as they tried to see where Sammis's mount had gone. Kevla realized she didn't know if they should be looking for a horse or a *sa'abah*.

"You should not be seen with me," hissed Jashemi, barely moving his lips.

The rebuke stung. She had thought...she had been foolish to think it.

"Two sets of eyes are better than one," she replied stubbornly. "I am a servant assisting the *khashimu*."

"Curse you, Kevla, it's more than that," Jashemi said, but did not elaborate. "There. It sought out the company of other *sa'abahs*."

The exhausted beast, a female, had indeed tried to join the herd of the House of Four Waters. They found her pacing mournfully back and forth outside the stone corral, bleating plaintively as she scented water and others of her own kind on the other side. Tahmu's *sa'abahs* had come up to her and were nuzzling her, their muzzles barely clearly the wall.

She started when Jashemi and Kevla hurried up to her, but Jashemi dove for the trailing reins. He spoke softly to the creature, patting her neck and sending a small cloud of dust into the air.

"Down, down," he urged the *sa'abah*, tugging on the reins. Obediently, she crouched so that Jashemi could reach the saddle and the small bundle tied securely to it. So tightly was the leather pouch bound to the saddle that Jashemi had to use the small knife he always wore to cut it free. He removed the saddle, opened the gate, and let the exhausted *sa'abah* inside. She headed straight for the trough, lowered her head, and began to drink. The others crowded around her, reaching to touch her with their small, stubby arms, as if they understood that she had been through a terrible ordeal.

Although she had lived at the House for some time now, Kevla still found the *sa'abahs* fascinating, and watched them as Jashemi fumbled through the sack. She heard a rustling, then silence, then a deep sigh.

She turned around just in time to catch him wiping his eyes with his sleeve. Her heart ached in sympathy. Without thinking she touched his arm gently.

Jashemi jerked away, and immediately Kevla dropped to her knees. Again, she had assumed too much.

"Forgive me, young lord! I transgressed, I did not mean—"

A gentle hand on her shoulder urged her to rise. "It's all right," he assured her. "I just...."

"What does the letter say?"

His face crumpled and he looked down. "My uncle and all of my male cousins are dead. Slaughtered while they slept off the wine they had drunk in celebration of Kur."

Kevla listened, remaining silent.

Jashemi cleared his throat and continued in a more normal tone of voice. "The women were…were assaulted and then taken. Probably they are five-scores now. My cousin Sammis was sent by my uncle to summon help." He looked at her now, and she did not like the expression on his face. "The first thing the raiders did was burn the aerie, so that no warning hawks could be sent out to gather reinforcements. The *Sa'abah* Clan has probably taken what they want and are long gone."

"The *Sa'abah* Clan?" Kevla repeated, incredulous. She looked over at the milling creatures. They seemed gentle, intelligent. They had welcomed a stranger.

"It is ironic that the people who breed the most peaceful of animals are the ones most thirsty for blood," said Jashemi, bitterly. He looked down at the parchment in his hand. Kevla followed his gaze and saw that he had crumpled the missive.

Jashemi composed himself. "We will attack in retaliation. Father will want to see this. Return to the House, Kevla. My mother will be distraught to hear of the death of her brother."

Without another word he turned and trudged slowly back toward the healer's hut. Kevla wanted to follow. She had no desire to be in Yeshi's company when the *khashima* received such dreadful news.

For the third time in the span of a few months, the House of Four Waters was thrown into a flurry of activity. This time, though, the preparations were not for a welcome-home feast, or the wild celebration of a favorite holiday, but for battle.

Kevla continued her lessons in healing. Maluuk explained that he would be going with the warriors, as his skills would be needed to treat the injured.

"And there will be," he said, seeming suddenly very old. "There are always injured. Too many, even in a victory."

Asha would stay behind, to assume his master's position. Kevla would become his apprentice, assisting him in treating the household and preparing bandages, salves, ointments, and tinctures. Although it was uncommon for a woman to be placed in such an important position as apprentice healer, the usual niceties could not be observed. Asha seemed happy enough to take on the role of a full healer, and apparently didn't object to Kevla's gender.

She had always looked upon these sessions as play, an escape from the world of the household, a time to be with Jashemi. But Jashemi no longer attended the lessons, as he would be expected to accompany his father into battle. Her time with Maluuk had a new sense of urgency to it, and there was no more play involved.

Still, it was better than being with Yeshi. Kevla had not been present when Tahmu had told his wife that her brother was murdered and her nieces and nephews dead or captured. But she had heard the scream of anguish as she waited outside the door, and exchanged helpless glances with Tiah and Ranna. For the first time, she had felt a kinship with the other women as they listened to their mistress shriek and sob.

For nearly a day, Yeshi would not speak to them. She permitted them to bring her food, but nothing more, and she never looked at them when they entered quietly. When at last she did rouse herself to let them bathe and dress her, there was a new harshness to her mien. The three women moved quietly around their mistress, frightened for themselves, frightened for their household.

The war party was assembled with astonishing rapidity. The warriors would need to travel well and quickly, as the *Sa'abah* Clan was nomadic. Every bit of preserved food was brought forth and packed, and dozens of animals were slaughtered to replenish the stores. Weapons were brought out of storage, sharpened, cleaned, repaired, and set aside. Craftsmen worked from sunrise to sunrise making more arrows, more swords, more knives. Falcons flew back and forth from the House, as Tahmu called in his allies and they responded.

They trickled in, clan by clan, and Kevla gaped in amazement at the numbers. Within a few days, over five hundred men from the Sheep Clan, the River Clan, the Horserider Clan, the Star Clan, and the Cattle Clan had arrived to assist the Clan of Four Waters. None of the household's women had a chance to visit the caverns, as they were constantly teeming with warriors set on enjoying the House of Four Waters' famous bathing pool before they left for battle.

Kevla would have been glad to see them go had not she feared for Jashemi and Tahmu. What would happen if either one of them was killed? If *both* were killed? The thought was so dreadful that Kevla always drove it from her mind. But at night, she had dreams, and though she never remembered them, she would awaken with tears on her face.

The night before the warriors were to depart was not marked by revelry. It was too grim an occasion. Yeshi had dismissed her women and Kevla, wanting to do something to help, assisted in distributing freshly-filled waterskins to the men camped out on the grounds.

They were all of a kind: angry-looking or solemn-faced men, clad not in finery but in weather-worn *rhias,* who barely acknowledged her presence, though they took the waterskins she offered readily enough. They were crowded together, and Kevla heard conversations consisting of low mutterings and angry cries, the jingling of tack, the crackle of small fires. There was a smell of leather, fur, and sweat that after an hour or so made her stomach roil.

She had turned and was headed back to the House for more waterskins when a hand clamped down on her arm. She started to cry out, but turned and saw that it was Jashemi. He held a finger to his lips and she nodded. He tugged on her arm, leading her away from the bustle of the House.

Kevla trotted after him, confused and a little alarmed. Why would the *khashimu* want to see her alone, at night? Finally, Jashemi stopped.

"We are far enough away, we won't be overheard. And the moon is new."

Kevla kept her gaze on the ground. "What does my lord wish?" she asked.

"To apologize."

She was so startled that her head whipped up and she stared at him. "My lord, a *khashimu* never apologizes to a servant!"

"But Jashemi can and will apologize to Kevla," Jashemi countered. She had no response, merely looked at him in confusion. What was going on?

She heard him swallow. "You felt sorry for me the day that Sammis came. You wanted to help. I was rude to you. I wish I could explain why. Maybe someday."

Kevla lowered her eyes again. "I do not understand."

"I saw the hurt on your face," he said gently, stepping closer to her. She felt the soft puff of his breath on her cheek. "When I said you shouldn't be with me."

"My lord, you were right to say that. I overstepped."

He made an annoyed sound. "Kevla, please let me apologize!"

"Of course. As the *khashimu* wishes."

There was a pause. Then he said, "I am leaving tomorrow. Will—will you miss me?"

Her heart almost stopped. "Of course. I shall say prayers for the safety of my lord and my lord's son."

"Kevla, I—" She would not—could not—look at him. She knew what he wanted to hear, and she couldn't speak it. Not when she was Bai-sha and he was *khashimu*.

"Never mind. I'm sorry. I shouldn't have brought you here. I don't know what I was—" He turned and strode off.

Kevla's knees buckled and she fell hard to the earth. A quick sob escaped her and she clapped her hand over her mouth. He was already several paces away, but somehow he heard the soft sound. Kevla huddled on the sand, her head on her hands, willing him to go away. Before she realized what he had done, he was on his hands and knees in front of her.

"Kevla, talk to me," he implored.

She mustn't say it. She mustn't say anything. But the words seemed to have a life of their own.

"I'm afraid," she whispered. "I'm so afraid something will happen to you."

"Look at me," he said. She did, and found his face seemed blurry to her. She wiped angrily at the telltale tears. "I know you're afraid," he said softly. "I am, too. So is Father, and so are all the men. We all know we could be riding to our deaths."

He swore suddenly, a harsh curse that startled Kevla. "I hate these stupid raids! Why must people die like this? My uncle was not the most admirable of men, but he did not deserve to have his throat cut while he slept!"

"Perhaps the *Sa'abah* Clan—" began Kevla.

"It's not just them," he snarled. "It's *all* of them. We could just as easily be riding against the Star Clan or the Horserider Clan tonight as riding with them. They're our allies now, but we've fought them in the past. And we have allied with the *Sa'abah* Clan, and look what they've done." He continued to fume in silence, his lips pressed together in a thin line of anger.

"Come back," said Kevla, softly, shocked by her boldness.

His eyes searched hers, then he startled her by reaching out and taking her hands in his. Their palms pressed together, hot and moist in the darkness. Tears continued to slip down her cheeks. He leaned forward, releasing one hand to wipe the tears from her face with an odd mixture of grace and clumsiness. Starlight caught the glitter of tears in his own eyes.

"I will come back," he said firmly.

"But only the Great Dragon knows our destinies," she replied, her voice catching on the words.

Jashemi placed one hand on either side of her face, forcing her to look into his eyes.

"We are not done with each other yet," he said fiercely. "I don't know my destiny, but I know this much. I can feel it. Can't you?"

As she gazed into his eyes, she felt a sudden lightening. Her tense muscles eased, relaxing so that she almost slumped. He was right. Somehow, in a way that surpassed her understanding, she knew that he was right. What she felt swirling inside her now was not something as frail as hope. It was swift, certain knowledge.

Some would die in this retaliatory raid. Perhaps people she knew. Perhaps even Tahmu.

But not Jashemi.

We are not done with each other yet.

Chapter Nine

The warriors departed the next morning. Kevla had lined up with the other servants to watch the warriors march through the courtyard and down the road that led past the twining Four Waters and beyond.

As the ones who had issued the rallying cry, the members of the Clan of Four Waters were the last ones to depart. Kevla stood properly clad in the veil in front of so many male strangers at such a formal function. Most rode horses, a very few rode *sa'abahs*—Ranna nudged Tiah and muttered, "They'll likely come home with more of *those*"— and many walked. They almost danced as they passed, and the crowd cheered and whistled.

"It's as if they are going off to a game," Kevla said softly.

"No game," Sahlik sighed, "but you would not know it. Here come our people."

Tahmu, proudly astride Swift-over-Sand, led the procession. Beside him on a *sa'abah* rode Jashemi. Neither whooped or danced, although some of the other clansmen did. Tahmu smiled reassuringly at the assembled crowd of wives, children, and servants, and Jashemi emulated his father. He did not meet Kevla's gaze.

Yeshi stood at the gate. Kevla had helped her with her cosmetics that morning, but it was obvious the *khashima* had been crying in the intervening time. The kohl that had encircled her dark eyes had run down her face and been wiped away, smearing both the rivulet of black and the red rouge of the great lady's cheeks so that Yeshi almost appeared to have been assaulted. Her full, red lips trembled and her eyes were bright with tears. She wore no veil; as the highest ranking female present, the only one who outranked her was her husband.

Tahmu dismounted and embraced his wife. She hugged him, but it was for her son that Yeshi reserved her fiercest affections. She dropped to her knees and clung to him, the tears again flooding her face with black streams of grief. Jashemi wiped the tears away, as he had done with Kevla last night, and his expression as he regarded his mother was one of deep compassion. Kevla was too far away to hear what Yeshi said, but as the minutes passed and Yeshi did not rise nor release her son, she could feel the tension in the crowd.

Sahlik moved quickly toward her mistress, stepping behind Yeshi and placing her hands on her shoulders. Jashemi gently disengaged himself. Tahmu whispered something to his wife, who brightened and put a beringed hand on her gently swelling belly. She straightened and stepped away from husband and son.

They rode out, and as the gates closed behind them, Kevla felt a dreadful hollowness in her chest.

Yeshi stepped forward. "In the absence of the *khashim,*

his Second, and the heir," she said, her voice thick with grief but surprisingly strong, "All orders will come from me. The first order I will issue as present leader of the Clan of Four Waters is that every day we will petition the Great Dragon with offerings, so that he will be moved to bring our men safely home."

A murmur of approval went up. Yeshi nodded, pleased. "We will begin today."

The days dragged by. Yeshi did not seem to have a great deal of time for her women during the day, though at night she was more exhausted than Kevla had ever seen her. At that time, she wanted all three of them to massage her swollen feet, rub oil on her growing belly, and speak softly and kindly to her.

Each day, Kevla went to the aerie, to see if there were any messages from the war party. Sometimes there were, but the hawk master would hardly reveal their precious contents to so lowly a servant, although as Kevla's appearance became a regular occurrence, he grew fond of her. Sometimes Yeshi would share the news, sometimes not.

Kevla's lessons with Asha continued. He was particularly anxious for her to learn about childbirth, in case Yeshi's baby came before Maluuk and the others returned. While happy to be trusted with such information, Kevla found the hours spent in the healer's hut only served to emphasize Jashemi's absence.

Days stretched into weeks, and then months. Celebration days came and went, and Yeshi presided over the revelry. Although the unctuous Bahrim flirted heavily with the *khashima*—and he was not alone among the *uhlals* casting glances at the beautiful great lady—Yeshi's growing belly seemed to discourage further improper advances. With each moon she tired more easily, and spent more time sleeping. Asha and Kevla examined her every day, and at one point Asha announced with certainty, "The child could come very soon."

Yeshi shook her head. "The child will not come until his father returns home."

Asha bit his lip, hesitant to disagree, and finally said diplomatically, "Then let us pray that that day will be soon."

Not long after that, Kevla was in Yeshi's chambers, watching the morning processional heading out to the House's altar. Though she had never visited it, she knew that it was some miles distant. Each clan had an altar at the foot of the nearest mountain. The entire chain was sacred to the Great Dragon, and never to be crossed, although of course Mount Bari was the mighty creature's home. Some clan altars were only for show, but Tahmu-kha-Rakyn had always been particularly devout and eager to placate the Dragon. Household gossip held that this was why the House of Four Waters was so prosperous. His wife continued the tradition in her husband's absence, and each morning the party left, laden with gold, food, sweet herbs, jugs of water, and wine, all to please the Dragon. As her eye followed them, watching the group growing smaller as they headed down the road, Kevla noticed movement in the sky. She squinted against the sunlight, already harsh though it was still early, and saw that it was a bird.

It was a hawk.

Her heart leaped, as it always did whenever one of the winged messengers arrived. She raced out the doors, down the spiral stone stairs, out of the House and across the courtyard to the aerie. By the time she had ascended the stairs, breathless and sweaty, the bird had arrived and the hawk master was unfastening the small message.

He read it quickly, and a grin spread over his face. He turned to Kevla, thrust the message at her and said, "Give this to your mistress! Hurry!"

Kevla took the message and hurried down the stairs. The small, tightly rolled piece of parchment seemed to burn in her hand. As she reentered the coolness of the House, she ducked into a corner and unrolled the message with shaking hands.

Yeshi: We are victorious. The clan has scattered with only a few of their precious sa'abahs. *The rest, we have captured and will divide among the clans. We will also have many five-scores. Jashemi conducted himself with skill and honor. Halid, too, did the Clan and his* khashim *proud. Our allies worked well together and all are pleased with the results. We have lost men, but that was to be expected. If only it was not necessary to trade lives for pride and livestock. With* sa'abahs *enough so that all high-caste warriors may ride them, we will make good time returning home. I hope the baby and you are well.*

Kevla's knees suddenly went weak and she almost slid down the wall to the floor. Jashemi and Tahmu had survived. That was all she needed to know. Five-scores, *sa'abahs*, Clan honor—no doubt these things were important to others, but as far as she was concerned, they would have been bought at too dear a cost if it had meant having to ceremonially burn the corpses of the *khashim* and his heir.

She heard footsteps and the sound of voices. Quickly, Kevla rerolled the scrap of parchment and hastened along the corridor to the stairs. Yeshi was in her room, standing and bathing her face when Kevla burst the door open.

Yeshi turned to frown at the noisy interruption, but Kevla thrust the message at her. "The hawkmaster smiled when he read it," she said. "So it must be good news."

Yeshi snatched the parchment out of Kevla's hands. Her eyes flickered back and forth much more rapidly than Kevla's had when she had read the missive. Yeshi brought a hand to her lips, and although she began to weep she smiled broadly.

"Good news indeed," she said to Kevla. "They are victorious and they are coming home. My son and my husband are safe." She pressed the small letter to her chest. "Thank the Great Dragon. Kevla, run and fetch Sahlik. We must be about preparing for a celebration!"

Kevla wondered if Yeshi had read the part about *we have lost men*. Was it possible to celebrate and grieve at the same time? Would there be pyres blazing under the starlit skies the same night as celebratory torches flickered in the great hall?

As she hastened to the kitchens, she could not help but think about Jashemi. She had tried not to dwell overmuch on thoughts of the *khashimu* and the odd parting they had made. Now, with his arrival imminent, the memory of that night flooded back to her. He had wanted her to admit that she would miss him, would fear for him.

We are not done with each other yet. His prediction that he would return had come true, and her heart was glad of it. Yet now that he would soon be back, what would he want from her? They had crossed a line that night, when he knelt in front of a servant and wiped the tears from her face, and she feared what lay on the other side of it.

It was only three days later that Tahmu's colors of red and gold were spotted against the blue sky. The deep, resonant sound of the *shakaal* issued, and the weary but exultant scout announced that the *khashim* was only a few hours behind him.

Yeshi was sitting at her window, watching the horizon intently, while Kevla dusted her mistress's face with powder and Ranna and Tiah worked on her feet and hair respectively. "I want to be the first to see him," Yeshi had said.

As Kevla applied the kohl, Yeshi started. A black line went straight from her eye to her ear.

"They are coming!" Yeshi cried, leaping up. She knocked

over the basin of water at her feet, which splashed all over Ranna's lap. Oblivious to the chaos she was creating for her handmaidens, she pointed out the window. "They are—"

Suddenly, Yeshi doubled over, her hands clutching her belly. Kevla caught her as she stumbled and would have fallen. There was a puddle of liquid at Yeshi's feet. At first glance, Kevla thought it was the spilled water from the basin...but that had gone all over Ranna, not the floor....

"Help me," Kevla snapped. "The baby is coming!"

"What...what should we do?" Ranna stammered.

"Fetch Asha. He'll bring the birthing stool and herbs," said Kevla, reciting the steps Asha had drummed into her head. "And hot water—we need hot water and towels."

Yeshi's fingers dug into Kevla's shoulders and she moaned softly. Kevla looked up at her mistress and tried to smile reassuringly.

"The great lady said the baby would wait for his father," she reminded Yeshi. "Well, the one is coming, and now so is the other."

Ranna was dismissed after she became ill. Tiah seemed made of sterner stuff and stayed on. Sahlik arrived quickly, and was a deeply comforting presence. Asha, too, was calm and soothing, his long fingers gently probing the mother-to-be's body.

"It has turned," he said reassuringly. "This should be an easy birth."

The look Yeshi gave him at this comment made him cringe. Yeshi was sweating, her hair was a tangled mess, and she seemed beyond words. All Kevla heard from her were shrieks, moans and growls.

She steeled herself to the sounds of Yeshi's pain. Neither Sahlik nor Asha seemed disturbed by the noises, so Kevla assumed that this was simply part of a normal birth. Every few minutes, Kevla glanced anxiously out the window, to see how much closer the returning warriors had come.

After a few hours had passed, Kevla went to the window and saw a milling throng of people down in the courtyard. She could not see Tahmu, but he had to be there. Hastening back to Asha, she said, "The warriors are here!"

"Good," he said. "Great lady, get on the stool."

Whimpering, Yeshi straddled the wooden birthing stool, supported by the strong arms of Tiah and Sahlik. Kevla had prepared the tepid pool of water with scented herbs to catch the baby. She placed it between Yeshi's parted legs, risking a glimpse at Asha. His fingers were just inside Yeshi's body, and they were coated with dark fluids. Kevla gulped, and for a moment envied the absent Ranna.

Suddenly, Yeshi cried, "No! Tahmu must be here!"

"Great lady," stammered Asha, "the baby will come as it chooses. To try to halt—"

"Tahmu!" screamed Yeshi. *"Tahmu!"*

"Dragon's teeth," muttered Asha. "Kevla, go find Tahmu."

Kevla nodded and raced down the stairs, once slipping and almost falling in her haste. There was a huge commotion in the courtyard, and although she had grown considerably in her time at the House, she was still so short she could not see over the tall figures of the returning warriors.

"Tahmu!" she screamed, heedless of proper etiquette, pushing past large, *rhia*-clad torsos and the long legs of the *sa'abahs*. "Tahmu, where are you?"

"Great *khashim*," cried one of the men, "your little servant wants you!" Several men turned to regard Kevla and joined in their friend's laughter. She ignored them.

"I must find Tahmu! The baby is—"

"Here I am, Kevla," said a calm, familiar voice. "Take me to her."

Kevla turned to start fighting her way back through the crowd, but the warriors parted for their *khashim* as they had not done for her.

"Is she—all right?"

"Well enough," Kevla responded, "but the baby is almost here, and she wants you—"

"She wants me to catch the baby, for luck," Tahmu said. He pushed past her and raced up the stairs to Yeshi's chamber.

Kevla followed, only a few steps behind. Tahmu entered, grasped and kissed his wife's hand, and then took up a position beside Asha. The baby's head was already showing.

"Tahmu, you are here!" gasped Yeshi.

"I am here, my wife, and ready to catch our child," he said, his voice deep with emotion. He held the basin of herbs and flowers. Kevla stood by with clean cloths, ready to hand them to Tahmu once the baby had come. As Yeshi screamed and strained, more and more of the baby's head appeared.

She frowned at it, her heart speeding up. *No, please let this not be so....*

"The baby's face is red," she said, her voice trembling.

"All babies are red when they are born," snapped Asha. Sweat dappled his forehead. "Push again, Yeshi!"

With a cry that hurt Kevla's ears, Yeshi panted and did as she was told. More of the baby slipped out into the waiting world.

The redness was still there. On the baby's face, smeared with fluid but obviously there.

"Its face is *red!*" Kevla cried again, filled with horror.

"That is just the afterbirth," Asha said. "Once more, Yeshi, push and bring forth the baby!"

Yeshi tensed, then growled low in her throat and bore down. The baby surged forward to splash into the bowl that Tahmu held. At that moment, Maluuk rushed in and took over from Asha, who seemed relieved to relinquish his position. The baby took a deep breath and squalled.

"A girl-child," Maluuk said. "Whole and sound."

"A daughter," cried Yeshi as Tiah and Sahlik helped her to the bed and began to clean her. "I have a little girl..."

Kevla stared as if transfixed. The baby kicked and squirmed as Tahmu began to clean her. His smile started to fade as he washed her face, and the red marks that Asha had claimed were afterbirth did not come off on the towel.

"Maluuk—" he said, looking imploringly at the healer. Kevla's arms folded about herself. She was suddenly very cold.

"The blood mark," Maluuk whispered. Yeshi was still crying softly, but both Tiah and Sahlik had heard. Their eyes widened and they exchanged glances. Exhausted as she was, Yeshi caught the change of mood in the room. She propped herself up on her elbows.

"Tahmu? Give me our daughter!"

The baby was still shrieking. The blood mark covered fully half its face, an angry red blotch that spoke louder than any words of the displeasure of the Great Dragon.

"Tahmu..." Yeshi's voice was pleading. She was begging for her husband to give her their child, for him to say that it was all right, that their baby was beautiful, perfect....

Tahmu did not answer. He snatched a cloth from Kevla's stiff fingers and wrapped the baby in it, his eyes glued to the red blotch on his daughter's face, and said in a cold voice, "Leave us."

They hurried out, not wanting to see what had to happen next. Tahmu himself wished with every fiber of his being that he did not have to do this, but the traditions were clear. The baby was imperfect.

He rose unsteadily, clutching the crying, wriggling bundle to his heart. Tahmu met Yeshi's eyes, and he saw her dawning comprehension.

"The blood mark," he said heavily. He did not need to explain further. It was rare, but not unfamiliar to the people of Arukan, this bitter stain that sometimes singled out the unfortunate children of wretched parents.

He knew why this child was so marked. It was a sign that the Great Dragon was still angry with him. It had given him back a daughter he did not know he had, but it had cruelly taken away this precious little girl now clasped in his arms.

For a moment, Yeshi did not react. Then she said, "No."

"I am sorry, my wife. Perhaps this is the Dragon's price for bringing so many of our brave warriors safely home." The lie burned him, but he could not let Yeshi know the truth. There was no need to inflict more pain on her. She would know suffering aplenty in the next few moments, and for years to come.

"No," said Yeshi, again. She held out her arms imperiously. *"Give me my daughter."*

"It is best if I take her—it—now," Tahmu said, aware that he was pleading. "If you hold her, it will only hurt you more when I—"

"Give her to me!" With a strength that startled him she leaped up from the birthbed and lunged at him. He barely managed to turn in time to keep her from seizing the infant. Even so, he was not quick enough to prevent Yeshi from scoring his face with her long, sharp nails. One came perilously close to his eye and he jerked his head away.

Her small fists rained down upon his back, her hands scrabbled for the baby, her screams echoed in his ears. She ducked underneath him and seized the infant, clasping it close to breasts that were swollen and full of milk.

"She's mine! I won't let you take her!"

But she was a delicate woman, and weak from her ordeal, and Tahmu was a war-hardened man. Implacably, hating himself, hating her for making this so much more painful than it had to be for both of them, he wrested the baby from her and pushed her backward.

She fell onto the bed. He stood, clutching the bundled, crying baby, waiting for her to come at him again, but all the strength seemed to bleed out of her. She lay where she had fallen, sprawled on the lavish bed where this tragic child had been conceived, and mewled pitifully.

"My baby," she moaned, "my little girl...give her to me, Tahmu, please, I beg you, give her to me...."

His heart ached as he watched her, filled with his own grief at what he must do. "I'm sorry," he said uselessly, and left her, racing down the stairs into the courtyard and grabbing the reins of the nearest *sa'abah* from a startled Clansman.

For much of his trip, the baby continued to scream. It wanted sustenance, love, its parents, soft bedding. All the things a baby has a right to expect when it is brought into the world, all the things Tahmu had not given Kevla and could not give this little girl. Eventually, its cries subsided. It whimpered now and then, enough for Tahmu to know that his daughter was still alive.

By the time he reached the Clan's altar at the foot of the mountains, the girl made barely any sounds at all. He drew the *sa'abah* to a halt and slipped to the ground. Tahmu felt ill when he saw the remnants of all the offerings Yeshi had made to the Dragon in his absence. Dried leaves from fruit long since devoured, wilted flowers, empty water jugs—all pleas from the House of Four Waters to bring the warriors home safely.

Most of those pleas had been answered; they had lost few men. But the Great Dragon had a terrible price for his protection, and Tahmu's feet felt as heavy as if they were carved of stone as he approached the offering area.

He looked down at the baby. Her eyes were closed, but she was breathing.

"I'm so sorry," he said, illogically trying to explain what he was doing to her. "But this is the way of our people. The Great Dragon marks those it would have us give to him. He robs them of their sight, or the use of their legs, or their minds. He cleaves their mouths, or gives them only nine fingers, or," he paused, the lump in his throat preventing speech, "or stains their faces with the blood mark, as he has done with you."

Gently, he reached to touch the blotch on his child's otherwise perfect face. She opened her eyes and regarded him. Tahmu held the doomed infant close.

"Dragon!" he cried at last, his voice raw, "Dragon, you have tormented me for so long. I beg you, let this be your last judgment upon me and my House. You marked this child. She is yours. I have torn her from the arms of her mother to bring her to you, as our traditions demand. Now leave me and mine be!"

Gently, he placed her on the offering stone. She roused at the movement, and somehow summoned the strength to cry. He turned, willing himself not to hear the heartbreaking noise, although it seemed to echo in his head long after his mount had placed many miles of desert sand between them.

Chapter Ten

Kevla thought it would have been better if the household had been permitted to show its grief. Had the child been born clean, not so clearly marked by the Great Dragon's disfavor, and died during birth, it would have been deeply mourned. As it was, no one spoke of it. Things moved on as if all was normal, but there was a sickly, frightened, sorrowful pall that hung over the House as if storm clouds sat atop it.

Yeshi locked herself in her room and would see no one. Several times a day, Tahmu knocked on her door and asked permission to enter. All he received was silence. On the third day, he muttered something under his breath and burst open the door with his shoulder.

Kevla did not know in what condition he found Yeshi, but an hour later she, Tiah and Ranna were summoned to the room. Yeshi lay on the bed, still in the filthy, blood- and af-

terbirth-stained clothing she had worn on the day she had
borne her ill-fated child. She stared, unseeing, at the ceiling,
but as the day wore on the three women managed to coax
her into eating a few bites of food, shedding her soiled
clothing, and permitting herself to be bathed from a basin.

While Yeshi slowly and unwillingly returned to her
women, the rest of the House was kept busy with the flood
of new five-scores. Kevla did not interact with them, but she
passed them in the kitchens now and then and pitied them.
Most were not much older than she, and female. They
seemed terrified and spoke with a thick accent. Some of
them bore old scars. She wanted to let them know that it
was all right, that Tahmu was a good master, but when she
did try to speak to them, they shrank from her like frightened *liahs*. Kevla hoped that Sahlik's mixture of practicality
and kindness would reach them.

She saw little of Jashemi, and there was no talk from
Maluuk about resuming their lessons. She feared that going
to war had changed the young lord. Was that strange connection she had felt real? Or was she fooling herself into
thinking she meant anything to him other than as a servant?
He passed her in the halls with no acknowledgment, and at
such times she was buffeted with both relief and regret. She
told herself it was for the best; any closeness between a Bai-
sha and a *khashimu*, even a friendship, courted trouble.

But she did not believe it.

Several days after Tahmu had given the child to the Great
Dragon, Kevla was filling up Yeshi's tray with tidbits to
tempt her to eat when Sahlik came up behind her.

"No, no!" she scolded, pointing to a small cup of boiled
balan. "Yeshi hates this cooked. Give her the fresh root,
child. Like this."

She plopped a long yellow tuber onto the tray. Kevla was
startled at the rebuke, and then she noticed a small corner

of parchment peeking out from underneath the root. She sucked in her breath. Sahlik turned away.

"You! Come here, child. You seem to like cooking. Do you know how to make bread?"

Kevla's heart pounded so hard she thought it would burst through her chest. There was only one person who would send her a written message.

She shook so badly that she feared she would drop the tray, but managed to make it into a small room off the great hall which saw little activity. She unfolded the letter and read:

Sahlik has arranged for me to have time alone in the cavern. Go to the kitchen first, then come find me there when it is time for someone's afternoon nap.

Kevla felt weak as joy and apprehension flooded her. Was this not what she had hoped for? To see him again, alone? She wished he had said more, but the letter could be dangerous if it fell into the wrong hands. She read it again, trying to decipher his intentions. He had seemed so aloof when she saw him in the halls, and the letter was brusque. Perhaps she should not go, but did she dare refuse? Then, as if he were present, she seemed to feel again his hands on her face, see his eyes glinting with starlit tears.

She would go, as he had asked.

Kevla returned to the kitchen, and put another piece of fruit on Yeshi's tray. It was far too much for the *khashima* to eat; she barely tasted anything Kevla brought her, but Kevla needed an excuse. While she was there, she looked around. Everyone was busy doing something. She picked up a few crumbs from the floor and tossed them and the small piece of parchment into the fire. She watched it twist and curl up on itself, and then it was ash.

It was only midmorning. She had many hours to wait. Finally, Yeshi decided it was time to take a nap. The girls scattered, each anxious to seize time alone, and Kevla headed straight for the kitchen.

Sahlik was there, overseeing dinner preparations. Several loaves of bread were stacked high on platters. Roast meats turned on spits, supervised by dull-eyed five-scores. Other five-scores chopped vegetables for the huge pots of stew that bubbled on the fires.

Sahlik saw her and gave her a wineskin. "Take this," she said quietly. "If anyone notices you coming or going, say you are bringing wine to the young master."

Kevla couldn't help herself. The head servant of the House of Four Waters was actually encouraging the *khashimu* to meet secretly with a lowly servant.

"Sahlik," she whispered, "why are you—"

"I have my reasons," the old woman said curtly. "Go."

Kevla hurried toward the small building, opened the door, took the torch and descended the cool stone steps, both aching for and dreading this illicit encounter.

He was there. He was dressed in the men's *rhia*, which clung to his still-damp body. He sat on the pool's edge, his legs in the water. Droplets on his dark skin and hair glistened in the torchlight. He turned to see who had arrived and their eyes met.

"Did anyone see you?" She shook her head. "Good. Come, Kevla. Sit beside me."

Nervously, she did as she was told, dangling her own legs into the cool water. She waited for him to speak.

"I have seen...so much," he said at last. He didn't look at her. He stared down into the water, as if speaking to his own wavering reflection. "Kevla...I have killed a man. It was only a few moments into the raid. He charged at me, a dagger in each hand, screaming something—I can't remember what—and before I realized what I was doing the deed was done. I had drawn my sword and cut deeply into his neck."

Her heart ached for him, even as her mind filled with images of gore and death. *He was born to this,* she told herself. And yet, she wished he had not had to experience it.

"It didn't cut his head off, not quite. But the blood—by the Great Dragon, it was everywhere, on me, on my *sa'abah*, on the sand—so much blood. And he was just the first. I cannot tell you how many ran at me, how often I swung my sword, how many I struck. My hand ached, my arm grew tired, and still I swung. It was so fast to be so...so thorough. It took much longer to round up the scattered women and children, tie them up like sandcattle—"

He paused, swallowed hard. "Then when it was over, some of them men dipped their fingers in the blood and marked their faces. They laughed. They danced. I went behind a stone and was sick."

He looked at her then, his eyes haunted, expecting ridicule. Kevla bit her lip and her eyes filled with tears.

Suddenly, violently, he tugged off his *rhia,* exposing his thin boy's chest. An ugly scar snaked from his left nipple to his navel. Kevla gasped.

"My lord—are you—"

He smiled bitterly. "I'll be all right. It was a shallow, clean wound and Maluuk is a skilled healer. He said I should be proud of it. *Proud.*" He almost spat the word. "Father made me sit through the celebrations. But when I went to sleep that night all I could see was the face of the man I had killed...his head spoke to me, called me murderer...."

He buried his face in his hands. "And then to come back and discover I was about to have a brother or sister...I thought it was a blessing, a sign that life went on even after what we did. But Kevla, we—I—I lost a *sister!* My father left her to die on the mountain, and I can't even talk about her to anyone. My father walks as if his steps are dogged by ghosts. My mother will not see me, it's as if I'm dead to her now, too...."

He shuddered as a deep sob racked his thin frame. "My little sister...."

Kevla could keep the barrier between them no longer. Jashemi's torment called more loudly to her than her fear or her sense of propriety. He was in pain, and she had to do what she could to ease it. Deliberately, knowing full well she might regret it later, she put her arms around him.

Jashemi clung to her, burying his face in her neck. She felt the cool wetness of the water and the warm wetness of his tears. She ran her fingers through the thick softness of his hair, closing her eyes and opening to him, taking all the hurt and shock and angry grief into her own soft, compassionate body. She murmured nonsense words as if he were a baby, and rocked him until the violence of his grief was spent.

"My sister," he whispered, over and over, "My sister...."

The time passed. Each day that unfurled was a step away from the terrible tragedy that no one was permitted to mention. The servants stopped speaking in whispers. Tahmu started to laugh and carry himself with confidence again. Even Yeshi seemed to revive, though there was a hardness about her that Kevla had not seen before. Her tongue was sharp, her words cold, and her laughter, when she did laugh, had an edge to it that made Kevla's skin prickle. Yeshi had recovered, but she had not healed.

Nor did she ever call for her son.

Kevla suspected that she was the only one who knew how deeply Yeshi's avoidance of Jashemi cut the youth. He did not show it in word, expression, or deed, but she knew how badly the rejection pained him. They stole time where they could, with Sahlik acting as their touchstone, but it was difficult. He never referred to their embrace in the caverns, nor did she; but there was a new ease in their mannerisms with one another, as if some barrier had been lifted.

One day, as Kevla was gathering up Tahmu and Yeshi's bedclothes, she noticed certain stains on them. She stared, disbelieving. She knew exactly what sort of stains they were, having cleaned her mother's linens, and if Tahmu had not been gone for several days visiting the Star Clan's *khashim,* she would have thought nothing of it.

But Tahmu was gone. Had been gone since before these linens were put on the bed....

This could not be. Yeshi would not jeopardize her position. Infidelity to the *khashim* was treason. Tahmu could have her put to death for it. And why would Yeshi do such a thing? From all that Kevla could tell, Tahmu was a kind husband and probably a gentle lover.

Kevla felt a rush of anger at the betrayal which abated a moment later. It was not her place to either defend her lord or condemn her lady. She was a servant here, nothing more.

And perhaps these stains were something else. Perhaps she was making assumptions that weren't true. Quickly, she bundled them up and was about to take them downstairs when she paused. A half-filled glass of wine sat on a small table. She took the wine, opened the sheets to expose the telltale stain, and poured the wine over it. Better the women who washed Yeshi's sheets think her clumsy than adulterous.

Yeshi took to retiring early and dismissing her women. Tiah and Ranna were only too happy to be relieved of their duties, and immediately rushed to meet with their stable-boy lovers. But Kevla worried that Yeshi and her unknown lover—or lovers—would grow careless. She made it a point to be the first to attend Yeshi in the mornings, and sometimes she noticed something that would have given Yeshi away, such as finding two glasses of wine where there should be one.

To Kevla's great relief, the liaisons ceased when Tahmu was in residence. Yeshi might be indiscreet, but she was no fool. Sometimes she wondered who Yeshi was taking into her bed, but she had no real interest in learning the man's identity.

Yeshi moved as if she were a dead person trapped inside a living body.

The last thing she had felt, really felt, was overwhelming grief as Tahmu snatched their child from her arms. She had raged, sobbed, railed against the Dragon, screamed curses at her husband, beaten her still-swollen and sensitive belly with her fists for not housing a clean child.

Then the darkness descended. Later, she would find it difficult to believe that she had even been able to continue to draw breath, that her heart had not simply stopped beating. Despite her desperate wish to die, Yeshi lived.

She had vague recollections of soft skin, of concerned eyes, and gentle hands that pressed tidbits into her unwilling mouth, that bathed a soiled physical shell. Her body ate, used the food, excreted what it did not need, and demanded more. How strange, that it continued when her soul felt so dead.

The emotions that came afterward were pale in comparison to her grief, but she clung to them anyway. She hated Tahmu for what he had done. And she could not bear to lay eyes on her beautiful, healthy son. Why should he live, if his sister was born only to die of exposure on a mountainside? Why should Tahmu laugh and move forward with his duties, when he had been the one to execute the dreadful deed?

No matter that the traditions were clear on this point. No

matter that it would have been impossible to disguise her daughter's disfigurement. No matter that there was no other course for anyone to have taken. There was no sense in anything Yeshi felt now.

She took her lover not out of passion and desire, but of an urgent need to feel something. She would not let Tahmu touch her, but she wanted arms around her in the night, wanted to taste the salt of sweat and remember that she wasn't dead yet, even though she yearned for death's graces.

The one place where she felt even the faintest brush of peace was when she was alone in the caverns. Before the tragedy, she had not often liked to be alone. Now, she craved the solitude. She did not need women to scrub her back and dry her body. She needed a place to be embraced by cool water, where all was silent save her own racking sobs.

So when she descended the steps, padding softly on bare feet, she felt a lightening of the grief that clung to her like a burning shroud. She was just about to enter the cavern when she heard voices. She stopped, straining to listen.

"Why do you always pick red?" It was Jashemi's voice.

"I like it. It's pretty."

Kevla! She shouldn't be talking with Jashemi, she was just a servant. Yeshi straightened and turned the corner, her mouth open to rebuke both son and servant, when she went still as stone.

Her steps had been light, and they were too engrossed in their game of *Shamizan* to notice her approach. They sat with their dark heads bent over the board, foreheads nearly touching. Jashemi wore a cloth around his loins, and Kevla wore a damp, sleeveless *rhia*. Yeshi noted distractedly that her son had a scar across his chest, but Jashemi's war injuries were of no concern to her, not now.

The two children were of the same height and build.

Both had their gazes on the board, but simultaneously they looked up and grinned. Two mouths of the same shape pulled back from even, white teeth; two pairs of eyes the same color tilted up at the corners in an identical fashion. Jashemi said something, but Yeshi heard no words. Blood pounded in her veins.

How could she not have seen this? She knew every inch of her son's face since she had held him in her arms a few seconds after his birth. Kevla had attended her for almost two full years. She had thought the girl looked familiar when she had first laid eyes on her, but it had never occurred to Yeshi that Tahmu had...that he would....

Yeshi was so shocked that she had to lean against the stone steps for support. She was cold, so cold, and her stomach churned.

Betrayers. All of them. How they must have laughed at her ignorance, her stupidity, her inability to see what was right before her eyes. Did the whole household know? The whole *Clan?* Was she the only one who labored under the misapprehension that her husband had been faithful?

Shaking with anger and pain, Yeshi turned and made her way up the stairs as silently as she had come.

Tahmu had begun coming to bed late. It was easier on them both if he lay beside Yeshi while she was asleep rather than awake. He disrobed quietly in the bedroom, not lighting the lamp, when suddenly one flamed to life.

He turned, surprised. "Yeshi, I hope I did not...."

The words died on his lips at the expression on his wife's face. He had thought that he had seen the worst she could offer him when he had taken their daughter, but now he almost physically quailed. There was stone in that gaze, and a hatred that went much deeper than mere rage and grief.

"I saw them today," she said, her voice calm, almost conversational. "In the caverns, playing *Shamizan*. Talking. Laughing. Just like *brother and sister.*"

He should have known this day would come, but he had hoped…"I never wanted you to know," he said.

"Of course not!" Yeshi's voice cracked like a whip. "Of course you wanted me kept ignorant, wanted me to be laughed at by my son, my women, *your Bai-sha daughter—*"

"I did not want to hurt you," Tahmu said. "Jashemi and Sahlik are the only ones who know, and Sahlik tells me none of the other servants suspect. Not even Kevla knows."

"Well, then, that makes it all right, doesn't it, that you broke our vows, slept with—"

"Kevla is older than Jashemi, or haven't you noticed?" replied Tahmu defensively. "I never broke my vows to you."

"Then it's the *halaan's* child?"

Tahmu flinched at the crude word, sick that the epithet was truer than Yeshi knew.

"By the Dragon, Tahmu, that makes it worse….how could you do this? How could you take our daughter, born legitimate, and leave her to die, and yet bring your Bai-sha into our home?"

For a moment, she looked down at her hands, balled into small fists atop the silky sheets. She looked less angry and more hurt, and Tahmu felt pity stir in him. As he had said to Jashemi, Yeshi's only real crime was that she was not the woman he loved. He went to her and sat beside her on the bed, but as he reached to put his hand over one of hers, she jerked to life and struck him. He tasted blood.

"I want her out," she hissed between clenched teeth. "I want her beaten until the blood runs down her skinny little back, I want to scratch her face and—"

"No."

His conviction halted her flood of vitriol. She seemed startled. "What?"

"No. Kevla will not be beaten. She will not be sent away. She has done nothing wrong."

"She is your Bai-sha!"

He met her gaze levelly. "That is my wrongdoing, not hers. The only thing Kevla has done is to be a good servant to you. Until today you doted on her."

"She should not have been with Jashemi!"

"I suspect the boy is at fault, not Kevla. But I am responsible for the girl. I swore to keep her safe. That she would always have food, a place to sleep, protection. I will not break that vow, not even for you."

Yeshi's eyes flashed, then the light in them seemed to die. "I cannot order her from this house without your permission, *khashim*. But I will not have her attend me another moment. I will put her to work in the kitchens. I will find a place where she cannot have the comfort of other women to laugh and talk with. And I will forbid my son to ever, *ever* see her again."

Tahmu felt as if he had swallowed a heavy weight. This was not what he had envisioned, that day two years ago when he had set Kevla before him on Swift's back, when he had taken her away from everything she had known.

Now, he would have to do that to her again, except this time, she was not trading a difficult life for an easier one. This time, she was trading a life she had come to enjoy for one that would be harsh and trying. He had taught her to believe that she was worthy of a good life. Now, he would rip that away from her.

His voice breaking, he said to Yeshi, "You told me she was almost a daughter to you, Yeshi."

"'Almost,'" said Yeshi, "is a very big word."

* * *

Kevla was asleep when the door to the women's room burst open. There were startled shrieks as the women groggily realized that their sanctuary was being intruded upon by three men, all with torches.

"Which one is the Bai-sha?" their leader demanded.

Tiah and Ranna pointed to Kevla, who shrank back before the accusation. Gulping, she tried to appear calm.

"I am Kevla Bai-sha. Who asks for me?"

They did not reply. Instead, the leader jerked his head in Kevla's direction and the other two grabbed her and hauled her to her feet. She was wearing nothing but a light sleeping *rhia.*

"Stop!" she cried, "put me down! I am handmaiden to the *khashima,* you must—"

"It is by the *khashima's* orders that we are here, Bai-sha," one of the men snarled.

Kevla's heart sank at the words. She looked over her shoulder, and saw that Ranna looked stricken at what was happening to her. Even Tiah seemed upset.

"Where are you taking me?" she demanded as they dragged her down the stairs. A foot caught on a step and she winced.

"You are no longer to serve the great lady," one of the men said. "You are to stay in the kitchen. You will sleep in a small room, alone." They half carried, half dragged her up another increasingly narrow set of stairs.

"There must be a mistake!" she stammered. "I have not displeased the great lady. Please, let me speak to her and—"

The man clutching her right arm shook her so violently that her head snapped back. "You are never to directly address the *khashima* again! Do you understand?"

Terrified now, Kevla only nodded. The stairs came to an

abrupt end and the guard in front hauled open a heavy wooden door. They flung her inside. She stumbled and fell, hitting hard stone and cutting her hands and legs on sharp edges. She eased herself up to a sitting position and when the blow came it almost knocked her unconscious.

"That," said one of the men, leaning so close to her that she could smell his stale breath, "is from the *khashima*. She told me to tell you that it is but a taste of what you will experience if you speak to her son again."

He slammed the door shut, and Kevla was plunged into darkness.

For a moment, she huddled on the stone floor, trying to understand. She hurt all over, but her face hurt the worst. She reached to touch her mouth gingerly and winced as her fingers touched and probed. Then the import of the man's last words fully descended upon her.

There was only one conclusion. Yeshi had seen her with Jashemi. She had been so offended at the thought of her son with a lowly Bai-sha that she had ordered Kevla banished. Suddenly, Kevla couldn't breathe and her body went cold.

This was what she had dreaded; that she would lose her enviable position and be turned away in shame and disgrace. This was the fear that had tempered the pleasure of her time with the young lord, the shadow to the bright light of their moments together. Their secret meetings were forbidden, and she had known it. Now, she would have to pay.

Even so, somehow, the thought of never being with him again made her heart hurt worse than her battered body. She began to sob, loudly, violently, each paroxysm of grief and loss racking her body painfully. She pounded fists into the stone floor, welcoming the ache. She kicked and screamed and begged with the unseen, unfeeling *khashima*. And when at last she drifted into an exhausted slumber, her dreams were haunted by the image of Jashemi on one of the river rafts, drifting farther and farther away from her even as he extended his arms to her, crying out for rescue.

Chapter Eleven

The sound of the door swinging open woke Kevla early the next morning. She blinked sleepily, wondering why she was gazing directly at an old harvesting rake, and then memory came flooding back. She bolted upright, then sagged in relief when she saw Sahlik standing in the door.

Harshly, Sahlik said, "Get up, girl. You're to come work in the kitchens now."

Kevla felt the smile bleed from her face. There was no reprieve in Sahlik's grim mien. But Sahlik had always been kind to her, had been the one who arranged for her and Jashemi to meet....

Kevla got to her feet. Her *rhia* was wet in places, and even as she looked down at it and realized with shame what the wetness was, Sahlik said, "You've soiled yourself, girl."

"I'm sorry," Kevla whispered. She felt her face grow hot.

"There was no pot, and the door was locked... May I be permitted to bathe and change?"

Sahlik laughed without humor. "You are forbidden the use of the caverns. I'll send up a clean rag and some water. When you are done, come immediately to the kitchens. There's a beating in it for you if you are late."

She closed the door, but Kevla didn't hear the latch falling into place. Her stomach roiled. She choked the vomit down, knowing it would go badly for her if she added that to the mess she had already made. She gritted her teeth against the nausea and grief that welled up inside her.

A few moments later, one of the new five-scores brought up a basin of water and a clean *rhia*. Kevla remembered the girl. What was her name...Shara? Sharu, that was it. Kevla had attempted to make pleasant overtures to her, but the five-score had regarded her with terror. Now, though, Sharu gazed curiously at Kevla, with no sign of awe as she placed the items down the floor. Stories of Kevla's fall from grace had already begun their inevitable spread.

"Thank you," Kevla managed to say. Sharu stared, and then closed the door.

The water was clean at least, although the *rhia* was little more than the rag Sahlik had described. It had been repeatedly torn and remended, and there were deep stains in it that would never come out. Shaking, Kevla washed her groin and legs, willing herself not to think of the cool water of the caverns and how good it felt against her skin. She slipped into the stained garment with grim resignation.

It was still better. Whatever working in the kitchen entailed, it was still better to be here, at the House of Four Waters, with a remote possibility of seeing Jashemi, than to be anywhere else.

By nightfall, Kevla thought with longing of dancing on the street corner and crying her mother's skills.

There was no softening of Sahlik's demeanor. She put Kevla to work immediately, and it proved grueling. Kevla was forced to stand for hours in the hot sun, collecting the droppings of the sandcattle, horses, and *sa'abahs*. She spread them out to dry, and gathered the dried droppings to use as fuel for the cook fires. She was permitted to go into the caverns only to haul buckets full of water. She stirred, scrubbed, chopped, ground and carried until her arms burned with pain. Twice, she was permitted to stop and eat, and the meals were meager: dried bread, heels of cheeses, fruits that were overripe and unfit to serve the higher-caste servants or the lord and lady.

Through it all, Kevla caught Sharu watching her intently. She was too exhausted and broken-hearted to try to be friendly.

Every time she tried to steal a few moments to sit and rest or rub her aching limbs, Sahlik was there, barking orders and dragging her to her feet. By the time she ate what passed for an evening meal and was brusquely dismissed by Sahlik, it was all she could do to stumble out of the kitchen and crawl up the stairs to her room. She almost fell to the floor. Curled up on the hard stone, she fell asleep within minutes.

Such was her life for the next several weeks. She moved dazedly, doing what was asked of her, moving to the next thing, then collapsing, exhausted, in her tiny room. Sahlik continued to behave as if Kevla had never been anything other than the lowest-ranking of the House's servants. The girl saw nothing of Yeshi, Tahmu, or Jashemi, and turned away whenever Tiah or Ranna came to the kitchen to select treats for their mistress. She thought she could feel no worse, but when Tiah and Ranna came accompanied by Sharu, the five-score Kevla had thought to befriend, she had to bite her lip to keep scalding tears of disappointment from flowing down her dirty cheeks. The little five-score, who had once been so timid, was now elevated to Kevla's former status.

One day, while she was tending the fire, Sahlik did something completely incomprehensible. The elderly servant positioned herself so that no one could see what she was doing, then deliberately poured a cup of hot *eusho* on Kevla's hand.

Kevla cried out, staring in shock at Sahlik. Before she could say anything, Sahlik said sharply, "You clumsy girl! Look what you've done! Go see Maluuk right away. If that blisters you'll be of no use here at all."

Wide-eyed, Kevla clutched her burned hand and backed away from Sahlik, who continued to glower at her. Then she started running, pushing her way though the crowded kitchen and racing over the courtyard to the healer's small hut.

The scald was minor. What hurt more than the injury was the knowledge that Sahlik had intentionally inflicted it. Was the head servant trying to kill her? Kevla began to cry as she ran. She tried to stifle the sobs, but she might just as well have tried to dam the Four Waters with a walking stick.

She slowed as she approached the healing hut. She dragged her arm across her wet face and sniffed hard. Swallowing, Kevla straightened, composed herself, and opened the door.

"Maluuk, I—"

The words died in her throat. Standing there waiting for her was Jashemi. She stared at him, and then her legs refused to hold her. It was as if the last few weeks of pain, shame, and exhaustion caught up with her in the span of an instant. He caught her before she fell and carried her over to the table. Still weak, she did not protest.

"Kevla, I am so very sorry. I take full responsibility. Let me see the burn. Good, she didn't hurt you too badly. I will put something on it."

Kevla felt as though his words were coming from leagues away. Their meaning registered only slowly. She watched him as he removed the stopper from a jar and scooped out a fingerful of gray, pleasant-smelling ointment. He applied the salve with a delicate touch, and the pain subsided at once.

"Sahlik...she did this to me so I could meet you?"

Jashemi gave her a quick glance. "Of course. Did you think she simply wanted to hurt you?"

"I—I didn't know what to think," Kevla said, her voice thick. "I had thought that Yeshi liked me, and when she...then Sahlik was so mean to me...."

He paused in his treatment to look at her gravely. "My mother discovered us together," he said. "It is my fault. I was careless. I should have made sure that never happened." He finished applying salve and began to bind the wound with a clean cloth. Suddenly, his mouth twisted in a smile. "It seems as though I am always apologizing to you."

Despite the seriousness of the situation, Kevla couldn't help smiling in return. "You are a most unusual *khashimu*."

"And you are an unusual...." He paused. "Girl," he said. Kevla felt her cheeks flush. "Now, you need to finish tying this. Your story will be that you came to the hut and neither Maluuk nor Asha was here, so you treated yourself."

She complied, holding her arm against her body to better secure the bandage.

"Where are they?"

"Someone has been injured by the river. I saw them go and told Sahlik that we had a chance to meet."

"Why has Sahlik been so cruel? It seems as though she has been particularly hard on me."

Jashemi's face hardened. "My mother has a little spy. One of the five-scores we brought home from the raid. Shari, I think her name is."

"Sharu," Kevla corrected. "I tried to be kind to her."

"Of course you did. For several weeks, Sharu was in the kitchens, watching to make sure you were treated as badly as possible. Mother was satisfied and rewarded Sharu by making her a handmaiden. Now that she is no longer in the kitchen, Sahlik does not have to be so harsh with you."

"Thank the Dragon for that, at least," Kevla said softly.

She had not intended her words to be interpreted as criticism, but she saw Jashemi wince. When he spoke again, his voice was serious.

"Because of my carelessness, you lost your position," he said. "I don't want anything else to happen to you, but I can't lie to you. If we continue to meet, someone could find out."

Their eyes met, and she realized what he was saying. He was asking if she wanted to keep seeing him. He was not ordering, as was his birthright. Kevla realized that every moment of true happiness she had experienced at the House of Four Waters had occurred when the two of them were alone together. It had been good to be Yeshi's handmaiden, yes, but she had to be constantly on her guard. Over time and repeated encounters with Jashemi, she had learned to let the line between master and servant blur. There was a warmth in her heart for this boy that she had never felt with anyone else: a sense of safety despite the danger, an oasis of peace in a desert of apprehension.

He was letting her decide. She could choose safety, or she could choose him.

"Then we must make certain that doesn't happen," she said.

Knowing that Sahlik's abuse was a sham helped Kevla to accept it more easily. She cringed when berated, and Sahlik spared no opportunity to harass the girl. But there was no physical violence after the "accidental burn," and Kevla's duties suddenly became much less demanding. She ate better, and was able to rest for longer periods of time.

Yet it was still hard work. Her body grew strong from the physical demands, her slender build becoming more defined with muscles and her blossoming womanhood. Some of the young men she encountered on her errands stared at her growing chest, straining against the confines of her *rhia.* Sahlik made a point of complaining loudly when Kevla asked for a different garment, but the next morning Kevla was handed several fresh *rhias,* none of which clung quite so revealingly as her older ones.

She saw Jashemi infrequently, and it was always an unexpected delight. Their moments together were tense and exciting, the thought of discovery adding a sharp tang of adventure to an experience the two found both necessary and painfully happy. At the same time, she had never felt more comfortable in his presence.

One night, after a particularly grueling day, Kevla's body ached more than usual. She had quarreled with some of the five-scores over the preparation of a dish, and although she knew she was correct, Sahlik had sided with the other girls. Kevla understood the necessity of the pretense, but somehow, today she was sick of the act.

Her newly large breasts were tender and her belly hurt as well. Perhaps she had eaten something that disagreed with her. Her head ached. For no reason, she sat down on the stone floor of her small room and wept angrily.

It was all so awful, so unfair! She had tended Yeshi well. She had kept Yeshi's secrets, and this was how the *khashima* repaid her. It had been so long since she and Jashemi had played *Shamizan* that she was certain she'd forget the few rules.

Has there ever been anyone more wretched than I? she thought, misery overwhelming her. She stretched out onto the stone, felt its coolness against her hot, tearstained cheeks, and fell into an unhappy slumber.

Kevla opened her eyes to discover that she was surrounded by flames. They leaped up, walls of fire, forming an enclosure that trapped her inside their circle more firmly than if they had been made of stone. Smoke swirled around her, but it did not sting her eyes, nor make her gasp for breath. She turned, slowly, seeking a break in the enormous sheets of flame, and then screamed as she saw something more frightening than fire.

It seemed made of fire itself, all hues of red and yellow and orange. It moved with the same sinuous grace as the flames that surrounded it, but it seemed unaffected by their licking tongues. Slowly, it lifted its serpentine neck, reared up on its massive, scaly hind legs. Two membranous wings unfolded and beat the air, setting the flames to dancing wildly. It opened its mouth. For an instant, Kevla caught sight of teeth as long as her arm, and a flickering, forked tongue. Then fire spewed forth. Its massive tail raised and then came crashing down on the burned earth. The ground trembled and Kevla fell.

The Dragon lowered its horned, wedge-shaped head until it was mere inches from Kevla's face. She wanted to scream, close her eyes, turn away, but she remained transfixed, as the bird before the snake. She stared into its glowing yellow eyes.

It opened its mouth, and Kevla braced herself for the exquisite agony of its fiery breath. Instead, the monster spoke, and Kevla understood the words. Understood, but could not comprehend their meaning. The noise of the Dragon's voice shattered her ears, reverberated along her bones, dropped her to the ground in agony.

"DO YOU KNOW WHO YOU ARE?"

Kevla was brought awake by the sound of her own scream. She bolted upright, gasping for breath. Her heart threatened to burst out of her chest. Her *rhia* clung to her, and she realized that she was soaked with sweat.

The light of the full moon spilled in through the small window, silvering and softening the harsh angles of the stacked-up tools. Kevla wiped at her wet face, shivering with fear and mortification.

Even her dreams, it seemed, mirrored her fall from favor and the shame inherent in her very existence. The dragon in her dream had to be the Great Dragon, who lived in the heart of Mount Bari. According to legend, the Dragon sent his flames in the form of molten stone coursing down the steep sides of Mount Bari when the people of Arukan forgot their traditions and laws.

Forget who they were.

DO YOU KNOW WHO YOU ARE?

Kevla could hear the bellowing voice in her head even now and she put her hands to her ears, as if the voice were real and could be shut out by something as paltry as human flesh and bone.

Perhaps the dream meant that the Great Dragon was as displeased with Kevla as Yeshi. Perhaps the Dragon felt that Kevla had no right to presume to a friendship with a *khashimu,* heir to the most powerful Clan in Arukan. She was born of a *halaan.* She was Bai-sha, her father unknown to her, one of her mother's clients. She recalled the Dragon's ferocity in the dream and shuddered.

And then, as she moved to sit up, she saw more evidence of the Dragon's displeasure.

Blood was all over her thighs.

Kevla went through the motions of her day, but she almost felt as though she was standing outside her body. The only thing that brought her back to living in her own skin was the sensation of torn rags stuffed inside her, to absorb the telltale bleeding. Twice, she had to change them, and fought back tears of misery as she looked at the sodden, scarlet fabric.

Until the moment that the blood had begun flowing from her *sulim,* she had been cloaked in the safety of childhood. Kevla had dreaded being sent away from the House of Four Waters for disobedience, but now that fate was almost certain. She was now a viable female, able to conceive and bear children, and would no doubt be part of some negotiation with another clan; of the same value as a cart of vegetables or a brace of sandcattle. Or, she mused darkly, perhaps less, as she was Bai-sha.

Kevla shrank from the image. Her mother had never painted the joining of male and female as anything pleasant, and until this moment, Kevla had never given much thought to the subject. Now, it loomed over her like a grim shadow.

She thought she could bear even that, even lying in the darkness while a stranger roughly violated her body, if she could stay in the House of Four Waters. If she could play *Shamizan* with Jashemi now and then, who never made her feel worthless, and whose delight in her company was genuine.

She felt Sahlik's eyes on her and once even heard the head servant whisper, "Child, are you unwell?"

Telling Sahlik would only hasten the inevitable. The onset of womanhood varied from girl to girl, she knew. Perhaps, if she kept her bleeding secret, she could stay longer. So she looked up into the concerned face of the maternal woman with eyes that she knew looked dazed and haunted and murmured that nothing was wrong.

The seemingly interminable day finally crawled to a close. For the first time since Yeshi's commandment, Kevla hastened to return to the privacy of her room. Once there, she removed the soiled rag, replaced it with a clean one, and stared at the mute condemnation of the bloody cloth. What should she do with it? While she was working in the kitchens, Kevla had managed to excuse herself and change the cloths in private. When she returned, she bided her time until she could toss the rags into the fire. But here, there was no such option.

She would *not* start crying again. She bit her lip hard and willed her eyes to stop stinging, willed the lump in her throat to dissolve. She would have to hide the rags until such time as she could dispose of them.

She would also have to hide the water with which she scrubbed her thighs and *sulim* in a futile effort to clean herself. As she stretched out to try to get some sleep, Kevla thought that if Yeshi ever wanted to see her wretched and miserable, all she needed to do was poke her head in at this moment, and the great lady would be mightily pleased.

She slept, and again the Great Dragon appeared in her dreams, with its accusatory cry, *"DO YOU KNOW WHO YOU ARE?"*

The next day, the flow was still strong, but Kevla felt less pain. But she could not forget what was going on, nor the dreadful dreams that seemed so real. She had dreamed before; everyone dreamed. But never anything like this.

This time, when she retreated to her room, she staved off sleep as long as she could, frightened of the Dragon and his censure, but eventually her eyes closed of their own accord.

Again, Kevla stood in the center of a wall of fire. She was as terrified as she had been previously, familiarity with the scene making it no less horrific. Again, the Dragon reared up and spouted flame; again, it pressed its face close to hers. But this time, it reached out with a huge, scaly foreleg. Claws clamped on her shoulder and it shook her.

"Kevla!" it cried. "Kevla, wake up, you're dreaming—"

She bolted awake with a vengeance, squirming and clawing against the foreleg that grabbed her shoulder, that clamped down on her mouth to stifle her screams—

"Kevla, hush, it's me, Jashemi!"

She sagged in relief, and his hand left her mouth and he moved away slightly. It was then she remembered the Dragon's accusation. Remembered the blood still flowing from her body.

With a soft cry, she buried her face in her hands.

"Kevla, what is it? I can't bear to see you so unhappy. What can I do?"

Her heart swelled with affection and gratitude. Whatever had happened to her, she knew she had been blessed in having his friendship for as long as she had.

"I have to go," she said, her voice muffled by her hands.

She heard a swift intake of breath. "You...you are going to leave?"

"She will send me away. The blood and the Dragon have ordained it so." She risked a look at him.

His face was lit by moonlight, and he looked utterly confused. "I don't understand."

"It cannot be coincidence," she said thickly. "The Dragon has come to me in dreams and—"

"Dreams?" The word exploded from him. "Tell me."

So she did. He listened silently, attentively. The image of the beggar who had burned in the market came back to her. He had had dreams of the Dragon, too; he had been cursed by the *kulis*. And he had died horribly because of it.

Finally, when she was done, Jashemi said gently, "Your so-called fall from grace was not due to anything you did.

It was because my mother is an angry, unhappy, and jealous woman. When you fully believe that, I think the dreams will stop."

She gazed deeply into his eyes, black pools of compassion in the dim light. *I love him*, she thought. *I could not love him more if he were my brother, my own blood.*

Blood.

She stared down at their clasped hands. "There is more. I am bleeding," she whispered. "I am an adult woman now, and Yeshi will send me away to be married. The Dragon wants us all to remember our place, and I have forgotten. Even now, with you here, I am forgetting my place. He wants me to leave."

"I refuse to believe that," Jashemi said, his voice low and intense. "I refuse to believe that the Dragon would be so cruel. You have always performed your duties well, Kevla. And I know that Father will not permit you to be sent away. If you were going to be forced to leave, it would have happened before now. It was just a dream."

"It...Jashemi, the dream could have been sent by the *kulis!*" she whispered fearfully. "I could be—"

He reached and placed a finger over her mouth, silencing her as he had done before, but very gently. "That you are a woman is no shame. That you have bad dreams is no surprise. Do not fear, Kevla. All will be well."

As he lay in his bed after his midnight visit to Kevla, Jashemi felt no desire for sleep.

He blushed to think of Kevla speaking so freely of her bleeding. It was a deep mystery, one not discussed between men and women. Nonetheless, he was glad she had trusted him enough to tell him, so that he could assuage her fears of being sent away. Of much more concern to him were Kevla's dreams. He had dismissed them lightly enough when they were talking; Kevla did not need to worry about such things when her waking life was sufficiently trying. But privately, they troubled him deeply.

Troubled him, because on the night when he first spilled his seed in his sleep, he too had begun having disturbing dreams.

Moonlight slanted in through the window. He stared at it, hoping that its brightness would keep him awake.

The brightness of the sun was not dimmed by the rolling, pulsating darkness that loomed on the horizon.

Not dimmed yet, at least.

Jashemi huddled in the cold, his filthy, ragged clothes offering little protection against the cutting knife-edge of the wind. Part of him questioned why he was wearing such poor clothing; another part felt very much at home in the vermin-ridden scraps.

He drew strength from the woman beside him. She was tall, and dressed as finely as he was poorly. Atop her head she wore a circlet of gold. Her hair was long and flew in the wind. When he had first met her it had been black as night; now, there were streaks of gray.

"It's only been two weeks," Jashemi said.

The dream unfurled as it always did. It never varied. The great lady whispered the words that always frightened and puzzled Jashemi when he awoke:

"You alone will remember... It may well fall to you...do not forget."

And as always, Jashemi whispered as she held him tightly, "I won't."

And when he awoke at dawn, the brightness of sunlight replacing the subtler illumination of the moon, Jashemi-kha-Tahmu of the Clan of Four Waters asked himself:

"Do not forget what?"

Chapter Twelve

The knife was inches away from Jashemi's face. He clutched the arm of his attacker, his muscles trembling from the effort. Slowly, the blade came closer to his cheek.

With a grunt, Jashemi closed his legs around the other man's thigh and yanked. The knife disappeared from his vision as the man lost his balance. Smaller and lighter than his attacker, Jashemi twisted until he was atop the man. He still had the knife. Jashemi shoved his knee into the man's stomach and was rewarded with a grunt. The thick fingers relaxed on the dagger's hilt ever so slightly.

Jashemi clutched the hand that held the weapon. He squeezed, applying pressure exactly where Halid had taught him. The man beneath him yelped and his fingers flew open. The knife dropped to the earth.

Jashemi dove for it, rolling off his adversary as he felt the man move to seize him. He leaped lightly to his feet, knife at the ready, panting with exertion.

"Excellent!" cried Halid, pleasure on his sweaty face. "That's the first time you've gotten the knife away from me. You've been paying attention."

"You're...a good teacher," Jashemi gasped, grinning in return. He reached for his waterskin and took a long drink. Since he was eight years old, Jashemi had been training with Halid. Tahmu's Second had taught the *khashimu* how to fight with dagger, scimitar, club, rock, and bare hands. Jashemi was a natural with the scimitar; it had been that weapon with which he had taken a life on his first raid. Dagger work was trickier, and he had been having difficulty with it for some time now. He was pleased that he had wrested the knife from Halid, for he knew the man did not coddle him. If he had gotten the knife, it was because, at least this time, he had bested Halid.

"The *khashimu* is gracious to say so," said Halid. Then, with no warning, he kicked out and the knife went flying from Jashemi's grasp. Jashemi made a face and rubbed his stinging hand.

"But the *khashimu* also needs to be more alert," teased Halid, his eyes twinkling. He picked up the blade and in mock surprise said, "Why look! It seems I have the dagger again."

Jashemi grinned, readying himself for the next round. "And I'll take it from you again."

They had been practicing for some time, though, and Jashemi was growing tired. He did not get the knife, and instead wound up facedown in the sand, one arm yanked behind his back.

"I yield," he said, and immediately the pressure relaxed. Halid extended a hand to help his young master to his feet.

Tahmu had been gone for a few days now. He was visiting another clan and had taken with him servants and higher-ranking caste men. He was on a diplomatic mission, not on a raid, and Halid had remained behind as he always did at such times. As Second, he went with his master into battle, but in peacetime, he made sure Tahmu did not slip behind in his duties at the House. He disliked this intensely and Jashemi did not blame him. Most of what Tahmu had to do seemed very boring to him, and those aspects of being *khashim* held little appeal.

Halid sniffed at his *rhia* and whistled. "I'm for the caverns. Cold water, sweet soap, and clean clothes are what I need."

Jashemi wrinkled his nose as his own odor assaulted him. He, too, could use a bath. He wondered how the poorer clans, with no access to water, managed not to suffocate from the stench. As they walked back to the House, Halid briefly rested his hand on the boy's slim shoulder.

"You did well today," he said. "When you are a man full grown, you will be a warrior to be reckoned with."

Jashemi's smile faded a little. He hoped that by the time he was a man full grown, there would be less need for warriors and more need for good leaders.

He fought back a yawn. He had not been sleeping well; the dreams came every night. Most often it was the dream of the sad, beautiful woman looking out onto the roiling darkness and telling him not to forget. But there were other dreams, too. Other people, unlike any he had ever seen.

His thoughts were interrupted by a nudge from Halid. He looked where the Second pointed, and saw a hawk approaching the aerie.

The caverns would have to wait.

Tahmu returned home two days later, and his face was grim. He called for his son and Second even before he went in to bathe and refresh himself. Despite hours of hard riding, Tahmu insisted they all mount their *sa'abahs*. When they were well away from the House, Tahmu spoke.

"This morning, I received a falcon. The Star Clan and the Cattle Clan were supposed to ride together to raid the Horserider Clan. But the Star Clan and the Horserider Clan had made their own agreement. When the men of the Cattle Clan rode to battle alongside the Star Clan, they were shocked when their ally turned on them. They were downed by the joined forces of the Star Clan and the Horserider Clan. While they fought, another group of raiders from the Star Clan attacked their defenseless House."

He looked first at Halid, then Jashemi. It was the first time Jashemi had been brought in on so important a decision, and he sat straight in his saddle.

"We will ride against the Star Clan and the Horserider Clan. I have sent falcons to the Sheep Clan and the *Sa'abah* Clan, who—"

"But we just raided the *Sa'abah* Clan!" blurted Jashemi before he could censor himself. Halid and Tahmu exchanged amused glances.

"My son does not yet appreciate the pervasive power of gray, even though he is a master of *Shamizan*," Tahmu said, chuckling. "It is precisely because we so decimated the *Sa'abah* Clan that they will want to ally with us in this raid. They will at least be able to take many fine horses, and I have offered to return a few *Sa'abahs* to sweeten the drink."

"Do not look chagrined, young lord," Halid rumbled in his deep voice. "Politics is a delicate game, and there is never an absolute. Your father took many years to master it himself. I am lucky, I need only to follow his orders."

"Dragon willing," continued Tahmu, "you will have plenty of time to learn the subtler details. On this raid, stay close to me and Halid. We will include you in all the planning from this point onward."

As before, the clans assembled. The Clan of Four Waters was so formidable that Jashemi knew it was likely safe from any raid. There had never been one in his lifetime, and unless the House suddenly and unexpectedly weakened, he knew there never would be. The Clan of Four Waters was the one every other clan wanted on their side, not the one anyone wanted to attack.

He felt his mother's eyes upon him during this time, although she still barely spoke to him. When his blood-marked sister had left the House in her father's arms, to be abandoned to the Great Dragon, she had taken with her Yeshi's affection for her son. It still pained him, but at least he had Kevla.

His affection for his half sister deepened with each encounter. Jashemi wished desperately their father could acknowledge her, but that was impossible. A public revelation such as that would shake the Clan to its foundations, perhaps rendering it weak enough so that others would feel sufficiently emboldened to prey upon it.

He felt linked to her in a way he could not articulate. They would have been inseparable had they been true brother and sister. As it was, he craved her company like he craved water after a ride in the desert. Jashemi had known other families with many siblings. Some of them were close, but he had never seen anyone need a sister or brother the way he needed Kevla. Despite her sometimes stiff formality, she made him feel that she wanted his company for who he was, not what he was born to; she wanted to be with Jashemi, not "the young lord." Had they shared a womb together, been born at the same moment, he could not possibly care for her more.

That he was unable to say goodbye to her because of Yeshi's scrutiny was agony. But he dared not jeopardize her further. Kevla had already suffered because of his carelessness; better not to see her than to arouse Yeshi's wrath a second time.

This time, the ride across the desert to the Horserider Clan's House was much less exciting to Jashemi. He was only going to greet death again; to deal it out, to watch it claim friends and perhaps family. Without anticipation, the long procession seemed endless.

The first night out, weary with the long ride, Jashemi fell asleep quickly.

The man was tall. His face was the color of goat's milk and his eyes the color of the sky. His hair was as yellow as the sands. Jashemi had never seen a man that looked like him. He was obviously of high rank, as he was clean-shaven. Strange clothing adorned him, heavy and furred, as if he were some- how cold. When he breathed out, a white smoke encircled his head. He looked terribly sad, as if all the tragedies of the world had fallen on those broad shoulders. But there were laugh lines around his strange-hued eyes, and Jashemi liked him at once.

Jashemi heard a soft, low growl. His heart almost jumped into his throat as he beheld a simmar *curled like a tame beast at the man's feet. But such a strange* simmar... *its coat was not brown, but blue, and there were black and white stripes that ran along its body. The man leaned on a staff, and reached to pet the magnificent cat, then turned and looked straight at Jashemi.*

"You should remember," the man said, in a rich, pleasant voice. "You are a—"

Jashemi came awake with a spasm. He wiped his sweat-sheened face with a hand that trembled.

Even here, out in the desert, the dreams would not leave him be.

Tahmu wondered what was wrong with his son.

He was not sleeping well, that much was apparent, but

Tahmu wanted to know why. Jashemi had not displayed sleeplessness on the previous raid, a time when he well might have been expected to. What, then, was troubling his heir?

On the third day of the journey, Tahmu took the opportunity to ride close to his son. As they talked about ordinary things, he glanced around to make sure they were far enough away so as not to be overheard. Halid was riding behind them, talking to some of the men, but he was out of earshot.

Satisfied that their conversation would be private, Tahmu gently inquired, "I notice that you have not been sleeping well, Jashemi. Can you tell me what keeps you awake?"

Jashemi colored slightly and did not meet his father's eyes. "It is nothing, Father. Merely the toll of the ride."

Tahmu shook his head. "Do not lie to me, my son. It is not that."

Jashemi was silent for a time. Finally, hesitantly, he said, "I have...been having troubling dreams."

Tahmu nodded. Of course. The child was having nightmares. He was young yet, and this was only his second raid.

"That is nothing to be ashamed of," he reassured his son. "You have not yet seen enough battle so that it does not intrude upon your dreams."

To his surprise, Jashemi shook his kerchiefed head. "It is not dreams of battle that trouble me, Father."

For no reason, fear began to creep through the *khashim's* veins. Keeping his voice steady, he inquired, "Then what is the nature of these dreams?"

Again, Jashemi hesitated before replying. Then he spoke quickly, as if now that the decision to speak of the dreams had been made the words must be uttered all at once.

"I dreamed that I was a young beggar boy, standing beside a *khashima* whose finery outstrips even my mother's.

We stood watching a darkness hovering on the horizon, a darkness that was about to completely swallow us. She told me that it might all fall to me, that I must not forget. But I don't know what it was I was to remember! And there is sometimes a man as pale as milk with hair the color of sand, and a blue striped *simmar* crouches at his feet. Sometimes there is a sad-looking young woman, and a man who loves to laugh, and a horse that is not a horse, and someone all in shadows—

"Enough!" Tahmu spoke in a whisper, but the fierceness of his voice silenced Jashemi at once. The fear that had been threatening now descended full force. He felt cold, although the day was hot. "You will not speak of this again. These are no ordinary dreams."

"That much I know. But—

"They are sent by the *kulis*. The demons want to confuse you, to tempt you to stray from the ways of our people. Why else would you have visions of people so unlike us? And if you are having dreams sent by the *kulis,* and you speak of them as you have to me, you have marked yourself. You know what the punishment is for the *kuli*-cursed."

He looked at his son, searching the boy's eyes. "If this comes out, I can only do so much to protect you. I am bound to the ways of the Arukani."

Jashemi's face was unreadable. "You would be bound to condemn me," he said levelly, "just as you were bound to abandon my sister on the mountain."

Tahmu sighed. "Yes. Just like that."

"But what if the dreams *aren't* being sent by *kulis?*" Jashemi demanded. "What if they are good, are somehow warnings?"

"I will not listen to this," said Tahmu. He felt his entire being shutting down, closing up, withdrawing from even considering his son's words. "Our family has suffered enough as it is. I will bring no more torment upon it."

He kicked Swift, who snorted and bolted forward. Tahmu's heart was pounding and his eyes filled with tears as he left his son in the dust.

The sun had not yet cleared the horizon when Kevla went to the corrals, a basket hanging on her arm. This was the least pleasant task of the day, and it was growing more unpleasant as time passed. With so many horses and *sa'abahs* gone from the House of Four Waters, there was not a great deal of dried droppings to be had for the fires. Kevla scowled as she gathered up what she could find. A sandcattle calf nuzzled her and she petted its soft nose absently.

"Who would have thought I would ever wish for more dung," she told it, laughing a little.

Sahlik jokingly called the dried dung used for fuel "cakes." Right now, there were more piles of steaming droppings than cakes, and what cakes there were weren't terribly dry. Kevla wrinkled her nose as she brought them into the kitchens and began to set the fire.

It was early yet, and few people were in the kitchens. Most would not arrive until the fire was going well, their particular tasks requiring a steadily burning flame. Kevla began to strike sparks.

Nothing.

It was never an easy task, getting the cakes to burn at all, but today it seemed impossible. Again and again Kevla tried, striking spark after spark and blowing on it gently. But the cakes were simply too fresh and would not catch.

She heard the sounds of more people coming in behind her, talking in soft morning voices. Soon, they would need to begin baking and cooking.

She kept trying. Each time the spark would land on the cakes, flare for an instant, and then fizzle.

Suddenly, anger rushed through Kevla. Sahlik would chastise her for being tardy in getting the fires lit, and it wasn't really her fault at all.

"Burn, curse you!" she whispered, glowering at the pile of dried droppings.

With a sharp crack, a flame licked upward. A heartbeat later, the fire burned as if it had been lit an hour ago.

Kevla gasped, staring at the fire. How could this be? One moment it was stubborn, moist cattle cakes and now—

She felt sick as the realization broke over her, and sat down hard on the stone. There was only one answer. She *was kuli*-cursed, despite Jashemi's calm words. First the dreams, now this. No ordinary person could light a fire with a word.

The hand on her shoulder startled her. She looked up to see Sahlik smiling down at her.

"The cakes are not usually dry when the men go on raids," Sahlik said approvingly. "You must have a way with fire."

Swallowing, Kevla managed, "Yes. I must."

She went through the chores of her day in a state of near-panic, glancing repeatedly at the merrily burning fire. When her day was done, she lay awake in her room all night, dreading sleep, fearing that the Great Dragon would come for her and bear her away to his lake of fire in the heart of Mount Bari. She was surely an abomination, and the Dragon dealt swiftly with such monstrosities.

And yet she did sleep, and the dream was exactly the same: the leaping flames, the bellowed question, *"DO YOU KNOW WHO YOU ARE?"* It was terrifying—it was always terrifying—but there was no new frightening twist. Nor did the Dragon give any sign of leaving its home in Mount Bari to snatch up her waking self.

The next day, Kevla gathered the cakes with hands that trembled. She laid the fire and struck the spark. Again, the stubborn cakes refused to catch.

Kevla licked dry lips. Softly, she stared at the cakes and whispered, "Burn."

As before, where there had only been a sullen smolder- ing, now there was a steadily burning fire.

Despite her fear, Kevla smiled.

As the days passed, Kevla gradually began to believe that the Dragon wasn't going to punish her. Her skills seemed to be useful, not harmful. Each morning, she now lit the fire with ease, no matter how moist the cattle cakes were. Her room, which had previously grown chilly with the desert night, now became comfortably warm with a single word. She certainly didn't feel like she was *kuli*-cursed.

One morning, Kevla lingered a little bit longer than usual gazing at the fire she had lit by merely saying, "Burn." Its flickering flames always called to her, but this time, she seemed to see figures in the fire.

She blinked and rubbed her eyes. No, she was not imag- ining it. There was Jashemi! She smiled, happy just to see him. He seemed unaware of her presence, his expression troubled. He leaned forward, and the flames trembled. As he moved back, she saw that he held a stick. He had stirred his own fire with the stick, and Kevla had seen it at her fire.

From that moment on, Kevla seized every opportunity that came her way to gaze into the fire. Sometimes, she saw only flames. Other times she saw Sahlik, or Tahmu, or Yeshi. Sometimes she saw the faces of people she did not know at all; strangers somewhere, gazing into a fire, not knowing that the fire was gazing back at them.

The dreams intensified with each passing moon. The col- ors of the fire seemed brighter to her, the Dragon larger, more frightening. Senses other than sight and sound came into play; she could feel the heat of the flames, could smell the smoke, taste its acridness on her tongue. During the day, when she could think rationally about it, she wondered why the dreams never lost their terror. Surely, familiarity with what would unfold ought to lessen its impact.

But such was not the case. The dreams remained as alarming as ever, and each morning she awoke with her heart pounding as if she had been running all night.

The question the Dragon asked was always the same. Kevla never knew how to reply, but somehow she knew that, could she but manage the correct response, all the mysteries would have answers, and everything would fall into place.

She anxiously awaited Jashemi's safe return. The Clan came home three moons later, victorious as usual, and the House was once again thrown into a flurry of activity. As a kitchen worker, Kevla was now on her feet almost all day long, sweating profusely in the heat, collapsing late at night only to rise and do the same thing the next day.

Kevla was forbidden to attend the family or guests; her low status demanded that she remain in the kitchens. Now and then, though, unable to resist, she peeked out hoping to catch Jashemi's eye. They were halfway through the eight courses, having consumed dates and nuts, greens in oil and vinegar, fruit and cheese, and fowl in a glaze of fruit juice and garlic, when Sahlik bustled into the kitchen.

"The young master has taken ill," she told Kevla. "The servers are all busy. Bring him up a platter in case he awakens hungry in the night."

Kevla nodded as if this request was nothing special, but felt joy swell inside her. Moving casually, she arranged some light tidbits on a tray—fruit, nuts, cheese—and tried to disguise her eagerness as she ascended the stairs. A perfect plan—Yeshi would not leave the banquet hall for several more hours. They would have time to talk.

Trembling with anticipation, she knocked on the door. "Come," said Jashemi in a weak voice. Suddenly fearful that he might really be ill and not feigning in order to see her, Kevla burst through the door.

"Jashemi, are you—"

He lounged on the made bed, fully clothed, grinning wickedly at her. Slightly annoyed, she stamped on the floor, and he laughed aloud. Kevla couldn't stay angry with him. She set the tray on a small table, fighting a grin herself.

"You enjoyed scaring me like that," she accused.

"I had to sound convincing, in case Sahlik wasn't able to send you," he replied. "But I confess, the look on your face was most entertaining."

They smiled at one another for a moment, then Jashemi's grin faded.

"Was it bad?" Kevla whispered.

He shrugged, looking down at his hands. "Not as bad as the first time," he said. "Father says you get used to it."

Kevla winced at the hollow tone of his voice. She didn't want Jashemi to grow into a man who had "become used" to taking lives. She didn't think Jashemi did, either. But he had no choice.

"It's not the—the killing that troubles me, not this time," he continued, still looking at his fingers. He took a deep breath and raised his eyes. They seemed to bore into Kevla's soul.

"Before I left, you spoke of dreams. Are you still having them?"

She nodded. "Yes. The same dream. Every night."

"You have told no one?" At her look, he smiled a little. "That was a foolish question. Of course not." The smile faded. "I was not so wise."

She cocked her head. "You have been having dreams, too?"

He nodded. "Dreams in which I am a beggar boy, standing beside a great *khashima*. There is something I am supposed to remember, to prevent something dreadful from happening, but I don't know what it is. And other dreams. I see strange people, Kevla, people who look nothing like you and I. Their hair is yellow, and their faces are pale as milk. They have mighty creatures at their command—blue striped *simmars,* strange horses, dogs with wings. I can make sense of none of it. I confided in Father, who fears that I am *kuli*-cursed. As you feared you were."

Kevla felt cold. He did not know, yet, about her newly discovered ability with fire. She licked her lips and waited for him to continue.

"I don't know what they mean, but somehow I know they're not from the *kulis*. Nor, I think, are your dreams. Father told me to never mention them again. He fears he would have to denounce me."

Kevla gasped. "He wouldn't!"

"He would. He would have to, if it became general knowledge."

"Then you must never speak of it," she said promptly.

"Except to you. I can tell you anything."

Her heart swelled at the words, and she realized that it was time for her to confide her own secret.

"I have something to tell you, too," she said. "Or rather show you." She rose and went to the small brazier. A small bundle of dried grasses lay inside, more for decoration than for any real light or heat. She stood in front of it, her heart racing. She desperately hoped she was right, that the power of their bond would stretch to accommodate even this.

"I've been having more than dreams," she said, meeting his eyes evenly. "I have been able to...to do things." She pointed at the bundle.

"Burn," she said.

At once, the grasses burst into flame, burning quickly, writhing and turning to black soot within seconds. Jashemi stared, open-mouthed, and did not speak. Kevla's heart sank. She had misjudged him. He would scream and they would come for her and—

"When did this start?" His voice was astoundingly calm, although his still-wide eyes betrayed his shock.

"A few days after you left," she whispered. "I was having trouble getting a fire started, and I said, 'Burn, curse you,' and this happened." She gestured at the dying fire. "I can make the room warmer, too. Jashemi, I'm scared! I don't know what's happening to me!"

He looked at her searchingly and then held out his arms. For a moment, she could not move. They had crossed one barrier when she had embraced him in the caverns. Now, if she permitted him to hold and comfort her, they would cross another. Slowly, she went to him, and his arms closed gently around her. She could smell the sweet oils mixed with sweat on his skin, feel the warmth emanating from his slim boy's body as she rested her head on his chest. Kevla closed her eyes and accepted.

"I don't know what's happening to either of us, Kevla. But at least, we have each other." He folded her even closer. "We will always have each other."

Chapter Thirteen

Strange, Sahlik thought as she bent to stir the pot that hung over the fire, *how fast the years fly when one is old.*

It did not seem so long ago that Kevla had arrived at the House of Four Waters as a skinny, big-eyed girl of ten. Now, Sahlik rose and regarded the woman that girl had become.

Kevla had blossomed like a desert flower when given proper food and shelter. The long, lustrous black hair was still kept in a braid, but that was the only resemblance between girl and woman.

The once-scrawny child was now almost as tall as her father and brother. Despite the best efforts of the seamstress to create clothing that disguised Kevla's figure, it was apparent to anyone with eyes that beneath the shapeless *rhia* was a body that was slender yet ripe with womanly curves at hip and breast. Her face was exquisite, almost as perfect in its proportions as a carved statue's. But no statue could match the beauty of Kevla's face when it lit up in a smile.

Had Kevla been the *khashim's* legitimate daughter, she would have had suitors clamoring for her hand from sunrise to sunrise. Had she even been permitted to continue in Yeshi's service as a handmaiden, it was likely she would have been well-matched despite the stigma of Bai-sha. As it was, the men looked, the men lusted, but there was no talk of marriage.

Nor did Kevla express interest in such things. She appeared content in her role as low-caste servant, moving with grace from chore to chore. It seemed enough for her to have Sahlik and her work.

And, of course, Jashemi.

The youth had matured into a younger version of his father, with Tahmu's wise, dark eyes. He was, if such a thing was possible, even handsomer than his father had been at that age, his features softened by Yeshi's blood in him. Sahlik thought it odd that he had not yet been betrothed, but soon enough he would come of age, and then such matters would have to be addressed. Sahlik wondered how Kevla would react when she had to share Jashemi's attention.

There were moments when Sahlik wondered if conspiring with the two siblings was the right thing to do. They thrived on one another's company as if the moments together were meat and drink to them both. They were intelligent enough to be discreet in their clandestine meetings, but the keenness of their desire for one another was almost overwhelming to behold. Sahlik was confident that nothing improper was happening between the two young people; although Kevla did not know her parentage, Jashemi did, and Sahlik trusted him to respect such a profound taboo.

Still, sometimes it troubled her. But then she thought of how miserable the two would be if she did not assist them, and all thoughts of abandoning them evaporated like water under the sun. Things were hard enough on the poor creatures. Let them enjoy what they had while they could.

Holding that thought, Sahlik said, "Kevla, we are out of fresh mint and parsley for the stew. Go and gather some from Maluu—from Asha's garden." Maluuk had died in his sleep a few months ago, and it was still hard for Sahlik to think of young Asha as the Clan's healer.

Kevla kept her face neutral, but could not hide a brief flash of delight in her beautiful brown eyes.

"Yes, Sahlik." With a rustle of cloth, she was gone.

Sahlik watched her go, and as she did every time she sent Kevla off to meet Jashemi, said a brief prayer for both children's safety.

Asha had left several hours ago, when a falcon had come with a note requesting his aid. The Clan of Four Waters was spread over much territory, and Asha served all the Clanspeople. Jashemi didn't know and didn't care who Asha was assisting. He only cared that he and Kevla now had a time and place to meet.

He paced inside the little hut. Its familiar scents and decorations sang to him of the time when Kevla had first come through that door and he had taught her how to play *Shamizan*. He had the board and pieces now, just in case they had time for a game. He held it with hands that were sweaty, and he was aware that his heart was racing.

Was this how it was with other brothers and sisters? This sharp, almost painful pleasure? This anticipation that made one nervous and elated, made one's throat dry and one's palms moist? He could only guess. Perhaps the fact that he was forbidden Kevla's company made their time together sweeter, but he could not imagine a moment when he would not be delighted to see her.

For the hundredth time, he peered out the window. This time he saw her, and his heart surged. She was coming up the little hill at a quick pace, not daring to run lest she draw undue attention. She carried a small scythe in one hand and a basket in the other.

Gathering herbs was the excuse today, then. They must make sure she did not forget.

She pushed open the door and then closed it. Her eyes sparkled with pleasure. "I encountered no one," she said in answer to his unasked question.

"We should still keep away from the windows," Jashemi said, placing a hand on her back and leading her to the center of the room. He gazed fondly down at her. She was wearing an older *rhia* today, one that did not fit her well, and as he stood close to her, still touching her back, his eyes traveled down her throat to her breasts. He was suddenly, sharply aware of the headiness of her scent, of the curve of her body beneath his hand, of his instinctive masculine response.

His fingers tightened against her back as heat flooded him, a fierce combination of desire and shame. Quickly, he stepped away, hoping she was unaware of what had just happened. Her own face was flushed and her eyes bright. She too seemed uncomfortable suddenly, and looked away quickly. She didn't know what Jashemi knew, of course. She only knew that she was a servant, and he the heir to a mighty Clan.

To end the awkwardness, Jashemi rumpled her hair as he had done when she was younger. She giggled, and when she looked up at him, it was with the old affection.

Good. Very good.

"You are to harvest herbs," Jashemi said, indicating her

tools. "It should not take long. Do you have time for a game of *Shamizan?*"

"I always have time to win against you," she replied with an engaging smirk.

He grinned back. All was well between them, again.

As always, time with Kevla, however brief, buoyed Jashemi. But when he ran lightly up the stairs to his room, he overheard something that bled delight out of him. His parents, their voices raised in argument.

He had known for many years that his parents were bound by law and clan tradition, but not by love. He had accepted that, and the older he grew, the more he saw that such was the norm. But ever since Yeshi's second child had been born so ominously marked, there had been a gulf between the *khashima* and her family. There were few arguments between her and Jashemi for the simple reason that they barely spoke. But *khashim* and *khashima* could not indulge in such an easy solution, and over the years, the strife had escalated.

Unaware that he did so, Jashemi ducked his head, as if trying to pull his ears into his body so that he could not hear. His shoulders hunched and he quickened his pace. He could not understand the words, but he did not need to. The tone, especially his mother's, was sufficient.

The sick discomfort turned to anger. His time with Kevla was so rare and so precious, and all the joy it had brought him had been chased away by those sharp, raised voices. He could think of nothing worse they could have done to him.

Kevla, too, was not unaware of the growing tensions between the great lord and the great lady. Although she was no longer one of Yeshi's handmaidens, servants gossiped, and sometimes her duties took her within hearing of Yeshi's once-melodious, now-harsh voice. At such times, she made haste to finish whatever duty she had been charged with; to cross Yeshi's path when she was speaking so would be to invite disaster. She thought back to her suspicions that Yeshi was taking lovers, and wondered if it were still so.

It was a searingly hot morning as Kevla prepared a basket to take to Asha. The young healer preferred to have his meals delivered to him at daybreak and midday, joining the other servants only for the evening meal. She was heading out to his hut when she heard raised voices. Or rather, a raised voice—Yeshi's. She ducked back into a corridor as the mistress of the household stormed past.

"Foolish girl!" Kevla jumped at the sharp crack of palm striking flesh. "This stain will never come out!"

"Yes, it will, great lady, if I have to scrub it until my fingers bleed." Sharu, the little five-score, fear and pleading in her voice. Kevla felt a stab of pity for the girl.

"As if blood on the cloth will make it better. You are clumsy and lazy. Your five years of service are over, why are you still here troubling me so! Go to Tahmu and get your last score and leave this house by nightfall."

A sharp intake of breath and a little sob. "Great lady, I beg you, give me a chance to—"

"Another word from that ugly little mouth and I will have you beaten as well."

Silence. Quick, angry footsteps. A soft cry, a sniffle, and then slow, bare footsteps in the opposite direction.

Although Sharu had been Yeshi's spy and taken Kevla's place, Kevla could not find it in her to resent the girl. She was just trying to survive. Kevla, who had danced on a street corner extolling the sexual skills of her own mother, could understand that. She had no idea what Sharu had done to so offend Yeshi, but expected that it was no great crime.

Deep in thought, she made her way to Asha's hut. She

placed the basket of roasted fowl, bread and dates on a small stone, rapped on the door, and walked slowly back to the House. An idea was taking shape.

That night, she sat alone in her small room. She had gathered some sandcattle cakes and even a few sticks, so that the fire would burn longer. She was nervous at what she was about to do, but resolute.

She laid the fire in the small fireplace, and said quietly, "Burn."

Kevla was no longer startled or amazed by the fire that leaped into being at her verbal command. She stared into the fire, letting her vision soften around the edges. Faces and images started to form in the flame.

"Show me Yeshi," she whispered.

At first, there was nothing. Then the flames shimmered and twisted, reforming into a familiar face.

She had done it. She had ordered the flames to show her a specific person, and they had obeyed. She grinned a little, flushed with her achievement, then concentrated.

There was another figure. Kevla blinked and rubbed at her eyes, striving to distinguish features. But the flame was not as exact as the eye, and as the two lovers embraced the image became blurred. She wondered if her little fire was too small. Perhaps if she had a larger fire, she could see more detail.

But how would she do so? It was hard enough to have a fire in her room at all. She could try to see in the larger fires in the kitchen, but Yeshi would not be with her lover during those times.

Kevla sighed and poured water on the small fire to extinguish it. She would simply have to keep trying.

And so she did, every night for the next several nights. She was embarrassed at doing so, but she felt certain that it was important. The fire was limiting in that it only showed Kevla images that were directly in front of it. If Yeshi were in her bed, the fire would not show her. Only when Yeshi and her lover passed directly before the fireplace in the bedroom she shared with Tahmu did the flames reveal the two to Kevla, and that did not happen every time Kevla scried. And never did Yeshi's lover obligingly turn to look fully into the fire. Kevla couldn't even tell if she saw one man or many, only that she was certain none of them was Tahmu.

About two weeks after she had begun her nightly observation, as she blushingly watched Yeshi and her lover entwined before their fireplace, Kevla realized she could understand words. That was something new—up until this point she could only see people in the fire, not hear them. She bent forward, her ears straining for anything of import. Her blushing increased as she realized that the two lovers were not speaking of anything Kevla needed to hear, only murmuring endearments and crude words. If only Yeshi would speak her lover's name!

Some nights, Yeshi slept alone. Sometimes, she accepted Tahmu's caresses. On such nights, Kevla quickly ended her spying.

More time passed. Still Kevla learned nothing useful, and she grew to find the activity extremely distasteful. But then, something happened while Tahmu was away that vindicated her gut instinct that Yeshi needed to be watched.

The great lady and her lover were finished by the time Kevla sat down to observe. Kevla was grateful for that, even with the indistinct images the flame showed her. The man sat behind Yeshi and brushed her hair. Again, his face was too indistinct for Kevla to make out his features. He was bearded, of course; all the men wore beards save Tahmu and Jashemi. He was large and muscular, and Yeshi sometimes winced as he attended her. Kevla couldn't help but think that if any of her handmaidens had pulled her hair so often, Yeshi would have had them beaten.

"I like it when he is gone to a far corner of the land," said Yeshi. "We can take our time."

The man planted a kiss on Yeshi's naked shoulder. "It is still too short a time to lie with you, my beloved. A lifetime would be too short."

Kevla inhaled swiftly. She had heard that voice before, but where? She felt certain that she knew this man.

Yeshi did not reply, only continued gazing into the fire. Her lover moved on to rubbing her neck. She sighed and leaned against him.

"I can offer you no more than a lifetime," she said, "but we will have at least that. Have you thought more on it?"

Kevla was lost. There was no way to legally sever a marriage in Arukan. How, then, could Yeshi offer this man a lifetime with her?

"I have," the man replied. "It will be difficult but I think we can manage it."

"It would be best if you were nowhere near," Yeshi said.

"It would be best if neither of us was near," he replied. "That narrows our options."

"Time is growing short, too," Yeshi added. She looked younger, softer in the firelight, but there was nothing soft about her next words.

"We must kill Tahmu soon."

Kevla barely slept. The dreams came as they always did, but frightening as they were, her memories of what she had overheard terrified Kevla even more.

What to do? She could not accuse Yeshi, not without proof. Nor, she admitted, even *with* proof, not as low-caste as she was. She supposed she could tell Sahlik. But how would she explain how she came by the knowledge? She could not tell anyone about her abilities, even though she had learned something urgent and important through them.

There was only one person in whom she could confide, and she desperately hoped they would have time together soon.

She spent every waking moment in a state of heightened awareness, wondering if today would be the day when Yeshi and her unknown lover would strike. It did not matter to her if Tahmu were in the House or not, because until she knew who Yeshi's lover was, she had no idea how close he was to Tahmu.

The Great Dragon seemed to have no interest in Kevla's waking torments. Each night, it demanded, *"DO YOU KNOW WHO YOU ARE?"* And she continued to have no answer for it.

She stood again in the ring of fire, quaking in terror before the Dragon's overwhelming presence, when suddenly she bolted awake to find Jashemi sitting beside her on the floor.

"I am sorry to come in the night like this," he said, "but it has been so long since I saw you, and there seemed no other way."

They both took up a great deal more space on the floor of the tiny room than they had when they were children, and were forced to sit close together. Kevla sat up and clasped her hands about her knees.

"I'm glad you came," she said. "I have learned something awful, and I don't know what to do about it."

"What?"

"I have told you that I can see in the flame. See into other fires, and into the faces of those who sit around those fires." Her tongue would not cooperate and her mouth clamped shut of its own accord. How to tell this to Yeshi's son?

Gently, Jashemi urged, "Go on."

"I think I should have told you this earlier, but I thought no good would come of it if I did." She took a deep breath. "When I was still a handmaiden, I suspected Yeshi was taking lovers. Now, I am certain. I have seen them. Together."

Jashemi went very still. The moon was still close to new and there was little light. She was glad of that. She did not want to see the pain on his face.

Finally, he said, "I have suspected the same myself. I had hoped I was wrong. It could mean her life if Father learns of it. Do you know who it is?"

Kevla shook her head. "Scrying by the fire is difficult. It's unclear at best, and the man never looks directly into the flames so I can see his face. But the voice seems familiar, though I can't identify it. Jashemi, there's more," she blurted. "The other night, I saw them sitting together and they were talking—talking about killing Tahmu."

"*What?*"

She shushed him frantically, fearing that his outburst would draw attention. For the first time she was grateful that her small room was so far away from the other living areas. Quickly, in a hushed voice, she recounted the conversation.

"You're sure of this?"

She nodded miserably. "The words are branded in my head," she said. "I've been sick with worry. You're the only one I could tell."

He was silent. Gently, tentatively, she touched his arm. "I'm so sorry, Jashemi. I wish this weren't so."

"Kevla..." he said slowly, "you don't think...you are certain... You are certain your power is true? Perhaps you are seeing something that doesn't really exist."

"Do you think I'm a demon, then?" She hadn't meant the statement to sound so challenging, but his words hurt her deeply. He softened at once, and impulsively stroked her cheek.

"Of course not. I shouldn't have said that." A soft moan

escaped his lips and he buried his face in his hands. "If only you knew who it was," he said, his voice thick with pain.

"Maybe we can find out. I have an idea...."

Chapter Fourteen

Tahmu lazed in the cool water, letting it caress his body and wash away the dirt and aches of a hard day of riding. *Sa'abahs* were more comfortable than horses, but he had been riding since daybreak and it was nearly dusk. He was growing older and his body preferred beds to hard-packed desert soil.

He heard footsteps coming down the stairs and turned to see who it was. He smiled when he saw Jashemi.

"Have you come to join me in the waters, my son?"

"Indeed I have, Father, unless you wish to be alone."

"I always have time for you." The words were sincere. There had been a distance between them since Jashemi had spoken to Tahmu of his dreams. Jashemi had said nothing more about them since then and Tahmu desperately hoped the troubling dreams had ceased.

Jashemi stripped off his *rhia* and stepped into the cool water. He sank beneath the surface, then sat beside his father on the stone steps. The silence that fell between them was awkward, but Tahmu waited for Jashemi to break it.

"My birth festival is approaching," Jashemi said at last. Tahmu nodded. Jashemi would be turning twenty, the age at which an Arukani youth became a man. The Waiting would then begin, and within six months the Acknowledgment would occur. At that time, Jashemi would come into his own as heir. He would not receive all of his father's land, wealth or prestige, but much of it would be granted to him at that time.

"I have a request," Jashemi continued. "I would like to make the ceremony open to all members of the Clan and their servants. Even five-scores."

"We will be gathering everyone together for the Acknowledgment in six more months. They will not like having to make the trek twice."

"I know," his son said. "But I would like to do this."

"Why?"

"Perhaps we can change things around," Jashemi said, which was not an answer to the question. "Perhaps we can have everyone come for the birthday celebration instead."

Tahmu regarded his offspring with a mixture of affection and exasperation. Where had this streak of defiance come from? Why was Jashemi so bent on changing things, on defying—

And then he thought of a youth much like Jashemi, who had been hotheaded and passionate and set on much greater acts of defiance. Jashemi-kha-Tahmu had had bad dreams a few years ago, and now he wanted to change the order in which the Clan came to honor him. Tahmu-kha-Rakyn had wanted to marry a low-caste woman and had brought their Bai-sha child into the House of Four Waters. Who was he to judge his son?

Sighing, he said, "It can be done, but we will need to send falcons out tomorrow. Such a journey requires time to prepare, and we must make it as simple as possible for our people to obey. You are certain you must have it this way?"

Jashemi turned to face him. He smiled, but there was something sad in his eyes. "I have never been more certain of anything in my life," he said.

As he regarded his son and thought about the upcoming celebration, Tahmu realized that there were things he and Jashemi had never discussed; things that a father needed to tell his son.

"You are about to become a man according to the laws of our people," he said. "Soon after that, you will take a wife."

Jashemi's expression was unreadable. "I am not unaware of my duties to the Clan."

"It is not always a duty," Tahmu said. "With the right woman, it can be joyful."

"Forgive me for saying this, Father, but it seems to me from what you have told me that you know of both joy and duty, but not with the same woman."

Tahmu could not deny the truth of the statement. Instead he replied, "Let us hope that your mother finds you a wife with whom you can share both. Have you...lain with a woman?"

"No." The answer was short and harsh. Tahmu thought this just as well. He had fallen in love with the first woman he had lain with, and her face had haunted him ever since. "But don't worry. I know what needs to be done to get a child, Father."

"Producing an heir is important," said Tahmu, "but there is more to it than that. There is...tenderness, and pleasure."

Jashemi sighed and then laughed. "I sense you will not

let me leave until you have told me what you think I need to know."

Tahmu, too, laughed, and the tension between them eased. "I would feel better if I sent you to your wife's bed with a little knowledge, that much is true."

Still chuckling, Jashemi replied, "Speak then, and I will listen like a dutiful son."

So Tahmu shared what he knew about pleasuring a woman; where they liked to be touched, when to be gentle and when to be forceful. As he spoke, he thought of Keishla and the tender, too-brief time they had shared.

True to his word, Jashemi listened patiently. Emotions flickered over his face, but Tahmu could not interpret them. He asked no questions. When he had finished, Jashemi searched his father's face, as if trying to memorize it.

"Thank you, Father," he said formally, ducked underneath the water once more, then got out. "Enjoy your bath. I will see you at dinner."

As Tahmu watched his son ascend the stairs with a quick step, he wondered, half-ruefully, if all fathers felt as puzzled by their son's behavior as he.

Tahmu made the announcement at dinner that night. He did not inform Yeshi beforehand; he was in no mood for an argument before dinner, and he knew he would get one. He seemed to get an argument from Yeshi if he suggested that the sun might rise in the morning and set in the evening.

She was wise enough not to publicly contradict her husband, but the look she gave both Jashemi and Tahmu was openly hostile. She did venture, as she reached languidly for a piece of fruit, "Husband, do you truly believe there is time to notify all so they may come prepared?"

"The hawks will fly tomorrow," he said.

"And, Mother," Jashemi interjected, "my birthday comes

at a quiet time. The Acknowledgment will be in the midst of Second Harvest season. Our people will appreciate not having to let the fruits of their hard labor feed animals instead of their families."

Tahmu gave his son an admiring look. "Well spoken, Jashemi," he said. This had not occurred to him, but it was true. It would indeed be better to hold the ceremony sooner rather than later. Jashemi wasn't thinking like a hotheaded youth. He was thinking of his people's ease and comfort— thinking like a future *khashim*. Proud of his son, Tahmu clapped a hand on the boy's shoulder.

Yeshi glowered.

Yet again, the House of Four Waters began preparing for the descent of hundreds of people. This time, though, the gathering would be a purely celebratory occasion. No one would be riding off to a raid, perhaps never to return. Still, the event brought with it its own unique set of challenges. They would need places for the elderly, women, children, and servants to sleep, not merely healthy men of a certain age. Tahmu rode into the river valleys, asking higher-caste men if they would open their homes to other Clanspeople from far away. They would do as their *khashim* ordered, of course, but a personal request and thanks from their lord would ease the burden somewhat.

Kevla, as usual at times like this, was worked hard. But she went through her chores with composure and a sense of achievement. This was exactly what she and Jashemi wanted, and it could result in saving Tahmu's life.

They started trickling in several days before the actual date of the ceremony. Kevla knew that the Clan was large, but as the days passed and more and more throngs of people descended, she began to wonder how many people actually called themselves members of the Clan of Four

Waters. She asked Sahlik, who chuckled and replied, "Soon as count the hairs on your head, child. I can think of at least two hundred who are high-caste enough to be known to me. And they have families and servants of their own."

Kevla doubted that Clan members were as numerous as the hairs on one's head, but she understood Sahlik's reference. The numbers were constantly shifting, and whatever their eventual total, it was large.

Finally, the day arrived. Kevla and Jashemi had not had a chance to speak since they had come up with their plan, but at that time, they had worked most of it out. Kevla felt certain that if anything had happened to disrupt what they had planned, the resourceful Jashemi would have found a way to contact her. She was wide-awake long before the first summoning blast of the *shakaal* sounded, already in the kitchens tending the fire with the other servants.

Most of the food would not need to be cooked, because there would be no one to cook it as everyone, including the lowest servants, was required to appear before the *khashimu* today. While it would satisfy hunger, the feast would be light: breads baked yesterday, fruits, raw vegetables, and stews that could be left to slowly simmer all day long.

For the first time in her life, Kevla was grateful for the fact that she was Bai-sha. She would be among the last to come before Jashemi and pledge loyalty and devotion—which meant that she could remain alone in the kitchen, gaze into the fire and see and hear nearly everyone else who came before her.

She and Jashemi had decided that Yeshi would never take anyone low-caste as a lover. So that meant that the unknown man who shared Yeshi's bed whenever her husband was away was most likely of high rank, perhaps among the highest in the Clan. Kevla recalled Yeshi's repeated flirtation with Bahrim, and Jashemi sourly put forth several other likely candidates. Even the fact that the voice seemed familiar did not narrow the list much; Kevla had attended Yeshi at many important functions and had heard nearly every high-ranking *uhlal* address her lady at one time or another. Kevla desperately hoped that she would recognize him when she saw him. If this plan failed... It did not bear thinking about.

Jashemi had woken several hours ago, and per custom had descended into the caverns alone to bathe. He ducked under the water twenty times, once for each year he had been alive, and rubbed specially consecrated oils into his smooth brown skin until the sweet, spicy fragrance filled his nostrils and his body gleamed in the torchlight. Normally, he would be attended as he prepared for important gatherings, but today he was strictly left alone. The ceremony was centered around Jashemi entering adulthood; no one made such a passage in the company of others.

He was glad of this custom, as his thoughts were racing and time to himself was welcome. He let the oils dry on his skin, going over every step of the ceremony and looking for places where something might go wrong. The only problem would be if Kevla did not recognize the man, or if somehow the fire was extinguished. He took a deep breath and calmed his mind. Fortunately, everyone would expect him to be slightly nervous on this day.

He touched his arms, and found them sufficiently dry. It was time to don the ritual clothing. The garments were waiting for him in a basket, so white that they almost seemed to glow of their own accord.

For a moment, he panicked. What was the order? What were the words? Ah, yes, he remembered.

First the sandals. He slipped them on, taking a moment to feel the softness of the tanned leather against his skin.

Closing his eyes, he intoned softly: "I am a man. If the Dragon wills, my feet will walk leagues for the Clan of Four Waters."

Next, the breeches. They were soft as a whisper against his thighs as he donned them. What in the world had the weavers done, to create fabric as strong but seemingly delicate as this? He spoke the ritual words: "I am a man. If the Dragon wills, my *kurja* will sire many sons for the Clan of Four Waters."

Now, the *rhia,* embroidered with golden thread that seemed to twist like a snake in the flickering torchlight. He slipped it over his head, feeling the fabric caress his skin.

"I am a man. If the Dragon wills, my shoulders will carry great burdens for the Clan of Four Waters."

Finally, the head covering, light as a falcon's feather. He wound its length around his head, tucking it in here, letting it trail there.

"I am a man. If the Dragon wills, my thoughts will be always with the Clan of Four Waters."

The ritual calmed him and redirected his mind. This was more than a ruse to discover the identity of Yeshi's lover. This was the day he became a man, with all the joys, burdens, privileges and sorrows it entailed.

He had come down the stairs as a youth. He eyed them now as they stretched upward toward the surface. Jashemi straightened. He recalled all the times he had come here as a boy, most poignantly when he had wept in Kevla's arms for both of the sisters whom he could never acknowledge. He looked down at his body, clad in gleaming white fabric. He beheld muscular thighs, a flat belly, powerful chest and arms. He touched a face that needed shaving to be smooth with hands that had dealt lethal blows.

Not the body of a boy, not anymore.

Again, Jashemi looked at the steps. Deliberately, he strode

toward them, feeling the muscles work as he moved, taking each step with the full inner knowledge that at the top of the stairs, where a boy had descended, a man would emerge.

The blast of the *shakaal* startled Kevla so much that she nicked her hand. She jumped and brought the injured finger to her mouth.

"It is time to assemble," Sahlik said to her servants. "Kevla, are you all right? Let me see the cut."

"It is nothing," Kevla said, extending her finger so that Sahlik could examine the thin slice. It was already closing. "Sahlik, I will stay and watch the stews and keep preparing for the feast."

Sahlik searched her brown eyes. "You are a member of the Clan of Four Waters just as much as any of us, child. You will need to honor the future *khashim*."

Kevla wished she could tell Sahlik the truth, but both she and Jashemi had felt it was risky. Even Sahlik might quail at the thought of a serving girl who could scry in the fire.

"I am Bai-sha," she said bluntly. "I will be among the last to honor the young master."

Sahlik's face softened. "You will be among the last, that is true." She glanced over at the bubbling pot and pursed her lips. "It will be many hours before I can return," she said thoughtfully. "If you would stay for a while and then come out, that would be a great help."

"I am happy to serve," Kevla murmured. Sahlik eyed her curiously for a moment, then left to join the others.

When she was certain she was alone, Kevla went to one of the fireplaces. Quickly laying a few sandcattle cakes in it, she said, "Burn." The fire appeared at once, blazing brightly.

Kevla swallowed. She had never tried this before. Her voice quavering slightly, she said, "Burn a little brighter."

The fire did so, and she breathed a sigh of relief. She had

half feared she would burn the kitchen down, but while this size was far too large to cook on, it served Kevla's purpose well.

She seated herself in front of the fire, and watched it intently.

The raised dais had been built only a few days ago, but was as sturdy as if it were a permanent structure. Jashemi sat alone at the top; his father stood at the bottom of the wooden stairs. Tomorrow, they would resume their traditional roles, but today, Jashemi was the center of attention and honor, and even Tahmu deferred to him as the "future" *khashim.*

Jashemi looked out at the sea of faces, all turned expectantly toward him, and gripped the arms of his chair tightly to calm himself. He knew his father was a good leader. He had seen Tahmu hold his own in both battle and debate, but now his throat was dry and he wondered how Tahmu projected calm and confidence when faced with a crowd of this size. Thank the Great Dragon, Jashemi would not have to say anything, but simply sitting in the chair was intimidating enough.

He waited for the signal, one long blast from the *shakaal* followed by three shorter blasts. He swallowed hard, and then lifted his hand. The rite had begun.

Tahmu, as the highest-ranking member of the Clan, was the first to acknowledge Jashemi's passage to adulthood. He stood at the bottom of the steps and bowed deeply, then ascended. Before he could greet the future *khashim,* Tahmu, like all the Clan, would have to greet the Elements.

Each step had a symbol of the element. There were five in all, Earth, Air, Fire, Water, and Spirit. The last step would put the Clansman directly at the feet of his future lord.

Tahmu took the first step. He leaned down and lifted the

sizable rock that represented the element of Earth. He said nothing, but closed his eyes as if turning his attention inward, then replaced the rock. Others, Jashemi knew, would not be strong enough to lift the rock and would merely touch its rough surface with reverence.

The wing of a falcon lay on the next step. Tahmu picked it up, and swung it through the air, creating a brief, gentle breeze. Air was thus honored.

The third step had a brazier of coals next to a large pile of quick-burning twigs. Tahmu gathered a handful and dropped them into the brazier. The flames leaped up, and he gazed steadily into their light, not shrinking from the sudden heat, until the flames had burned themselves down to coals once again. Jashemi's heart sped up a little as he watched his father stare into the flames. It would be at this moment, when he gazed into the fire, that Yeshi's lover would reveal himself to Kevla.

Or so Jashemi desperately hoped.

His honoring of Fire complete, Tahmu took the next step. He dipped his fingers into a large ceramic bowl and sprinkled the precious Water on his face.

Spirit had no representation, because it was nothing solid. There was only a white circle painted on the next to last step, indicating where the supplicant would stand. Tahmu stepped into the white circle, and closed his eyes in concentration as he had done with the previous four Elements.

Now, he took the last step, and knelt before his son on a red and blue embroidered cushion. He spoke in soft tones, so that no one would overhear.

"You are a man today, my son. No father could be prouder of his child than I of you." He smiled gently, and Jashemi felt a lump well in his throat. Then, Tahmu's smile widened mischievously.

"Endure the heat as best you may—both from the sun and from those who approach you."

Jashemi felt his lips twitch as he suppressed a grin.

"I will step in if you need me. If you feel uncomfortable, look at me and nod imperiously." He winked, then bowed again and descended the second set of steps on Jashemi's left. He resumed his position at the foot of the steps and looked at the next supplicant who came forward.

Yeshi gazed steadily back at him, then she centered herself and greeted the representations of the Elements. She moved fluidly, observing all the proper etiquette, and yet Jashemi sensed that she was observing the form but not the substance.

When she knelt before him and he took her soft hands in his, she looked up at him. For a moment, their old connection was there.

Anxious to hold on to that instant, he squeezed her hands and opened his mouth to speak. But before words could escape his lips, Yeshi said in a flat voice, "Today my son is a man, with a man's responsibilities. Today his mother is but another woman in his life."

She rose and went down the stairs, back straight. He watched her go, feeling hollowness in his heart, the deep ache of regret. Then he faced forward again. Yeshi had made it plain how she wished things to be between them. He would not shame himself by begging.

The next person to ascend was Halid, Tahmu's Second. Halid honored all the elements as Tahmu had, then knelt before Jashemi and clasped the *khashimu's* hands.

"I hope to someday serve you as well as I have served your father. You are worthy to succeed him."

He knew he shouldn't extend the moment by speaking—it was going to be an achingly long day—but Jashemi said, "The Clan has been honored by your service. I will sleep better knowing you will be at my side, as you have been by my father's."

Nodding, Halid descended the stairs.

Jashemi felt the sun begin to beat down as the morning drew on, and was grateful for the coolness the white clothing provided. Three had pledged. At least two hundred more remained.

Jashemi sighed inwardly, and forced a smile as the next *uhlal* made his ascent. The day was going to be very, very long.

The sun grew higher, baking those gathered beneath its harsh glare. Jashemi drank at least a dozen full waterskins and ate only fruit, for the moisture. Some took only a few minutes; others, overcome with the opportunity to speak to the *khashimu,* took several. Every now and then, Jashemi would glance at his father, looking as imperious as possible, and Tahmu would encourage the supplicant to hasten his speech.

So many! The full import of what his father did settled on Jashemi in a way he had never experienced. All these lives, relying on their *khashim,* trusting Tahmu to guide them wisely and well. A grave responsibility.

Finally, the higher-ranking castes and their families gave way to lower. As the sun settled down toward sleep and blessed coolness began to tinge the air, the servants came forward. Jashemi had begun the day nervous and excited. Now he was weary, hungry, and thirsty, and wanted nothing more than to bathe in the caverns and then crawl into bed. It was difficult to even summon courteous interest as the servants bent over his feet, but then he saw something that brought him fully alert.

In the back, at the very end of the line, stood Kevla.

She was veiled, of course, and had her hair properly covered. But he knew it was her. He would know her slender, full form, her carriage, anywhere.

Had she learned what they hoped she would? Now Jashemi was even more impatient to be done with the ceremony, but he knew that each person who came up the stairs had value to him and to the Clan. He tried to return his attention to his duty, but he kept glancing back as the line grew shorter and Kevla, scorned servant and Bai-sha, his half sister and dearest person in the world to him, drew closer.

She trembled as she greeted the Elements, and once she nearly stumbled as the fire seemed to burn more brightly at her approach. Jashemi had to grip the arms of his chair to keep from going to her assistance. Finally, she made it and fell to a huddled heap at his feet. It was more difficult even than he had imagined to keep his face impassive as he leaned forward to take Kevla's outstretched hands.

"I honor my gracious young lord," she said, "who deigns to acknowledge the Bai-sha girl."

She said more, but he didn't hear it. His eyes were glued to her face, waiting for the signal.

Slowly, continuing to speak meaningless, proper-sounding words, Kevla blinked her eyes twice. He swallowed hard and felt sweat break out all over his body.

She had seen Yeshi's lover.

Chapter Fifteen

Kevla waited until the waning moon had made most of her path across the sky before leaving her small room. Barefoot, she padded down the cool stone steps, pausing now and then and straining to listen. Nothing. While the feasting and revelry had lasted long into the night, even the heartiest carousers had surrendered to too much drink and food by now.

The House was oddly silent. Kevla knew she had little time. Within an hour, the first servants would awaken and begin preparing the day's meals.

Like a small, secret animal, she scampered through the house, pausing in the shadows to make certain she was alone before darting into the open. She was panting by the time she reached the door to the caverns and had to stifle her urge to hurry.

Slowly, she opened the door, so it would not give her

away with a telltale sound, and made her silent way down the stairs. She did not take a lantern, but trailed her fingers lightly along the stone walls for guidance in the absolute darkness.

Gradually, she became aware of light at the bottom of the steps. Even now, she did not run; she could not be certain it was safe. She flattened her back against the cool stone and peeked around a curve in the stairway.

He was there, pacing like a caged *simmar*. She exhaled the breath she had been holding, and raced down the last few steps.

"You saw him?" Jashemi asked, his voice low and urgent. She nodded. As if steadying himself against the onslaught of a desert storm, Jashemi asked quietly, "Who is it?"

Oh, she did not want to tell him. Better it was some stranger, someone he did not know....

"Halid."

He stared, his mouth open, not wanting to believe her. "No, you must be mistaken, Kevla. Halid is devoted to my father. I see it every time—"

There was no time to indulge his doubt. "Jashemi, I am so sorry, I wish it were not so, but it *is*. He stared full into the fire and spoke clearly. I didn't want to believe it either, so I waited, and I watched...but his voice and features were the only ones that even came close to those of the man I saw with Yeshi. It is Halid. It can be none other."

Jashemi shut his eyes and breathed deeply through his nostrils. Kevla wanted to comfort him, as she had done in this same place so long ago, but a deeper instinct told her to step back. Jashemi needed to come to a point of acceptance on his own.

He sat at the pool's edge, gently kicking the water as he stared into its depths. Quietly, Kevla sat beside him.

At last, Jashemi spoke in a ragged voice. "It makes sense.

You told me that my...that Yeshi said something like time was running out. That they had to—had to kill Tahmu soon."

"Yes," Kevla whispered.

"Halid is Tahmu's Second. He will become *khashim* if anything happens to Tahmu before I have reached Acknowledgment. That gives them only six months from today. No wonder Yeshi was so upset that I wanted to push the ceremony up."

He shook his bare head in sorrow and disbelief. "My mother has betrayed my father with the one man he truly trusts, and the two of them are planning murder. This sounds like a fireside tale, not my life."

Kevla watched as the pain gave way to anger. It was subtle; his nostrils flared and his eyes narrowed, but she knew every expression that flitted across his face.

"They will not succeed," he said through clenched teeth.

"How do we stop them? Are you going to tell your father?"

Jashemi shook his head. "No. How would I explain knowing this? I cannot mention your...abilities. I have to have my own proof. I must somehow catch her with him." A blistering oath escaped his lips and he pounded the stone floor with a fist. "*Halid!* How could they *do* this?"

Gently guiding his thoughts back to action rather than anger, Kevla asked, "How do you plan to accomplish this? You cannot lurk at Yeshi's door every night."

He turned to her, and Kevla shrank from the coldness of his smile.

"No," he said, "but you can."

"Yes," she said thoughtfully, "I can."

For the next several nights, Kevla got very little sleep. Every night, she would light a fire in her room, gaze into the flames, and say quietly, "Show me Yeshi."

If Yeshi was near a fire, be it in her bedroom or elsewhere in the House, Kevla would see her. Sometimes she was too far away, other times her face was as clear to Kevla as if the woman were standing right in front of her. She found that the more she practiced, the clearer even the vague impressions became.

She was not overly concerned on nights when Tahmu was in the House. Not even Yeshi would dare invite a lover in when her husband might enter at any moment. Those nights, Kevla slept gratefully, her dreams troubled only by the appearance of the Great Dragon and his unceasing question.

Inevitably, Tahmu would have to leave. He did so a few weeks after Jashemi's birthday celebration, and Kevla knew that Yeshi would not let the bed grow cold.

It took several hours after nightfall, and Kevla was beginning to nod off when a voice came from the fire.

"I thought you would never come," breathed Yeshi. Kevla snapped awake and stared into the fire. Sure enough, there was Halid, crushing Yeshi to him in a tight embrace.

Kevla swallowed hard, hoping the plan would work. She closed her eyes, calmed her racing thoughts, and said softly, "Show me Jashemi."

The flames shimmered and crackled. The forms of Yeshi and Halid gave way to the image of a bed with only one occupant. Jashemi's face was turned away from the fire that had burned in his room every night since they had learned that Halid was the man they sought.

"Jashemi," whispered Kevla. There was no response. He was deeply asleep. Kevla didn't know what to do. She didn't want to speak so loudly that she might be overheard, but saw no other course.

"Jashemi!" she said, more loudly. "Wake up!"

He started, and looked around. His eyes widened when they looked at the fire.

"Kevla! I can see you!"

That was alarming. Up until this point, Kevla had not realized that she could be seen by those she watched. She had been very lucky to escape detection until now.

"He's with her," she said.

Jashemi nodded and rose from the bed. Kevla looked away, her cheeks burning. She had not realized Jashemi slept unclothed. She did not extinguish the fire, however, and after a moment, asked of it, "Show me Yeshi."

Jashemi threw on a *rhia* and went silently through the House to his parents' sleeping chamber. As he stood outside, he wondered what would be the best course of action. To knock and feign surprise at seeing Halid there? No, that might give Yeshi a chance to hide him, or he might climb out through the window.

As he hesitated, he heard voices. Soft, lustful murmurings. Laughter.

A red haze fell down over his vision. He heard blood thundering in his ears, and before he realized what he had done he had placed his shoulder to the door and broken it open.

They rushed to pull the sheets up, to cover themselves. Furious, Jashemi grabbed the sheets and yanked them back. He stared, anger mixing with contempt, as hands went to cover groins and breasts.

He reached for Halid, seizing the bigger man's wrists. Halid's knee slammed into Jashemi's stomach, knocking the breath out of him. Jashemi's hands opened and he staggered back. Halid came after him. He clutched a wicked-looking dagger. It glinted in the firelight. Of course. Halid would not be so foolish as to sleep with his master's wife without a weapon immediately to hand.

The blade arced down. Gasping, Jashemi darted to the side and felt the breeze as Halid struck only air. He whirled and angled his body, ramming Halid with his shoulder with all his strength. Halid's bare feet slipped on one of the rugs and he went down, still gripping the knife. He managed to roll over before Jashemi bore down on him, and Jashemi felt the tip of the blade slice through his *rhia* and graze his ribs. He slammed his elbow into Halid's throat, then gripped the hand that held the knife. He squeezed and Halid's hands opened. Jashemi seized the knife. Halid grabbed his arm, but Jashemi easily twisted out of it. In a smooth motion, the blade was at Halid's throat.

For a long moment, they lay there, Jashemi atop Halid, gasping for breath. Jashemi stared into the eyes of his father's most trusted friend, and saw there none of the affectionate warmth he had seen for the last twenty years. He saw only hatred and treachery.

He pressed down with the dagger. A thin trickle of red seeped out from beneath the bright blade. Halid had committed treason against his *khashim*. The punishment was death.

Halid's eyes grew wider as the pressure on his throat increased, but uttered no word. With a low oath, Jashemi leaped to his feet. He still held the dagger.

He could not do it. He could not murder in cold blood, not even when it was deserved. The crime was committed against Tahmu, and Tahmu must be the one to order punishment. Jashemi would abide by the laws of his people, despite the rage that surged along his veins.

Halid's hand went to his throat and found it whole. Slowly, he grinned.

"I knew you wouldn't have the stomach for it," he said.

Jashemi felt his face flush but ignored the taunt. "I will send a falcon to my father describing in detail what I saw here tonight. Your lives will be in his hands, not mine. May the Dragon have mercy on you, for you'll get none from Tahmu or me."

He turned and was about to make good his threat when Yeshi's voice stopped him cold.

"What notice will Tahmu take of lies told by a son who is possessed by demons?"

"What do you mean?"

Halid grinned, his teeth white in the firelight. "A few years ago, it seems you were having some very bad dreams. Dreams of people with yellow hair and pale skin, of blue *simmars* with stripes. Dreams that your father knew were sent by *kulis*."

Hotly, Jashemi retorted, "My father will believe me, no matter what dreams I—" The words died in his throat as the true import of Yeshi's and Halid's words registered.

They knew Tahmu would believe him. That was not the issue. Their words were a threat that they would reveal to others what Jashemi had confided to his father when he thought they were alone. If word got out about Jashemi's strange dreams, the best he could hope for from his father was disinheritance. At worst, he would be executed.

"My bright boy," purred Yeshi. "One breath of scandal, and you are immediately disowned, like that little slut you keep company with." Her eyes narrowed. "Go to Tahmu with tales, sweet son of mine, and they will be the last words you speak as a member of the Clan of Four Waters—perhaps the last words you speak as a living man!"

Jashemi made his decision. Kevla had lived as a Bai-sha. So could he, if it meant his father's life would be saved.

"For my father's safety, I will risk it!" he cried.

"Ah, but what about the safety of your little friend? Accidents happen in the kitchen, Jashemi. Burns. Cuts. It would be a shame if Kevla hurt herself—or worse."

Jashemi felt as if he had been struck in the stomach. He trembled, but not from fear. Outrage at the wild miscarriage of justice made him shake.

"Believe this, Mother, if you believe nothing else. If Kevla comes to any harm, I will kill you myself."

"You'll have to get past Halid first, and Kevla will still be dead," Yeshi said, shrugging.

The two lovers looked at one another and grinned in satisfaction as Jashemi struggled to make sense of it all. If he told his father, Halid and Yeshi would make public Jashemi's dreams. Tahmu's hands would be tied. Jashemi would be either disowned or executed. Tahmu could not even act on the news his son had given him, or else the stigma of *kuli*-cursed would be attached to him as well. And then, one day, when Tahmu's guard was down, they would kill him. With he, Jashemi, so conveniently out of the way, it would be easy for Halid to become *khashim* and wed the widowed *khashima*.

And Kevla... He could not permit anything to happen to her. As he stared at Yeshi's face, gloating, twisted in a smirk, he realized Yeshi would have no qualms about murdering Kevla.

A low growl escaped him. He rushed the bed on his mother's side, hands raised to strike her, and had the brief satisfaction of watching her quail. Then, he clenched his fist and brought it to his side with an effort.

He turned and marched out of the room, the scornful laughter of the lovers and would-be murderers following him.

The next few days that followed were the most anguished of Jashemi's young life. He could not tell his own father that his life was in danger. He could not see Kevla, or even try to contact her through the fire, to confide in her and seek comfort; to do so would put her at risk. Worst of all, he saw his powerlessness reflected in Yeshi's dark, knowing eyes every time he saw her. He lay awake at night, trying desperately to think of a way out.

It was at the evening meal when she made the announcement that would change his life forever.

They were halfway through a simple meal, just the *khashim* and his family, Halid and Asha, when Yeshi set down her goblet and straightened. She seemed calmer and happier than Jashemi had seen her in years.

"A few days ago, my little boy became a man," she said. Her voice was warm and affectionate, but Jashemi knew how false such sentiments were. He was on the alert at once.

"And a man needs a wife," Yeshi continued, addressing Tahmu and ignoring Jashemi. "I have found an excellent candidate, my husband. For too long we have been the enemies of the *Sa'abah* Clan, when we should have been their friends. *Sa'abahs* mean wealth, and the Clan of Four Waters deserves as much wealth as it can obtain. It is my understanding that the clan leader has a daughter who is of age. I have sent falcons to her mother, and she has agreed to the match."

Sickly, Jashemi realized he ought to have expected this. Now that Yeshi knew Jashemi knew about her and Halid, she would want him out as quickly as possible. Out, and as far away as she could contrive to send him. As *khashima*, she had the sole and undisputed right to arrange marriages for every male in the household. Tahmu had the same rights with regard to the women. Her choice could not be debated; it was absolute. And when the heir was wed, custom demanded that he live for one year with his wife's clan. He felt sweat start under his arms, felt it gathering at his hairline and on his shaved upper lip.

"This is sudden, wife," Tahmu said uncertainly, looking from Yeshi to Jashemi.

"Not at all," Yeshi replied, reaching for a date and taking a small, dainty bite. "Jashemi has come of age, he is able to take a wife."

"But he is still Waiting. He has not had the Acknowledgment ceremony yet, nor spent sufficient time in battle to—"

Yeshi paused, the date halfway to her mouth. Her dark eyes flashed. "You gainsay my decision, *husband?*"

"I have no right to. But I would ask you to reconsider."

"I have spent a great deal of time thinking on this, believe me," she said, her gaze flickering to Jashemi. He met her stare for stare. He had no doubt that she spoke the truth. "Jashemi will leave in two days' time. His bride is eager for him." Yeshi smiled. "She will no doubt count herself among the most fortunate of women."

Jashemi had known that one day this moment would come. He would have no say in who his bride would be, any more than Tahmu had had a say in his own marriage. He knew that it was unlikely he would even have had a chance to meet the woman in question before the wedding. He knew this, and had accepted it.

But to be sent away so that his mother could more conveniently murder his father—to be sent away from *Kevla*—this could not be. She watched him with her clever eyes, searching for any hint that he would explode in anger and bring his own doom upon himself. Doubtless, she considered marrying the daughter of the *Sa'abah* Clan *khashim* too easy a fate for him.

He would not give her the satisfaction. He rose and bowed. "Excuse me, Father, Mother. I think my meat was spoiled."

In the privacy of his room, he forced his anger into a corner of his soul, and began to think furiously about what, if any, alternative there might be.

Yeshi watched him go, then said calmly to Sahlik who waited on them, "My son's food was spoiled. Beat the one who prepared it."

Kevla ached.

Not from the beating that Sahlik had been forced to give her, for the old woman had gone gently on her back so that it barely stung. No, she ached from something else Sahlik had given her—news that Jashemi was to be married and live far from the House of Four Waters for a full year.

Far from Kevla Bai-Sha.

Sahlik had whispered the awful words in her ear before she began the beating, so that Kevla's sobs and wails would be heartfelt and convincing. Kevla was strangely grateful for the opportunity to grieve aloud. She did not know if she could have feigned indifference in front of others.

She screamed and wept and sobbed, feeling her heart break in her chest. All these years, she had denied her feelings for the young lord, and her emotions would be silent no longer. *Jashemi! Jashemi!* She wanted to cry his name over and over, as if uttering it might make it possible for him to stay, but instead bit her lip till it bled to hold back the telltale word.

Now she sobbed into the cold stone floor and beat on it with her hands, for she, too, knew why Yeshi had chosen to do what she did. She had continued to watch in the fire, that night when Jashemi had confronted Yeshi and Halid. And she also knew Jashemi would not be able to steal away to meet her before he was forced to leave, for Yeshi would be watching them both.

The pain inside her was so extreme that she thought she would never sleep again. Yet sleep she did, exhausting herself with weeping. And when as always she stood before the Great Dragon, for the first time she felt more grief than fear.

When it reared up and demanded, *"DO YOU KNOW WHO YOU ARE?"* she had an answer ready for it.

"I am nothing without Jashemi," she cried, collapsing in front of the mammoth creature and weeping tears that were as hot as the flames.

And strangely, the Great Dragon seemed placated by her words.

PART II

In the Shadow of Mount Bari

Chapter Sixteen

The advisor hastened along the stone corridors. He was late, and his lord would not like that. But he hoped that the news he bore, extracted from the latest prisoner by various means of persuasion, would placate the Emperor.

Though it was daylight, the castle was dark, as it ever was. A thunderstorm outside rendered the skies a dull pewter shade. Portraits glowered from the stone walls. Torches burned a dull orange red in sconces, illuminating little. The cold from the stone floor seemed to seep through the advisor's thick boots and into his feet.

The corridor wound deeper into the bowels of the castle. Windows disappeared; even the cheerless light of the stormy sky was now gone. The advisor quickened his pace, almost running.

At the end of the corridor stood two huge wooden doors. They were mammoth things, carved with a variety of designs and inlaid with precious stones. They seemed as though they would be impossible to move. Such was their craftsmanship, however, that a single finger's pressure would open them. But the advisor was not fool enough to apply that pressure uninvited.

"Your Excellency," he called in a voice that quavered slightly. "I have come as you asked."

"Enter." He could read nothing in the voice; it was cold, flat. Dead. Settling himself and putting a pleasing expression on his face, the advisor did as he was bid.

In this room, the Emperor's private refuge, the only light came from a crackling fire whose friendly glow was disconcertingly cheery in the dark place. The Emperor sat in shadow, in a wine-colored, overstuffed chair. Statuary crowded the room, images from mythology and history, and the paintings that adorned the walls were barely visible in the dim light.

The fire cast shadows which danced grotesquely, like capering demons, against the walls. But there was enough light to see the Emperor's creature that cowered against his legs.

The advisor eyed it briefly. The beast was ancient, and powerful enough to destroy anyone in a heartbeat. Yet it was timid and often frightened. A thin golden chain wrapped around its slender, graceful neck. The end of that chain disappeared into shadow. The advisor knew it was clutched in the Emperor's left hand, as always. He never inquired as to why the Emperor felt such a shy creature must be constantly chained. One didn't ask the Emperor such questions.

The beast, about the size and shape of a small deer, looked up at the advisor with limpid brown eyes. Its single horn and the scales on back and face caught the glow of the firelight, and its brown coat looked chestnut. It lowered its head, the golden chain jingling with the movement, and closed its eyes.

The advisor was relieved. Despite—or perhaps because of—its docility, the creature always unnerved him.

"I hope," said the Emperor in his flat voice, "that you bring good news this time."

"News, Your Excellency, but whether it is good or bad remains to be seen."

The Emperor waved a slender, beringed hand. "Speak."

The advisor did. When he had finished, the Emperor remained silent, and then he, too, spoke at great length, of armies, and conquest, and crushing all who opposed him.

And at his feet, enduring her master's petting, the beast sighed heavily, as if it understood every word.

Jashemi was so wrapped in misery that he later recalled very little of his arrival and wedding ceremony. He spoke, moved, laughed as if someone else were commanding and directing his gestures. No doubt the food was good, but he did not taste it; no doubt the wine was strong, but it did not intoxicate. When the time came to stand before the veiled woman he was to take as his bride he found the words came without much effort. He was too far lost in his wretchedness to even will them away.

He lifted the veil, seeing Shali's face for the first time, and had no reaction. She was not pretty, but neither was she plain; not fat, but not slim. She was in every way ordinary, but Jashemi knew that even had his bride possessed the sort of beauty that inspired ballads, he would not have desired her.

The men of the Clan, and his father as well, followed him to the prepared bedchamber. For the first time, Jashemi felt real emotion penetrate his dulled senses.

Of course. This was part of the tradition, that the high-ranking men of both clans would demand to see this union consummated. There were many solid reasons for this: proof that the woman was a virgin, proof that the man had claimed his rights and could not later deny it.

Jashemi had never felt less like lying with a woman than at this moment. He stared at Shali, feeling the mask of pleasantness melt from his face, and her own face fell.

She put her arms around his neck and whispered, "I have a small wineskin prepared for this, my husband. I am a true virgin, but my handmaidens tell me that sometimes women do not bleed sufficiently to impress the onlookers."

Overcome with gratitude, he buried his face in her neck and whispered, "Thank you."

They stood while servants stripped them, and Jashemi's face burned as the men saw his limpness. There was much joking, but the girl's father, Terku, who had drunk too much wine, was insulted.

"He does not find my precious jewel of a daughter attractive!" the *khashim* of the *Sa'abah* Clan bellowed.

"You plied him with much wine, my friend," Tahmu said smoothly. "Give the boy a moment. Touch often rouses what sight does not."

As quickly as possible, Jashemi and his naked bride went to the bed and pulled the covers around them. Again, Shali spoke into his ear, "The skin is under the pillows."

"Get it ready," Jashemi whispered back, hoarse from embarrassment. He maneuvered so that he was on top of Shali and pretended to thrust. She cried out in seeming pain and her arms reached under the pillow. Jashemi remained unaroused, even as his *kurjah* brushed against her *sulim* and thigh, but continued his movements. Around him, he heard laughter and cries of approval. He felt the rough leather of the wineskin press into his hand, maneuvered its stopper, and was rewarded by dampness. He smeared the fluid on himself and between her thighs, then uttered a long, low groan and collapsed on Shali. He barely had time to hide the evidence before Shali's father had whipped off the bedclothes to reveal a small amount of blood on the sheets and on the loins of the new husband and wife.

"Well done!" exclaimed Terku, and Jashemi was unsure if he was referring to his daughter or Jashemi. "Let us leave them alone to recover...and beget a child tonight, Dragon willing!"

They left in a wave of raucous laughter, and the door slammed shut after them.

Jashemi rolled away from his new wife. Shame, anger, and regret flooded him. They lay for a while, neither speaking. At last, Jashemi said, "I'm sorry, Shali. You did not deserve this."

"Deserve what?" she said, rising and walking to the small basin of water on the table. She wet a cloth and began to wash.

"A man who could not truly make you a wife on your wedding night."

"I would rather have that than be taken by force, as many brides are," she said, rinsing the bloody cloth, wringing it out, and resuming her task. "There is time enough for consummation." She turned to look at him. "Unless you prefer men to women?"

He laughed bitterly. "This would be easier to understand if that were so," he replied. The blood drying on his thighs and *kurjah* was sticky and uncomfortable. When Shali had finished, he rose and cleaned himself, not enjoying being the object of her scrutiny but seeing no other option. She propped herself up on one elbow on the bed and regarded him.

"You are a beautiful man, Jashemi-kha-Tahmu," she said softly. "And they say you are kind. I am happy that you are my husband."

He finished his ablutions and went to her, sitting beside her on the bed. "Shali," he said earnestly, "I must tell you that I did not wish this marriage."

Her not-pretty, not-ugly face smiled. "The resting warrior between your thighs tells me that, my husband."

Husband. Jashemi forced himself not to cringe from the word. "I will do what I can to make this...bearable for you. Know that I will never raise my hand to you, nor take you against your will. I will treat you with honor and respect."

Her muddy brown eyes shone. "Husband," she whispered, "what you have said moves me greatly. In return, I will never deny you your right to my body, I will never speak against you, and I will tell my handmaidens that you are the most virile man in the world."

Coyly, she glanced down at his groin. "Perhaps you did have a bit too much wine," she said. "And perhaps some loving attention will rouse this warrior."

Shyly, gently, with hands that were clearly inexperienced, she reached to touch his flaccid *kurjah.* He wanted to pull away; every fiber of his being screamed that this was wrong, was a betrayal—

A betrayal? Of whom?

And of course, he knew. Kevla's face flashed into his mind. Desire welled inside him like liquid fire, and for an instant, before he could redirect his thoughts, he imagined that it was her work-callused hand caressing him, her full breasts he now reached to fondle, her lips he tasted. And even as he knew this flood of passion was wrong, he surrendered to it, permitted himself to be carried along like a reed in a swollen river. He moved to lie atop the willing Shali, parted her legs and thrust into her moist warmth, moving as gently as he could as she cried out first with pain and then pleasure. It was the first joining for both of them.

The tide crested, engulfed him. Fire, he was on fire, his skin prickled from the scalding heat. His eyes were squeezed shut, his mind filled with images of Kevla, and he climaxed with an intensity he had never before experienced.

Sweating, gasping for breath, he rolled over and wiped his face. Shali muttered something about not having to lie to her women after all, and he almost wept.

Jashemi had known the truth for years now, but he had denied it. Denied it to protect and honor Kevla, to keep the sacred order of things, to not violate the worst taboo the Dragon had laid upon his people.

He not only desired Kevla Bai-sha, his half sister.

He was helplessly, thoroughly, eternally in love with her.

That night he dreamed. He saw again the yellow-haired, milky-skinned warrior with a clean-shaven face. His strange *simmar* walked beside him, and the world around him was white. But this time, Kevla, too, walked beside the man. She seemed to know him, and was pleasant to him and smiled. But Jashemi knew her better than anyone on the world, and he saw that a shadow lay across her beautiful features. She looked older, as if she bore a burden she did not bear now.

The man wore heavy furs, but Kevla wore only a red *rhia*. She did not seem cold in the slightest. The warrior, the beast and Kevla walked across the strange white stuff—like sand, but cold and wet—their feet sinking deep and leaving footprints. They were just cresting the rise of a hill.

Then Jashemi's heart spasmed. Rising behind the three, unseen by any of them, was an enormous red dragon.

He screamed and bolted awake, wondering for a moment where he was, surprised to see a shape in the bed beside him. He recoiled from Shali's touch at first, thoroughly disoriented, and then memory crashed upon him like an avalanche.

"Husband, what is it?" Her hands were calm, soothing. She rose and wet a cloth to wipe his sweaty face.

"It is nothing," he said, "merely a dream."

She dabbed his face gently with the cloth. "I am troubled that your dreams are so disturbing, my lord."

He lay back down, opening his arms so she could lie on

his chest. With an intensity so powerful it made him weak, he wished that it were Kevla in his arms.

"I am troubled, too," he said.

He walked alone with his father while Tahmu's *sa'abah* was being readied for the journey home. They chatted about small, inconsequential things for a time, and then Jashemi said, "I suspect I will greatly miss my home and you, Father."

"Perhaps," Tahmu acquiesced, "but this is the way of things. And it is only a year. Before you know it, you will be home again, with your bride."

Jashemi grit his teeth, looking down to hide his expression until he could get it under control. *If only I could warn him, tell him!*

"Father," he began, feeling his way carefully, "There are some who might think you growing old and feeble, with a son already of age. There might be...plots against you."

"There have always been plots against me," Tahmu laughed. "But I have Halid to watch my back. That's what a Second is for, after all."

"Yes," said Jashemi, dully, "That is what a Second is for."

"I leave two hawks with you," Tahmu continued. "If you have need of me, send a message."

"I will. Father...please take care of Kevla."

Tahmu stopped in midstride and regarded his son. "So," he said, "you have been seeing her, haven't you?"

Jashemi smiled slightly. "Come, Father. I can't believe you didn't know."

"Of course I knew," Tahmu said, smiling himself now. The smile faded as he added, "I only wish there had been no need for secrecy. You are brother and sister. You should have been raised as such."

I wish we were not, Jashemi thought, a heady yet painful mixture of desire and guilt sweeping through him. *I wish she were anyone in the world but my sister.*

"It is time," said Tahmu, and Jashemi realized their walk together had brought them to the corral. Tahmu's *sa'abah* had been saddled, and as it turned bright eyes to them its tack jingled.

They stood looking at one another, father and son, yet two men grown. Tahmu held open his arms and they embraced tightly.

"You have a great opportunity here, my son," Tahmu whispered. "Relations with the *Sa'abah* Clan have never been good, but I can think of no better ambassador than you."

They parted, hands still on one another's shoulders. "You share my vision," Tahmu continued. "You desire peace more than war. Let us see if we can bring this about."

With a final clap on Jashemi's shoulder, Tahmu mounted. His entourage was waiting for this signal, and they mounted as well. Tahmu did not give a last wave or shout a farewell; he had said all he meant to say. Jashemi watched as his father rode into the desert, and his throat closed up.

Be careful, Father.

Life among the *Sa'abah* Clan was very different from what Jashemi was accustomed to. They were nomadic, so there was no Great House. The tents of the *khashim* and the higher-caste members of the clan were as ornate as could be managed, but even they were nowhere as fine as even the poorest room in the House of Four Waters. Because there was little opportunity to grow crops and store meats, the clan subsisted mostly on the meat they could hunt and the fruits they happened upon. Jashemi found he missed fresh vegetables terribly. The entire atmosphere was much more rough-and-tumble, and Jashemi was reminded more of his uncle's household than his father's. The greatest single privation, though, was a lack of water. He was used to bathing every day, sometimes even twice a day if he had been out hunting or in the sun for a long time. Now, he realized that the basin of water he and Shali had used to cleanse themselves on the night of their wedding was as much of a bath as he would ever have here. The resource was finite; it was whatever the clan stumbled upon in their travels and whatever they could carry.

But more than the comforts of a proper bed or water to bathe in, Jashemi missed Kevla. All the other things could have been borne had she been present. Their time together had been infrequent and laced with fear of discovery, but now, denied even this, Jashemi realized how much he had grown to count on his sister. She understood him, accepted him…loved him, he was sure of it, though they had not spoken of such things.

He did not dare even to be close to a fire, and was thankful none had been kindled in his tent during his wedding night. He did not want Kevla to risk giving herself away, nor did he want her to see him with his new wife. On even the coldest of nights, Jashemi made certain to be well away from the crackling flames.

He was a stranger here, even though he was now kin to the clan leader, and the clansmen never let him forget it. They laughed at him when he asked for a spoon to eat the thick, meaty stew, stared aghast the first time he inquired about water. It was no wonder the clans were always at each others' throats. They were so different, and made so little effort to try to understand each other.

To ease the ache of Kevla's absence, Jashemi strove to fill the void with information. His wife was the one person he felt he could comfortably ask potentially embarrassing questions of, and when they were alone he bent her ear. This served several purposes. First, he learned about his new family and their customs; second, he forged a closer relationship with the stranger who was now his wife, and third, he filled their time together with this new sort of bonding instead of the more common union between man and wife.

He was racked with guilt over what had transpired on their wedding night; the only reason he had been able to satisfy her as a man should was that he pretended she was Kevla. That was an insult to both her and the beloved woman who was his sister. Since then, he ruthlessly drove all images of Kevla that were not innocent from his mind, and did not touch his wife in a sexual manner. Better to abstain from both than to sully either.

At first, Shali seemed perplexed by his lack of desire. But she warmed to him when she saw his genuine interest in learning about her people, and seemed willing to make this intimacy an acceptable substitute.

"Do your people not grow weary of traveling?" Jashemi inquired one night as he sipped a goblet of wine with Shali. The wine was excellent; Tahmu had brought it from the House of Four Waters. It tasted of home.

"Oh, no," Shali replied, taking a drink from her own goblet. "It is in our blood, this wandering. We would feel trapped if we were to stay in one place too long." She leaned forward. "Tell me again of your House," she said.

So Jashemi spoke of the House and its never-ending supply of water, its strong stone foundations and brightly painted hues, its enormous kitchens and gardens. Shali's eyes shone as she listened. They had been speaking like this for weeks now, and Jashemi thought it was safe to move on to other topics.

"My father has long wanted to be counted a friend of the *Sa'abah* Clan," he ventured.

"Then giving us his son was a good thing to do," she said, smiling sweetly.

"It seems to me your people are very skilled at warfare."

"We have to be," she replied. "Everyone wants our *sa'abahs*. But they do not breed well when kept in a corral."

Jashemi wondered if the so-called "wanderlust" Shali had attributed to her tribe was dictated not from within but from the *sa'abahs*. They were as valuable as water, and if they only bred readily when on the move, well then, it made sense to become a traveling clan.

"Of course everyone wants them," he said, "but some would prefer not to fight to obtain them. Why does your father oppose trade?" He kept his voice light, as if the conversation meant little to him personally, but he hung on her answer.

"What is to stop another clan from trading and then descending at night to reclaim what they had given?"

"Trust," Jashemi said simply.

She looked sharply at him then. "Trust," she said, "is a luxury that perhaps those in your Clan can afford." He marveled at the bluntness of her words; the wine was having an effect. "It is easy to trust when you are in no danger. When was the last time the House of Four Waters came under attack?"

"Not in my lifetime or in my father's," he admitted.

She shrugged, the gesture conveying more than words could. She drained her cup and poured more wine. "Besides," she said, "it keeps our warriors ready for battle from all sides."

"You mean, from all clans."

She shook her head, the looseness of the gesture revealing that she had indeed drunk too much tonight.

"No," Shali said, "from all *sides*. Our scouts have returned with rumors of war from other lands. Lands on the other side of the mountains."

Jashemi was completely alert. He had never even given any thought as to what lay beyond the mountain range.

Arukan was all he knew, was all he thought there was. There were other people, other lands? The mountains and of course the Great Dragon had kept them safe until now.

Casually, he inquired, "What lands? I have not heard of this."

She smiled proudly. "When you have to fight as often as we do, you learn where your enemies will come from. I don't know the names of the places, but people have been coming from the mountains and killing some of those who live too close to the Northern range."

Shali yawned and stretched, then got up and went on her hands and knees to him. She settled her head in his lap.

"My husband," she murmured, the words beginning to slur, "will you not make love to me tonight?"

Jashemi closed his eyes and stroked her hair softly. "No, my wife," he said, very gently. "But I will take you to bed and tuck the covers around you and sing you to sleep, if you like."

She smiled sleepily. "That sounds pleasant," she said.

He picked her up in his strong arms and did as he promised her, singing children's songs in a soft voice. He watched her sleep for a few long moments. He wished he could love her, or at least make love to her, but to do so would be to court thoughts that he knew were forbidden.

Sighing, he rolled over and soon went to sleep himself.

Again, he dreamed of the sad, elegant woman with whom he regarded the Shadow that lurked on the edge of the world. If only he knew what it meant. An image flashed into his mind, like a memory; an image of a boy just into manhood, lying dead on a stone street.

Jashemi had never met this youth, but he knew him. Knew of him. Why? Who was he?

He saw the laughing horse creature, the elegant hound with claws and wings, and another being unlike any he had ever seen. He could not even properly describe it. A horn and cloven feet like a *liah*, scales like a snake, beard like a goat—it ought to be ugly, hideous, a monstrous thing. Instead it struck him as exquisite, and his heart ached to behold it.

There was a thin golden chain around its slim neck, a chain that trailed off into shadow. And despite the creature's apparent delicacy and great beauty, he knew that it was a harbinger of terrible danger.

He awoke covered in sweat, his throat so tight that he knew he could not possibly have cried out. Anger replaced fear as he wished desperately he could make sense of these dreams. He was suddenly unable to bear sleeping next to Shali, a woman he could not love, could not confide in. It was not her fault; she was a good person and tried so hard to comply with his desires. He took the pillow and stretched out on the cold stone floor.

Kevla. Oh, Kevla, I wish I could talk to you about this.

He had no more dreams that night.

Unto the Great Khashim,

I am sorry to hear that you were not able to come to better terms with the Shining Clan. It is unfortunate that we seem to be the only ones who prefer peace to war.

I have heard news that might interest you. It seems that not only must my wife's clan defend themselves against attack from other clans, but there is a new enemy to be wary of as well. I am now in a position to command informants, and they have corroborated the rumors.

Arukan is no longer alone. It appears that there are lands on the other side of the mountains that have thus far protected Arukan so well. I have not seen this with my own eyes, but the stories keep coming of attacks on those who live too close to the Northern range.

Have you heard of such things? I am certain that you keep at least as informed as I. We have long desired to unite the clans, in order to bring about prosperity and peace for all. Now I wonder if we ought to try to unite them so that we present a strong force to this mysterious enemy. He will easily be able to pick us off one by one, like the simmars *do the* liahs, *if we continue to be fragmented and conduct these petty raids.*

Please take care of the One we both know. I understand you can tell her nothing, but keep a kind eye upon her.

My deepest regards to you and wishes for your continued good health.

Tahmu read and reread the note. Jashemi had not written names or any identifying terms, as they had agreed, and had used a code they had contrived when Jashemi was young. For a long moment he thought that some of the comments were in another sort of code, so strange did they seem to him.

Other lands beyond the mountains? No one had ever heard of such a thing. Of course, most clan leaders had very specific priorities that did not go beyond which other clan they would raid this season. But even he, who prided himself on being more farseeing than others, had never entertained such a thought.

For a moment, he wondered if Terku wasn't playing a cruel trick on Jashemi. It would not be out of character for the wily old man. But Jashemi would not be taken in so easily. He would have tried to verify something on his own, as he had said in the letter he had done.

But Tahmu had heard nothing of this! He had spies far and wide, in every clan. He had scouts who had ranged to every corner of the country and returned. He had....

Despite the heat, Tahmu suddenly felt a chill. Such people were his, of course, as he was Clan Leader, but Halid commanded them.

One of four things was true, and none of them was pleasant.

Jashemi had been the victim of a cruel joke, one that Terku had gone to great lengths to execute.

Tahmu's scouts and spies were idiots, failing to listen and report properly.

Halid was controlling the information he received from the spies and not reporting it to Tahmu.

And worst of all: Jashemi could be hearing the *kulis* again.

A knot formed in Tahmu's belly. Of the four, the best option was the first, that somehow an elaborate prank was being played on his son. He hoped that was the case, but Jashemi was no fool.

The other three were unthinkable. He passed a hand over his face, wiping away sweat that felt cold to him, and began to compose a reply to his son.

Chapter Seventeen

The weeks crawled by, and not an hour passed that Jashemi did not think of Kevla. He missed her more than he thought possible.

His discussions with Shali had proven enlightening, and having gotten what information he could from her, Jashemi began to befriend some of the men who were close to his station, Shali's brothers and Terku's Second, a man named Melaan. Melaan seemed to Jashemi at first to be a peculiar choice for a Second. Halid was an enormous bull of a man, heavily muscled, tall, and powerful, if treacherous. Melaan was tall but slender, and seemed perpetually lost in thought.

But if Terku trusts him with so important a position, then there must be something there that I am not seeing, Jashemi thought as he sat under the stars, sated from the evening meal.

He, Melaan, and Terku's youngest sons Raka and Kelem were all enjoying the slightly inebriated feeling that a full belly often produced. They stared up at the stars, and for a moment Jashemi permitted himself to become lost in their beauty and the old tales: of the First Clan Leader kneeling before the Great Dragon, who dictated how the clans should live; of the eight spirits who guarded the rain and river waters; of the Sand Maiden who tempted the First Clan Leader into lying with her, resulting in, logically enough, the First Clan.

He closed his eyes, wishing he had not thought of the last myth. For it was no Sand Maiden he saw, but Kevla, her face alight, reaching for him. Jashemi took a deep breath and deliberately turned his thoughts away from that dangerous path.

"It is a peaceful night," he said, "to think that somewhere men are fighting."

"The stars are above us all," said Melaan. "They care nothing for our petty joys and quarrels. They shine on death and birth all the same."

Jashemi turned and regarded him in the dim light. Melaan met his gaze evenly.

"You are quite the philosopher, Melaan," Jashemi observed.

"I have seen much, my lord," said Melaan.

Deciding to be daring, Jashemi pressed, "Have you seen armies from another land?"

The uncomfortable silence told him more than any words. Propping himself up on his elbows, Jashemi continued, "I've heard rumors. I know some of what your scouts are reporting. I am the son of a *khashim*, as are all here save you, and you are Terku's Second. I have a right to know what you know."

Melaan did not reply at once. Raka, the youngest, quipped, "Be careful with Melaan, Jashemi! His bad dreams sour his temper some days."

A shiver ran through Jashemi. Bad dreams?

"If I have bad dreams," drawled Melaan, "it is only when I think of either of you leading the *Sa'abah* Clan."

The two brothers laughed. They were indeed young; their eldest brother had been killed in the same raid that was Jashemi's first, so long ago. There were times when he wondered if his was the hand that had dealt the deadly blow to his future brother-in-law; times when Jashemi wondered if they wondered that, too.

"We have done battle with men who do not call themselves members of any clan," Melaan admitted. "We have never been able to take prisoners. They seem somehow to be able to imbibe poison once they realize they have lost."

"Sometimes," said Kelem, the more sober of the two youths, "they have not lost."

Again a silence fell, so profound Jashemi could hear the *sa'abahs* snuffling on their leads in the distance.

"I know," he said slowly, "that you think of me as an outsider. Perhaps even as an enemy. My clan has ridden against yours more than once, and there have been deaths on both sides." He could sense them listening, and wondered if he dared utter what was in his heart—that he wished that there could be an end to all the fighting, between all the clans. He decided that now was not the time.

"But our clans are now allies through marriage. I am a warrior and the son of a warrior. What concerns my wife's clan concerns me. I would have you confide in me, so that I might be able offer what help I could."

No one spoke. Jashemi suddenly felt embarrassed and was grateful for the caress of the night air that cooled his cheeks.

"It is difficult for us to trust," said Melaan at last. "Too much is at stake. You could tell your father what we tell you, and lead a raid against us."

"I would not slay the father of my wife!" Jashemi was indignant, and the words were the truth. Not even in self-defense would he do such a thing.

"She's just a woman," Raka said casually.

The anger that shot through Jashemi turned his vision red, and before he realized what he was doing he had seized Raka and was shaking him as a hound worries a hare.

"She is your *sister!*" he cried. "Think you so little of her?"

Melaan and Kelem pulled Jashemi off the startled Raka, and shoved him hard into the baked earth. The air went out of him with a *whoosh* and he braced for the beating.

It did not come. Melaan towered above him, a dark figure against the starlit sky, and Jashemi saw that he had extended an arm to hold Kelem back.

"Either you are more cunning than you appear, or you speak truly," Melaan said. "Terku adores his daughter, woman though she be. That you come so quickly to her defense, even against her blood brother, speaks well of you. I will talk with my *khashim*. Perhaps it is indeed time for you to be permitted into the inner circle of advisors."

The next day, Jashemi was summoned to Terku's tent. He was the last to arrive, and as he entered, several men looked at him with varying degrees of mistrust etched plain on their faces.

One of them spoke. "Great *khashim,* I say again, the boy from the House of Four Waters may be no friend to us."

Terku raised his hand. "I have heard your words, Baram, and given them the attention they deserve. Cease repeating yourself. I have made my decision. Jashemi-kha-Tahmu, will you swear to be my man?" The eyes that peered out of the wrinkled face were bright.

Jashemi sensed a trap. He stood up straighter. "I am the son of a *khashim,* one day to lead the Clan of Four Waters.

I am no one's 'man.' I would, however, come to this circle to listen, to speak truly, and to honor you and your clan."

Terku's lined face creased into a smile. "A good and true answer, Jashemi. I can ask for no more. Had you agreed, I would never have trusted you."

He had passed some sort of test. He thanked the Great Dragon, for he sensed that what he would learn would affect everyone in Arukan...and perhaps beyond. Unbidden, the milk-skinned, sand-haired man came into his thoughts. He forced the face away. The circle made room for him, and he sat on the rug that covered the sand. Terku turned to Melaan, who began to speak.

"We have always thought that we were alone," said Melaan. Clearly, he was restating what the others already knew for Jashemi's benefit. "We were wrong. Some of the more northerly clans, such as the Clan of the Mountain and the Warcry Clan, have reportedly been attacked by men unlike any they have ever seen. They are pale, with light skin and eyes. Sometimes their hair is pale as well."

Jashemi's breath caught in his throat, but he was careful that his expression reflect the surprise he was no doubt expected to show, not the horror of certainty he felt.

"They crash upon us like an avalanche from the mountains, and the clans they have attacked have been all but destroyed. They do not take water or goods, but slaughter merely for the purpose of killing. They take prisoners, and force them to fight in their army. The few Arukani who have escaped capture or death have fled their own lands, fearing recapture by this dreadful enemy. This is painful to these clans; unlike us, they have a bond with their land."

Jashemi nodded his comprehension. The *Sa'abah* Clan was nomadic, but he had spent all his life in the same place, as had his father before him. As would his son, should he have one. He was already pining for home after a short time away; he could not conceive of being frightened enough to flee the land which had succored him.

"They have weapons such as we have never seen. Though they have taken many clansmen, we have never been able to take one of them prisoner, to interrogate him; they ingest poison before they can be captured. But we managed to take this."

He gestured, and a servant approached bearing a wooden box. Melaan opened the box to reveal a piece of folded fabric. The other men leaned in; clearly, they had not seen this yet either. Jashemi licked lips suddenly gone dry.

"It is their standard," Melaan said, "the symbol of their Emperor." Grimly, the Second unfolded the fabric, and Jashemi's heart spasmed.

Prancing on a field of white, stained by the blood of the fallen, was a graceful creature that appeared to be a combination of many other beings. It was the general shape of a *liah*, with cloven feet and a single, curved horn in its forehead. It was covered in light brown fur, save where scales encrusted its back and neck. The tail of a *simmar* curved around it, and a long mane streamed in the wind. The slight, tufted beard of a goat adorned its chin, and its eyes were large and brown. A gold chain encircled its neck.

For a moment, Jashemi couldn't even see, so overcome with horror was he. He blinked hard, swallowing to force down the bitter fluid that suddenly rose in his throat.

While the craftsmanship of the flag was admirable, it didn't even come close to capturing the beauty of the creature as it had appeared to him while he slept. But there it was, complete with a golden chain, which in his dreams had trailed off into shadow.

Now he knew why he had felt such a dreadful sense of impending danger when he had seen the beast. It was the symbol of the unknown Emperor, who seemed poised to descend upon Arukan with all the merciless force of a desert storm.

A name came to him. *Ki-lyn.* Somehow, he understood that this was the name of the creature. Where had he learned that? Had he heard it in his dream?

Jashemi stared at the ki-lyn, as did all the other men gathered. No, not quite all the other men. Jashemi felt a prickling at the back of his neck that told him he was being watched. Slowly, he lifted his head to see Melaan, Terku's Second, regarding him with knowing eyes.

Akana, fourth son of the *khashim* of the Hawk Clan, crouched low over his laboring horse. He gasped for air as the beast did, his heartbeat thudding in his ears, his mind almost numbed with horror at what he had witnessed.

They had come with unbelievable swiftness in the night, pouring down the mountains in staggering numbers. They would not have been seen at all if it were not for a full, revealing moon that exposed them. Still, even with that much of a warning, the outcome was inevitable.

That they were even men was uncertain. The warriors wore metal covering their bodies, metal that clung to them and moved like the flow of a river. They had long, sharp swords that seemed almost too big for a man to wield. Some wore head coverings of metal that completely encased their heads; others let their strange, milky faces and pale hair be seen, causing still more fear. The beasts they rode had no proper tusks, but came in a staggering variety of hues. They, too, wore the flowing metal, and they were completely unafraid of battle.

Arrows did little damage, and the army moved so quickly that soon the Hawk Clan was frantically engaged in hand-to-hand combat. The weapons of scimitar and spear, wielded by men who had not even time to mount their own horses, were of little avail.

The *khashim* had found his youngest son in the furor and had practically thrown the boy onto a horse.

"Ride!" he had screamed to his son. "Ride and get help, or at least warn the nearest clan!"

"No, Father! I want to fight!"

His father then did something he had never done before; he struck his beloved youngest child across the face. Akana fell at the force of the blow.

"You are the only chance we have!" he bellowed. "Ride, *kulis* take you!"

And, sobbing, Akana obeyed what he knew was his father's last wish. There was no time to saddle the beast, only time to leap onto the horse's back and cling to its increasingly sweat-soaked hide and ride into the desert, ride as if the earth had cracked open and all the *kulis* in the world were clamoring at his heels.

Akana had no sense of time, no idea how long the horse had been running at a full gallop, but it was slowing now. He screamed at it, he who had never raised his voice above a murmur when talking to animals, and kicked its ribs until he was certain he had left bruises.

He felt a wet warmth on his cheek as the horse blew, and wiped the foam away. The horse's sides heaved between his legs, and part of him ached for what he was demanding of the creature.

But he saw his brother fall again in his mind's eye, slashed nearly in two by the impossibly enormous swords. He saw the flood of enemies descending, heard the cries of the women. He didn't know how he knew, but he was certain that no member of the Hawk Clan would be spared.

Only he would survive. If he survived.

He suddenly, sickly realized that he didn't even know

where the horse was going. He hoped that the mute creature was wiser than he, heading for another settlement instead of out into the open, and deadly, desert.

The horse stumbled. Swearing, Akana kicked it again, but it did not lurch forward. Instead, it let out a low groan and collapsed. Akana was barely able to leap clear as it fell heavily on its side. For a moment, he kicked the horse repeatedly, shrieking incoherently. It cringed from the blows, but did not rise.

Shaking, Akana passed a hand over his face. What was he doing? The beast was exhausted, if not dying. It could go no farther. Gently, he placed a hand on its wet neck, whispered, "I am sorry," and began to run.

He was slim and strong, and the terror of what he had witnessed gave him extra speed. He settled into a rhythm, arms and legs pumping, sandaled feet flying over the hard, bare rock. Sweat poured forth, cooling him, but his mouth was parched.

He ran until he could run no farther, and then he walked, swaying like a drunken man. Just when he was about to give up and surrender to the earth as the horse had done, he saw it.

A gray tendril of smoke curled up into the moonlit sky. He stumbled into the encampment, of which clan, he did not know. He summoned enough breath to croak a single word, "Warriors!"

They tumbled out of bed with lit torches and weapons, seemingly confused at the sight of an exhausted boy in their midst. A well-dressed man in his middle years approached. No doubt he was this clan's *khashim*. Akana stumbled to a stop in front of him, and then to his surprise fell into the man's arms. He opened his mouth to speak, but nothing came out. His lips and tongue felt thick and leathery.

"Water, quickly," ordered the *khashim*. Blessed wetness splashed over Akana's mouth and he gulped greedily.

"Warriors," he repeated, "from another land." He gasped for breath. "They—came in the night and—slew us all."

"Another land?" the *khashim* repeated, puzzled.

"He is ill," came another voice. "Having visions. Dreams."

"No," Akana managed to say, struggling in the *khashim's* arms. "They have metal on their bodies, and mighty weapons. No clan has such things. They are—"

He fell silent, staring out into the desert. A dark cloud headed straight for the clan's encampment.

Akana had not warned this clan. He had led the strange warriors directly to them.

The *khashim* dropped Akana at once, whirling to face the enemy. They descended swiftly, efficiently, but Akana did not see it. He had seen too much this night, and he huddled on the earth in a tight ball, covering his ears and whimpering as horse's hooves thudded dangerously close. Despite his efforts to block the sounds, he heard the screams and the sickening noise of blades impaling flesh. The stench of blood, urine, and feces assaulted his nose and he uncurled enough to vomit.

It lasted forever. It lasted a heartbeat. Finally, there was a lull in the noise. Akana uncurled, daring to hope that the strange army had departed and he had survived.

He looked up to find one of them standing directly above him, holding a sword a hand's breadth from Akana's throat. The warrior said something, but Akana shook his head. Then the warrior grabbed him by the front of his *rhia* and hauled him to his feet. This, Akana understood, and he shuffled forward, the sword at his back. He was past terror and now felt more curiosity than fear. He expected to be dead. They had left him alive. To what end?

Following the prod of the sword at his back, he was directed toward the corral in which the clan had until now kept their horses. The beasts had been taken by the warriors, and now the corral contained men. Only men; Akana saw no women or children, and shuddered as he realized what must have happened to them. A sharp prick at his back urged him forward into the corral.

The men stared at him with empty eyes. He did not recognize any of them. He had been right; apparently no one else from his clan had survived. Some had blood on their clothing, but all were relatively unharmed. There were three men with swords guarding the others; they wore a mismatched combination of traditional Arukani garb and the metal clothing of the conquerors.

Akana said nothing. More men came into the corral. There was a shout in a language Akana did not understand, and the houses and outbuildings of the clan began to burn. Beside Akana, a man let out a low, guttural sound and covered his face.

A tall man clad in metal stepped forward. He removed his head covering. His hair was close-cropped and pale, as was his face; pale as the moon. But even in that light Akana could see the scar that twisted down the man's face like a snake. The blow had claimed an eye.

The man spoke. He had a thick accent, but the words were clear enough.

"My name is Captain Kayle," he cried over the crackling of the fire. "I serve the Emperor. You are now his prisoners. You have a choice. If you join the ranks of the Emperor and fight in his name, under his flag, you will be spared. If you refuse, you will be executed immediately. Those who wish to die, step forward, and I will grant that wish."

At first, no one moved. Then, sobbing, the man standing next to Akana cried, "You murdered my wife and children! I will never fight for you!"

With no weapon save his bare hands, he charged. Kayle, moving easily, readied his massive sword and cut off the man's head in a single, almost lazy-looking blow.

A horrified murmur rippled through the crowd. A few more sobs broke out.

"Anyone else?" Kayle invited, grinning a little. When no one else stepped forward, he said, "Good. It is not so hard a decision, after all. Now, warriors of the Empire, turn and honor your new standard!"

Numbly, Akana turned with the others and watched as a flag on a pole was brought forward. He stared with listless eyes as the white fabric, easy to see in the moonlight, fluttered in the wind. It looked as though the strange beast, part *liah* and part dragon, was capering with delight.

Chapter Eighteen

After the meeting, Jashemi wanted nothing more than to return to his tent. He longed to bathe; he knew well the calming properties of cool water lapping at his body. But that was no option here. All he could do was seize some time to himself, and try to reason out the strange, elusive dreams.

He heard a rustle of clothing. Turning, he saw Melaan, and tensed.

"Walk with me," said Melaan without preamble. They walked together for a while, the sun beating down on their covered heads. Jashemi held his tongue. Melaan had initiated the encounter; Melaan would speak first.

At last, the Second broke the silence. "I watched your face when you saw the creature," he said.

"We all watched one another's faces," Jashemi replied.

"You have seen the standard before."

"No!" Jashemi whirled on his companion. "I have never seen it—" And then he realized how Melaan had tricked him.

"No," Melaan said softly. "But you recognized it."

Jashemi said nothing, then something Raka had said floated back to him. On the defensive with the other man, Jashemi quoted the boy's words. "'Be careful with Melaan, Jashemi! His bad dreams sour his temper some days.'"

"My young master has a loose tongue," Melaan said. "I am fortunate that only you understood what it meant."

"You have been having strange dreams."

Melaan nodded. "As, I think, have you."

Jashemi searched Melaan's eyes, and then nodded. "Since you were about twelve." It was a statement, not a question, and again Jashemi nodded. "That's when they begin. Let me guess what you have been dreaming: of being on a vast expanse of water, with no end in sight, and of a strange Shadow closing in on you. Wiping you out, as easily as this."

Melaan knelt on the sand and traced a circle with his finger, then with one quick movement erased the image as if it had never been.

"Yes...and no," Jashemi said. "I do indeed dream of the Shadow approaching. But I am not on a boat; I am on an open area in a great House. Standing next to me is a *khashima,* who tells me that I must not forget. But I don't know what it is I'm supposed to remember!"

He slammed a fist into his hand in impotent anger, and yet was keenly aware of relief that he was not the only person who had dreams of the devastating Shadow.

"There are others like us," said Melaan.

"How do you know? To speak of such things is to condemn yourself as *kuli*-cursed."

"But there are hints," said Melaan. "Hints, like the one you noticed. This is no *kuli*-curse, Jashemi. This is a warning.

Those of us who have these dreams are being given them as a warning to stop the Shadow."

"I have seen no such Shadow."

"Not yet," Melaan admitted. "But we are only now learning of people who live beyond the mountains."

"You think our dreams and this Emperor are connected?"

"I have seen the ki-lyn in my dreams."

Jashemi lowered his gaze. "I, too, have seen it. And know its name."

"I know of other dreamers," said Melaan. "We must seek them out."

"We must do more than that," said Jashemi. He regarded Melaan intently. "We must find a way to unite the clans."

Melaan snorted. "Compared to that, holding back the Shadow seems like child's play."

Holding back the Shadow...there was a way to do that... there were people *who could do that....*

"We must," he repeated firmly. "They have a massive army, one that swells with each clan they defeat. Together, we might be able to stand against them. Alone, we will be easy prey, and the clans will be trampled one by one beneath the cloven hooves of the Emperor's ki-lyn."

Melaan sighed heavily. "I will speak to Terku," he said, "and I will do what I can."

He held out his hand, and Jashemi grasped it. Despite the direness of the situation, he was filled with elation.

He was no longer alone.

Kevla's misery changed, but did not disappear. It went from an almost unbearable, stabbing agony to a dull, aching throb in her chest. Jashemi's absence left a gaping hole that nothing could fill, certainly not her mundane and thankless duties in the kitchen.

She still dreamed of the Dragon every night, but there

were other dreams: dreams of playing with Jashemi when they were children, dreams of touching him before he left for his first battle, dreams of looking into his deep brown eyes and knowing that she was truly seen.

How did anyone live when a loved one was gone? she wondered. How did her own body continue to function, when all that gave it light and life was so terribly far away?

She refused to think of him lying with another woman. While in her heart she knew she yearned for his physical embrace as much as his presence and voice, that was a longing she had never dared utter. She was Bai-sha, he was a *khashim's* son, and he would never be able to take her as wife. She had known of this reality since childhood.

But she was fiercely jealous that this unknown Shali, daughter of a *khashim,* had Jashemi's presence. She could talk to him as she wished, without hiding and deception, without fear of repercussions. She could wrap her arms around him, fall into the warm, strong comfort of him. This, Kevla had known, had tasted, and as with honey on the tongue, she wanted more.

The single thing that kept her sane was knowing that now, she was the only person who could protect Tahmu. She and Jashemi knew of Yeshi's betrayal and Halid's treason, and Jashemi was many leagues away. He could do nothing. Kevla knew that there was very little even she could do, but at least she was here, at the House. When Tahmu rode to a raid, she begged the Great Dragon every day to send him home safely. She knew, as the other household members could not, that Tahmu was a target not just for rival clans, but for his own Second. It would be easy for Halid to slip into Tahmu's tent at night, a sharp knife between his teeth....

Pain blossomed in her hand and she bit back a cry. She had become so lost in her thoughts that she had not paid attention while she was chopping vegetables, and had nicked her finger. She stuck it in her mouth and sucked on it, her eyes darting about to make sure no one had noticed her slip, but the kitchen was busy and noisy.

He came home safely, Kevla, she chastised herself as she rinsed her bloody hand until it stopped bleeding. *You should be thanking the Dragon, not imagining frightening scenes.*

Indeed, that was the reason the kitchen was bustling so. Tahmu had returned, without losing a single man, in the raid against the Sandcattle Clan. Such an event warranted a special feast, and the household was eager to give him one.

Kevla returned to her task and was chopping vegetables with renewed concentration when the kitchen suddenly fell silent. Along with everyone else, she looked up, and her eyes went wide with shock.

Standing in the entrance to the kitchens, her clothing and person both spotless and elegant, was Yeshi. She smiled at Sahlik. The elderly servant hastened to her mistress and bowed.

"Great lady," said Sahlik, "what do you desire? Some *paraah,* perhaps?"

All the other servants had stopped what they were doing, but did not dare look directly at the *khashima.* Kevla, too, bowed her head, but watched Yeshi out of the corner of her eye. She knew her mistress well enough to know that Yeshi rarely visited the kitchens, and in fact had not done so in several years. That was what she had servants for. Why had she not sent them today to fetch her favorite tidbits?

"No, thank you, Sahlik. I just wanted to see and taste for myself how well the feast is progressing."

Kevla's eyes widened and her breathing quickened. Something was definitely afoot.

Sahlik clapped her hands. "Return to your duties," she called, and the servants obeyed. No one dared look at Yeshi except for Sahlik. Kevla continued to chop vegetables, but unlike the others, did not let Yeshi out of her sight.

"What have you prepared?" Yeshi inquired. As Sahlik told her, she nodded, listening. She stepped over to where a girl was carving a decorative bird out of a gourd, removing the fleshy, deliciously sweet fruit with a spoon.

"That looks lovely, child," Yeshi said, causing the girl to blush and smile. "Tahmu will be pleased. Oh, and is this *balaan* stew?" She bent over the cauldron and smelled. "Delicious!" she pronounced. "Worthy of such a celebration."

Kevla clenched her teeth, willing Yeshi not to come to her. She had not looked the woman in the face for years and did not want to do so now. Fortunately, Yeshi seemed to share her sentiment, and brushed past Kevla as if the girl was not there. Kevla caught a faint whiff of scented oils, and for a moment was transported back to when she was eleven years old and massaging the *khashima*. It seemed like a lifetime ago.

She continued to watch Yeshi as one of the aerie's hawks might. Looking as out of place as a silver goblet in a sand-cattle pen, Yeshi made her way through the kitchen, stopping in front of the plate that would be the *khashim's* that evening.

"Will the gourd-bird sit here, on my husband's plate?" Yeshi inquired.

The girl looked alarmed at being directly addressed and glanced at Sahlik, who nodded. "Yes, great lady. On the *khashim's* plate, if it pleases you."

"It does indeed," Yeshi said, smiling warmly. "I see you are almost done. Finish it quickly, and I will fill it with delicious treats myself."

The girl whirled around and began to carve rapidly. Kevla hoped she did not cut herself. She averted her eyes momentarily as she heard the rustle of Yeshi's clothing and knew that the woman was regarding her. Then Yeshi turned, and began to fill the gourd from a bowl full of delicacies placed next to it.

Again, Kevla lifted her gaze just slightly and watched as Yeshi worked. Sahlik was tasting the stew, and the other servants had their eyes on their tasks. Into the hollow went dates, nuts, cleverly fashioned pastries—

—and something else, a green powder that poured from Yeshi's sleeve and dissolved when it hit the juicy fruit—

A gray mist swirled before Kevla's eyes as she realized what was happening. The scream welled up and ripped free from her throat.

"No!"

Righteous fury and a terrible fear for Tahmu shuddered through Kevla as she lifted her hand and pointed at the tray, pointed at the poison-soaked fruit that a supposedly devoted wife was going to feed to her unsuspecting husband, pointed at the evidence that would save Tahmu's life and expose Yeshi's crime for all to see—

The thin ribbon of fire began at the tip of her finger and sped across the room like a lightning strike.

It struck the gourd and the small table exploded. A curtain of flame leaped upward. Sparks scattered across the room to ignite hair and clothing. Kevla heard the screams of terrified servants and saw Yeshi leap backward, staring first at her burned hands and then at Kevla. Smoke filled the room. Others coughed and shrieked, but Kevla felt no sting from the smoke. The only thing she felt was a sickening horror as Yeshi pointed a red, oozing finger at her and cried, *"Kuli!"*

"No," Kevla said again, her voice a hoarse whisper. She knew she should run, should flee before they could catch her, but she remained rooted to the spot, her eyes locked with Yeshi's, and she saw in those dark orbs a hot blaze of triumph.

Kevla suddenly snapped out of her paralysis. The kitchen was chaos. Servants were screaming, fighting to escape. The walls were of stone, but everything that could catch fire had, and the smoke was thick and acrid. She turned and tried to run with the others, but felt strong hands close on her arms and shoulders.

"Sahlik!" she screamed as she twisted in the implacable grasp of two of Yeshi's servants. "Sahlik, help me, she tried to poison Tahmu...please! *Help me!*"

She screamed the last two words over and over, craning her neck to try to find the elderly servant. Hard hands clamped over her mouth. Kevla squirmed, fighting to escape, fighting to warn someone, fighting to breathe. Her eyes rolled back in her head and she knew no more.

Tahmu was pleased with the new irrigation system his men had devised. It would be a good year for the crops. He smiled as he turned Swift from the Four Waters and headed home.

The smile faded as he saw black smoke curling up from the house. He clapped heels to Swift and the horse sprang into a gallop. As he drew closer, he realized that the fire was coming from the kitchens. His heart contracted.

Kevla....

A small figure was running toward him. He recognized the youth as one of the kitchen servants. The boy was now waving frantically, and Tahmu slowed as he approached.

"Fire!" the boy gasped.

"I can see that," Tahmu snapped. "Was anyone hurt?"

The boy nodded, leaning forward with his hands on his knees as he gulped air. "Your wife, great *khashim*. Her hands were burned. Asha is with her now."

Tahmu saw that his *rhia* had been singed. "Is it bad?"

"Yes, *khashim*."

Tahmu felt sick. "Will she have the use of her hands? What does Asha say?"

"I have not spoken with him, great lord."

When he was done talking to the boy, he would ride to Asha's hut. The youth was skilled and had been well taught. He would do all he could. It would have to be enough. Pleas to the Great Dragon would be in order.

"How did it start?"

The boy's eyes were enormous as he replied, "Kevla."

Tahmu's heart sank. Yeshi would surely insist on a terrible punishment. Curse the girl's carelessness! "What happened? Did she get too close to the fire?"

The boy shook his head solemnly. "Great lord...she *made* the fire. It flew from her hand like an arrow of flame." Tears of fear filled his eyes. "The *khashima* named her...*kuli*."

This could not be. Tahmu refused to believe it. Kevla was just a girl, a Bai-sha, not a demon. His mind raced back to that day so many years ago, when he had held her in front of him as they rode, just as he would a pure-blooded daughter. He thought of watching her dance in the square, of standing demurely by Yeshi, of her uncomplaining adaptation to life in the kitchens.

This was not a *kuli*. This was just a young woman.

"Yeshi said this?" he asked. "You are certain?" He knew he was grasping at straws, but perhaps, just perhaps, Yeshi was trying to turn a common kitchen accident into a way to destroy the young woman she hated.

The boy nodded. "Yes, great lord. But we all saw it. Yeshi just said it first."

Tahmu began to tremble. Was it possible? Had he truly unleashed a *kuli* upon his household?

"There is one more thing, great lord," said the boy. He looked even more frightened now than he had earlier, if such a thing was possible.

"Speak," Tahmu said, in a hoarse voice.

"Kevla said that the *khashima* was trying to poison you."

"Poison me?" The words were yet another blow. Yeshi disliked him, he knew that much, but poison him? Surely not. If Kevla had done what this boy said she had done— and he would speak to Sahlik, she would not participate in any slanderous campaign Yeshi had contrived to start against Kevla—then she was indeed a *kuli*, and her words were lies.

Asha was waiting outside the House for him. Anticipating his lord's question, he said, "Great lord, Yeshi will recover. The burns are bad, and will leave their mark, but if Yeshi will let me tend her properly and obey me when I ask her to move her hands in certain ways, she will not lose the use of them."

"Good," Tahmu said. "May I see her?"

"Yes, but only briefly, my lord. Rest will help her heal."

Tahmu nodded his understanding. A crowd was starting to gather. It was to be expected. He was the head of the Clan; when something like this happened, they would look to him to make things right.

He turned and regarded them. It seemed that everyone had stopped what they were doing to come to him; he could not blame them. He regarded the sea of upturned, frightened faces. They were expecting him to pronounce swift judgment. But he could not bear to do so, not yet.

He followed Asha up the stairs to Yeshi's quarters. His wife lay on the silken sheets. Her hair was loose on the pillow, her face pale, her hands swathed with bandages. Despite the fact that there was little affection between them, Tahmu felt a stab of sympathy. He sat down beside her and her eyelids fluttered open.

"Leave us," he told the healer. When the door had closed, Tahmu said gently, "Asha tells me you will recover." She tried to smile, but it turned into a grimace. "Tell me what happened."

Tears filled her eyes. "I was in the kitchens, thinking to make you a special treat with my own hands, my husband," she said. "Then Kevla screamed out and—fire came from her hands! She was trying to kill me! I am lucky I am alive."

He didn't look at her. "You think she is a *kuli?*"

"What else could she be? We have burned men for less than this, my husband. Everyone saw it! I know you are fond of her because she is your Bai-sha, but you must not let that cloud your mind against what you know you must do. You must protect your people."

Now Tahmu did look at her. He wanted to see her reaction to his next words. "She accused you of trying to poison me."

Yeshi smiled sadly. "And does that not make it even more obvious what she is? You and I are not in love, Tahmu, but that does not make me a murderer. Even if I hated you with all my heart, why would I try to kill you? I could not be *khashima* without a *khashim.*"

Tahmu had to admit that she spoke the truth. While he could stretch his imagination to accommodate Yeshi as hate-filled enough to kill, he could not see her jeopardizing her luxurious life as *khashima.*

He bent to kiss her forehead with a heart that grew heavier by the moment. "Rest, now," he said.

"Where is she?" he demanded as he strode into the courtyard. "Bring her before me."

Everyone knew who he meant, and a ripple of surprise ran through the crowd. They were curious as to why he would even bother seeing the *kuli*-cursed girl.

He spotted Sahlik and waved her forward. The old woman forced her way through the crowd. He extended a hand and helped her up the steps. Placing his lips close to her ear, he whispered, "Tell me that this was a simple kitchen accident."

Sahlik had begun looking old to him when he was twelve. Since then, it seemed to him that she had not aged. Now, though, all the years seemed to have descended upon her at once. Her eyes were red, and not, he suspected, just from the smoke.

"Great lord," she said, "I would that I could. But I saw it with my own eyes. Kevla extended a hand, and fire came from it."

Tahmu let out a low groan. "I had hoped this was nothing more than Yeshi's jealousies," he whispered.

Sahlik clutched his hand. "Perhaps it was a divine blessing from the Dragon," she said. "Kevla said that Yeshi had put poison in your dish. Perhaps the Dragon gave her his fire to protect you."

"The Dragon is a distant god," Tahmu said, his face impassive. "He doesn't come when he is needed." He squeezed her hand, and gently touched her arm to indicate that she rejoin the crowd. Tears filled the old woman's eyes, but she obeyed.

It was then that Tahmu saw his daughter.

Halid had taken charge of the *kuli* masquerading as a beautiful, illegitimate young woman. She had been beaten, he saw, and his heart ached. But he was not surprised. A rough cloth had been tied around her mouth, and her hands were tightly bound. Halid clutched another rope that snaked around her waist. She limped as she moved forward, and the crowd parted to give her a wide berth. Tahmu heard muttered curses and watched as someone spat upon her. Step by slow, unsteady step, Kevla Bai-Sha made her way toward the House. Halid led her as he might a cow or goat, but with far less gentleness.

Finally, she stood before him, and before he could say anything she had collapsed at his feet. Her bound hands, the hands that had supposedly shot fire across the room, reached to touch his sandals. Reacting instinctively, he jerked back, and heard the murmur of the crowd.

He swallowed hard. "Speak," he ordered his daughter.

She was crying so hard that she could not. Her hair had come undone from its customary braid and fell like a black river down her back and face. Her body shook with each sob.

Tahmu could not help himself. Knowing full well that he should not, he stepped forward and raised her, shaking her gently to get her attention.

Her head came up and she looked him full in the face. He had not looked at her so for many years, and with a pang realized that she had blossomed into a true beauty. There was much of him in her face still, but more of the radiant, exquisite Keishla.

His words to her came back to haunt him as he stared at their child: *This I swear to you—she will never want for food or a safe place to sleep. No man will dare lay a hand on her without my permission.*

He had lied to his true love, had betrayed her trust in him. Now, he feared he would have to do something every bone in his body screamed at him not to do.

"Kevla," he said, for her ears alone, "give me something, anything, to defend you with. Tell me you didn't do this thing and I will believe you."

Her eyes filled with fresh tears. They spilled down her cheeks as she replied, "I wasn't trying to hurt her, great lord. I was trying to save you. Yeshi and Halid have been conspiring against—"

Her voice continued speaking, but Tahmu didn't hear another word. Even she had confessed to her evil.

My daughter has become a demon.

He let her go and with a sudden rush of pain and anger shoved her. She fell backward hard; no one rushed to break the *kuli*'s fall.

"Take her," he ordered, fighting to keep his composure. "Take her and build the fire. Lock her in her room and bring her out when it is time. No food, no water. The Great Dragon is clear about what to do with *kulis* and those whom they have cursed."

He looked her in the eye. He owed her that much.

"The *kuli* will burn."

The color left her face, but she made no sound. She stared at him. Her lips parted as if to speak, but if she said anything, he did not hear it; it was drowned out by the cries of the crowd. They were jubilant, angry, ready to see justice done. Tahmu stood rigid, his knees locked lest they tremble and betray him, and watched as Halid dragged the lost girl away. The crowd dispersed, returning to their duties. They would be in the courtyard on the morrow, ready to watch the demon die, knowing that their *khashim* was keeping them safe.

Tahmu went inside and closed the door. Moving quickly, he ducked down a corridor and into a little-used room. There, where no one could see him, Tahmu-kha-Rakyn, the most powerful *khashim* in Arukan, slid slowly down the cool stone wall to the floor. He wept silently, as he had not done since he had abandoned Keishla for the good of the Clan. Now he had pronounced a death sentence on the living symbol of their passionate, forbidden love.

Alone in her bedroom, hearing the cheers of the crowd as she drifted in and out of consciousness, Yeshi smiled through her pain.

Jashemi enjoyed riding alone. The last few weeks, he had hardly been able to seize any time for himself. Not that he regretted his decision. He and Melaan had shared everything they remembered about their dreams, and the Second had supported him in his desire to unite the clans. A year ago, this vision that both he and his father shared had seemed like a child's tale. Now, faced with the threat of the strange armies from over the mountains, the clans seemed much more inclined to talk. Several of them had already come for a meeting, and things sounded promising.

It caught him in midgallop.

Suddenly his chest constricted and his vision swam. Fear with no name washed through him, causing him to gasp and his *sa'abah* to slow, sensing a change in its rider. One hand crept up to clutch his chest.

An image of Kevla rose in front of him that was so real he almost believed she was present. He saw her bound, sobbing, beaten. He cried her name, reached out for her. Then she was gone, and he saw only the desert sand.

He was chilled despite the heat, covered with cold sweat. The *sa'abah* had come to a complete halt, and craned its neck to look back at its rider inquiringly.

Something dreadful had happened to Kevla. He knew it in his bones. He loved her. He had to go to her.

His new family would worry when he did not return, and he had no food and little water for a very long ride. None of that mattered. Time enough to send a hawk back once he had arrived at the House of Four Waters. Once he had saved Kevla from whatever was happening to her.

"Come on," he said gently to his mount, turned its head, and set off as fast as the beast could go.

Chapter Nineteen

Kevla had not resisted when Halid and the others had hauled her away from Tahmu; she had been too stunned by his words to resist. They literally threw her into her room and slammed the door. She looked around her tiny room, and for the first time was glad that she struggled for space on a floor that was crowded with tools. Most of them were dulled with use, but she sat down next to an old scythe, maneuvered it into position, and began to cut her bonds.

It took time, and the sun moved across the sky. Kevla continued; time was nothing to her now. At last the ropes fell free. She rubbed her hands to bring life back into them and assessed her situation.

Kevla knew she was no *kuli*. What she had always known was that others would fear her abilities if they knew of them. If only she'd been thinking! She could have dropped a pot to create a distraction and then "accidentally" knocked over the poisoned food. But she had not thought, she had reacted on instinct, and tomorrow, she would pay the price.

She studied the door. It was made of wood. If she could send a bolt of flame leaping from her fingers that could ignite a table, the wooden door to her room should be no challenge. Then again, she would probably simply trap herself in the room and burn to death, or choke on the smoke. She knew she could start a fire, and could see through it; she feared fire was not friend enough to leave her flesh unscathed.

Besides, where could she run to? Tales would spread of the *kuli* in woman-shape. How would she live? She could not go to Jashemi; he had a family now, and if he took her in, they would call him *kuli*-cursed.

As she thought about him, tears welled in her eyes. She had never gotten to say goodbye to him. She wiped the tears away angrily. Crying served nothing. Kevla got unsteadily to her feet and looked out the window. In the dying light of the day, she could see the pyre being built, and watched with detached interest as piles of wood began to appear. There was a platform and a long pole in the center.

It didn't seem real. She simply seemed unable to fully comprehend that tomorrow she would be tied to that pole, smoke filling her lungs, heat assaulting her, flames licking her body—

Unbidden, her mind went back to the time when she had just arrived at the House, when she, Yeshi and Tiah had gone to the market and the *kuli*-cursed man had approached them. She remembered the rush to gather wood for the fire, how Yeshi had been willing to pay for it in order that the man burn quickly. Then, Yeshi had been acting to protect her; now, the great lady of the House of Four Waters was doing all she could to condemn Kevla. They were taking their time, in order that a huge crowd would have time to assemble. Kevla thought of the man, rushing at her. Had that beggar truly been cursed by demons, or was he as innocent of taint as she? She smelled again the stench of burning flesh and suddenly her stomach heaved.

Kevla turned away from the window and covered her mouth, willing herself not to be sick. She crawled to a corner of the room and sat there, drifting into an uneasy slumber as night came. For the first time since she began to bleed from her *sulim,* she did not dream.

She was startled awake by the sound of the door opening. Halid stood in the doorway, his massive frame almost filling it completely. He sneered, and for a moment she felt hatred blaze inside her. He entered, followed by three other men. Kevla extended her hands for them to tie. Halid's gaze flickered from her chafed wrists to the bits of rope to the old scythe. The other men seemed surprised at her calmness, but Halid just looked irritated.

"Come, *kuli,* your death awaits you."

"I do not fear death," Kevla lied. *Don't show your fear, Kevla. Don't give this dog anything to hold over you.*

"You'll be begging for it by the time the fire has burned away your feet," Halid said. Kevla's stomach clenched, but she forced her face to reveal nothing.

The sun was bright and Kevla squinted against the glare. Halid prodded her with the tip of his sword and she stumbled on the steps, catching her balance awkwardly.

A huge crowd had assembled to watch her execution. She guessed there were well over a hundred, perhaps double that. There had been time for the news to spread, and clearly as many as could had come to watch the *kuli* burn. Such executions served as warnings to the people, to prompt them to honor the ways of their traditions, to never stray from the path.

Again, Halid prodded her, and she walked slowly toward

the pyre. She climbed up the short ladder to the platform. It was tricky, as it was difficult to use her hands. She stumbled more than once and would have fallen had not one of the guards caught her. He seemed startled at his instinctive reaction; no doubt he suddenly remembered that she was a *kuli* and merely touching her could be dangerous. She gave him a quick smile, and saw emotions warring on his face.

At last, she stood atop the platform. Halid had come up behind her and was now tying her to the pole. He cinched the ropes unnecessarily tight, and as he bent over her to check the knots, she whispered, "I know about you and Yeshi. You won't get away with it."

He looked at her and laughed. "Brave words, but empty," he said. "Jashemi is gone and you will be dead soon."

"If I'm a *kuli*," she challenged, "how do you know I won't destroy all of you? How do you know I won't escape?"

He grinned, showing white teeth. "You're not a *kuli*," he said. "I don't know what you are, but you're not that. A *kuli* would never have let itself get caught in such a foolish manner." He pulled the last rope so tight that the air went out of her in a *whoosh*, knotted it, and left without another word.

Kevla searched the crowd for Tahmu, thinking even now that somehow she could warn him and that he might believe her. Finally she saw him. He was dressed in white, his arms folded across his chest, regarding her. He was too far away for her to make out the expression on his face, but she didn't need to. The position of his body told her enough. Any pleas she might have made died in her throat. Tahmu-kha-Rakyn had made his decision, and in ordering her death, had sealed his own.

Tears stung her eyes and she blinked them back, realizing that it only made those about to witness her murder more excited. She swallowed hard and tried to stand as erect as possible. She had had so little dignity in her life; she would at least meet death with it.

Tahmu's voice drifted to her. "It is our law, that all *kulis* and anyone who has been influenced by them shall be put to death by the cleansing fire. Kevla Bai-sha was witnessed creating fire from her own hand, and attacking the *khashima* with the demonic flame. Kevla has been *kuli*-cursed at the very least, if she is not an actual demon herself. We honor the traditions of our people, and the laws of our Dragon, as today we witness her execution. Let this serve as a reminder to all to obey the Dragon."

Did she detect a tremor in that powerful voice? No, it must have been her imagination. Her gaze traveled to Yeshi, standing beside her husband, and she felt a faint petty pleasure stir as she noticed that Yeshi's hands were bandaged.

Yeshi was trying hard to look fragile and worthy of sympathy, but Kevla was not fooled. This was her day, her victory, and Kevla knew she and Halid would be celebrating.

Kevla looked out into the crowd, desperate to find a kind face, and her eyes met those of Sahlik. The older woman looked ancient, and her eyes were red. Kevla smiled sadly. At least someone would mourn her passing.

Four men approached with lit torches, and the fear she had thought dulled sprang to life. Futilely, she squirmed against her bonds, found them far too tight, and sagged against them.

This is my fate. This is my destiny. Great Dragon, I still don't know who I am.

The wood was dry, and the fire well-prepared. It lit almost at once. Tongues of flame licked upward, and Kevla felt their heat. Smoke began to rise, engulfing her in a black and gray cloud. Through the smoke she could see orange and red flames beneath her. The wooden platform beneath her bare feet began to grow hot, then it, too, erupted into flames.

* * *

The *sa'abah* was exhausted. It had been running for a full day and night with only infrequent, brief breaks, but Jashemi was merciless. Something was happening to Kevla, and every heartbeat was precious. He too was exhausted, but fear flooded his veins and kept him going.

They were almost there. The riverside and the road to the House were oddly deserted, adding to Jashemi's apprehension. The beast grunted in protest, but Jashemi would not ease up on it. It surged up the hill, through the open gates, and into the packed courtyard of the House of Four Waters.

Jashemi cried aloud at what he beheld.

Kevla was tied to a stake in the center of the courtyard. Flames leaped around her, so high and so smoky that he could barely see her body.

"Douse the fires!" he shrieked, sliding off his mount. "I order you, douse the fires!"

But no one obeyed his orders. His own father's guards seized him and shouted into his ear, "The *kuli* must burn!"

Jashemi was not a weak man, and his terror for his sister gave him added strength. He wrested his arm free from the guard and started pushing his way through the crowd. Two more guards slammed into him, knocking him down. He surged up, startling them, but their grip on him was firm. He used every fighting technique that Halid had taught him, but could not break free from three guards.

There was a mighty crackle from the deadly fire, and a new sheet of flame leaped skyward. The cheers of the crowd swelled gleefully, and Jashemi finally realized with a slow, sickening horror that he had arrived too late.

"No!" he screamed, coughing from the smoke, "No! *Kevla!*" Tears filled his eyes and streamed down his cheeks. He sagged forward in the guards' grip and fell to his knees, sobbing. Whether from pity or contempt, he did not know or care which, they released him.

While the crowd around him celebrated and the deadly fire crackled as if shouting a victory, the *khashim's* son knelt in the dust, lost in his rage and grief.

Kevla...Kevla, I should have kept you safe....

Suddenly, the crowd's shrieks of delight fell silent. Shaking and wiping his wet face, Jashemi looked up.

The flames were beginning to die down. He could see through their red-orange curtain, expecting the agonizing sight of a charred skeleton. Instead, impossibly, Kevla stood untouched atop the blackened branches and logs. Even as he watched, her clothing twisted and burned, turning black and dropping off her unharmed body. She seemed as surprised as the crowd to find herself alive.

For an instant, Jashemi was so dizzy with relief that he could not move. Kevla lifted her head, stared at the crowd—and their eyes met.

"Jashemi!"

It was the sweetest sound in the world. Jashemi leaped forward like an arrow shot from a bow, rushing toward his sister. He struck and pushed his way through the press of people. Out of the corner of his eye, he saw two women carrying full earthenware water jugs, staring slack-jawed as Kevla strained against her bonds. As he raced past the oblivious pair, Jashemi grabbed the jugs and hurled them onto what was left of the pyre. The water splashed the hot wood and hissed. Everyone seemed too startled by what they had just witnessed to try to stop him.

Kevla struggled with the burned remains of the rope, and just as he reached her she pulled the last blackened coil free. He stumbled on the burned branches that cracked and gave beneath his weight and she caught him before he fell. For an instant they clung fiercely to one another. Then Jashemi whirled, grasping Kevla by the hand. He felt the remaining heat start to scorch his sandals and breeches, and held his breath against the choking smoke. He looked frantically for a mount, knowing his was too exhausted to continue. If he did not find one—

He spied a *sa'abah* on the edge of the crowd. It wore the livery of the House of Four Waters and probably belonged to one of the guards. Jashemi and Kevla sprinted for the beast.

The crowd was starting to recover from its shock. Tahmu's voice rang out and Jashemi faltered for just an instant.

"Stop, Jashemi! Return the *kuli* for punishment! It is the law!"

He clenched his jaw and kept running. The law and everyone who would enforce it be cursed. He would die before he let anyone hurt Kevla. At the same time, he felt a stab of pain as he realized that his father had authorized this, had likely ordered it; had spoken the words that would send his own daughter to the flames.

Father, how could you?

They barely made it to the *sa'abah* before strong hands clapped down on Jashemi's shoulders. He let go of Kevla, who quickly scrambled atop the animal.

Other guards were coming. "Go!" Jashemi cried.

"Not without you!" Kevla screamed, reaching a hand down to him. Her once-carefully guarded expression was as naked as her body now, and in it he saw love and fear commingled. His heart surged. With renewed strength, Jashemi twisted in the guard's grip, turned sharply, and yanked the man's arm behind his back. The guard cried out and dropped like a stone. In an instant, Jashemi had leaped onto the *sa'abah*, pulled its head around, and sped down the road, Kevla behind him holding on for dear life.

* * *

Tahmu watched them go. Emotions warred within him: relief that Kevla was alive, pride in his son for rescuing his sister, worry that he had permitted a demon to live.

"What are you doing?" snarled Yeshi in his ear. She was furious, her color high, her teeth bared. "Go after them!"

"Yeshi, I—"

She swore, then composed herself. Very loudly, she said, "Yes, my husband, you are right!"

Tahmu stared at her, not comprehending.

"You and your Second must indeed make haste and ride after the *kuli*. She has turned the flames to be her allies; you must kill her yourselves."

Tahmu couldn't believe what he was hearing, but what she said next took the breath out of him.

"And what is truly tragic is that she has obviously cursed our beautiful son Jashemi as well," Yeshi said theatrically. "Now, he, too, must die."

He could only stare. Had be truly been so blind as to not see what hatred of her former rival had done to her? Could she really have sunk so deeply into her jealousy and pain that she would condemn not only Kevla, but the son she had once loved above all things?

"They are no longer children," she continued, "but things of evil. If they are permitted to go free, think of the harm they will do! My husband, painful as it is, you must slay both of them. Otherwise, anything they do will be your responsibility. The other clans will blame the Clan of Four Waters, and they will unite against you and bring you down."

She smiled then, a satisfied, hateful smile, and he wished he could strike her down where she stood.

How could he hunt his own children, murder them in cold blood? No ordinary person could command fire, or have survived such a conflagration unscathed, this much was true. Also true was that in freeing his condemned sister, Jashemi had gone against the law and his life was forfeit. Yet the girl who admitted her own guilt seemed so unlike a demon that he wondered if perhaps Sahlik was right—that this had nothing to do with *kulis* and everything to do with a warning.

The Dragon was angry with Tahmu, that much was certain, but for what? Conceiving Kevla out of wedlock? Bringing her to the House? Marrying Yeshi and not Keishla? He had done so many things he thought right, but that felt wrong. The opposite was true, as well. How could he atone when he did not know which was the true sin?

Confusion whirled in his brain, but there was one thing that stood out above all else: he loved his children. Kevla had given him reason enough to condemn her, according to their laws. And yet, fire was the Dragon's symbol. Was the Dragon protecting the girl, or issuing a challenge to Tahmu? Surely, the Dragon would not want Tahmu to slay his own progeny—or would it?

If he did not pursue them, his people would turn on him. They were frightened; he needed to allay the fears that his wife had stirred up in them. He would hunt his children. But that did not mean he needed to find them.

"Yeshi," he whispered, bending in as if to kiss her, "you are dead to me with these words."

Straightening, he said aloud, "My wife is right. Jashemi and Kevla must be found...and killed." His voice broke on the last word and he dared say no more.

He moved forward, heading for the corral to find a *sa'abah*. His way was blocked by the figure of a small, old woman. She was the last person Tahmu wanted to see right now.

"Sahlik, out of my way," he warned.

She stood her ground and looked up at him. "I will not move," she said, "until you refute what you have just said."

"The Clan—"

"You know in your heart that Kevla is not a demon! And Jashemi is only being a good brother to his sister. His mind is his own, as are his actions. Do not go after them, Tahmu, or you will regret it for the rest of your life!"

"I must," he said, trying to push past her.

Then Sahlik did something she had never done to him before. Slowly, with difficulty, she lowered herself to her hands and knees and bent her gray head into the dirt. One gnarled hand reached to touch his sandal imploringly.

"Great Tahmu," she said, her voice trembling, "I beg of you. I *beg* of you. Let the children go."

"It is not my wish," he said, kneeling and lifting her up gently. "You of all people know that, Sahlik. But they are my responsibility, both of them. I sired them, and they have been cursed by *kulis*. If I skirt this, if I let them go because they are my children, any who are not content in the Clan will turn on me. The Clan will be ripped apart."

Sahlik's old body shook with one violent sob. Then she lifted her head, and her eyes blazed. Before he realized what she was doing, she had reached for the ceremonial knife he always carried. For a wild instant he thought she would try to attack him, but instead she shoved up the sleeve of her *rhia*, baring her forearm, exposing the four old scars that marked her place in the household. Looking defiantly into the eyes of her lord, she sliced into her own arm with his blade, cutting a fifth score and emphatically ending over fifty years of service to the House of Four Waters.

Sahlik spat on the ground, looked at Tahmu with contempt, and tossed the knife to the earth. Her head high, blood dripping from the cut that marked her as a free woman, Sahlik turned and strode out the gates.

Tahmu watched her go, raising a commanding hand when one of the guards would have stopped her. He was beyond anger, rage, grief. He knew only a deep, profound sorrow that made him feel older than Sahlik.

I would I were a lesser man, he thought.

"Bring *sa'abahs* and weapons," he said to the guard who had appeared at his elbow. "We ride after the *kulis*."

Chapter Twenty

Kevla clung to Jashemi, her skin, protected only by the shade of the *sa'abah's* tail, exposed to the sun and wind, and tightened her lips against the increasing thirst. How long they rode without stopping, she did not know. Neither of them spoke; the brutal pace of their flight did not lend itself to conversation. She had experienced a rush of joy at his unexpected appearance and her salvation, but the euphoria had faded and fearful thoughts were taking its place.

Jashemi had left the main road early, as if he had a specific destination in mind. He was riding toward the mountains, and at one point Kevla caught a bright gleam in the distance. She knew what it was: the sun flashing off the large golden disk that marked the site of the Clan of Four Water's altar to the Great Dragon.

She thought about her dreams, and trembled, tightening her grip around Jashemi's waist. They had transgressed, both of them. The Great Dragon, the strict keeper of the laws and traditions of their people, would exact punishment.

After they had passed the altar, Jashemi guided the *sa'abah* westward. The creature climbed the small hills at the foot of the mountain. But the beast was tiring, and the hills grew increasingly steep.

Jashemi brought the *sa'abah* to a halt and slipped off. Not looking at Kevla, he held up a hand to indicate that she should stay mounted. He tugged off his *rhia* and stood clad only in breeches. He handed the garment up to her.

"Put this on, and then dismount," he said. "It will be easier if we walk."

Surprised by the blunt tone of his voice, she did as he instructed. He reached to help her down and as her bare feet touched the warmed earth, their bodies were but a hand's width apart. She risked a look up at him and saw an expression in his eyes she could not comprehend. He touched her cheek with his forefinger, gently, then turned and grasped the *sa'abah*'s lead.

"Come. This way."

She followed him down a tricky patch of stones and was glad that she was no longer riding. The *sa'abah*'s long, powerful toes found secure grips, but it would have been thrown off balance with two riders atop its back.

Suddenly, Jashemi stopped so abruptly she almost walked into him. He looked back, puzzled, then smiled. Her heart lifted to see that expression on his face.

"I walked right past it," he said. "Good. No one who doesn't know what to look for will find it."

He retraced his steps and Kevla now saw, hidden by an apparently random group of stones, a narrow entrance into the mountain.

"The *sa'abah* won't want to go in," Jashemi said. "Hold

him, Kevla." She did so and he slipped inside, reappearing a moment later with hands that were cupped to hold—

"Water!" she cried.

"Yes," he said. "There's a natural spring in here. I found this place when I was a boy." He held out his dripping hands to the creature. Its long purple tongue crept out and lapped the precious liquid, and when Jashemi coaxed it with soft words, it sniffed, scented the water, and hesitantly entered the cave.

Kevla followed, stepping into a cool darkness that was startling after the glare of the sun. It took her several blinks before her eyes adjusted. The cave wasn't large, and the little spring was nothing compared to the luxurious pool at the House of Four Waters. But the cave was big enough for the three of them, and it had water.

Kevla rushed toward the pool and began to drink. Jashemi and the *sa'abah* joined her. Kevla splashed some on her face and closed her eyes at how good it felt.

"I'm sorry I have no food," Jashemi said as he leaned back against the stone wall. "But at least there is water."

Kevla looked down at her wet hands. She did not know where to begin. The *sa'abah*, its thirst slaked for the moment, loped back toward the entrance of the cave, settled its bulk down, and closed its eyes.

"You may bathe if you like," he said. When she hesitated, he said, "I'll turn around."

"It's not that," she began, "but Jashemi, you—"

The odd look on his face stopped her. "Wash, Kevla," he said gently. "We'll talk afterward."

He turned around as he had promised. Kevla felt utterly miserable. Everything had changed so suddenly, and so completely. She was alive because of Jashemi, but she had never wanted him to be put at risk.

She did not immerse herself, but stood and sluiced down

her sun-heated skin with the cool fluid as best she could. She felt a little better, a little cleaner, and shrugged into the *rhia*. "I am done, my lord," she said softly. He whirled as if stung, and this time she had no trouble reading his expression. He was angry.

"Don't call me that!"

Startled and hurt by the outburst, Kevla went to sit with the *sa'abah* while Jashemi took his turn in the pool. She heard him splash in the water. Finally, he said, "You can turn around now."

She turned and looked at him. The fine fabric of his breeches clung to his damp legs. His torso glistened in the faint light and his dark, wet hair curled.

Seldom had she beheld him so, out of his well-made clothing, without a kerchief or wrap around his head. She remembered when he had been a boy, come home from his first battle, the first time he had taken a life. She had seen the healing scar that snaked across his chest and had held him while he wept. That scar had faded now, but new ones had joined it, marring the otherwise smooth, brown skin. His body was beautifully fashioned, his chest broad, his hips narrow. A thin trail of dark hair traveled from his belly and disappeared into his breeches, and she averted her eyes.

Kevla understood how men were made. Her mother had seen to it that Kevla knew just about all there was to know about how men and women came together. But knowing something and seeing it, or even imagining it—that was something different.

He padded over to her and sat. "Kevla," he said gently, "tell me what happened."

"I didn't mean to hurt the *khashima*," she said.

His eyes widened slightly. "I am sure you didn't, but...she was hurt? Was it bad?"

Kevla took a deep breath, and as calmly as she could

she explained what had happened. He listened without interrupting, his eyes fastened on her face, nodding from time to time. When she had finished, she pulled her knees into her chest and clasped them. He put a strong hand on her shoulder and squeezed reassuringly, then let it fall.

"I, too, have had something happen to me," he said. "I have learned that I am not alone in my dreaming. We all stayed quiet for fear we would be condemned. There is an army of an Emperor gathering force on the other side of the mountains. His standard has a strange creature on it called a ki-lyn. I have seen this beast in my dreams. Many have died. I am doing what I can to unite the clans and stand against this, and I know that somehow my dreams and your abilities have manifested at this time for this reason— to protect our people."

She buried her face in her arms. "I wish I could believe you. I wish I did not have these powers."

"Kevla, look at me." She did and found him smiling. His gaze seemed to bore right through her. Why was it so hard to breathe?

"I know," he said, slowly and deliberately, "that your powers are not from the *kulis*, any more than my dreams are. I know you only wanted to save our—our Clan leader. There is nothing evil about you." He reached to brush a strand of damp hair from her face. "Nothing."

Tears filled her eyes and blurred her vision. "Oh, Jashemi," she said thickly, "I am so sorry. Your father will be angry with you for helping me."

A shadow fell over his face and he looked away. A terrible suspicion filled her. "Jashemi," she said slowly. "Jashemi, what will happen to you?"

He sighed heavily. "He will disown me. I will be Jashemi Bai-kha, who has no father or mother. And he will track us down until he finds us and puts us both to death."

Kevla's hand went to her mouth, and for a moment she couldn't speak. Then a cry burst from her.

"No!" she screamed. "No! I will not be the one to bring this on you!" She leaped to her feet and reached for the *sa'abah*.

"What are you doing?" Jashemi's hand closed on her arm.

"I'm going to ride back to the House," she said. "Persuade him to take you back. If they have me they won't need to kill you, too."

"But you'll die!"

"Better that than live with having done this to you!"

He had both her wrists now. She struggled against him. Why had he come for her? *Why?*

"Kevla, listen to me!" He shook her roughly. "*Listen!* I knew exactly what would happen! I chose this! I saw that you were in trouble and I came. I had to because—" His voice broke and then softly he said, "Because I love you."

She stared at him, stunned. He released her and went to the other side of the cave, not looking at her. Sighing, he sat down and put his head in his hands.

"I should not have said that," he said. "For many reasons. Kevla, there is something I have to tell you. Something I should have told you long ago."

The tone of his voice filled her with dread. "I don't want to hear it," she said.

"Kevla—"

"No." She rushed to his side and dropped down beside him. "You have a wife, Jashemi."

"Not any more. Not now. I am dead to her." He didn't look at her. "And I did not love her. On our wedding night, when we—when I—all I could think of was how much I wished it was you instead. She deserves better."

"Oh," said Kevla, weakly.

"And when they came for you—I saw you, as if you were right there. You were in trouble." He shrugged. "I came. I could have done nothing else."

He knew he spoke the truth. He could no more have refused to ride to her than he could have grasped the sun in his fist. The bond that he had sensed between them the moment they had first locked gazes at the feast had only strengthened with time. It was stronger than a blood tie; stronger even than a love bond. He was a part of her, and she of him.

He had intended to tell her of their common parentage. Instead, what had come out was a confession of a love that should never have been.

Jashemi tried again. "Kevla, we—"

"Are bound to each other," she whispered. At the tone of her voice, he looked up at her.

"But how could that be? I tried to resist it. You were the *khashim's* son, and I a lowly Bai-sha. There was no way in the world that we could be together, and so I did not even dare dream of it. Yet you kept pushing, kept creating ways for us to be together. So I saw you in secret, touched your hand, embraced you when you wept." She smiled slightly. "Played *Shamizan* with you. And I convinced myself to be content with that."

A terrible, wonderful hope rose in him, a hope that made him feel weak and powerful at the same time. It was possible, now....

"But you are no longer a *khashim's* son," she continued. She moved toward him, sat down beside him. His throat was dry and he could not speak. "The world has changed. There is no life for us here, only death. You speak of a land over the mountains—we could go there, Jashemi. We could go there and start again."

Kevla's gaze held him. "We have nothing left but each other. Am...am I being a fool to think that we have that?"

He shook his head, still unable to find words. Licking dry lips, he said hoarsely, "No."

She held out her hand to him and he took it. Palm to palm, fingers slowly entwining, Jashemi trembled from even this simple touch. He had held her before, but everything was different now.

As they gazed into one another's eyes, Jashemi made his decision. He would not tell her. He couldn't, not now that he knew she loved him in return. There was no need for her to know that she was his half sister. All who cared about such things considered them already dead. Jashemi would not let this stand in the way of their happiness. Surely, even the Great Dragon would feel they had suffered enough.

Slowly, she brought his hand between her breasts as she leaned forward and placed her hand over his heart. He felt her heartbeat, strong and fast, against his fingers, and knew she could feel his own heart racing. He covered her hand with his, pressing her fingers into his smooth skin.

Kevla moved closer, kissing his hand with soft lips and then releasing it. Her fingers traveled over his chest, caressing the old and new scars, brushing his unshaven cheeks, slowly discovering him. When she ran a finger over his lips he jumped, nerves on fire. A smile touched her face, and he knew that for the first time she was experiencing the power a woman had over the man who loved her. It was impossible for him to resist touching her in return. He ran his fingers through her thick hair, savoring its softness even as he gently undid the snarls the wind had wrought.

She closed her eyes and leaned toward him. Their lips brushed lightly, and the pleasure was torment, taut and lingering. He breathed her in through his open mouth; scents and tastes of smoke and honey. Unable to bear it any longer,

Jashemi permitted himself to do what he had dreamed of for almost half his life; he tangled his fingers in her hair, pulled her to him and kissed her deeply.

Her response excited him even more. She opened her sweetness to him and pressed into him so they sat heart to heart. Kevla still wore his *rhia,* and he felt her breasts through the fabric that scratched his bare chest.

Kevla was lost in pleasure, lost in love for this man. He had always been such a profound presence in her life, and always, she had buried any feelings that were not acceptable. Now, she finally gave free rein to her passion.

We are one. We always have been. Why did it take this for us to dare to claim that?

Jashemi broke the kiss and she made a soft sound of protest. She fell silent in delight as he kissed her throat where the vein pulsed, flicking his tongue lightly over the vulnerable hollow at the base of her neck. She pulled him tighter, gripping his thick hair. She felt a tentative brush of his hands on her breasts through the *rhia* and suddenly ached for him to touch her.

The garment was a barrier to the contact she so urgently needed, and she moved away and struggled out of it. Kevla heard a gasp of breath and found Jashemi staring at her, full of awe at beholding what the *rhia* had hidden from him. She had been naked earlier, when he had ridden to her and helped her escape. She remembered the strength of his body as he clutched her briefly, saw the love in his eyes when she reached down from the *sa'abah,* refusing to abandon him as he had refused to abandon her. But then, survival had been the pressing need. Now, she offered herself to him, her nakedness her gift, her choice.

He lifted her eyes to hers and for a long moment neither moved, not touching, only their gazes locked together.

Then Jashemi's face flushed and he reached for her again. Kevla went joyfully into his arms, shuddering with pleasure as her nipples brushed his chest. She was dizzy as her senses were flooded and surrendered to the sensations. His kiss this time was fierce, but she responded with an intensity that matched his.

Jashemi had never imagined it could be like this; this pleasure so intense it was pain; this joy making his heart swell until he thought surely it must burst. The gentleness was gone and he knew he was being rough with her, but she seemed to want this as much as he.

Her hands moved down his chest, over his flat stomach. He tensed in anticipation. When her fingers lightly stroked him through the thin fabric of his breeches, he cried aloud in surprised delight.

She drew her hand back and asked, "Have I hurt you? I thought men enjoyed—"

"We do," he gasped. "*I* do. You heard my pleasure, beloved, not my pain."

Kevla looked unconvinced. By the Dragon, he could take her right now; could have taken her easily before she had even laid one of those exquisite fingers on him. He swallowed hard and asked gently, "Please...touch me again."

She did, at first hesitantly and then with growing confidence, and he shuddered. His *kurjah* strained against the breeches and impatiently he sat up to remove them. He heard a slight intake of breath.

"There is nothing to fear, my love," he said hoarsely. "But I will stop at a word."

She looked at him then, with eyes that smoldered. "I want this," she whispered. Tears filled her eyes. "Oh, Jashemi, I want you...I have wanted you for so long...."

Growling in the back of his throat he pulled her down on

top of him. His freed *kurjah* pressed hard against the softness of her belly as their mouths met and the sensation was
so intense he almost climaxed. He tensed, holding himself
back, wanting to make this first joining exquisite and bring
her as much pleasure as she was giving him.

He sat up, taking her with him, and kissed her between
her breasts. She folded him close and laid her cheek on his
hair. For a moment, they clung to one another, eager to continue exploring and discovering, loath to relinquish the
sweetness of this moment.

Holding Kevla securely with one strong arm, Jashemi
reached for the *rhia* she had discarded. He spread it on the
cold stone. She smiled at the gesture.

"I would it were the softest bed in the land for you, my
love," he said, easing her onto her back and moving away
from her slightly. "I would feed you dates and honey from
my lips, like so," he said, kissing her repeatedly, "and cover
you with rare and precious oils, thus," and his hands moved
over her perfect body, worshipping her as she lay naked and
opening to him.

Kevla closed her eyes and drank in the sensations of his
hands on her. She gasped as he touched her breasts gently,
then more firmly, and quivered in anticipation as he bent to
take the hard peaks into his mouth. Already flooded with
pleasure, she jumped when she felt his strong, sensitive fingers reach between her thighs to touch her with the light-
est of strokes. She pulled his face to hers, closing her lips on
his in a kiss that was as much a devouring as a caress.

She felt him trembling as though he stood in a strong
wind, he, Jashemi, son of a *khashim*, was trembling in her
embrace. He pulled back and she reached to stroke the
beloved face that was, after so many years of desiring and
denial, finally hers to touch.

* * *

Tears stung Jashemi's eyes as her fingers brushed his cheek, and all playfulness fled before the power of his adoration of her.

Oh, Kevla. I love you so much. I will never let any harm come to you.

Jashemi's skin prickled with a sudden, swift knowing. He grasped her face between his hands, locking his gaze with hers, and when he spoke, his words were laced with a passionate urgency.

"There is destiny here. I feel it...I know it. We were meant to be together. I belong to you completely, Kevla. I always have, and I always will. No matter what happens—no matter who or what we are—know that I am yours."

His knees parted her thighs and she opened willingly to him. He could hold back no longer.

"You are my soul," he whispered.

His mind, heart and senses ablaze with love for this woman, he pressed gently at her entrance. He wanted to go slowly, to cause her as little pain as possible, but he was not sure he—

Kevla uttered a deep, primal sound, and then moved her own hips fiercely, deliberately impaling herself on him.

Jashemi cried out in ecstasy as he entered her. She was so wet, so hot, he felt as if he was being engulfed by the molten fire that sometimes streamed from Mount Bari. She hissed in pain and he kissed her, sorry to have hurt her, regretting nothing else about this joining.

Slowly, Jashemi moved his hips, building a rhythm, bracing himself on his arms to watch her face. She opened her eyes and their gazes locked as he moved inside her.

"I love you," she whispered, caressing his face with one hand as the other gripped his arm, her fingers digging into the flesh.

I love you, he thought wildly. But he was beyond words now, though he ached to say them. He let his body speak for him, communicated his desire and need for her with each increasingly urgent thrust. She was breathing quickly now, her breasts rising and falling, the sight of her passion heightening his own.

Jashemi wanted this moment to last forever, and he tried to hold back the cresting tide. But then Kevla made a soft sound and bit her lower lip, and the powerful surge of love he felt for her swept him over the precipice.

Heat, and wetness, and tightness—

He cried aloud as his climax overtook him. His eyes squeezed shut and he surrendered to the exquisite pleasure.

Merging. Union. One. Heat and—

His eyes flew open, but he did not see Kevla or the cave. He saw only darkness at first, but then realized that this darkness was pulsating. A word came to him: *Shadow.*

The queen stood next to him, her presence a comfort, although not even a woman as magnificent as she could hold back the Shadow's onslaught. The boy thought about the dead youth he had found, whom he had seen in a vision. He felt drawn to the young man, bonded with him, even though he had died—been murdered—before they had even met. Hard to believe it had been only two weeks since he had seen the youth; harder to believe that in a short hour or less, he, the queen, this solid stone parapet, their entire world would be gone—

"—wiping you out, as easily as this." Melaan knelt on the sand and traced a circle with his finger, then with one quick movement erased the image as if it had never been. He understood, he was one of them, was a—

The ship was tossed by the storm, but it was no cloud that was rushing toward the elderly captain's vessel now. The Shadow was nothing natural, and he knew when he saw it that his son had failed, and the pain of that knowledge stabbed his heart and he fell to the deck—

The woman whooped with glee, and ran to embrace her friend as she stood with her other four companions. The Shadow was fading, evaporating like mist on a hot day. But it could not be gone soon enough for her. She shook her fist as it retreated—

The girl gasped as she clutched her chest. Blood spurted out through the hole the man had made with his knife. Vainly, she tried to stop the flood, but it dribbled between her fingers. As she fell to the wet cobblestones, her blond hair pooling beneath her head as the blood pooled beneath her body, she held fast to one thought and smiled through her agony: The bastard had attacked the wrong woman. She was not one of the five, only a—

Jashemi arched above Kevla, staring into the lives he had lived, swift, sure knowledge flowing into his being even as his seed flowed into his beloved. He remembered everything now. He had to tell Kevla, had to let her know....

Her legs locked around him and as he blinked and again saw her face, he realized that she was lost in her own cresting passion. Brokenly, he cried, "Kevla, my love, you are fire!"

The words Jashemi uttered floated to Kevla's ears, but she did not acknowledge them. Her eyes were shut and she was so deep in sensation that she could not tell where she ended and he began. She had not expected that physical union would be so painfully, powerfully sweet.

Her heart slammed against her chest and suddenly a wave of ecstasy washed over her. She clenched hard against him, wrapping her arms about him and pulling him into her even more as her body exploded with delight. Heat burned through her, she could feel it emanating from her, and for a long, taut moment everything went away except this molten sensation of bliss.

Suddenly Jashemi's weight disappeared and her arms were empty. Still gasping and trembling from release, Kevla opened her eyes.

Jashemi was gone.

For a mercifully long, uncomprehending moment, she simply stared at the fine gray powder that coated her body. Then the devastating reality crashed upon her.

Covered in the ashes of her beloved, Kevla Bai-sha began to scream.

Chapter Twenty-One

How long she laid on the floor of the cave, sobbing and shrieking her agony, Kevla did not know. At some point, she drifted into a restless slumber, and as always when she slept, she saw the Great Dragon. This time, for only the second time she could recall, it did not bellow its challenge at her. Instead, it lowered its head and crooned softly.

She awoke sometime later, sick and dizzy from grief and lack of food, to find the *sa'abah* tapping her with one stubby forepaw. It smelled of warm, musky fur. Kevla did not move. She willed the creature away, for if she sat up and acknowledged it, she would have to also acknowledge that life went on after...and she could not bring herself to do that. Better far to lie here in a stupor, surrendering to the mourning until at last death claimed her as well as Jashemi.

She curled up in a tight ball at the mere thought of his name. Part of her was aware that she was still covered in his ashes, but another part could not admit that or else she knew she would go mad.

So Kevla lay unresponsive, and the *sa'abah* grew annoyed. After a few moments, it shoved her hard with its snout, blew mucous on her neck, and uttered a loud bleating sound right in her ear.

She bolted upright, wiping at the offending fluid and covering her ringing ears. "You stupid creature!" she yelled at it. It seemed unperturbed by her outburst, rocking back on its hind legs and surveying her with what looked like satisfaction.

Kevla sagged. The beast had foiled her plan to lie here on the cave floor and die. She gazed at it and tears filled her eyes. It swiveled its ears expectantly. She tried to stand and couldn't, so she crawled to the spring and washed herself with hands that trembled. For a long time, she sat in the cool waters, wondering if she would ever feel clean again.

Oh, my love. I killed you. I killed you.

The tears came again, flooding down her face, the hot moisture a contrast to the cool water, and she sobbed until she could cry no more.

On unsteady feet, she reached for Jashemi's discarded clothes. She swallowed hard as she picked up the *rhia*. Bringing it to her face, she inhaled the musky, spicy scent. Kevla sank to the ground, the garment still pressed to her face. *I'll just lie down again and pretend he is here, I can smell him, he's right here....*

Another irritated bleat from the *sa'abah* roused her, and, surrendering to the torment that continuing to live brought her, she donned Jashemi's clothes.

I should have known better. I should have known, somehow, that this would hurt you. Oh, Jashemi....

How had it happened, that she had destroyed her love? It was not through her kiss, or her touch; he had entered her fully, spilled his seed inside her. When was the deadly moment, and why?

The memory was agony, and she pushed it away. A thought came to her mind, and her heart lifted slightly. Yes. Yes, this was the right thing to do. The *sa'abah* was hungry and wanted food. She was in pain, and wanted release.

She would make a pilgrimage to Mount Bari, and finally come face to face with the Great Dragon.

She would offer herself as a sacrifice. And then, perhaps, she would have atoned sufficiently for what she had done....

Kevla gave the *sa'abah* its head, trusting the creature to scent out food and society, for *sa'abahs* were herd animals and felt most comfortable with those of their kind. Where there were *sa'abahs*, there would likely be people, and where there were people, there would be a chance to steal food and clothing.

Tahmu would have sent out hawks by now, warning other clans of the dreaded *kulis* in human form they might encounter. She did not want to be caught by Tahmu; she did not want to cheat the Great Dragon out of his sacrifice. So she decided to make her way carefully, walking in the shadows.

Kevla looked to the North. There it was, Mount Bari, the most sacred place in the world to her people. There, the Great Dragon made his home. There, she would end her brief, pain-filled life.

The thought brought some small shred of comfort.

She approached the outskirts of a small town at dusk, and was surprised to find her stomach growling as she smelled roasting meat. Kevla heard the tinkling of bells and caught snatches of song, and for a moment ached to join the singers.

Stop it, she told herself sharply. *You never belonged. You*

*were born Bai-sha, and any chance you had at earning a place
among ordinary people was destroyed when you—*

Kevla gulped hard. The pain, horror and racking guilt almost brought made her start crying again, but she fought
the grief back.

The *sa'abah* sniffed the air and bleated. It had caught
the scent of other *sa'abahs.* Kevla had never ridden one
of the creatures before her escape, and the fact that she
had been able to stay on its back at all was testimony to
how easy the creatures were to ride. Now, though, it set
off at a brisk pace and she found herself bouncing,
clutching its long neck. The reins slipped from her grasp
and she swore. Any hope of controlling the beast was
now gone.

She debated whether to slide off and take her chances in
a fall, but the ground looked very far away. And without
the *sa'abah,* she'd never make it to Mount Bari. So she hung
on grimly, hoping desperately they would not run across
any people.

A girl's shout quashed that hope. Kevla couldn't make out
the words. The creature slowed, making a chattering noise,
and within a heartbeat Kevla was surrounded by at least a
dozen other *sa'abahs.*

"Here, sweet one," came the female voice. "What is it
that you—oh!"

Kevla looked down and right into the startled brown
eyes of a woman about five years younger than she. They
stared at each other for a moment, and an observer would
have been hard-pressed to say who was the most fearful.

Kevla put a finger to her lips and slid off the *sa'abah.* Her
legs were stiff and numb from the long ride and they buckled beneath her. She went down hard on the earth and the
girl watching her giggled.

Kevla got to her feet. The girl was much shorter than she

as well as younger, and in the fading light Kevla could just glimpse the two scores on her arm.

"Who are you?" the girl said in a whisper, mindful of Kevla's gesture. "Why are you wearing a man's *rhia*?" Before Kevla could answer, her eyes widened and she added, "Are you an escaping five-score?"

Kevla shook her head, rubbing her sore behind. "No," she whispered. "But...I need your help. I'm in trouble and I need some food and some proper women's clothing."

The girl glanced back at the town. Small fires were being lit and their lights were orange and cheery.

Fire. Kevla closed her eyes in remembered pain, then opened them when she felt a gentle touch on her arm.

"I see that something lies heavy on your heart, *uhlala,*" she said, her gaze searching Kevla's face. Kevla blinked. No one had ever addressed her as *uhlala* before. "You have the look of one who has suffered." One hand reached to touch the scars on her own arm, then she forced it down.

"Only one who has known suffering can see it in another," said Kevla, and it was true. The girl's master had not been as kind to his five-scores as Tahmu was to his, and the child's haunted eyes reflected that.

Kevla made a decision. "I have no wish to get you into trouble. Let me water my mount and I will go."

"No," the girl said. "Wait here until it is full dark. Then I can help you. I tend the *sa'abahs,* I am not generally permitted in the town."

Kevla's eyes brimmed with tears. She was moved to encounter so much kindness from a stranger. "Thank you," she said.

The *sa'abah*-tender was as good as her word. Once darkness had fallen, she sneaked into the village and returned with a sack and a waterskin.

"They are all drunk," she said. "Our *khashim* is celebrating a great victory against the Star Clan. Tomorrow when things are missing, everyone will be accusing the other. Here. I got you some bread, some dried meat, some fruit and water. The best I could do is give you some of my clothing. It is not befitting your station, but it will cover you properly."

Kevla accepted the offering. "I don't know how to thank you," she said.

The girl inclined her head. "It is little enough. *Uhlala*—I do not know you, nor your errand. But somehow I feel as if I needed to do this for you. Perhaps one day, we will both understand why."

Impulsively, Kevla reached and hugged the girl. The child felt stiff in her embrace at first, then relaxed, and after a moment's hesitation, hugged Kevla back.

Kevla mounted and turned her beast to the North. She would live a few more days at least; with luck, long enough to complete her fatal mission. She wondered if the girl would have been so forthcoming with gifts and aid if she had known Kevla's true intentions.

She rode until the moon was high in the sky, then stopped to rest for the night. As she slipped off her mount, she realized that she had no way of restraining him. Kevla looked at the *sa'abah,* and he returned her gaze with interest.

"Are you going to stay with me, or are you going to run back and join your friends?"

It cocked its head and grunted.

"Which does that mean?" She wondered if she was going mad, talking to an animal. But it was better than being alone with her silent thoughts. Jashemi's face appeared in her mind's eye and she squeezed her eyes shut as pain constricted her heart.

I am coming, Jashemi. I will be with you soon.

She sat and the beast settled down beside her amiably. As

she unwrapped the food the girl had stolen for her, the smell of it hit her nostrils and moisture flooded her mouth. She ate ravenously, chewing and swallowing great chunks of the bread. The animal had drunk his fill with the other *sa'abahs*, and she knew that it could now go without water for several days. She took a small sip and tried not to think of the water in the cave where Jashemi had taken her, tried not to think of his hands on her body, tried not to think of—

And then she understood. Jashemi had not died from anything *he* had done, from taking her virginity. He had died when she had fully surrendered to her feelings, allowed herself to be caught up in the passion they shared. Her release, her moment of supreme pleasure, of lack of control over these unsought powers was what had claimed him.

Suddenly, she was on her knees, vomiting up the half-masticated bread and crying. It was too much to be borne. Surely, the Dragon would come and take her right now. But no, the night sky did not suddenly fill with the sound of beating wings; no shadow blotted out the moon to descend upon her. The Great Dragon was not going to make it easy.

Gulping salty tears, she sat up straighter. Slowly, deliberately, she took another bite of bread and forced it down. She wiped her eyes. She would eat, and drink, and sleep, and meet the Dragon in his own lair.

And then he would end this torment.

Kevla woke in the predawn to find that the *sa'abah*, far from attempting to leave in the night, had snuggled up to her. Its fur was so soft. She stroked it absently, wondering why it had felt the need to be so close to her. Surely it could not be cold—

Frowning, Kevla touched the fur again, paying attention to it this time. It felt cold to the touch. Another "gift," she thought bitterly; she no longer felt the cold, even when a furred creature did. Her head and her heart ached, but she forced herself to eat some dried fruit and drink water. She wondered dully if Tahmu had gone riding out after her, or if he had merely sent out falcons warning other clans against the *"kulis."* That thought sluggishly led to another; that Tahmu's life was still in danger. How could she have forgotten this?

If Yeshi and Halid wanted to take over the clan, they would rejoice that Jashemi was—

Dead, dead....

—discredited and could not lay claim to leading the Clan of Four Waters. There would be no one else to challenge Halid; Jashemi's cousins, who would have been next in line, had been killed long ago in a raid. Tradition would side with a seemingly loyal Second who knew how to lead the Clan, rather than a distant, perhaps common, relative. But Tahmu was still very much alive.

The first emotion other than raw, ragged grief crept into Kevla's heart. Despite what he had done, she still knew Tahmu to be a good man. He was only obeying the laws of his people, doing his best to protect them. He did not deserve to be murdered by a faithless wife and her deceitful lover.

She hesitated before she did what she knew had to be done. She hated her fire abilities now. They had cost her the single most precious thing in her life, and she was loath to make use of them. But she was already doing so without being able to control it; she was warm and comfortable in an environment that made a *sa'abah* shiver. She might as well deliberately use her abilities to help save a man's life.

Kevla scouted for a scrap of dried grass, found a few sorry blades, and placed them down in front of her. She took a deep breath, then said quietly, "Burn."

As it had always done since she began to bleed, the fire obeyed her command. A small flame crackled to life.

"Show me Tahmu."

It revealed nothing. Kevla tried not to be too worried. The fire-scrying only worked if the person she was trying to locate was near a fire himself. It was morning. She should have tried last night; the odds that Tahmu would be close to a fire would have increased. She would try again tonight.

After getting some food and water in her stomach, Kevla stretched, trying to ease the soreness of riding all day, then mounted. She set her eyes on the sacred mountain, and rode.

She stopped only briefly to eat and stretch. She talked to the *sa'abah* a great deal in an effort to push down the pain. It was starting to abate, only, she suspected, because she was focused so intently on her own impending death. It made her feel better to think that it would all be over soon.

When she made camp that night, the first thing she did was create a fire and ask to see Tahmu. She watched it intently for some time, eating and drinking with her eyes glued to the flickering flames.

Suddenly, she saw a blur and sat up straighter, leaning forward and straining to listen.

"I wonder if there was anything I could have done," she heard the *khashim* of the Clan of Four Waters say in a heavy voice. Tears sprung to Kevla's eyes. She had not fully appreciated how much son resembled father; Tahmu's voice and face were so like Jashemi's. She swallowed the lump in her throat. Tahmu tossed something into the fire moodily.

"Done how?" The voice was Halid's, and Kevla tensed. "Prevented someone from being taken by *kulis?* Great *khashim,* if you knew how to do that, you would be more honored among our people than even the Great Dragon."

Tahmu's lips thinned. "I...suspected. But I did not act. I was blinded by love."

Jashemi's dreams, thought Kevla. Jashemi had tried to tell

Tahmu of his dreams, but his father had refused to listen. Fear now warred with anger. If only Tahmu had trusted his son! She thought about what Jashemi had said, that her powers and his dreams—the dreams of others like him— were manifesting now to save their people. She wondered if he was right, and if Tahmu was hastening the destruction of all of Arukan.

But now Tahmu was speaking again and she turned her attention back to him.

"...have been warned," he was saying. "Yet I have heard nothing."

"Perhaps they have not been spotted," Halid said. "Or perhaps the other clans think you have made this up, to hide your shame at a son who has run away with a Bai-sha."

Tahmu's gaze went stone cold and his head whipped up to look at Halid, who was out of Kevla's view.

"You speak freely for a Second, Halid," he said in a low voice. "Don't forget your position, or I shall name another in your place."

Kevla's hand flew to her mouth. *Don't get him angry with you, my lord! You don't know what he's capable of!*

There was a strained silence, then Halid's gruff voice. "I humbly apologize, my lord. This has been a trying time for everyone in the Clan."

"That it has been," said Tahmu. "It is forgotten, Halid."

She watched the fire for a long time. The two men and a few others cooked a meal over its flames, convincing Kevla that they were indeed on the hunt for her and Jashemi and not staying at the House. She learned nothing more of import, but was not comforted by the idle chatter of men around a fire.

She had no way of knowing how many men Tahmu had brought with him, but it didn't matter. All that concerned her was that one of those men was Halid. It would be easy now for the Second to get his lord alone, away from the other men, and cause an accident or—

She was surprised at how much she cared. This was the man who had decreed her death, but she knew he hadn't wanted to. Knew he certainly hadn't wanted to hunt down his son like a *liah*. Kevla felt an odd sort of compassion for him. She did not want to see him dead, regardless of what he had done.

Besides, perhaps Tahmu was right. Maybe she was a *kuli*. The only one who thought she was not was Jashemi, and he had been a victim of her deadly powers. She fell into an uneasy sleep, and when she awoke in the morning was suddenly aware that she had not had any dreams of the Great Dragon since Jashemi's—since Jashemi. She wondered why. Perhaps he knew that she was coming to see him, and soon she would be face to face with him. Then he could torment her to his dragon heart's content. But she had to admit, she was relieved that she did not have to stand before the Great Dragon every night. Sleep was now her escape; living was her nightmare.

Her little five-score friend had done well by her; Kevla had plenty to eat and drink. Each day, she traveled closer to the sacred mountain, and each night, she sat and called fire, to see where Tahmu was. Kevla started to look forward to it; why, she did not know. She supposed it was that this was her last connection to this world, and she wanted to make sure Tahmu was safe before she gave herself to the Dragon.

Tahmu had taken to sitting and staring into the fire, as if he could see the same things Kevla could. She knew he simply wanted some time to think. One night as he did so, she locked gazes with him. She and Jashemi had been able to speak through the fire; she wondered if, should she will it, she and Tahmu could.

Just as she was thinking this, she saw something move behind Tahmu.

Someone was approaching him, raising an arm—

"Behind you!" Kevla shrieked.

Startled, Tahmu leaped to his feet and whirled around. The shape behind him was now revealed to Kevla. Firelight glinted off the blade Halid carried, the blade that now slashed down—

Kevla moved forward, as if she was there with Tahmu, leaning into the fire. Suddenly, his face took on more natural tones. She saw stars and sand and realized that somehow she had stepped into her own fire many leagues away and was now standing in the center of Tahmu's. The fire had transported her.

She gasped, shocked. The two men struggling in deathly silence were startled by her abrupt manifestation as well. Halid gaped openly at her, and Tahmu took that precious second of inattention and twisted Halid's wrist. As his Second arched in pain, Tahmu seized the blade from Halid's nerveless hands, flipped it so he grasped the leather-wrapped hilt, and shoved it deep into his adversary's midsection.

Halid grunted. Gritting his teeth, Tahmu jerked the knife upward, piercing Halid's heart. Blood fountained onto the *khashim's* hand. Halid's face displayed an expression of shock, and when Tahmu pulled out the knife, he fell to the earth.

For a long moment, neither Kevla nor Tahmu moved or spoke. She stood, still in the center of a burning fire, her hands to her mouth. She wondered how long it would take for Tahmu's men to rush out and seize her, but apparently, the confrontation had awakened no one. The men had fought in silence, and she had to assume that no one but Tahmu had heard her warning cry.

Tahmu stared at his trusted Second, lying dead by the fire,

then slowly looked up at the woman whose warning had saved his life.

Kevla stepped out of the flames. This was not how she had willed it, but the moment had arrived. She stood tall and straight, then bent her long, slender neck back, exposing her throat. Her hair fell like a dark cloud almost to her knees.

"Kill me," she said.

Chapter Twenty-Two

Tahmu stared at his daughter standing before him, her long neck stretched back to receive the blade.

He was still panting from the deadly fight. The knife that Halid would have used to kill him was red with the traitor's own blood, and the night was so still and his senses so heightened he could hear the scarlet fluid dripping into the sand.

Tahmu had been the one to take the watch; he would have stood, stretched, and awakened the next man in a few moments, had Halid not come. None of his men had yet roused. His thoughts were jumbled and confused. There was only one thing that was clear to him: Kevla had been right. Halid had indeed planned to kill him.

When no blow was immediately forthcoming, Kevla lowered her head and looked at him questioningly. He motioned to her and they walked away from the encampment, where their voices would not be heard.

"You saved my life," he said.

Uncertainly, she nodded.

"Did you also speak the truth about Yeshi? That she was trying to poison me when you...attacked her?"

"Yes," Kevla said. "I would not lie to you now. Not when I have come to you to be killed."

Tahmu looked at her. The moon's light permitted him to see her face clearly, even though they were away from the fire's light.

The fire....

"No," he said. He flung the bloody knife onto the ground. "You have saved my life. I will not take yours."

They were silent for a moment. "You do not think I am a *kuli?*" Kevla asked.

Suddenly feeling very old, Tahmu sat on the sand. "I don't know what to think anymore. I thought my wife faithful, if not happy; I thought my Second worthy to be trusted with my Clan. Now I learn they have conspired against me, and tonight I killed Halid. I thought my son obedient to the law, but he has dreamed strange dreams and defied my orders. I thought you a demon, and even now you walk through fire as easily as through a door. Yet you saved my life. My world is not what it once was. But your life is spared."

"No it isn't," Kevla said softly, sitting beside him. "There is something you must know, great *khashim*. I was on a pilgrimage tonight. I was going to go to the Great Dragon and offer myself as a sacrifice. I have committed a terrible crime, and I can think of no better way to atone."

Tahmu softened. "You attacked Yeshi to try to save me, and these powers of yours—"

She cut him off. He was surprised at her boldness in doing so. "No," she said. "I did not intend to hurt her, but I stopped her from putting poison in your food, and I don't regret that. What I have done...oh, great lord, you will have no wish to spare me once I have finished speaking."

A sudden fear clenched his heart. She had not left the House of Four Waters alone, and he suddenly realized that Jashemi was not here....

Quietly, in a somber voice, Kevla told her father of her awakening abilities. She spoke of the strange dreams that began coming to Jashemi at the same age. She told him of their stolen moments, of the bond that grew between them. There was something final in her words, and Tahmu's apprehension grew.

Dragon, no...not him...curse me, but do not harm him....

"We found a cave, where we rested and drank," Kevla continued. "He told me that he had met others like him— others who had the strange dreams, which he believed were not dreams at all but visions. Jashemi felt that my powers and these visions were connected, that they were growing in strength now as part of a way to defeat this Emperor who has been decimating the clans. He wanted to gather these Seers, gather the clans, and stand united against this new threat."

Her usage of the past tense did not go unnoticed. A wave of unspeakable sorrow washed over Tahmu. He had agreed to Yeshi's demands to hunt down his children, but what he had not told anyone, not even Halid, was that he never intended to find them. He would let them go, and return having appeared to have made the attempt. Kevla and Jashemi would live—

The sharpness of the pain would come later, he supposed; right now, the ache was dull and heavy and wrapped with regrets, with bitter knowledge of opportunities missed.

"How did he die, Kevla?" he said, his voice deep and sad.

She didn't answer for a long time. When he turned to look at her, he saw she had buried her face in her hands.

"Tell me," he said.

Kevla took a deep breath. "There was a bond between us," she said, "and we knew it to be both wrong and powerful. He was a *khashim's* son and I a Bai-sha. And yet, we loved one another. We knew could never be together, so neither of us spoke of our feelings. But in the cave, when we thought we had nothing to lose, that there were no more obstacles between us, we—he loved me as a man loves a woman, and in those moments I have never been happier."

He stared at her in dawning horror. The girl was innocent of the wrongdoing, ignorant as she was of her identity, but Jashemi....

Kevla's voice was hollow as she continued. "He brought me great pleasure, and as that joy washed over me, the Dragon exacted his revenge for our transgression. I opened my eyes, and he was gone."

"He died...in your arms," Tahmu said. Such things happened, but usually not to one so young.

Kevla shook her head. "I killed him," she said. "All that was left was ash." She turned to look at him with eyes that glinted in the moonlight. "He burned as if with the heat of a thousand pyres, great lord. Fire came through me and took your son in the space of a heartbeat."

Tahmu's mind reeled. His stomach churned. Incest and death in the same single, passionate act— He trembled and put his sweat-slick, chilled face in his hands, trying to grasp it all. Kevla sat beside him, making no effort to flee.

"I am cursed," he whispered. "The Dragon has taken everyone that I ever loved. There is none in this world more wretched than I."

"Yes, there is," Kevla whispered.

He did not roar his anger. He did not scream his grief. Swiftly, and in terrible silence, he reached for the knife he had dropped, seized Kevla, forced her to the ground and pressed the blade against her throat.

And yet still he hesitated.

"Do it, great lord," Kevla whispered. "End my misery and avenge your son."

He straddled her, as his son had before him, trembling not with passion but with agony. Her face remained calm and she closed her eyes. With a bitter oath, he hurled the dagger into the night and rose.

"I cannot kill you," he said, "My life is yours this night. But oh, Kevla, you do not know what you have done!"

She sat up. Her hand went to her throat and he saw a thin trickle of blood that looked black in the moonlight. Rising, she said, "You mistake me. I know full well what I have done."

He turned away, shaking his head. "You know only part of it. The rest—by the Great Dragon, it seems I have made mistakes at every turn of my life. Your mother was right."

The mention of Keishla seemed to jolt Kevla out of her stony grief. "My mother? What does she have to do with this?"

He made his decision and faced her then, looking her in the eye. He observed with dull surprise that she was almost as tall as he was, and he was no short man.

"Your name is not Kevla Bai-sha," he said. "In a better world, it would have been Kevla-sha-Tahmu."

Her eyes widened. "You—you are my father?" At his nod, her hand flew to her mouth and she whispered, "Then Jashemi...did he...?"

"He knew," Tahmu said heavily.

"By the Dragon...that was what he tried to tell me, and I would not let him speak...." She began to cry, sinking slowly to the earth. "*That* was the bond between us. *That* was what we felt, not...."

Tahmu had thought he would enjoy seeing her suffer, but the sight gave him no pleasure. The fury in him was spent. Kevla had not known, and Jashemi had obviously made a deliberate choice to rebel against the laws. The boy's desire for Kevla—his *love*, Tahmu mentally amended, for he knew that Jashemi would not be tempted by any lesser emotion to violate so primal a taboo—had driven him to it. To his surprise, Tahmu found himself kneeling beside his daughter and putting a tentative hand on her bowed shoulder.

"Your mother wanted me to tell you, when you came of age," he said. "Tell you that you were conceived in love, not out of a base desire. Sahlik wanted you and...and your brother to be together, to know one another. I should not have tried to hide you—hide my own shame, bury my mistakes. And now, I have paid for that, with betrayal in my family and the death of my son."

Her slim shoulders shook. He rose, looking at her sadly. He had no comfort to offer her.

"You're not a *kuli*," he said at last. "Nor was Jashemi. *Kulis* have no hearts with which to feel love—or to break. Get up, Kevla. Return to your own fireside, and leave me to my men and my wife."

She sat up, wiping at her wet face. "Please kill me," she said. "I can't—I cannot bear this!"

"Your life or death belongs to the Great Dragon now."

He watched her stumble to her feet, and then slowly walk back toward the encampment. Tahmu's breath caught as she stepped into the heart of the fire, and disappeared.

He sat for a while, alone in the dark, thinking about his life and the choices he had made. What if he had married Keishla? Would the Clan really have been damaged past repair? What if he had brought Kevla openly into the House, not caring what Yeshi thought? Or if, after his wife had discovered Kevla's identity, he had acknowledged his daughter then?

He knew Jashemi's heart, and knew that at the beginning the boy had only wanted to know his sister. If he had been openly encouraged to do so, perhaps this sibling bond would have stayed innocent.

Jashemi... what if Tahmu had listened to his son's hesitant confession about his dreams instead of threatening? The boy had had no one to turn to who would listen. His traditions offered no acceptance. There was no one for Jashemi, except Kevla.

Decisions made. Opportunities missed. Roads not taken.

And then an image of his son's face swam into his head, and emotions came crashing down on Tahmu. His knees gave way and he fell to the sand and wept, wept for all the poor choices, the lack of faith, the turning away instead of opening. Wept for his son's misplaced passion; wept for his daughter, the unknowing instrument of her brother's death.

Oh my boy, you were the best of us. I am sorry I was not there for you. I'm sorry at my lack of faith, in myself and in you. And now it's too late.

Sounds reached his ears and he realized that someone had awakened. Halid's corpse had no doubt been discovered. It was time to return and explain.

His body felt heavy, stiff. But as he walked slowly back to the now-awakened encampment, something resembling clarity formed in his mind.

Perhaps there was, after all, something he could do to honor his dead son.

The advisor stood and surveyed the troops. It would be fanciful to say their solid, well-trained ranks advanced as far as the eye could see, but it was almost accurate. There were thousands of them, at any rate. Their number swelled daily as they conscripted their prisoners from various lands. Fear might not be the best motivator that had ever been conceived, but it served for now. He nodded to the general, indicating his approval.

Horns blew and the troops cheered as their Emperor advanced. It was strange, thought the advisor as he regarded his young lord. The Emperor always looked out of place when he was not indoors. He seemed to gather strength from the shadowed, musty rooms, seeming larger and more intimidating.

But he was the Emperor, and he commanded this magnificent army, and that army had already conquered two lands. If he looked slighter in the sunlight, it was no one's concern. Certainly not his advisor's.

The Emperor rode a magnificent white stallion. It blew and snorted, pink nostrils flaring, and champed at its golden bit. The Emperor sat straight on his steed, the jeweled crown he wore catching the light and almost blinding the advisor.

The Emperor waited patiently for the cheers to die down. When he spoke, his voice carried much farther than it had any right to, and the advisor felt a chill run down his spine. Just when he was ready to dismiss the Emperor, he did something like this to remind all gathered of his tremendous power.

"We stand poised on the precipice of yet another victory," he intoned. "Two countries have already fallen before our standard. Arukan must follow. Its people are scattered, and our raids over the mountains have been fruitful indeed. Though a barrier, the mountains are not impossible for our army to cross. We will find these isolated clans and sweep across their desert landscape like a sandstorm. Their pathetic weapons are no match for ours; their warriors pale in comparison to you, my army. We will take their women and goods, settle their lands, and continue to move until this world knows no place that

does not fly my standard. I, your Emperor, will ride with you on this glorious moment in our land's history. Arukan will fall!"

"Arukan will fall!" came the cry, uttered with fervor from several thousand male voices. Another chorus of cheers welled up, and the Emperor, looking down at the sea of men in armor from his perch higher on the mountains they were all about to cross, smiled slightly and waved.

The advisor's gray eyes flickered from the Emperor to the animal huddled at the stallion's feet. The ki-lyn's golden chain, so thin and yet apparently so unbreakable, went around its slender neck and arced upward to the Emperor's waist, where it was securely fastened.

As he regarded it, it craned its neck to look up at its master. Its blue eyes welled with tears and it sighed, deeply.

And as the tears rolled down the soft, golden-brown fur of its face, they turned to diamonds in the sand.

Chapter Twenty-Three

Kevla did not sleep after her encounter with Tahmu. The violence of Halid's killing, justified as it was, combined with the revelations that the *khashim* was her father and that Jashemi had been her half brother, kept her awake. The *sa'abah* curled up next to her, seeking her warmth and wheezing softly, and she tried to take what comfort she could from another living being.

She did not weep. She wondered if she would ever do so again. She felt desiccated and empty, only her mind alive, gnawing like a starving dog on a dry bone.

She made a decision. Both the heat and the cold were hard on her mount, but it seemed most affected by the chilly desert nights. *Sa'abahs* were herd animals, and no doubt at night they curled up together to keep one another warm. She would ride at night and sleep during the day; the exertion would keep her mount more comfortable. Clucking her tongue, she roused the sleepy *sa'abah*, mounted, and rode.

The days and nights blended into one another until Kevla lost count of how long she had been on this, her final journey. The hard ride and lack of food and water were starting to take their toll on the *sa'abah*. The path would not get easier, either. Few made the pilgrimage to Mount Bari itself, preferring instead to erect local shrines and altars to the Great Dragon as the Clan of Four Waters had done.

Compassion for the mute creature flooded her. The next settlement she came to, she traded the beast for a sack of dried fruit and meat and as many filled water skins as she could carry. She was not challenged; either the greedy clansmen did not recognize her or else, more likely, Tahmu had called off the hunt for her. The *khashim* had gotten a bargain, for a young, healthy *sa'abah* was usually an expensive acquisition.

Kevla patted its long neck, kissed its soft nose, and continued on.

Her bare feet hardened to the task, and with each day the pack on her back grew lighter. She walked and slept as the desire took her, regardless of the time of day, and slowly the massive shape of Mount Bari, jagged and forbidding, drew closer.

From time to time, she rested and conjured fire. She had no need of it for warmth or cooking purposes, nor did she have any desire to see her father.

"Show me the Great Dragon," she asked, but the fire never complied. She felt certain, though, when the time was right, she would see in the flames the enormous, terrifying creature that until so recently had haunted her dreams.

She also was aware that she was falling into a pattern that offered its own sort of comfort. She ate much less now than she had when she was at the House. A thin strip of dried meat and a handful of dried fruit seemed to be enough to get her through an entire day. Even though she was walking out in the desert, under an unforgiving sun, she seemed to need very little water as well.

She realized she was slowly detaching herself from the world of the living. She was not walking toward anything of this life; she was walking toward death. Bit by bit, she was deliberately pulling back, shedding things that kept her in this existence. To her shock, she sometimes felt a stab of happiness as she strode steadily along and the wind tousled her hair. The pain and the guilt were still there, but there was a lightness to her being that increased with each day that brought her closer to Mount Bari.

Gradually, Kevla worked her way through her supplies. She felt a brief stab of worry as she squeezed the last few drops of water into her mouth, washing down the last bite of dried fruit, then calmed herself. She knew she was on the right path. Whatever the Dragon decreed to be her end, she would accept.

She fell into an exhausted, dreamless slumber and awoke to a smell teasing her nostrils; a crisp, citrus scent that made her mouth water. She slowly opened her eyes, then started upright when she saw a plate of *paraah* spread before her. Four of her waterskins had been refilled.

Kevla's heart raced. She glanced around, trying to see who had done this for her. She saw no one, only the vast expanse of sand to the south and the ring of mountains on all other sides. No clan lived here, not even the nomadic ones. Who, then had—

She smiled, softly. "Thank you, Dragon," she said as she reached for the fruit. He had provided, as she had trusted he would.

Her steps that day were sure and strong. The food and water strengthened and sustained her, and her purpose guided her. Food continued to appear each morning. Every time she stopped now, she tried to see the Dragon in the flames. Just as dusk was approaching one night, she realized that her steps were gradually going uphill. She was now at the foothills of Mount Bari.

Her mouth went dry. Dropping her pack, she quickly conjured fire. Her heart was beating wildly. She stared into the flames for a long moment, dreading and craving what she knew she was about to see.

Licking dry lips, she whispered, "Show me the Great Dragon."

And he was there, his massive, reptilian face no larger than her palm, but every bit as frightening as it had been in her dreams. Kevla gasped. As she looked into his eyes, she knew he was looking back at her.

For you, Jashemi. My brother. My love.

She shook so badly that she almost fell as she stumbled to her feet. She wanted to stride boldly into the fire, but for a moment, she couldn't move.

Coward! she thought. *This is your fate, Kevla. Accept it!*

Closing her eyes and taking a deep breath, Kevla stepped forward into the circle of flame.

She emerged on a rock ledge. Kevla was confused. Before, when she had stepped from her fire into Tahmu's encampment, it had been from her fire to his fire pit. Where, then, were the flames?

It was only then that she realized that she was surrounded by flickering sheets of orange and red. She took a step forward. Her foot stepped onto nothing. Kevla flailed to regain her balance, leaning back and clutching the sheer rock behind her. The ledge upon which she stood was only about as wide as her extended arm. It dropped off several feet into a liquid pool of fire.

Fascinated and terrified at the same time, Kevla gazed into

the bubbling orange pool. Heat blasted her, and though she did not feel it on her skin, she felt the fabric of her clothing begin to burn and catch fire, as it had done when she stood on the pyre in the courtyard of the Great House. Feeling no shame, she plucked off what clothing remained and stood naked in the heart of Mount Bari.

As the moments passed, Kevla's fear abated somewhat. The narrow ledge, the pool of molten rock, the dancing flames that formed a circle and cast grotesque shadows— all were frightening. But the one thing she had most hoped and feared to find here had not appeared.

Where was the Great Dragon?

She shifted position on the ledge. A small pebble tumbled into the orange-yellow pool.

"Dragon!" she called. She tried to sound brave, but her voice quivered and she could barely hear it in her own ears. "Dragon, I have come! Where are you?"

There was no response.

Then, the pool beneath Kevla began to churn. Slowly, something forced its way through, swimming upward like the monsters of the river. The Great Dragon's head broke the surface of the viscous, liquid rock. Orange rolled down its long, scaly neck as it rose upward. Mammoth shoulders appeared next, and Kevla instinctively cried out and shielded her face as leathery wings beat and scattered molten droplets.

Kevla fell hard to her knees, lowering her arms from her head and wrapping them around her body. She shook so badly she feared she would topple forward into the pool of fire. It kept coming, a gargantuan creature birthed from flame. Its head towered over her. Kevla could not tear her gaze from it. All was unfolding as it had a thousand times and more, in dream after dream after dream....

Its sinuous neck twisted and the Dragon lowered its

head down to her. She stared into the glowing depths of eyes that were as broad as her hand, mesmerized, the bird before the snake.

Its mouth opened, exposing sharp, white teeth the size and sharpness of daggers. Kevla stared into its maw. A forked tongue flickered in and out. She waited, breathless, terrified, for the question.

"DO YOU KNOW WHO YOU ARE?"

She opened her mouth, and found it dry. No words came forth. Her gut clenched in horror. She had expected that at this moment, she would know the answer to this question, but she was as ignorant and frightened now as when she first dreamed this.

She shook her head mutely. The Great Dragon shook its own scaly head, opened its mouth again and then suddenly Kevla was engulfed in fire. She screamed in agony and curled in on herself. Surely this was its judgment, its punishment for lying with Jashemi, her own blood—

The fire was gone. Shaking, she opened her eyes to see the Dragon still staring at her with its horrible, yellow, implacable gaze.

"DO YOU KNOW WHO YOU ARE?"

Kevla had thought she would never again weep, but felt her eyes burn with tears as she answered, tentatively, "I— I am Kevla Bai-sha."

And she screamed as the wave of fire from the Dragon's mouth washed over her again, causing no injury but terrible pain. She clapped her hands over her ears, sobbing, trying not to hear the question; perhaps if she didn't hear it she wouldn't have to respond to it—

"DO YOU KNOW WHO YOU ARE?"

She couldn't look at the Dragon. Curled on the ledge, she whispered, "I am the daughter of Tahmu-kha-Rakyn."

A third time the fire enveloped her, and she almost lost

consciousness. But the merciful blackness only teased her, and again came the question.

And again, and again. Each time, she tried to say something, anything, that might satisfy the fearful creature. Each time, she failed.

Sister of Jashemi. Daughter of Keishla. Servant of the House of Four Waters. Nothing was right, nothing appeased the horrible monster, and Kevla wished that her father had cut her throat when he had the chance.

"DO YOU KNOW WHO YOU ARE?"

Kevla was not even looking at it now. She was lost in agony and fear, her mind dancing on the brink of madness. She was nothing without her name, her beloved brother, her work, her identity in this world. She wondered if the pain she was enduring each time the Dragon breathed a sheet of flame upon her naked skin was anything like what Jashemi had felt when she had unwittingly killed him, unleashing the full force of her passion upon the one person in the world she cherished most.

She heard his voice again, the last words Jashemi-kha-Tahmu had uttered before she had reduced his beautiful body to a handful of ash, as he arched above and inside her—

My love, you are fire!

Kevla's breath caught. She blinked and wiped her hair, salty and stiff with dried sweat, from her face. The words echoed again, almost as if he were here with her, speaking them to her.

Oh, Jashemi....

My love, you are Fire!

"DO YOU KNOW WHO YOU ARE?"

Her lips barely moving, terrified of giving the wrong answer yet again, Kevla whispered, "I am Fire."

The silence was absolute. Kevla could hear her ragged breathing, her own heart thundering in her ears.

Slowly, fearfully, she lifted her head, and gazed into the face of the Great Dragon. She sensed that he waited, that she needed to say this again, to claim it, to believe it.

Slightly louder, she said, "I am Fire!"

And then the Dragon opened its jaws and she cringed, bracing herself for the inevitable assault of flame. Instead, the Dragon roared, its tail splashing the liquid fire, its wings beating and sending a powerful wind that lifted Kevla's hair. The sound assaulted her ears, penetrated to her bones, and Kevla opened her mouth in a soundless cry.

The ledge beneath her crumbled and she fell. Her body limp, she plunged into the liquid fire without struggling. She had expected the scalding heat of the Dragon's flame, but instead the thick fluid wrapped her like a blanket. She floated in its depths, eyes closed, feeling the liquid slowly flow into her mouth and ears, muffling sound, silencing speech. She was drowning in fire, but there was no fear, no struggle. She felt like she had come home.

Then something solid and hotter than the lava of the volcano's heart positioned itself beneath her, and she felt herself lifted out of the molten fire and pressed tightly to a scaly surface.

The Dragon held her in his forepaws as if it cradled an infant. Somehow, in her dazed state, she felt it probing at her mind. It nuzzled her thoughts like the *sa'abah* had nuzzled her face, tentatively asking admittance.

Euphoric, almost unconscious, Kevla permitted it inside.

The darkness was physical, calming, and soothing. Out of the blackness appeared a small light. It flickered, a tiny flame, then it grew until the light filled her field of vision. When it dimmed slightly, Kevla found herself standing on a mountainside. The sun blazed and the sky was a brilliant blue. A breeze blew, ruffling her clothes.

Her clothes? She looked down at herself and for a moment it looked as though she was wrapped in a sheet of fire. Then she realized that the rhia *that draped her was made of a red material that felt soft as water to the touch.*

She looked up and gasped as she saw a wide expanse of still water. It reflected the blue of the sky, and she wished she could wade forward and immerse her body in its cool depths. Somehow she knew this water was not for bathing.

As she continued to gaze at the blue depths, seeing herself reflected in its surface, she saw something else.

It was the Dragon, on all fours, sitting quietly at her side. Their reflected gazes met, and suddenly Kevla laughed with delight. She turned to the creature beside her, remembering everything they had shared in times before. This was no monster, no stern, implacable "guardian" of a frightened people's controlling beliefs. This was her old friend, a part of her, given flesh as she was given flesh. Four times before, they had been together. Four times before, they had laughed and cried with delight, or faced destruction with a brave face, taking comfort from one another. Images flashed before her, reflected in the water.

"I'm so sorry," she said, holding out her arms to her friend, companion, ally, comforter, other Self. "How could I have forgotten you?"

It lowered its head so she could throw her arms around his sinuous neck. She felt a huge, warm tear splash on her shoulder, soaking her new garment.

"It has been hard, waiting for you," he said, his voice booming in her ear even as he tried to whisper. "I could not come to you. You had to find me, to remember who you are."

"I am Fire," she replied, knowing now it was true. But what it meant....

"Open your mind and heart, dear friend," the Dragon urged. "Gaze into the water, and remember."

*She obeyed. She saw herself, but the image in the water
looked nothing like Kevla Bai-sha. She was a woman about the
age of her mother, with long yellow hair; a man with a powerful build; a youth with his first downy growth of beard; a little boy who had never lived past five summers. The Dragon
was with her at every turn.*

*"I understand that…that I have lived before," she said to her
friend, one hand reaching out to caress his smooth red scales.
But the fire….*

*"Watch," the Dragon remonstrated. Kevla watched as the
yellow-haired woman's image shifted and reformed into a
leaping flame. It rippled again, and the flame stretched out four
streams that formed into legs and arms, solidifying into the second figure Kevla had seen, the strong young man. His shape
in turn became fire, then reformed into the youth, then the
child. Comprehension dawned.*

*"I am Fire," she breathed, understanding now. "I truly am
Fire, Fire made into human form." Almost unaware that she did
so, she brought one hand to her arm, touching the soft skin, half
expecting to find the liquid fire that had almost drowned her.*

*"As am I," the Dragon said. "You are the element of Fire
given flesh, and I am your Companion. Four times we have
been given shape and form; this is the last time it will be so."*

*The number was important, Kevla knew. She also knew
something else, and that knowledge descended with a swiftness that almost brought her to her knees:*

*"We're not alone," she said, steadying herself against the
Dragon. "There are others, aren't there?"*

*"It is coming back to you now," the Dragon said, nodding his
head approvingly. "Yes. There are four more. Name them to me."*

*"Earth, Air, Water…and Spirit," she said. As she spoke the
words, images of each element began to appear in the water.
They whirled about the flame, twisting, leaping, chasing each
other in a wild—*

"Dance," she whispered. "We are the Dancers. We're the Guardians." She sat down hard on the ground, unable to stand any longer even in this fantastical place that she knew existed only in her mind. "Twice won, twice lost...this is our last chance."

"It is the last chance for everyone," came a voice that she knew beside her, a voice she had thought she would never hear again. Uttering a soft cry, she turned to behold Jashemi sitting in the Dragon's place. His eyes shone and his full lips were parted in a smile.

A wave of joy and gratitude washed over her. "You've been with me, too," she said thickly. "Haven't you?"

He nodded. "Every time. The last time...I was too late." Sorrow furrowed his brow, and Kevla had a dim, fear-laced memory of a man attacking from the shadows. "I am your Lorekeeper. My task, and that of the others—and Kevla, there are many of us—is to seek you out and give you back your memories."

"Your dreams," Kevla said. "They weren't dreams, or even visions—they were memories!"

He nodded. "Memories of all the times before. Memories only the Lorekeepers had. We find the Dancers, help them discover—"

"Who they are," Kevla said, her voice breaking. My love, you are Fire! "You died so that I could know who I was...what I was born to do."

He reached to touch her cheek and she closed her eyes, trembling at the contact.

"I gladly died, this time and before this time, for you. For this world. Do you remember what is at stake, Kevla, my lover, my sister, my friend, my soul?"

She reached for the knowledge, and it appeared:

"Everything," she whispered.

"Everything," he confirmed. "I do not understand it all yet myself, but I know this: Our world, and the other four that have

*come before, are not real. They were created, crafted, as a pot-
ter crafts a pitcher. Civilizations appear, whole and complete.
Some know about the Dancers and their task; others, like
Arukan, are utterly ignorant. After each world has existed for
five thousand years, the Dancers are born, and each world
faces a crisis. If the Dancers can unite and use their powers to
defeat this evil, their world is permitted to continue. If not, then
it is—"*

"Gone," Kevla finished softly, tearing her gaze away from
her Lorekeeper's face to look upon the water again. Its surface
was now cloudy and gray, and fear closed her throat.

She knew she beheld the Shadow, the dreadful agent of destruction that would slowly cover every facet of her world and
simply erase it as if it had never been.

"I have seen the Shadow," the Lorekeeper said. He now
looked to her like a little boy in poor clothes, his eyes preter-
naturally wise, his face smudged and dirty. "You have seen it
too. If you fail, all will be lost—not just this world, but all the
others that have won a temporary victory against obliteration."

Kevla's gaze was still locked on the Shadow in the water. She
sagged. The responsibility was too much. All those worlds, all
those people, and everything she knew in this world were in
jeopardy.

"I can't do it," she whispered.

"Yes, you can," the Lorekeeper insisted. His voice sounded
different, and when she looked at him, the being who had been
born as Jashemi looked like a woman her own age, with short
brown hair and green eyes.

"You know who you are. You are more powerful even than
you can understand right now. You have remembered your
Companion, and soon you will join with the other Dancers. You
were never meant to be alone, Flame Dancer. You were always
meant to have allies. Find them."

Kevla was confused and suddenly angry. She stared at the

Lorekeeper, not wanting to see what this entity had been to her in the past, wanting to see Jashemi, whom she loved desperately. The Lorekeeper's face changed yet again, into the visage of an old man with a grizzled beard.

"I want you back, Jashemi!" she cried. "I can't do this without you!"

The Lorekeeper cocked his head, and the old man's face bled into that of another woman.

"I am no longer Jashemi. I am all these people you once loved, and none...."

"Please," she begged. "Please come back. Let me say goodbye to you."

With a visible effort, the Lorekeeper resumed the form of her brother and lover. She sobbed as she beheld the dear face.

"Our love is beyond the physical, Flame Dancer," Jashemi whispered. "Death cannot stop it. It hasn't before and it won't now. But if you wish to have the Lorekeeper with you, you must learn to let go of the form I took when I was flesh. The form that loved Kevla Bai-sha is dead. Only I exist now."

"Do you even remember?" she cried. "Do you even...." She couldn't speak anymore.

His hands shot out to seize her wrists and when she looked into the Lorekeeper's eyes, she saw, truly saw, Jashemi.

"Of course I remember!" he said, his voice hoarse with intensity. "But our love was not meant to be that of a man and woman. Not this time. I was born to be your brother and friend, to be close to you and love and support you in that fashion. We became lovers because we had to. Because our people stamped out anything else that we could have used to discover the truth. Think of a tree planted among stones, Kevla. Think how its roots twist and turn, seeking sustenance any way it can. You needed to learn your true nature, and I needed to help you do that. In a country where my dreams and your powers condemned us to death, we connected with each other the only way we could."

He touched her cheek, and it was Jashemi's touch. "Our love was right, Kevla. How it expressed itself was not. Do you understand?"

"No. Yes. I don't know." Even as she held his hand, he began to fade. "No...! Jashemi, don't leave me, don't go—"

"I must," he said regretfully. "I ever existed to love and serve you, Flame Dancer. And even though I am no longer flesh...I still do."

Kevla opened her eyes and air filled her lungs. Jashemi and the scrying pool were gone. She was awake and still held in the arms of the Dragon. He bent his head and re-garded her, concern plain on his reptilian face.

She found the strength to meet his gaze and nod. He cra-dled her closer, and her head fell back against his strong, pro-tective forepaws as the Flame Dancer fell into sweet unconsciousness.

Chapter Twenty-Four

Kevla awoke feeling rested and famished. For a moment, she kept her eyes closed, unwilling to open them and see what was reality and what was surely a dream. Beneath her, she felt hard stone, yet she knew she had slept as well as if she had been in a *khashim's* bed. A scent wafted to her nostrils...cooking meat?

She opened her eyes and sat up, realizing with a strange mixture of joy and dismay that her "dreams" had not been dreams at all. She was still inside Mount Bari, the only light coming from the leaping flames and the lava pool. The Dragon had moved her to a safer place away from the pool. As she moved, she observed that the *rhia* she had worn in her vision was real as well. She touched the soft, scarlet fabric.

She sniffed again. She was not imagining it; somewhere close by someone was roasting meat. She rose, stiff and sore, and stretched, following the scent around a corner where a small fire burned quietly. On a spit, the proper distance from the flame, was a whole roasting fowl. On plates around it were bread, fruits, nuts, and wine and water skins.

Kevla's stomach growled and she fell ravenously upon the food. She ate and drank with an intensity that surprised her, reaching into the fire and pulling off chunks of meat with her bare hands. There was no pain from the heat. Finally, sighing with contentment, she rubbed her full belly and leaned back against the stone walls.

Her hunger sated, she turned her attention to all that she had so recently discovered. There was so much in her mind that she felt overwhelmed. Her own identity and purpose, Jashemi's true Self, the Dragon—it was hard to sort it all out.

"Flame Dancer?" The deep voice rumbled and echoed. Kevla wondered how she could ever have found that voice frightening. Now, it caressed her ears and warmed her heart.

"Yes, Dragon," she called. "I am here."

He rounded the corner, enormous and red, his long tail snaking behind him. His wings were folded against his sloping mountain of a back, and his eyes were bright.

"I thought you were going to sleep the century away, but I did not want to wake you."

"How long have I been asleep?"

"Two days and two nights."

"No wonder I was so hungry."

"Mmmm," said the Dragon, surveying what little remained of the meal. "Perhaps you would like an entire sand-cow for dinner?"

Kevla's tentative smile broadened into a grin, and impulsively she ran and threw her arms around his long neck.

"How did I ever get along without you?" she asked, squeezing him one final time and then letting go.

He cocked his head and raised an eyebrow. "I was wondering," he said mildly, with a twinkle of humor in his golden eyes.

Kevla's smile faded. The trio was not complete, would never again be complete. Jashemi, the Lorekeeper, had passed from flesh. Still, she could have sworn she felt his presence, gentle as a kiss, in her mind before she awoke.

Her somberness did not escape her friend's notice. He knew what she was thinking.

"I regret," rumbled the Dragon, "that things unfolded as they did. I wish the people of Arukan had been wiser."

His words reminded Kevla of something Jashemi had said, something he had thought was important.

"Jashemi believed that our powers were manifesting now for a reason," she said. "He thinks—thought—that it had something to do with the Emperor who is attacking our people."

The Dragon nodded. "Jashemi was correct. Your destiny and that of all the worlds are entwined with the Emperor."

She rubbed her temples. "I'm not ready to face that yet. I am still so... Dragon, tell me of our past. I remember much, but so much more is lost to me."

The Dragon brightened. "I love a good tale," he mused, "and this is a marvelous one, for it is all true."

He settled back on his haunches, exposing his lighter-hued orange-yellow belly. Like a child seeking comfort from a loved parent, Kevla crawled over and nestled against him. His scales were smooth, like glazed pots, and so warm. She felt the tentative pat of a mammoth claw and relaxed even further. Safe, she felt so safe with this new, old friend.

"You found me first when I was still in the egg," the Dragon began.

* * *

Each day, he told her of a different life they had lived. She listened attentively, hoping to glean information that would be of use in this life, this final Dance that she and the others, as of yet unknown to her, would perform. Some things she remembered, others felt more like stories than memories.

Food mysteriously continued to appear when she slept, and she ate and drank without questioning. Finally, on the fifth day, she knew it was time to turn her attention to the present.

"Jashemi spoke of other Lorekeepers, here in Arukan," she told the Dragon. Her chest ached as she spoke. It still hurt so much to speak of him, to think of him, but she continued. "Like him, they probably are afraid to speak of their dreams. It could condemn them to death."

The Dragon nodded and made a sour face. To one who did not know him, it would be terrifying to behold. Kevla recalled the expression from a life before, and to her it was amusing and endearing.

"It would indeed. Foolish Arukani," he muttered.

"So how do I find them? How do I let them know what Jashemi knew—what we know?"

He looked at her intently. "How do you find out anything, Flame Dancer?"

Of course. She should have thought of it sooner. Easily, without even thinking, she conjured fire and asked it, "Show me the Lorekeepers of Arukan."

The fire suddenly flamed up, almost as tall as the Dragon. Several faces were in its heart, flickering and shifting. Jashemi had been right; there were indeed many others.

"Well," said the Dragon. "It seems you have an embarrassment of riches. And these are only the ones who happen to be near fires right now. Perhaps you'd best narrow it down."

"I agree," said Kevla. "Show me...show me the Lore-keepers in the Clan of Four Waters."

The fire subsided, and two faces appeared. One was unknown to Kevla, but the second was familiar indeed. It was her old adversary, Tiah.

"If we had only known," Kevla said softly, thinking of the time they had both wasted in their confrontations. Who cared about petty household politics when their entire world was at stake? Tiah was carrying a candle. She looked older than Kevla remembered her, and unhappy, and Kevla found it in her to pity the woman.

One by one, Kevla went through every one of the Arukani clans. The Dragon explained that not all of the Lorekeepers would be as close to her as Jashemi had been, but each carried a piece of the puzzle. She thought with a stab of anguish that no one could have been closer than Jashemi, but said nothing. Her grief was hers alone; it belonged to Kevla Bai-sha, not the Flame Dancer. She would not strain the Dragon's sympathy by continuing to focus on her personal loss.

As she sat and gazed into the fire, memorizing faces and listening to conversations, Kevla was startled to realize that the young *sa'abah*-tender who had stolen food and water for her was among them. Then she recalled the girl's words: *I do not know you, or your errand. But somehow I feel as if I needed to do this for you. Perhaps one day, we will both understand why.*

It made perfect sense. The Lorekeepers were born to help the Dancers. Even when neither she nor Kevla understood their link, both had sensed their connection.

She observed and listened. Most of the Lorekeepers were of the lower or middle castes, but there were two Seconds, one in the *Sa'abah* Clan and one in the Horserider Clan, and the *khashim* of the Star Clan was a Lorekeeper as well.

Some of them did not speak of their dreams; others did. No one understood them, and all were frightened by them. They felt alone, isolated. Kevla was moved. If only they knew that there were many others like them, that they were special and to be honored, not feared.

For the first time since she had made love with Jashemi, she felt hope rise in her. Jashemi's dream had been to unite the clans so that they could stand against this Emperor from over the mountains. It had seemed like a fool's errand when he spoke of it, but now Kevla thought it possible. Every clan had at least one Lorekeeper. Every Lorekeeper would have been having strange dreams. Once they were made to understand the truth about their dreams, to realize that they could no longer stand separately and continue their petty quarrels, perhaps they would see the wisdom in union.

She spoke of this to the Great Dragon. "I hope you are right," he said. "It will be difficult for them to listen to a Bai-sha, though. You understand that."

She grinned at him. "It will be easier for them if the Bai-sha is riding the Great Dragon of Mount Bari."

"Hmph," was all the Dragon had to say, but he looked pleased.

She looked down at the handful of dates she was munching. "Dragon," she said, "I was wondering...how did you get this food?"

"I?" He seemed surprised. "I have not been bringing you food."

"Then who has?"

"The *kulis,*" the Dragon replied.

Kevla almost choked. *"What?"* She stared in horror at the innocent-looking dates. She had been eating the food that demons had brought her for days!

Repulsed, she threw the handful of uneaten dates as far

from her as she could, wiping her hands on her red *rhia*. Her stomach roiled.

"Now you're just being stupid," the Dragon said mildly.

"Stupid?" she spat. "Stupid, to not eat the food demons have been bringing me?"

He sighed and shook his head sadly, as if she were nothing more than a petulant child having a tantrum. "The *kulis* saved your life. It is they who have been bringing you food and water, when you would have died alone in the desert on your pilgrimage. Your contempt is poor thanks. They're not demons, Kevla. They're not evil. I thought you were intelligent enough to learn that on your own, but apparently twenty-one years of living in this country has addled your Fire-given wits." He perused her thoughtfully, then said, "Perhaps it is time you met them."

Her anger at him shifted into fear. He was going to give her to the *kulis*....

"Dragon," she said, her voice shaking. "Dragon, no, don't do this...."

"You're afraid," he said gently. "You're afraid of something you don't understand. You are the element of Fire, Kevla. If you are to succeed, there is much you will need to face...and learn not to fear."

His head was close to her level, as it always was when they conversed. Now he lifted it and extended his neck. Closing his great eyes, he opened his mouth and let out a long, crooning noise.

Kevla leaped to her feet and pressed back against the solid comfort of the stone walls. Her mouth was dry. She had learned so much, seen so much, but *this*—

She bit back a cry as long, distorted shadows moved along the walls.

And the *kulis* came.

* * *

Kayle, Captain of the Emperor's Guardsmen and overseer of the conscription of the Arukani prisoners, had literally been born into this life.

The son of a camp follower and a soldier, he had been left outside the nearest fort on the day of his birth. The soldiers had brought the infant in and given him to one of their wives to raise along with her own offspring. Kayle's earliest memory was that of wanting to play with the gleaming weapons lining the walls of the room he shared with four other children.

As soon as he could lift a sword, the woman who had raised him gave him back to the guards. He slept with other boys who did nothing but eat, sleep, train, and assist the older men. He had killed his first man when he was eleven, and had lost count of how many had fallen beneath his blade since then.

Kayle knew nothing of love, or politics, or literature, or art. He knew war, and tactics, and how to kill efficiently both on the field and by stealth in the depths of night. He was strong, tall and powerful, and the scars that crisscrossed his body and face were myriad, but old. No enemy's sword had touched Kayle's body for the last ten years.

Kayle had no particular love for his Emperor, but did know that the young ruler was the one who had provided the best weapons, horses, and men for his army, and permission to kill when Kayle felt like it.

Kayle liked to kill. When he was younger, killing had excited him. Now, after familiarity with the act, his pleasure had abated somewhat, but he always enjoyed it. Although he knew his task was to get more warriors for his Emperor's army, Kayle was secretly pleased when some of the captured Arukani men resisted and he was therefore able to make an example of one of them. The women and children were not as much fun to slaughter.

He had listened attentively as the Emperor spoke, inspiring

the troops with assurances of victory. He had not seen his ruler since then, but did not much care. He supervised his own unit, rode where and when the general ordered him, and moved steadily forward. Now, after a hard day of riding, Kayle sat by the crackling fire. He extended his powerful hands to the warmth, and looked up at the mountains they had yet to cross. It was night, so he couldn't actually see them; but he knew they were there by the way they blotted out the starfield. It would be difficult, moving so many men, beasts and pieces of equipment over those looming barriers, but it could be done.

He smiled, and the gesture twisted his scarred mouth into a grimace that made most men quail.

On the other side of the mountains, he was certain, good slaughtering would be had. Good slaughtering indeed. Kayle was looking forward to killing in the name of the Emperor.

Chapter Twenty-Five

By the time Tahmu reached the encampment, men were shouting and reaching for weapons. When he appeared out of the darkness, a cry of relief went up. Some of his men even rushed to touch him, to convince themselves that their *khashim* was truly unharmed.

"My lord!" cried Dumah. "When we found poor Halid slain, we thought there were bandits about! Did you see anything?"

"Put away your weapons," Tahmu ordered. He gazed at the body of his former friend. "You need not fear a bandit attack. I myself killed Halid."

The men fell silent as they stared first at their leader, then at his slain Second.

"He attacked me when I sat by the fire, unarmed," Tahmu continued. "He has been sleeping with the *khashima* and plotting my downfall." He lifted his eyes from the body and searched the faces of his men. "Just as Kevla said."

They gasped. "My lord," ventured Dumah, "surely this attack has distressed you...perhaps you...."

"I know what I know," Tahmu said, raising his voice slightly. "Whatever...abilities...Kevla has, she has only ever used them to protect me. She saved me when my own wife tried to poison me, and she saved me again when she appeared here last night in time to warn me."

The men looked at each other uneasily. Tahmu understood their conflict. They honored and trusted him, but he was asking a great deal.

"I don't ask you to believe it," he said. "But you will obey my orders, as is your duty. We return home. I will not hunt Kevla, and Jashemi...." He suddenly could not speak. They waited for him, and finally he managed to say, "Jashemi is dead. Dumah, prepare a message for the hawk. I want to make sure that no one tries to harm Kevla if she encounters anyone."

The men did not protest, but he saw their grief for their young master and their unhappiness with his pronouncement. He hoped that he had earned enough admiration and respect so that he could keep his clan together when he refused to kill a *kuli* in his own household.

They would need something from him in order to do that, some sign that he was still their leader, still unafraid to do the unpleasant things that a *khashim* must do.

He felt certain he could oblige them.

Yeshi was waiting for him as he and his men entered the courtyard a few days later. She was clad in her best finery. Her long hair was braided and bound atop her head, woven with jewelry throughout. Her lips, eyes, and cheeks were decorated. Her *rhia* was of blue and gold material, heavily embroidered. She stood atop the steps to the House, beautiful and furious, her eyes snapping with anger.

Tahmu had been wary about the encounter, but now he smiled to himself. She was going to make this easy. He looked her full in the eye as he marched toward her and climbed the steps.

Breaking protocol, certain in her power, Yeshi spoke first.

"My husband, you disappoint me," she announced. There were many assembled in the courtyard, and all heard the words.

He kept the small smile on his lips, tacitly encouraging her to continue her rant.

"You left to slay *kulis.* Then you send me a message saying that you have chosen to shirk your duty. How could you leave your people so defenseless? How could you betray them so?" As she spoke, her eyes flickered over the men and he saw her face tighten slightly when she did not see Halid.

She had given him his opening. "It is interesting, wife, that you should speak of slaying and betrayal," Tahmu said, his voice carrying. "I think you did not expect me to come home with the slain bodies of my child and the Bai-sha. I think you did not expect me to come home at all."

Yeshi stiffened. It would be imperceptible to anyone who did not know her well, but Tahmu didn't miss it.

Rallying, she cried, "Yes! I would think that if you failed to catch the demons, you would be ashamed to come home to me, to your Clan, empty-handed!"

"Ah," he said conversationally, "but I have not returned empty-handed. I have flushed my quarry, but it is not a *kuli.* Here is what I bring home to my *khashima!*"

Knowing all eyes were riveted on him, he gestured to Dumah. Pale and large-eyed, Dumah handed his lord a small sack. Tahmu opened it, reached in, grasped his prize, and brandished it in his wife's face.

It was the rotting head of Halid.

Yeshi screamed and shrank back, her hand to her mouth. Her shock was echoed around the courtyard as everyone else stared at the grisly trophy. Tahmu turned, holding the head by the hair so that all gathered could see it.

"Behold the head of a traitor!" he cried. "This man attacked me at my own fire, by stealth, when I was alone and unarmed. He has conspired with my *khashima* to take over the Clan. Many of you were here in this courtyard several days ago. Forfeiting everything, Jashemi prevented what he perceived to be a murder. Do you recall how Yeshi urged me to kill our own son for that one act of compassion? She knew what I now know, that Jashemi was not *kuli*-cursed. With the rightful heir discredited and hunted, and her husband apparently murdered by bandits in the night, she and my Second would be free to take over the Clan of Four Waters! You, my people, would have been lead by a traitor and a murderer!"

Disgusted, Tahmu hurled the head down. It bounced down the steps with a hollow sound, coming to rest on the hard-backed earth of the courtyard. Sightless eyes stared up at the crowd, who drew back.

"That is how I deal with treacherous Seconds," Tahmu said. He turned, slowly, to look at Yeshi. "The question before me now is, how do I deal with treacherous *khashimas?*"

He knew what he intended to do. What he did not know was how Yeshi would react. He hoped that she would compose herself, hold her head high, and accept whatever fate he decreed. In her face, he could still see the features that she had bestowed on her son; and for the powerful love he bore his child, he wanted her to behave with dignity.

Her nostrils flared. "I condemn Halid for his treachery, but I had no part in it. Jashemi will defend me. He will know that I have acted only for the Clan's best interest."

He laughed harshly, pain and fury battling inside him. "Then you will be distressed to learn that your son is dead, my lady. You have no defenders now."

Show me that this hurts you, he thought fiercely. *Show our son, that wise and beautiful boy, that you loved him.*

Yeshi went pale. She fell to her knees, and Tahmu dared to hope that perhaps true grief was at last penetrating the wall of bitterness and hate she had built around herself for so long.

She prostrated herself in front of him. But instead of the hoped-for words of pain and mourning for her dead child, Yeshi cried, "My lord, forgive a weak and foolish woman! It was Halid's idea. He frightened me, he threatened me—"

Any shred of fondness he had left for his wife evaporated like water in the sun. She clutched at his *rhia,* and to his disgust was actually kissing his sandals and feet.

He stepped backward and gestured to his guards. Their faces showing no emotion, they stepped in, seized Yeshi, and hauled her to her feet. Her pretty face was twisted with her sobs, the kohl running down her artificially reddened cheeks. As he stared at her, Tahmu wondered how in the world he had ever been persuaded to give up his beloved Keishla for this cunning, vengeful woman. One had turned to prostitution to keep herself and her daughter alive. The other had bartered her body for vengeance and power. Who was the real *halaan?*

She had not ceased babbling. Tahmu twined his fingers in her hair and pulled her head back sharply. She yelped, then fell silent, her eyes staring. He could see the vein beating in her neck.

"How is it possible that someone like Jashemi could spring from your body?" he hissed, tears standing in his eyes. "I won't ask why you did what you did. I know part of it had to do with our blood-marked child, and I cannot blame you for hating me for that. But Jashemi—your own son—"

Repulsed, he let her go. "It is within my rights and the laws of this land to have you burned, as you would have had Kevla burned, or cut off your head, as I have done to your lover. But that's not enough. I want you to taste suffering, Yeshi. The sort of suffering you've brought on so many others during your wasted life."

He stepped back and spoke more loudly, so that all could hear. "I decree this woman to no longer be Yeshi-sha-Rusan. She is no longer *khashima* of the Clan of Four Waters. I strip her of her name, her title, of all that she was born into or married into. Henceforth, this woman shall be known as Yeshi Bai-sha. Get from my sight before I change my mind."

She stared at him, as if she couldn't comprehend what he had just said. His eyes narrowed.

"Go!" he cried. When she did not move, the two guards again stepped in and grasped her arms. Tahmu watched, unmoved, as the mother of his son was dragged, screaming, from the courtyard. Without power, she was as toothless as an old *simmar.* Tahmu felt certain her malice had no more ability to harm anyone he loved.

When at last her cries had faded, Tahmu regarded the upturned faces in the courtyard. They displayed a variety of emotions, but most were turning to him eagerly, wanting a sign as to how best to proceed after this upheaval.

He nodded. Yeshi had brought everything on herself, and was indirectly responsible for Jashemi's death. *As am I.* There was much for him to think about. But for now, he dismissed his household and stepped into the comforting coolness of the House of Four Waters.

As Second of the *Sa'abah* Clan, Melaan had earned the right to a tent of his own. It was comfortable and well-appointed, but he tossed restlessly. Sleep eluded him, and he was not sure that was a bad thing as the dreams had been particularly intense as of late. Also, he was worried about Jashemi.

Terku, of course, had received the hawk with the dreadful message from Tahmu-kha-Rakyn. The *khashim* had read it aloud at council: *If Jashemi-kha-Tahmu or a woman who answers to the name of Kevla Bai-sha should approach your Clan, capture them and notify me immediately. They are under* kuli *influence. The woman is particularly dangerous and should be gagged, bound, and watched at all times.*

Melaan had said nothing unusual, only muttered the appropriate surprised and regretful words that all spoke. But he felt a sick feeling in the pit of his stomach, and was more careful than usual that he said nothing of his strange dreams to anyone.

Jashemi was not under *kuli* influence, nor, Melaan suspected, was the Bai-sha woman he was traveling with. Jashemi was wanted, and feared, for his dreams. Poor Shali had wept uncontrollably after the news was broken to her. She had begun to fall in love with her gentle husband. To learn that she was, perhaps, carrying the child of a *kuli* was devastating.

Melaan hoped that Jashemi and this Kevla had the sense to avoid the clans. On a personal level, he was sorry for the boy, but on another level, he feared for his Clan's existence. Men like he and Jashemi were needed now, desperately.

He heard a sound outside his tent. He kept his breathing steady, and slowly his fingers crept toward the knife he always kept under his pillow.

The sound came closer, a soft step, a tentative rustling as the tent was opened. He sensed a presence. He waited, feigning sleep, as it approached. Then in silence Melaan sprang, clutching the knife, and leaped upon the intruder.

She, for it was a woman, fell beneath him and did not resist. He pressed the knife to her throat.

"Who are you?" he demanded.

She didn't answer, but suddenly the knife grew unbearably hot and he dropped it with a cry.

The woman sat up and extended a hand. Before Melaan could think to do anything else, a small flicker of flame appeared in her palm.

Frightened, he scuttled backward. She lifted her other hand in a pleading gesture and said, "Please don't call for anyone. I'm here to speak with you. I am Kevla Bai-Sha, a friend of Jashemi's."

He regarded her cautiously, his eyes flickering from her shadowed features to the fire dancing in her hand. She brought the flame closer to her face, so he could see her better. He found her beautiful, but her face was drawn in sorrow.

"I know about your dreams," she continued, speaking quickly in a low voice. "I know they're not sent by demons. You're a Lorekeeper, Melaan. So was Jashemi, and so are the others. What you are dreaming are memories of the past and visions of the future."

"How do you know about this?" he rasped. The name she had called him resonated. *Lorekeeper.* Somehow it was familiar.

She extended a hand to him. "Because I am one of the Dancers," she said. "I am the Flame Dancer." She looked at him intently. "It means nothing to you, I see. Here. Take my hand, Melaan."

Slowly, he reached to do so, then hesitated. "You mentioned Jashemi," he said. "You said, 'Jashemi *was* a Lorekeeper.'"

By the firelight dancing in her palm, he saw her eyes glisten with tears. "Jashemi is dead," she said, "But I misspoke.

He remains a Lorekeeper. I know this is all confusing, but—
Please, Melaan. If you want to save your people, you must
trust me—trust yourself."

He had recognized her name. This, then, was the
woman Tahmu-kha-Rakyn had warned them about.
Reason screamed to Melaan to spring on her, tie her up
and bring her to his lord, as the *khashim* of the Clan of
Four Waters had requested. But the words she said resonated beyond reason. Tentatively, he reached and took
her hand.

As if in a waking dream, he relived the memories of the
people he had been; watched the Shadow come and destroy; saw it defeated and dissolve into nothingness. He
saw this woman dressed in different flesh as she might dress
in different clothing. And he knew her.

The remembering took but a moment, then she squeezed
his hand and let it go. Drifting back to the present, he stared
at her, then bowed in homage.

"Flame Dancer," he whispered. "I live to serve you. What
do you ask of me?"

She gave him the names of three other Lorekeepers in his
clan. "Find these people. I will go to them tonight also. Do
what you can to persuade your *khashim* to meet me in three
weeks' time at the foot of Mount Bari. Your task is to convince him to come. Once you have brought him," and she
smiled a little, "I will convince him of other things. Arukan
must have an army to fight the Emperor from over the
mountain, or all of Arukan will fall."

He nodded, and watched her in awe as she rose and
gracefully walked out of the tent.

Lorekeeper. At last, he had a name to put to that part of
himself. Knowing this gave him a comfort, a sense of peace,
he had never tasted in his adult life. He returned to his sleeping mat, fell asleep quickly, and had no dreams.

* * *

Tiah made no haste to return to her sleeping quarters. It was late, she knew the guard who stood watch at the entrance to the House, and she and her lover had been meeting unchallenged for some time. What had worried Tiah the most was the thought of Yeshi discovering her illicit encounters, and Yeshi was now gone. Tiah's nose wrinkled in contempt. Yeshi had been so intent that all of her handmaidens be "pure," and yet she was the one who had been taking a lover and plotting to kill her husband.

Tiah didn't miss her much at all.

Her feet padded along the road up to the House, and she breathed the still night air deeply. She swung the lit lantern she carried to light her way in the dark night, and hummed as she walked.

"Tiah," came a voice.

Tiah stopped dead in her tracks and whirled, trying to see who had called her.

"Who's there?"

"An old friend, or perhaps an old enemy." The voice belonged to a woman. Her thoughts scattered and clouded with guilt, Tiah took several heartbeats before she recognized the voice. When she did, she dropped the lantern with a soft cry. The little flame inside it ought to have been snuffed out, but instead blazed to a greater height.

Impossibly, a woman stepped out of the flames. She smiled gently.

"Hello, Tiah," said Kevla Bai-sha.

A few days after his arrival, Tahmu was approached by one of Yeshi's former handmaidens. Tiah, he thought she was called. Like all the other servants, she had said nothing when he had banished her mistress. He had put her and the other girl, the smaller, shyer one, to work keeping the house clean. They would also attend to any visiting *khashimas*, although he had entertained no one since his return. The House was in mourning for the fallen *khashimu*, and it would be some time before the Great Hall would ring again with music and laughter.

So he was surprised when Tiah approached him as he was preparing to ride down to the rivers. She hurried to him and prostrated herself in the dirt.

One hand on Swift's neck, Tahmu asked, "What is it?"

"My lord, I must speak with you. It is dire!"

The tone of her voice alerted him. "Rise and speak, then," he ordered.

She did so, not looking up at him. "My lord, last night...." She twisted her hands together, clearly at a loss as to how to proceed.

Handing the reins to an attendant, Tahmu told her, "Walk with me." She followed him dutifully, sniffing and gulping as if fighting back tears.

"No one will hear," he said, not unkindly. "Speak...Tiah, is it not?"

"Yes, lord. Lord...last night...last night Kevla came to me!"

His eyes widened. "Kevla? You are certain this was not a dream?"

Now she did look up at him and shook her head vigorously. "No, my lord. I was returning from—" Her cheeks reddened.

He almost laughed at her consternation. Such things were so unimportant to him now. "Yeshi might have cared if you took a lover, Tiah," he said, thinking that Yeshi was a consummate hypocrite. "I don't. Tell me the truth."

"Yes, lord. I was coming back from—from a meeting, as you say." She continued to blush, but thankfully also continued to speak. "I have been having dreams, my lord. Strange dreams of an approaching Shadow, that covers and destroys everything."

Gooseflesh prickled Tahmu's arms as a chill shivered over him. The words Jashemi had spoken so long ago came back to him: *We stood watching a darkness hovering on the horizon, a darkness that was about to completely swallow us. She told me that it might all fall to me, that I must not forget.*

If only he had listened! If only...but it was too late for Jashemi. It might not be too late for this girl, for Kevla. "I have heard of these dreams," he said quietly. "My son had them. I did not listen to him. I will listen to you."

Relieved, she rewarded him with a smile and continued. "Kevla told me that these dreams are actually visions and memories. She said I am something called a Lorekeeper, and that the young lord had been one, too. She wants all the clans to meet in three weeks at the base of Mount Bari, so that we can work together to stand against the Emperor from over the mountain. She also said—"

The frightened look descended on Tiah's round face again. He had bent to her with an attentiveness that clearly alarmed her, and gentled his expression.

"Don't fear, child. Speak what Kevla told you to say."

"She said to say thank-you for sparing her life."

Tahmu smiled sadly. "That might have been the wisest decision I ever made," he told her. "Thank you for coming to me, Tiah. If Kevla comes to you again, tell her that she may count on the support of the Clan of Four Waters."

She bowed low and scurried off. He watched her go and for the first time since he had ordered Kevla's death by fire, he felt a lightening in his heart.

As he had told his daughter, that bitter night when she had saved his life for the second time, it seemed to him that he had made the wrong choice at every turn. He married Yeshi instead of Keishla, and that had ended with treachery. He did not acknowledge Kevla openly as his child and permit her and Jashemi to play together as siblings ought, and that had perhaps forced them into a relationship that was as forbidden as it was powerful. He had exposed the inno-cent child that was his blood-marked daughter, fueling Yeshi's hatred and condemning a baby. He decreed a terri-ble punishment on his illegitimate daughter and discredited his legitimate son.

But despite these mistakes, Kevla yet lived, with powers that Jashemi was convinced were sent to heal. She wanted the same thing Tahmu and his son had: a union of the clans.

There were decisions ahead. He hoped he would be able, this time, to make the right ones.

He would not ride to the rivers today. If Kevla wanted the Clan at the foot of Mount Bari in so short a time, he would have to prepare right away.

Chapter Twenty-Six

Two weeks and four days later, as the sky turned orange and purple and the sun sank beneath the horizon, Tahmu and every able-bodied man in his Clan reached the foot of Mount Bari.

They were not the first clan to arrive, and Dumah, Tahmu's new Second, looked uneasily around at the dozens of campfires that were just starting to be kindled at the approach of night.

"So many," he said. "My lord, what if this is a trap? What if Kevla is not the woman she pretended to be? Her powers—"

"Are frightening," Tahmu agreed. He was pleased that the reticent Dumah was learning to speak openly with him. "But think, Dumah. With all those powers, she could have killed me or anyone else by simply pointing a finger. Even when she wounded Yeshi, it was an accident."

"So she told you, lord," Dumah said.

"So she told me," he agreed mildly, "and so I believe. I should have believed my son when he first came to me speaking of powers; I won't make that mistake again. Besides, there is sense in what she is trying to do."

"Who knows what she told the others," Dumah said nervously, still looking at the vast number of clanspeople who had at one time or another been the enemies of the Clan of Four Waters.

"Perhaps you had best send someone to find out," Tahmu said, and grinned at Dumah's expression.

Dumah did as he was told. While the rest of the Clan began setting up tents and lighting their own campfires, Dumah rounded up several men to act as representatives to each of the other clans assembled. Tiah and the other Lorekeeper from the Clan of Four Waters, an old beggar, accompanied the representatives. They met with the other Lorekeepers, and when Tiah returned to report to Tahmu well into the night, her eyes shone and she stood straighter than he had ever seen her.

He brought her and Dumah into his tent and bade them be seated. He called for *eusho*, and when the servant left to prepare it, he asked quietly, "Tell me what you have learned."

"The stories are exactly the same," Melaan said to Terku as they drank *eusho* together in the *khashim's* tent. "We have had the same visions and memories. Each of us knows something a little different, and I believe it would be wise for us to have a meeting of all the Lorekeepers and write down as complete a history as we can manage."

Terku raised a bushy white eyebrow. "A history," he repeated, "of four other lives you have lived. Four other worlds that were created. Two of which were destroyed, two of which survived. Do I have it right?"

Melaan felt the blood come to his face. "I know how it sounds, but... Yes, my lord."

Terku sighed and put the cup down. "Melaan," he said, "You have been my trusted Second for almost twenty years. If you told me that I would fly if I leaped off the peak of Mount Bari, I would jump."

Melaan's lips curved at the image. "I would not ask you to do such a thing, my lord."

"And yet you have me come to this place, with my finest warriors, to hear what someone who claims to be the embodiment of fire has to tell you. A woman, no less. You stretch the limits of my patience, my old friend."

Melaan regarded him intently. "I know what I know," he said. "Jashemi knew it. Fully twenty-and-two others scattered throughout all the clans know it. The stories are the same. The woman Kevla has demonstrated powerful magic, magic that seems to be limited to controlling fire and heat. I can't believe this is all a trick. Who could do such a thing?"

"A dreadful enemy," replied his *khashim*.

"We are already facing a dreadful enemy," Melaan replied somewhat shortly. "He flies the flag of the ki-lyn, another image with which all the Lorekeepers are familiar. I would rather face a foe I know to be my enemy than turn a possible friend into one."

Terku did not reply at once. Finally, he sighed in resignation. "I hope you are right," Terku said, "for all our sakes."

"Do you think he's right?" asked Jalik, Second of the Star Clan.

"He's always been a good leader," said Yumar as they walked together under the stars for which their clan had been named.

"That's not an answer."

"I know." Yumar shot his friend a quick grin, then grew sober. "There are some who say that this is a trick. That this fire-woman has gulled us here with tales of a foe who threatens us all, when really she wants us to fight each other. Maybe this so-called great battle will be between all the clans."

Jalik snorted. "To what end?"

"I don't know. She's a fire-woman, who knows what she's thinking?"

"But if our own *khashim* has had the same visions as twenty others, how can we deny the power in that?"

Yumar frowned. "I just don't trust this woman."

"You don't trust any woman, Yumar."

"True. But I don't have any reason to."

An uncomfortable silence fell between them. Yumar had had his heart broken many times. Jalik sometimes felt guilty, for he had a faithful and loving wife and two healthy children. He thought of his mate, and knew that he would trust her with anything. Even his life. If a woman told Yumar the sky was blue, he would feel compelled to look up just to make sure.

Finally, Jalik said, "Our *khashim* has ordered us here. We obey him."

"Let us hope that we will not need a new *khashim* by the time all is done," muttered Yumar darkly.

Melaan walked somewhat nervously up to the tent of Tahmu-kha-Rakyn. Following behind him were the Lore-keepers of the Horserider Clan and the Sandcattle Clan. Melaan had not seen Tahmu since Jashemi's wedding. The man was intimidating and powerful, and Melaan had no idea how his son's death might have affected him. The fact that the *khashim* had brought his clan to this meeting, several dozen warriors strong, boded well, but Melaan still worried.

He identified himself to the stone-faced man who guarded the *khashim's* tent, and a moment later was permitted to enter.

Sorrow washed over Melaan as Tahmu looked up from reading a scroll. The *khashim* of the Clan of Four Waters was fit and handsome, and had always looked much younger than his true years. Now, he looked old. His eyes were haunted.

Melaan bowed. "Great lord," he said, "as one who is what your son was, let me offer my deepest condolences on your loss. Jashemi was well-loved and respected by the *Sa'abah* Clan."

Tahmu nodded curtly and his lips tightened. "Thank you, Melaan. What is your purpose here?"

"Many of us—the Lorekeepers—" by the Dragon, the title still seemed strange "—desire to meet with one another. We each have a little knowledge of what has gone before, and we feel it would be valuable to set as much as we can down plainly."

Tahmu again nodded. "Has anyone resisted this?"

"A few, my lord. They fear what will happen when a *khashim* sits next to a *sa'abah* herder and listens to her words."

Tahmu laughed shortly. "If we are lucky, then perhaps the same thing as when a stubborn *khashim* listened to a Bai-sha."

"My lord?"

Tahmu waved the question away. "Do not mind me, Melaan. There are two Lorekeepers in my Clan, a beggar and a serving girl. They have my permission to attend this...council. But you must promise to share what you know."

"We will, lord. We will share everything with everyone."

Somewhat to Tahmu's surprise, he learned that every clan had agreed to send their Lorekeepers to the meeting.

Much was written down, but according to Tiah, there would need to be more meetings in order to complete the sharing of knowledge, and there were many other clans who had not yet arrived. Even so, the document would read as a tale with more left out than set down. While the Lore-keepers seemed to have bonded, the rest of the clans remained deeply suspicious of one another. Tahmu said a quick prayer to the Dragon that no accident or incident that might spark violence would occur. Tensions were tight as a bowstring, and it would not take much for this "meeting of the clans" to become a bloodbath.

The night passed without incident, as did the next day. More clans arrived; more opportunities for disaster. They kept coming, until at last Tahmu thought he saw nearly every clan represented. Some had come with men, ready to fight; others were smaller delegations, sent by their leaders to gather information and assess the situation before the clan would commit to anything.

The appointed day Kevla had given them came and went. That night, no one slept. Dumah begged Tahmu to leave, but Tiah, growing more and more confident in her Lore-keeper knowledge, insisted that they remain.

Then it happened.

The following day, shortly before sunset, four members of the Horserider Clan encountered six members of the Sandcattle Clan at the only available fresh spring. The Horseriders insisted that they needed to fill their water containers before the Sandcattle Clan. One of the Sandcattle Clansmen reasonably replied that there was room for several to fill their jugs and waterskins at a time. The biggest, most aggressive of the Horseriders replied that if the Sandcattle dogs wanted water, they could wait downstream while the Horseriders relieved themselves in it, because that was all Sandcattle Clansmen were fit to drink.

Later, witnesses said they weren't sure who had first struck whom, but a fight ensued in which two Horseriders were severely beaten and one Sandcattle Clansmen stabbed. The noise drew the attention of others, and what had begun as a brawl born of tension escalated into a multi-clan battle.

Tahmu bolted from his tent at the sound of the cries and cursed. "Dumah, saddle Swift, then alert all the other *khashims*. We have to stop this before—"

But Dumah was paying no attention to his lord. He stood as if carved of rock, staring up at the sky, awe and horror commingled on his face. Others, too, had stopped in mid-stride and were gazing upward. Tahmu followed their gaze, and his heart leaped.

It came from inside Mount Bari, seemingly made of the dark, twisting smoke which arose from that most sacred of places. But this was no smoky illusion. Enormous, graceful wings beat the sky steadily, keeping aloft a dark shape that seemed to be a blending of lizard and snake. Tahmu's heart began to race as the creature drew nearer.

There was no mistaking it now. Morning sun glinted off red scales, and even as he watched it opened its mouth and spouted flame.

The Great Dragon was descending from the mountain.

He heard screams of fear and joy commingled, and all around him members of every clan fell to their hands and knees. His own legs seemed to be locked into place, but when the Dragon drew nearer, he, Tahmu-kha-Rakyn, dropped to the dust beside the lowliest of his Clan.

Closer it drew, and he found he could not tear his gaze away. Now he could see that there was something on its back. A heartbeat later, he realized with a fresh shock whom he beheld: his daughter, Kevla, clad in a *rhia* the same hue as the mighty Dragon, sitting erect and calm on the Great Dragon's back, her black hair flying in the wind the creature's wings created.

Chapter Twenty-Seven

The Great Dragon had no trouble finding a place to come to earth. The clanspeople had fled from his descent, creating a clearing. It landed gracefully for so mammoth a creature, and folded its wings with the delicacy and fastidiousness of a sparrow. It raised its mighty head and surveyed them with yellow eyes.

Moving as surely and as gracefully as the Dragon, Kevla Bai-sha dismounted easily. She stood straight and tall, no sign of fear or arrogance in her gaze. Instead, Tahmu noticed a confidence he had never before seen in her.

She stood patiently, waiting for the cries of fear and wonder to fade. When at last there was silence, she spoke.

"We all know the stories," she said in a clear voice that carried on the still desert air. "It is said that when the Great Dragon leaves his home in Mount Bari, the end of the world is near. But I am here to tell you that this is only partially true.

The world will indeed end, if something is not done to prevent it. And we can do something to prevent it."

She began to walk the circumference of the crowd, her eyes singling out those Tahmu knew to be Lorekeepers. "You were born to prevent it," she said to a young five-score girl. The girl smiled tremulously. "And you," she said to the *khashim* of the Star Clan, "and you," to Melaan. "All of you who have had the dreams that have made you afraid to speak your truth. You have dreamed the fate of worlds before, and the possible fate of this one. I honor you, Lorekeepers."

She brought her hands to her heart and bowed deeply. "The creature before you is indeed the Great Dragon of our legends, but he is also part of me. He is Fire, and I am Fire, sent to heal.

"I am the Flame Dancer, the element of fire clothed in flesh. I have kindred—the Stone Dancer, the Sea Dancer, the Wind Dancer, and the Soul Dancer. We five and our Companions, beings like the Dragon, will stand to save this world from the coming of the Shadow. But we cannot do it without our Lorekeepers. Melaan, take up this tale."

Melaan rose to her challenge and began to speak. "Four times before, a world has been created and the Dancers have tried to earn it permanence. Twice they have succeeded. Twice, they have failed. This time is the final Dance. If the Dancers succeed, then this world and the two others who have been spared will be allowed to continue. If they fail, all will be obliterated."

"Mirya, take up the tale," Kevla said, turning to the little five-score girl.

She swallowed hard, and spoke in a nervous voice. "The Lorekeepers have the knowledge of what has gone before. We were born to help the Dancers succeed by keeping that lore from being forgotten and lost forever."

Kevla smiled approvingly at the girl. "It's my understanding from the Dragon, and from what the Lorekeepers have told me, that other civilizations were wiser than we," she said. "They respected what their Lorekeepers said, they sought out and protected their Dancers. But we here in Arukan have been foolish. We suppressed our Lorekeepers. Called them mad."

Her eyes met those of her father's, and it was with difficulty that Tahmu did not avert his gaze.

"Called them *kulis*," Kevla said. "When I came into my powers, I was afraid and ashamed of them. It is only thanks to Jashemi-kha-Tahmu, the man who began this uniting of the clans, that I can now stand before you." She paused, and Tahmu saw her swallow hard, saw the pain in her eyes; pain he knew matched his own. Perhaps even exceeded it.

"It is with deep grief that I tell you that Jashemi is dead. He gave his life in order that I might finally understand who and what I am—who and what the Lorekeepers are. He believed that our powers had surfaced at this time because Arukan is in great danger. Our enemies have long been one another, but that cannot be allowed to continue. We must stand together, stand strong, against the enemy that approaches from over the mountains.

"Some of you may have noticed that there are a few clans who are not represented here today. It's not because they were afraid to come. It is because the armies of the Emperor have destroyed them. Those who did not die were taken and forced to serve beneath the standard of the kilyn. You know the flag I speak of, and yes, that strange creature has a name. There is a saying that we all know."

She paused and turned to the Dragon, who was watching her attentively. Kevla smiled at him and stroked him affectionately. "'When the Great Dragon rouses,'" she quoted, "'None shall stand against his flame.'"

Tahmu could have sworn the creature winked. Kevla turned to face the crowd again.

"That saying is true. The Dragon has roused, and the armies of the Emperor shall not stand against his flame."

"How do we know this is true?" came a frightened voice from the crowd. All heads turned to see who had spoken. It was a high-caste youth from the *Sa'abah* Clan. He was a little younger than Kevla and looked both defiant and frightened.

"Raka," Melaan began.

"No! How do we know this isn't all a lie? How do we know that she *isn't* a *kuli,* casting some sort of spell on us to dream the dreams she wants?"

"You see before you the Great Dragon," Kevla answered calmly. "Do you doubt the evidence of your own eyes?"

The boy lifted his chin defiantly, but Tahmu could see that he trembled.

"No one can subdue the Great Dragon. Maybe this is a spell, too. Maybe this isn't the Great Dragon at all, but an illusion that—"

The Dragon's serpentine head whipped around and he snorted, smoke erupting from his nostrils. Faster than Tahmu would have thought possible for so huge a creature, the Dragon moved toward the boy. It reached out a clawed foreleg, closed it around the terrified Raka, and lifted him high off the ground as it sat on its haunches. Raka was too frightened even to resist, and stared slack-jawed into the Great Dragon's golden eyes.

"Do I *look* like an illusion, boy?"

Raka started crying. The Dragon rolled his eyes. He gently put the boy back down on the sand and gave him an absent-minded pat. Raka's legs gave way and he sat down hard on the sand. He was completely unharmed; the Dragon had obviously intended only to intimidate. Which,

Tahmu mused as he looked at the faces around him, it had done very effectively.

"I can prove to you that what I say is true," said Kevla quickly, hastening to the Dragon and laying a tempering hand on his foreleg. "Tonight, the *khashim* of each clan will select someone he trusts. We will fly over the mountain and I will show you the army that is coming."

The Dragon turned to look at Kevla. He seemed displeased. "None but the Flame Dancer has ever sat upon my back," he said in a warning voice.

"Dragon," she said pleadingly, "you know as well as I what awaits these people. We cannot waste precious time convincing them that what we say is true. Please. As a favor to me."

If Tahmu had not seen it, he would not have believed it. The Great Dragon's harsh expression, for it had expressions as versatile as any human's, softened with affection.

"I can deny you nothing, Flame Dancer," he said. Turning back to the crowd, the Dragon bellowed, "Those of you who will sit upon my back tonight are honored beyond any men before. Burn this voyage into your memory, for your children's children will tell the tale of this night and the battle that awaits."

While they waited for nightfall, Kevla permitted herself to be amused by the homage the people paid their Great Dragon. Once they had gotten over the initial shock of seeing a creature out of legend in the flesh, many felt compelled to prostrate themselves at his feet. With a glint of laughter in his golden eyes, he respectfully listened to them, absolved them of any wrongdoings, real or imagined, and told them to listen to Kevla, for she was in charge now. They came with offerings of beautiful carvings and pots, water, and food, all of which the Dragon graciously refused.

"Your people need this more than I," he said. "Your sacrifice is noted, but take it back now that I have witnessed it. Feed your people."

When the last supplicant had reluctantly gathered his food and returned to his clan, the Dragon looked at Kevla ruefully.

"Is it hard, being a god?" she said with mock sympathy.

He sighed, blowing a gust of fiery breath over her. "You have no idea."

She also approached and welcomed her Lorekeepers. Some of them still seemed reticent, others eagerly went to her, even embraced her. She found she gravitated to Melaan. This was the man Jashemi had trusted, and as Second of a powerful clan, he had no small amount of influence. At one point, their eyes met and he nodded. Even without words, she knew what he was communicating: he would be there for her, at her right hand, no matter what came.

At last, Kevla judged that it was sufficiently dark. She was pleased that the moon was well on the wane. The last thing she wanted was to alert the Emperor or his armies that the foolish, scattered clans of Arukan knew about their approach—and had a dragon at their disposal.

She created several pillars of free-standing flame to illuminate the clearing in which the Dragon sat. She did so with an extra flamboyance, so that those gathered could see her powers.

Oh, Jashemi. Once, we were so afraid of our abilities; we hid them, we lied about them. Now, look at what I am doing. Look at how proud these people are to be Lorekeepers. I wish I could share this sweet moment with you.

Kevla stepped forward and surveyed the crowd. "The time has come," she said. "Who among you is brave enough to ride the Dragon?"

One person strode forward boldly. "I will ride the Dragon, with the Flame Dancer," said Tahmu-kha-Rakyn.

She gave him a grateful smile. Now others too came forward, until there were over a dozen. Still more came.

The Dragon arched an eyebrow. "My, you people have a lot of clans, don't you?"

"Dragon, can you bear so many?" Kevla asked solicitously.

He looked indignant. "I am not a mere *sa'abah*. I am the Great Dragon, a creature of magic. I will bear what I need to bear, as, my dear, will you. Well, let's be about it then."

With a grunt, he lowered himself to the earth, crouching on his haunches with his forelegs extended straight out in front of him. Even so, it was no easy feat for the men to clamber aboard his back. Kevla waited until they had all mounted, watching with satisfaction as fear turned into awed delight. Then she stepped astride the Dragon's lowered neck. Her father—*ai*, it was still so strange to think of the powerful Tahmu-kha-Rakyn that way—sat behind her.

Turning to look at the men, she called, "You must hold tightly to one another. You have been enemies before, but now your life depends on the man in front of and behind you. Grasp the Dragon's spine ridges as well, you won't hurt him."

When her father made no move to secure himself to her, she looked over her shoulder at him.

"It's all right," she said softly, for his ears alone. "You once put your arm around me like this to keep me from falling from Swift. Let me return the favor now."

An odd look passed over his face, then he nodded impassively. His strong arms went around her waist, and for an instant, she became that little girl again, spinning a marvelous fantasy about being the *khashim*'s daughter. She wondered if he, too, was reliving that moment.

But that was long ago, and the success of her journey now would affect more lives than those of herself and her father. She faced forward. When she was convinced they were ready, she nodded to the Dragon. She felt him gather himself, trying to adjust to the extra weight of so many riders. His big sides swelled, then subsided as he drew and expelled a breath. He lowered his head, and she sensed—there was no other word for it—the Dragon willing himself to carry this strange new weight. Then, as gently and smoothly as he could, the mighty creature leaped skyward.

Kevla smothered a grin as she heard gasps and oaths behind her. Her father tightened his grip around her waist reflexively, then she felt him force himself to relax.

She permitted herself to close her eyes and enjoy the feeling of the night wind on her face. How she loved this! The moment she had first tentatively mounted the Dragon, she felt an immediate sense of familiarity. She knew exactly how to balance herself and had a complete trust in her friend. The men behind her quieted, but she knew they were still anxious.

It was so peaceful, so quiet up here, away from the noises of the earth. The only sound was the steady, powerful rhythm of the Dragon's wings, and her own breath. Upward he went, until the campfires of the clans were nothing but tiny specks.

Now the Dragon gently turned toward the mountain range. It was strange to behold them, seemingly so tiny, when for so many centuries their fearsome, jagged peaks had effectively protected Arukan from the rest of the world. Mount Bari loomed over the rest as the Dragon approached the place that had been his home for so long.

Kevla craned her neck. "Look down," she cried to the men behind her. They all did so, and Kevla smiled. Through the haze of black smoke, she could see directly into the heart of the molten pool of liquid rock. Where she had submerged only to be reborn. Where the Dragon had slept for centuries, awaiting her.

But now the Dragon's deceptively easy wingbeats carried them smoothly over the Sacred Mountain, and Kevla felt her heart speed up as for the first time she, indeed any Arukani, beheld what lay on the other side of the mountain chain.

At first, this far side looked much like its twin in Arukan. Then, she caught sight of something in the distance.

They might not have believed words, she thought with a combination of exhilaration and apprehension, *but surely they will believe this.*

They would likely have no clear sight of the armies tonight, no soldiers or tents or engines of war. It was too dark for that; too dark, as well, for the Emperor's forces to see a mighty Dragon wheeling above them in the sky.

But the men perched atop that Dragon could see the army's fires.

Tiny little sparks they were, and at first, the eye could not be certain as to their identity. Gradually, the Dragon dove closer, and the small orange sparks became campfires.

There were hundreds on the other side of the mountain, several in each encampment.

The army of the Emperor from over the mountain had thousands.

Again, Kevla heard gasps and murmurings. The Dragon went lower still, sailing silently above a vast army that was almost invisible save for their campfires. Now they could glimpse movement, see the faint outlines of tents.

When at last the men behind her fell silent, Kevla patted the Dragon's neck. Obediently the great beast wheeled smoothly and returned the way he had come.

No one spoke on that journey back to the encampments. Tahmu kept his arms around his daughter, and at one point she could have sworn he pulled her closer to him. She did not think it was because he feared for his own safety.

Finally, the Dragon headed for the clearing, easily recognizable because of the circle of fires Kevla had left burning, and settled down gently. The men were in no hurry to dismount. Slowly, they did so, not speaking. Kevla remained atop the Dragon, waiting for their decision. Would they join her and fight for their own lives? Or would they scatter, seeing in their isolation an ability to escape from so terrible a foe?

Her mouth was dry and she was aware that she trembled. If they fled, there was no hope.

"Well?" she said finally. "You have seen the campfires with your own eyes. You know what is coming. The army will be here very soon. Will you stand and fight together, or will you scatter like frightened *liahs?*"

The first to step forward was Tahmu. "The Clan of Four Waters will fight with the Great Dragon and the Flame Dancer," he cried.

"As will the Star Clan!"

"And the *Sa'abah* Clan!"

"The Horseriders will prepare for war!"

"As will the Sandcattle Clan!"

One after another, the cries went up and the pledges were made. Not a single clan chose to abandon the others. Kevla felt her heart fill to almost bursting. They believed her. They trusted her.

Jashemi, this is your moment. This is your dream. I wish you could see them.

"We will have a council of war," announced Tahmu. He turned to his daughter. "Kevla Flame Dancer—will you join us?"

Kevla's eyes widened. This would be a council unlike any ever seen in Arukan before. All of the *khashims,* their Seconds, and their most trusted advisors would be present.

A female had never been permitted to participate.

Slowly, she nodded. "Of course," she said, and slipped off

the Dragon. Tahmu extended a hand to help her down. They stood face to face for a long minute, each searching the other's eyes.

In Tahmu's face, Kevla saw Jashemi. The two men, father and son, had been so alike, she now realized. They had shared the dream that was coming true at this moment, and she would be a part of that.

She squeezed her father's hand, and went to the council of war.

Chapter Twenty-Eight

*K*ayle's attendant Parneth stuck his head inside the captain's tent, grinning fiercely. "Captain? The scouts have returned."

"Excellent," said Kayle. "A moment more and I will meet with them." He took another bite of bread and honey. If Kayle had anything resembling a weakness, it was his fondness for sweet things. The golden liquid dripped off the bread onto his fingers and he sucked it off. He had gone ahead of the army with seven of his most trusted scouts, to find the best path through the mountains and, perhaps, to see if there were any unsuspecting Arukani clans within easy attack distance. Even though the army had many men, they could always use a few more.

"Captain." Parneth hesitated. "I think you had best meet with them now. They come with an extra prize for the Emperor."

Kayle sighed and rose, still licking his fingers. Parneth knew his master well, and would not push so if it were not important. However, when he stepped outside into the moonlight *and saw the "extra prize," Kayle thought he might enjoy see-ing Parneth beaten.*

He whirled on the younger man. "You interrupt my meal for a camp follower?" Other men might rush eagerly into the arms of such a lovely woman, but Kayle cared little for the pleasures offered by either sex. His passion was slaughter, and he pre-ferred to save his energies for that.

Admittedly, they'd found a good one. Not a maiden, but a woman, still in the prime of her beauty. She looked tired and hungry, but bore herself erectly.

"She is not what you think, my lord," said one of his scouts, exchanging grins with his companions. "We will let her speak for herself."

The woman stepped forward, and for an instant Kayle felt a strong urge to kneel in front of her, so commanding was her presence. The desire passed quickly.

"I have come to you with news for your Emperor, which he will wish to hear. You will take me to him."

"No, lady, I will not. You will speak your news to me, or I will cut out your tongue and you will speak it to no one."

She looked at him, a half smile on her lips. "Do you know, I believe you."

"You should," said Kayle. He had been in deadly earnest. "I have many things that demand my attention, lady. Speak quickly."

"I know you recognize what I once was," she said. "I hear it in your voice. You know nobility when you see it, what-ever tattered rags it comes dressed in. I was once the khashima of a great House in Arukan—the greatest House. Now, I am nothing but a camp follower. How I fell to this is not important. What is important is that you believe that my desire to have revenge upon my husband and his peo-ple is real."

Kayle's single eye searched her, taking her in, from her long hair to her elegant features to her body. The clothing she wore had indeed been fine once, but was now filthy and stank of sweat. While she was thin, she did not have the aged, emaciated look of one who had lived a step away from starvation all her life. This was a woman who had once lived in luxury.

"Go on."

"You have been preying on the clans one by one," she said, "but they have seen your numbers and know what you have planned. In turn, they have abandoned their differences and will greet your army united."

Kayle scowled and looked to his scouts for confirmation.

"It is true, sir," said the head scout. "We were shocked when we cleared the range and saw so many campfires. Somehow, they know. I saw hundreds."

"We have thousands," retorted Kayle, but still he felt a quiver of doubt. It was one thing to descend upon small groups and conquer them one by one. To face all the Arukani clans together would necessitate different tactics. The Emperor needed to know as soon as possible.

But apparently, the woman was not yet done. "I have followed my former Clan to this meeting place. I have watched what has transpired there. I have listened in the shadows and I know their numbers, their plans, their weapons, and I know of an enemy that would make even your Emperor quail where he stands."

"Then tell me, lady. My meal is not getting any warmer."

"In exchange for safe passage in your country," she replied. "Food, water, clothing, money. I will not return to the land of my shame."

He had thought to kill her; it was just easier that way. But the honey had sweetened more than his tongue tonight, and he was in a good mood. While the news she bore was not good, her coming was welcomed in that the Emperor would have time to change his approach. Kayle decided that if what she had to say pleased him, he would give her what she wanted. If not, he'd carry out his original plan.

Kayle turned to his scouts and again raised an eyebrow in question. "We have been able to verify some of what she told us, sir," their leader replied. "And the information is valuable indeed."

"Very well," he said. "Come into my tent and eat and drink your fill. And then, traitor, tell me all you know, and how best I can use this information to slaughter your people."

For a moment, he thought he saw hesitation flicker across her lovely features. Then her face hardened and her eyes looked bright with an emotion he recognized as pure hatred.

"Do you have eusho?" *she asked.*

The council had gone well. Not only was Kevla present, but she had insisted that all the Lorekeepers—men and women—and the Great Dragon be in attendance as well. Some of the *khashims* looked as if they would have seizures when she spoke her conditions, but they gave in.

First, Melaan spoke briefly as to the history of the situation. Two others who had managed to elude the Emperor on a previous occasion told of what they saw. Each clan leader told how many men, weapons and provisions he had brought to contribute to the cause.

Preparations for war began in earnest. While many, such as the Clan of Four Waters, had listened to Kevla's plea and arrived ready for battle, others had simply come to hear what she had to say. Now, these clans sent out dozens of hawks, calling for reinforcements. Some would arrive in time, others would not.

Each night, Kevla and the Dragon soared over Mount Bari to spy on the approaching troops. The army was massive, and because of its size it moved slowly. Also, the mountain chain was not forgiving, and it was difficult to move so many men, beasts and pieces of equipment up its forbidding slopes.

On the third night, Kevla and the Dragon were return- ing to the clan encampments when the Dragon said, "Kevla. Look down. Do you see them?"

"What am I looking for?" asked Kevla. There was an odd note in the Dragon's voice and she did not think he was trying to draw her attention to a herd of *liahs*.

"Men," the Dragon said simply.

She looked harder and then she saw them: eight or so, clad in the strange metal clothing of the Emperor's army. They had only two horses and moved with purpose. At first, Kevla thought they were coming to attack the clans, but then she realized that they were moving up the moun- tain, not down it.

"They're a scouting party," she said. "They've seen us."

The Dragon craned his neck to look at her, his golden eyes glowing in the darkness. "Until now, the Emperor has assumed that the clans could be picked off one by one," he said. "If these scouts report what they have seen—"

"They'll know we're waiting for them," she finished.

"They can't be allowed to report back."

"I know, but...."

"I understand this is difficult for you," said the Dragon, "but you have done this before."

Suddenly Kevla had had her fill of these reminders of lives past. Of people she had been, who Jashemi had been, who had lived and died and still lived and—

"No, I haven't!" she cried. "I, Kevla Bai-sha, have killed no one! I haven't even deliberately hurt anyone! I don't want to kill these people, Dragon. I just want—"

"I know what you want," the Dragon said harshly, "*who* you want. But you can't have him, Kevla. Jashemi is dead. Your old life is dead. And your new life and the lives of almost everyone else down there are going to be lost if you don't accept the responsibility that comes with being who you are! You're the leader, Flame Dancer, and you've got to be bigger now than Kevla has ever been. The boy died so you could become the Flame Dancer. Don't let his death be in vain!"

Kevla was as startled as if he had splashed cold water on her face. She was terribly hurt, and very angry. How dare he speak to her like this!

"A few more moments, Flame Dancer," said the Dragon in a soft, angry voice, "and you will lose the chance. They will be far enough up the mountain so that the enemy will see our fire."

Kevla's lower lip quivered. "I can't murder them."

"Then they will reach the Emperor, and he will learn the truth about the force that faces him, and more of your people will die."

Kevla swallowed hard. "What do I do? How do I fight them?"

"Like this," said the Dragon, and dove.

Kayle had been more than pleased at what the Arukani woman had told him. She had a good eye for what mattered; she said she had been married to a clan leader and was familiar with such things. His luck. He was so delighted with the information that he kept his word and sent her walking off with food and gold. Privately, he thought she would die in the mountains before she reached the other side, but he didn't care.

He wished he'd thought to bring a hawk, so the news would reach his Emperor even more swiftly. As it was, it would take most of the night for the men to rejoin the main army.

Parneth's high-pitched shriek was the first warning he had of death from the sky.

Kayle whirled, sword at the ready, to behold a sight that froze him in place. The female traitor had warned him of this, but he had only half believed her. In the sky flew an enormous beast, its huge wings bringing it closer more rapidly than he had thought possible for something so big. He put a name to it, that of a creature out of legend: Dragon. *A heartbeat later the monster opened its mouth and a sheet of flame spewed forth.*

The blast of heat knocked Kayle off his feet. He could smell burning flesh and realized that some of his men had not escaped the blast. He dove for cover, frantically trying to wedge his large, muscular body in among the rocks.

The dragon's mouth closed and it turned, wheeling around for a second dive. Thinking he had a few moments before the next attack, Kayle got to his feet and scrambled for a more protected area.

But more fire came. How was that possible? The dragon was facing away, it couldn't—

Glanced up wildly, Kayle now saw that the dragon had an ally. This, then, was the Flame Dancer the woman had warned him about. The traitor had not been exaggerating. How could the Emperor stand against this? Even as Kayle watched, motionless with fear and knowing he needed to find shelter, the figure lifted its arms. Fire came from its hands—her hands—and rushed toward him in an orange-red ball.

In the instant before his death, Kayle did not think of his Emperor, or the warning he needed to bring him, or anything else remotely related to war or death.

He thought about the look on his adopted mother's face as she left him with the captain of the guards, and realized that she had loved him.

Atop the Great Dragon out of legend, the Flame Dancer continued to hurl fireballs at the scouts of the Emperor from over the mountain. She kept up the attack until the Dragon banked sharply to the right and rose even higher.

"It's done now," he said gently. "They're all dead."

They're all dead.

"You did what you had to do to protect your people."

She realized that she had been holding every muscle in her body taut as a bow string. Suddenly she shivered and leaned down on the Dragon's neck, wrapping both arms and legs about it. Kevla began to shudder and sob, hearing and feeling the Dragon utter soothing words.

They're all dead.

Father says you get used to it.

Slowly, she sat up and dried her tears. This was but a taste of what would come later. She had to be strong. She couldn't let herself feel the enormity of what she had just done.

"Take me back, Dragon," she said.

Chapter Twenty-Nine

*T*he advisor pulled aside the tent flap cautiously. "Your Excellency," he said, "you do not sleep?"

The Emperor scowled at the brazier that still glowed brightly and kept the chill of the desert night at bay. That was one thing they had not counted on: how very cold it got here at night. The contrasts were startling, to say the least. The ki-lyn, too, was wide-awake, huddled and shivering, but from cold or fear, the advisor could not say. He did not care to speculate.

"Do I look as though I am asleep?" the Emperor snapped. He glanced up, and the advisor was startled at the hollows underneath the Emperor's eyes. "One of them *is* there. I know it."

Fear flooded the advisor. "Surely, not, Your Excellency. You are weary. Perhaps your…intuition is playing tricks on you."

The Emperor shook his head. "It's faint. It shouldn't be. I should know which one it is, who it is. I ought to be able to sense—"

He slammed his fist down on the small table next to him and his cup of wine went flying. The ki-lyn started and tried to avoid the object. It pulled away it but was caught up short, gasping as the collar around its neck halted its movement and the ever-present chain that connected it to the Emperor pulled taut. The ceramic cup struck its head. Red wine splashed and trickled down its long neck, looking for all the world like blood. The creature folded its delicate, graceful legs beneath it again and simply sat, shivering.

"It's stopping me, somehow," said the Emperor, glaring at the ki-lyn. "It hates me. It wants me to fail." The creature shrank back from the loathing in that gaze.

"Why must you keep it?" asked the advisor. "If you just had it killed—"

The look the Emperor gave him made his legs quiver. "If you suggest that again," the Emperor said with deceptive calm, "I'll cut off your head myself and stick it on a pike."

"Yes, Your Excellency," stammered the advisor.

The Emperor sighed and rubbed his eyes. "I imagine you had a reason for coming here?"

"Yes, of course. We have had several desertions."

"That's to be expected, this close to their homes."

"It's not helping morale, Your Excellency. Should I make an example of the ones who remain?"

"Did they try to desert?"

The advisor was flustered. "Well, no, but they are Arukani and—"

"And we need every one of them right now. We don't know what's going to greet us on the other side of the mountains."

The advisor swallowed hard. "Speaking of that, Your Excellency....the scouts have not yet returned."

The Emperor stared at him. "No, of course they haven't," he said softly. "He's gotten to them. That's how I knew he was here—he attacked." Harshly, he jerked the golden chain and

*the ki-lyn made a strangled sound. "Why won't you let me
see him?"*

*The advisor eyed the creature with distaste. "Your powers
will grow with time, Your Excellency. Surely, even that creature
will not be able to hold you back much longer."*

*"That is true," said the Emperor thoughtfully. "Go to bed.
We will march in the morning. I still have the advantage of
numbers, even if my magic is stifled. We will hurt the Arukani
badly and take their country. If one of them is there, I will deal
with him when I see him, this pathetic thing be damned."*

Kevla kept her face as calm as possible when she told the
khashims about the attack on the scouts. They were
alarmed that the enemy had gotten this far, but praised her
and the Dragon for their quick thinking in destroying the
threat.

"There is more," she said, trying not to curl protectively
in on herself. On the way back, something had brushed her
thoughts that still made her quail. Something that was
angry, and dark, and powerful.

"I do not think we are dealing with an ordinary army. I
sense...I sense that there is magic here as well. Abilities that
haven't shown themselves yet."

"We cannot fight magic," protested young Raka.

Kevla turned to him. "Yes, we can," she insisted. "There
are many toiling up the sides of these mountains now who
eat, sleep, sweat, and bleed just like you do." *Just like the
scouts did.* "If you deal them a lethal blow, they will most
certainly die."

The words came easily out of her mouth, but inwardly
she grieved their utterance. It was so strange, to be talking
so comfortably about killing. Only a few weeks ago, she was
merely a servant in a great house, her only concern when
she would next see Jashemi. Now, she rode the Great

Dragon of story and song as comfortably as she had ridden a *sa'abah*, and had used her fire skills to take lives. The love and light of her life was dead by the same magic that now needed to be turned against the advancing army, and all the leaders of all the clans were looking to her to save them.

Her power was great. Startling, wondrous, amazing, and she knew she had not begun to probe its limits. But she would have traded it all for one more conversation with Jashemi, alone in the cavern at the House of Four Waters, ignorant of the blood bond between them and feeling only a deep and profound connection.

She blinked and came out of her reverie as one of the *khashims* was speaking and, blushing, had to ask him to repeat his question.

"When will they arrive?"

She and the Dragon had discussed this. "Judging by the progress they have made so far, we have until the day after tomorrow."

"Then we must make haste," said Tahmu, "to get everything in place. We must be ready for them."

That night, Kevla curled up close to the Dragon, and away from the prying eyes of the clansmen of Arukan grieved for all that she had lost.

The day of the battle dawned clear and bright, one of the loveliest mornings Kevla had ever seen. She had been awake for some time, addressing each of the separate forces in turn, sending them off to fight with inspirational words that she wasn't sure she believed. Her exchange with her father, who was leading one group, had been stiff and formal. She was not sure that was how she wanted it, but any conversation with him would be highly emotional, and instinctively she knew she needed to guard against that right now. She needed to keep everything tightly in check, or else, like Mount Bari, she would erupt.

Melaan accompanied her as she walked to where the Dragon waited. At one point, he said, "It was supposed to be Jashemi, wasn't it?"

Color rushed to her cheeks. "What do you mean?"

"Over these last few days, I have become the closest Lorekeeper to you. I'm the one you turn to when you need information, when you need to have word spread among the Lorekeepers. You have trusted me, and you honor me beyond words with that trust. But it wasn't supposed to be me. It was supposed to be Jashemi."

"Yes. It was."

"Kevla—how did he die?"

She didn't want to answer, but she looked at him with such a stricken expression that she felt sure he guessed at some of the truth. His face softened and he reached to squeeze her arm. "Be careful, Flame Dancer. Any of us is expendable. Even Jashemi was. But you aren't."

His words were obviously meant to comfort, but they had the opposite effect. Kevla didn't want any of this. She didn't want to be the leader of a force of armed men more than three thousand strong. She didn't want to be perched atop a dragon, knowing that she had almost unimaginable power at her fingertips, getting ready to use that magic to kill.

But she had to be here. She had to do what she didn't want to do, so that her people would survive. This strange Emperor had little mercy, and she harbored no illusions that he would accept anything other than complete victory.

She was shaking and her stomach roiled as she mounted the Dragon. Her mouth was dry as the sand, and no amount of liquid from a waterskin eased it.

The Dragon crouched, then leaped into the sky. The earth fell away from them. Kevla looked down, watching as the tents grew smaller, and the warriors looked like small white dots on the sand. As they went higher, Kevla was able to see all four of the separate fronts the gathered clans had formed standing ready to meet the enemy. The Dragon's wings beat the air steadily and they flew even higher. The faint sunlight touched the white stuff on the top of the mountains, turning it a delicate shade of rose-gold. Kevla laughed aloud at the thought of such a pretty color heralding a morning that would end with blood spilled on the sands. She clapped her hand to her mouth, stifling the hysteria.

It was at that moment that the first wave of soldiers crested the mountain ridge.

The Dragon said nothing; he must have felt her subtly tighten her legs as she sat astride him. For a long moment, Kevla looked at the men as she and the *khashims* had discussed. She was trying to guess their numbers, but the sheer mass of them was so great it overwhelmed her senses. It was like a flood, a river, a—

"At least five thousand in this first wave," came the Dragon's calm, deep voice, cutting through her shock. "They are the vanguard, making preparations for the second, third and fourth waves."

Twenty thousand men to the Arukani's three thousand, then. Kevla took a deep breath and tried not to give in to despair and panic.

As she and the *khashims* had discussed in their strategy sessions, the Emperor's army was using the only pass between the mountains. It curved around the peak of Mount Bari, creating a flat saddle for a few leagues, and then wound down through the jutting, raw-looking areas of the mountain and into the softer, swelling foothills.

The first line of Arukan's defense was waiting along that pass. Kevla could not see them now, but she knew they were there. They had taken position well before dawn, and would stay in hiding until the moment was right to attack. The enemy was approaching slowly, about ten abreast through the narrow passage. The ones in front had long, sharp spears. The ones who followed managed horses which pulled wagons covered with blankets to conceal their cargo. Other machines of war came into sight now, cresting the mountain and moving along the flat part of the pass. Many of them she could not put names to. One looked like a giant bow, lying flat across the wagon instead of being held properly upright, the arrows which were lashed to it twice the length of ordinary ones. For an instant, Kevla let herself wonder how such a thing could be aimed and released.

Suddenly the Arukani archers leaped from hiding. Arrows rained upon the approaching army so thickly that for a moment Kevla's vision was obscured. The strange metal the men wore protected them from some of the arrows, but not all; many fell, as did their unprotected horses, amid shrieks and screams of pain.

"First line, fire!" cried Melaan. Two dozen archers leaped up from where they had been hiding. Their clothing had been carefully chosen to blend in with the natural hues of the stone, and Melaan felt hope rekindle in him as every one of the Arukani archers took down an enemy. He stood behind a large boulder, which protected him and allowed him to see in almost every direction.

"Drop! Second line, fire!" The first line fell back into hiding, to refit arrows to their string, and the second line erupted. More of the Emperor's men fell.

"Drop! Third line, fire!"

But this time, as the third line of defense leaped up, the Emperor's men were ready for them. Some fired their own arrows almost as quickly as the Arukani. Others headed to where they knew the archers lay in concealment. Leaping over the stony ground, they jumped headlong into the Arukani hiding places. An arrow was no match for a sword at close range, and Melaan heard the grunts and screams as his men began to die.

He had expected this. It was why he had volunteered to lead this front, insisting that his *khashim* fight elsewhere. Melaan had no wife or family, unlike Terku. The men who had agreed to hold this first line of defense had done so in the full knowledge that they would be the first to die.

"Drop! Fourth line, fi—"

He never saw the arrow, nor heard it sing as it flew with deadly accuracy. Suddenly, he found himself facedown on the stone, unable to move. Breathing was agony and his legs felt cold.

From where he had fallen, he could see boots running toward him. They stopped in front of him and then he heard a sound he knew; the sound of a sword slicing through the air.

Be careful, Kevla.

Kevla watched in horror as the balance shifted abruptly and the Emperor's men began firing on the Arukani. Some ducked back to safety; others clutched their chests and toppled from Kevla's sight among the boulders.

The attack continued, and while the advance was slowed, it was not stopped. Fewer arrows came from the Arukani side; fewer men rose to fire them.

Kevla swallowed hard and tried not to count up the dead. The rest of the clans' warriors waited in plain sight, at the base of the mountain, armed and silent. Their numbers were a handful compared to what was spilling over the mountainside. Her people were waiting to be slaughtered.

Suddenly, a fierce protectiveness welled inside Kevla. It snuffed out her panic, her fear, her sense of inadequacy, as easily as she might snuff out a candle. She felt as if there was something deep inside her, growing larger, pushing her to extend and open. She was bigger than Kevla Bai-sha. She was bigger than any of the other lives she had ever lived. Her people needed her to be there for them, to fight for them, to embrace every bit of what it meant to be the Flame Dancer, both the light and the dark. She didn't have the luxury of being small anymore, of being afraid of her powers, of being unwilling to use everything she could to defend and protect. And with that surrender, she felt power and knowledge flow into her.

She had been clutching the Dragon's spine ridge so tightly that her hands ached, but now she released her grip. She did not need to worry about balance. She was the Dragon, and it was her. There was no risk of falling.

Kevla lifted her hands, feeling the movement as sensuous and graceful, and for the first time understood on a primal level why the guardians of the worlds were called Dancers.

It is like a dance, she marveled. *I know each step, but I don't know that I know it—*

Suddenly her mind was filled with images of Jashemi holding her, kissing her, making love to her. That fire that had burned in her, roused by his touch, smoldered inside her still. She could call on it, control it. Use it to protect her people.

Her eyes flew open. Her vision took on a clarity it had never had before. Her skin sensed the wind caressing it with vibrant intensity. Everything was heightened, sensitive—ready to accept Fire.

Attuned to her as he was, the Dragon sensed her readiness and swooped down toward the Sacred Mountain. Kevla stared at it, at the smoke that drifted upward. In her mind's eye, she saw again the pool of red-orange liquid. She reached out toward it with her mind and her hands as if to embrace it.

"Not yet," cautioned the Dragon. Kevla blinked as if emerging from a trance and saw the wisdom in his words. The army had only begun to come down the mountain. She looked over her shoulder at the tiny figures of the clans of Arukan.

"Dragon, they're dying down there!"

"I know," he said, gently. "But you must wait."

Kevla kept the simmering energy bottled inside her. Wait. Wait.

The sun rose higher and more soldiers flooded down the mountainside. Tahmu, atop Swift-Over-Sand, tensed, but did not charge.

"Hold your ground!" he cried. His men, many from his own Clan but a greater number from the Star Clan and the Horserider Clan, shifted uneasily. He shared their feelings. He had sent his best archers up to the pass, and had watched them kill and be killed with pain and resignation. This was the first place where the Arukani army—strange, to think of it that way—had tried to dam the flood of warriors. They had slowed it, but not stopped it.

Now, it was Tahmu's turn to try to hold them before they reached the open plains. His heart pounded in his chest and every sense was alert as he watched them come, some on foot, some on horses. *Wait. Wait. Let them come to us, waste their energy in running.*

"Now!" he cried, and kicked Swift. The warhorse charged, snorting. A hundred other mounted warriors did likewise. Scimitars glinted in the bright morning light as Tahmu's men surged forward, greeting the enemy with naked steel and the resolve that can only come from defending one's homeland.

Tahmu grunted as he swung his scimitar. The men were armed and armed well, and some of the men he led had already fallen beneath their blades, but they were not invincible. Their metal was vulnerable at the joints of neck and shoulder, and once he had spotted the weakness he did not hesitate to exploit it.

Suddenly, Swift screamed and collapsed beneath him. Tahmu barely leaped clear in time. Landing on his feet, he whirled to look at his mount. Swift had been eviscerated by a single long stroke. The blow had missed Tahmu's leg by a hair's breadth. Now the mighty beast churned up sand with its frantic kicking, his entrails spilling forth in a glistening red pool.

Pain sliced through Tahmu's heart. He had ridden Swift for over two decades. Even as he mourned his fallen friend, his heightened senses alerted him to danger and he whirled, bringing up the scimitar just in time to block a sword stroke.

For the briefest span of time, he thought about allowing the enemy to take him. He would make a good end that way, dying in battle. The way he died would be more honorable, more respected, than the way he had lived. It would be sweet, to put down the burden of guilt he bore for all the wrong choices, the lives lost.

But no. That was a coward's way out. Whatever his flaws, Tahmu knew he was a strong and cunning warrior, and Kevla needed every one of her warriors now if she was to succeed. Her success, the protection of their people, was more important to Tahmu than any false peace he could achieve by bowing his neck to the enemy's blade.

He parried his foe's next stroke, calmly eyed the gap in the enemy's armor, and with powerful arms that were strong and sure he struck.

It was then that the sheets of flame erupted.

Kevla watched as the Arukani battled the flank that charged forward, but her attention was caught by the second flank. They busied themselves digging ditches and pouring barrels of fluid into the channels. One of them touched a torch to the shiny pools and leaped back.

Fire sped along the pool and Kevla realized what they were doing. The warriors in the first wave were a sacrifice, a distraction. Now the army had made what they perceived to be a successful defense against the gathered Arukani— a wall of flame with a heavily guarded break.

They're protecting themselves from attack until the rest of them get here, Kevla thought. She felt her lips twist in a harsh smile.

"Take me closer," she called to the Dragon.

"Kevla, I don't—"

"Take me closer!" she cried, anger flooding her. The Dragon obeyed, tucking his wings and diving down at a staggering speed. Kevla extended her arms out to her sides, her movements fluid and in control. She fastened her eyes on the leaping flames, concentrating on them.

As if they were living things, the sheets of flame dove for their tenders. Men staggered and fell, uselessly beating their bodies in an attempt to douse the fire. Others, seeing what was happening, turned to behold the Great Dragon swooping down. He opened his mouth and breathed a long sheet of flame, further adding to the conflagration.

Kevla heard a strange noise. It was a sharp pinging sound. It took her a moment to realize what it was as an arrow whizzed past her ear. The sound was that of arrows striking the Dragon's heavily scaled frame.

Suddenly, she felt giddy, indestructible. The fire blazed through her and she had never felt more alive in her life. She began singling out men, taking aim and reaching out to them, the fire forming at her fingertips to rush in a glowing orange ball toward their chests.

Abruptly the Dragon began climbing upward again. The pinging diminished.

"Why did you—" Kevla began, but the Dragon interrupted her.

"Look at the pass," he cried. She did as he asked. Many more had come over in the time she had spent battling the front line. It was at least double, perhaps triple the numbers. She could see that the Arukani line of defense was falling back; could see fallen bodies in _rhias_ being trampled upon in the melee.

Now.

Rage boiled inside her, and she turned again to face Mount Bari, to summon in her mind's eye the image of the boiling pits of liquid fire.

Come forth!

She heard the rumbling even from this distance, and knew that those with their feet on the earth could feel it. Perspiration dewed her forehead and she began to breathe raggedly. It was harder to control than she had expected, but she called it, and it came.

Lava erupted from the depths of the earth with a terrible roar. Bright orange flowed down the mountainside.

"Take me down," she called to the Dragon. "I need to be closer!"

He obliged. She could see the individual rocks in the tide of liquid fire now, darker spots being swept along in the glowing yellow-orange flow. With a flick of her fingers, she summoned more lava. It spilled over another side of Mount Bari, this flow streaming over the pass. Anyone who had not yet crossed into Arukani lands now was completely cut off. A good quarter of the army would now never make it down the mountain.

The first stream twisted and snaked downward. It chased the men, who screamed and ran before it, into the waiting arms of the Arukani clans. Those who were not swift enough were engulfed in its lethal wave. Men, horses, wagons, casks of oil that exploded on contact, weapons—all fell beneath the merciless lava flow.

She heard the cries of the armies as they met in battle, heard the clash of steel on steel, but suddenly her attention was directed to a handful of men. Some of them clustered around the enormous bow and were pointing up at the dragon. Straining, they tilted the weapon skyward and fitted an arrow. One of them leaned forward, using his weight to pull back the string and—

Numbed with horror, it seemed forever until Kevla regained the use of her tongue.

"Dragon, watch—"

She felt the impact of the enormous arrow as it plunged into the Dragon's body. He let out a dreadful cry and bucked. Kevla clung to his neck, and looking down she could see the awful thing impaled in his left side, between his mighty forepaw and his wing. It had gone deep, and for a long, terrible moment, the Dragon's wings stopped beating.

He bellowed in pain and began to stroke the air once again, desperately trying to keep them both aloft and alive, turning away from the dreadful bow.

Fear for her friend erased everything else. She hugged him, leaning on his neck to cry to him, "Get down, get down! You're hurt!"

Kevla heard a stinging sound and felt a hard blow to her back that almost knocked her off the Dragon. Searing pain ripped through her and she couldn't breathe. Something wet was tricking down her right breast. She looked down and for a moment didn't see the blood, the same color as her flame-created clothing. There was a lump where there shouldn't be and—

A wave of dizziness and white-hot agony swept over her

as she reached with her left hand and her questing fingers found the sharp metal tip of an arrow protruding through her shoulder.

"Kevla!" roared the Dragon. "Fight it, Kevla...."

But she couldn't. The world began to turn gray. Kevla swayed forward and tumbled from the Dragon's back.

Chapter Thirty

Tahmu had watched in awe along with everyone else as Kevla turned the army's own fire against them and caused Mount Bari to erupt.

The sight had rejuvenated the forces he commanded. They now shrieked their battle cries and fell upon their foes with fresh passion. The Emperor's men, by contrast, seemed stunned by the unexpected and shocking turn of events. Some dropped their weapons. Others surrendered eagerly, and Tahmu realized that several of the men they were fighting were actually Arukani.

One boy fell to his feet in front of Tahmu and begged, "Please, lord, they forced us to fight, spare me, spare me!"

"Get up!" cried Tahmu. "Drop your weapons. Keep your hands in front of you so no one will think you armed and head for the tents!"

Others, overhearing, imitated the boy, dropping their

weapons and rushing gratefully to safety. Tahmu wondered if this was a battle or a rescue mission.

There came a brief lull in the battle and as Tahmu wiped sweat and blood from his face, his gaze traveled skyward. He saw the Dragon wheeling, saw Kevla as a tiny shape atop it.

Tahmu frowned. Something was wrong.

The Dragon was flying erratically, and as Tahmu watched in horror, a small shape toppled forward from the safety of the Dragon's broad back.

"Kevla!" he cried in impotent horror as his daughter hurtled toward the earth. There was nothing he could do for her, nothing to stop her downward plummet.

The Dragon dove, extending his enormous forepaws and catching the falling woman just in time. Relief washed over Tahmu.

She was safe. His daughter was safe.

"My lord!" The voice was Dumah's. Recovering himself, Tahmu whirled just in time to parry a stroke and begin a counterattack.

Kevla awoke from dreams of pain to the reality of agony. She was lying on her side, and as she tried to draw breath the pain increased a thousandfold.

"Gently," came a familiar voice. "Don't move. Asha is working on your injury now."

Kevla blinked, trying to keep still. "My lord?"

Tahmu was there, kneeling in front of her, tenderly holding one of her hands in his. "Don't speak, Kevla."

But she had to. "The Dragon...he's hurt, too...."

"Do not fear for me, I am all right." Despite the reassuring words, the Dragon's voice was laced with pain. He moved so she could see him. "They were able to remove the arrow. I will heal."

Tears trickled down her face. "I'm glad," she whispered,

then arched in torment as behind her, someone touched her back.

"Careful, Asha!" cried Tahmu.

"My lord, I am sorry, but—may I speak with you?"

Tahmu squeezed Kevla's hand and then rose. He and his healer walked off a few steps and conversed in whispers. Kevla locked eyes with the Dragon.

"Make them tell me," she whispered. "I need to know."

He nodded his understanding, lifted his head and bellowed, "Tell her what is wrong, Asha!"

The healer knelt in front of her, looking more sorrowful and frightened than she had ever seen him.

"It's bad, Kevla," he said. "An arrow entered your back at an angle. The shaft runs all through your body. The tip comes out in your shoulder. I fear that I will be unable to remove it without causing fatal damage."

Kevla blinked, not comprehending. To have come this far, to have endured so much, and now one arrow would take her life? Doom the whole world?

She started to shake her head, then hissed as the movement exacerbated the pain. She licked her lips and spoke.

"No. There has to be a way."

"Truly, there is not. Nothing has been pierced yet, but the arrow's shaft...." Aware that he was repeating himself, Asha fell silent. Tahmu shoved him aside and again gripped his daughter's hand, his gaze roaming over her face.

"Dragon," Kevla whispered, looking into her father's eyes. "Dragon, you know more about me than I know about myself. Is there nothing that can be done?"

"Yes, there is. But it will be difficult."

Hope swelled inside her, dimming the pain ever so slightly. Tahmu looked up at the Dragon.

"Save her."

"She must save herself."

"How is she to do that?" Tahmu demanded. "She lies near death, an arrow running the length of her body!"

Kevla closed her eyes, drifting. The Dragon continued to speak, but she barely heard him.

"The arrow is made of wood. You are the Flame Dancer. You must burn it, Kevla. Burn it to ashes inside of you. Burn it away to nothing. You know how to do this."

Because I did it to Jashemi. Tears leaked past her closed lids.

"Fire destroys," said the Dragon, as if she had spoken aloud, "but it also cleanses and purifies. Burn the arrow shaft, and cauterize your wounds."

It sounded so easy and so difficult at the same time. She was holding on to consciousness by a thread, only faintly aware of the pressure of her father's hand on hers.

"Kevla, you must do as the Dragon says," Tahmu said softly. "I have forsaken Keishla and lost Jashemi. Don't let the Emperor take my daughter, too."

Slowly, she opened her eyes. She had never seen him look like this; not when she told him about Jashemi, not when he had taken his blood-marked daughter to give to the Dragon. On his strong, handsome face were mingled hope and fear and...love?

Quickly, before she lost her courage, she squeezed her eyes shut and visualized the arrow that had pierced her body. It sprang to her mind's eye immediately. She could see its harsh wooden shaft embedded in her flesh. She understood now the reason for Asha's concern; it would indeed have been impossible to remove.

But not to immolate.

Kevla, my love, you are fire!

She gasped and arched her body as the heat began to burn from deep inside her. It spread rapidly through her body, and she felt her father drop her hand; no doubt it was too hot for him to continue to hold. She willed her body to consume the wooden arrow shaft, and she screamed aloud as the internal heat increased. She felt the shaft catch fire and burn to ashes in the space of one heartbeat to the next.

More. She needed to do more.

The ashes inside her continued to be consumed. Burned away until they had completely dissolved. Now she turned her attention to the entry wound in her lower back, willing her body to concentrate the heat there. She heard gasps and low talking as her father, Asha and the Dragon, and whoever else had clustered around to witness, saw what they could only call a miracle. One final, excruciatingly hot burst, and then it was over.

She had been sweating profusely, but her skin was dry. It was so hot that her sweat had evaporated instantly. Kevla gasped in short, harsh breaths, willing the fire to fade, to leave, to return to wherever it dwelt deep inside of her until she called it again. Slowly, the nearly unbearable heat subsided.

Kevla opened her eyes. "Asha," she whispered, her hands fluttering to her shoulder. "You can cut out the arrowhead now."

She closed her eyes and knew no more.

The man resembled those who had attacked her people, but Kevla knew he was not one of them. Tall, with yellow hair, he waited for her on a hill covered with white. She walked toward him, and the strange whiteness melted at her footsteps.

His face had laugh lines around the bright blue eyes, but now those eyes were hardened with pain and anger. This was a man who understood suffering, and who also understood the desire for vengeance.

And sitting at his feet, blue stripes running along its body, was a creature that resembled a simmar.

Jashemi's dream, she thought; I am dreaming Jashemi's dream. Floating toward her as she slowly swam toward the waking world came a voice she knew and loved. Jashemi's.

"You must hurry, Flame Dancer. Hurry, or you will be too late."

When she awoke, it was to find the Dragon gazing down at her. "You'd sleep through an avalanche, wouldn't you?"

She grinned up at him. The grin faded as memories flooded back: the memory of fireballs leaving her hands to destroy an enemy, the memory of a flow of molten stone that obeyed her commands to engulf hundreds, perhaps thousands, in its flood.

The memory of turning an arrow shaft to ashes inside her own body.

He helped her sit up. "How are you feeling?"

"Better," she said. Her garment had been cut away so that Asha could tend to her injured shoulder. It was bandaged securely. She winced. "It hurts."

"I imagine it would," said the Dragon. "You melted the arrowhead itself. When Asha removed it, it was but a molten lump of metal." He eyed her. "You can heal the wound, too, if you choose to do so."

She shrank from invoking that power again so soon. It was still so strange and frightening to her. But her dream had been laced with urgency, and she would not serve her great duty if she were injured and taking time to heal.

"I don't want to leave so soon," she said softly.

"I know," said the Dragon. "But the other Dancers are ready, and you have made an enemy here."

"The Emperor," she said, and he nodded. "I felt him. He is full of hatred. He—he wants the Dancers dead, doesn't he?"

Slowly, the Dragon nodded. "I am not certain, but thus far, I think he is only aware of you. You need to find the other four, Kevla. Trust me, they are ready. Fire has always been the leader, the most passionate of the four Dancers. They will follow you."

She let out a shaky laugh. "Follow me, Kevla Bai-sha. It seems absurd."

"But you know it is not undeserved," he said. "You know how well you fought today."

Bile rose in her throat as she heard again the cries of the dying. She would probably never know exactly how many lives she had taken today, and she did not want to.

"I did what I had to do."

"As the Dancers and Lorekeepers ever have," he said gently. "Call on the power again, Kevla. Heal yourself."

Slowly, she put her left hand to her right shoulder and, wincing, undid the bandages. The wound was clean, but deep where Asha had dug out the arrowhead. The heat came so quickly it was startling. She confined it to her hand, felt it penetrate deeply. Her skin began to crackle and smoke, then suddenly, the heat abated. The wound was seared closed. After a moment, even that redness faded, leaving her skin unscarred.

"Behold the healing power of Fire," the Dragon said softly.

"Fire, then," said the Emperor. "He was the Flame Dancer."

The advisor nodded, then said hesitantly, "Our men said they saw a woman riding the Dragon, Your Excellency."

"Man, woman, it matters not. What matters is that it was one of them. It is no wonder we were defeated so abysmally. I did not appreciate how powerful she was. We will not fail again."

The advisor blanched. "Lord, she decimated our troops. Nearly half of them are dead, and all of the Arukani captives fled back to their Clans. The pass is blocked with stone that yet smokes. We cannot try again!"

"Not a full assault, no," the Emperor agreed. He glanced down at the imprisoned ki-lyn. "But there are other ways to attack the Dancers. Aren't there, my little friend, hmmm?"

The ki-lyn lowered its head and wept diamond tears.

Chapter Thirty-One

When she met with the *khashims* two days later, who were almost drunk with their victory, Kevla learned that the casualties on the Emperor's side had been high, as high as perhaps ten or twelve thousand. Many of the dead, and some of the living from the Emperor's army, had been Arukani who had been captured in raids and forced to fight. Their return to their families had been moving to behold, they told Kevla.

"I have no doubt," she said. She hesitated, then told them, "The Dragon and I must leave you."

"When?" demanded Terku.

"Tomorrow."

"But we need you!" cried another *khashim*. She looked at her father and saw that his face was impassive, but his eyes sad. "We could not stand against the army without you. If the Emperor attacks again—"

"He won't," Kevla said with certainty. "He knows that I

am here now, and I'm the one he's after. You have learned how to work together. You stood side by side, clan by clan, to defeat a common foe. If you continue to rely on one another, there is nothing you will be unable to do."

She smiled, sadly. "That was Jashemi's dream, and that of at least one *khashim* here. You will be all right without us." Before they could protest further, she stood. "Gather the clans. I would speak to them before I leave."

It took a while, but at last everyone who had come to Mount Bari to stand against the Emperor was present. Kevla had insisted that everyone come, women and children as well as men of all castes. Standing beside her friend the Dragon, she looked out over the sea of upturned faces and was moved by what she saw.

"You have dared so much," Kevla told them. "You have not shirked your duty, and you have paid a painful price for your continued freedom. You have accepted that there are things you did not know before, and have grown to look upon the Lorekeepers as true bearers of wisdom, not as madmen and women. You listened to me, a woman, and followed my counsel. You have learned that the Dragon is very real, and has a kinder heart than some of the laws you attribute to him would indicate.

"All of these things speak to the quality of the people you are. Arukani are passionate and proud. We will not be dominated by the will of outsiders. We will tend to our own, and when we see injuries and injustices, we will heal them. The Great Dragon helped us see the path, and now you have chosen to walk it. You don't need us anymore.

"But there is one thing you need," she continued. "One thing you must reconcile."

She nodded to the Dragon. He raised his head, closed his eyes, and uttered a long, crooning call. Even though

Kevla knew what to expect, the hairs on her arms lifted at the sound.

"It is time for you all to understand the beings that you have called...the *kulis*."

A cry went up. Exhausted and injured as they were, they were not beyond fear. Kevla hoped they would give their eyes time to see, to comprehend, before they acted. She knew she was taking a great risk, but after all she had witnessed over the last several days, she believed her people could be trusted to do the right thing.

They came forth from their hiding places in the mountain. Some of them limped, their legs twisted or missing altogether. Some held withered arms close to their chests. Some had faces that were beautiful and whole; some had faces that were twisted and deformed. Some had eyes that stared vacantly into nothingness. They carried their smaller brethren; their clothing was nothing but scraps of cloth left behind on altars scattered throughout Arukan. They winced in the daylight, denizens of darkness that they were, but they came when their friend the Dragon called. The Dragon, who had taken care of the very first *kulis*, who had fed them and taught them to speak and care for one another.

The murmurings fell silent as the Arukani, after centuries, finally beheld the *kulis* who had so frightened them. The *kulis* in return stared back, their eyes round with terror. Some of them looked as though they were about to flee, to return to the safety of the mountain caves.

"Do you see?" Kevla cried. "Look not with the eyes of fear, but the eyes of understanding...of compassion!"

On the stones of the foothills of Mount Bari, wrapped in pathetic clothing, lean and pale and haggard looking, stood the abandoned children of Arukan.

Kevla went to one of them and took her hand. The girl,

about eight years old, looked up trustingly at the Flame Dancer as their fingers entwined. Kevla stroked her hair.

"For thousands of years, we thought the Dragon wanted us to expose any child born with a withered arm, or without sight or speech, or..."

She gently touched a large red patch on the child's sweet face.

"Or the so-called blood mark. We left them on the altars, and the older ones, the ones abandoned a generation before, and a generation before that, came to take care of them. They ate the food we left for the Dragon, made clothing from the fabric used to wrap that food. And they huddled in the darkness, afraid. As afraid of the Arukani as we were of our created demons."

Still holding the girl's hand, she walked to where Tahmu-kha-Rakyn stood. His eyes were wide and shone with unshed tears.

"For five thousand years," Kevla said, her voice trembling, "the Arukani people have been afraid of their own children."

Tahmu stared at the girl, who looked back shyly at him. Slowly, the *khashim* of the Clan of Four Waters knelt and opened his arms to the daughter he had left lying on the Clan's altar eight years ago.

The girl hesitated, looking up at Kevla.

"Go on, my sister," said Kevla. She looked at Tahmu and smiled. "It's all right. He will take good care of you."

The girl moved forward into her father's embrace, wrapping her arms around him as he folded her close and buried his face in her small, slim neck.

Kevla put her hand to her mouth, fearful of sobbing out loud with joy. She turned to see what the others were doing, and despite her efforts, the tears slipped freely down her face.

One by one, the men and women of Arukan were stepping forward hesitantly, trying to seek out their own lost children, looking first for the distinguishing mark or deformity and then holding on to the whole child. She watched as some continued to search in vain, and pity welled up inside her. For these parents, reconciliation had come too late. Not all the *kulis* survived.

Some of the children hung back, clinging to the older ones and to the Dragon, but Kevla knew in her heart that with time, there would be no more *kulis*. No mother had willingly surrendered the infant suckling at her breast; no father had wanted to place a baby at the foot of a mountain to die. This was a second chance, for all of them.

She did not know how long she stood, watching the reunions and feeling deeply content. A touch on her arm roused her from her reverie, and she turned to see Sahlik.

With a cry of delight, Kevla flung her arms around the old woman. "Sahlik...I am so happy to see you!"

"And I you, child. And I you."

They drew apart and regarded one another with moist eyes. A cough behind them caused them to look up. Tahmu stood there, holding his daughter's hand.

"There is much I would say to you both," he said. "Sahlik...I should have listened to you. You spoke wisdom, and I was too caught up in my own pride to hear it. Much has happened since you took your fifth score."

"I know, my lord," Sahlik said, softening. "I have heard what happened to the *khashimu*...and the *khashima*."

Tahmu reached to stroke his daughter's hair as he continued. "Jashemi and Kevla benefited greatly from your presence in their lives. I...I would that this little one know you, too. Would you consider returning to the House of Four Waters?"

Sahlik's answer was quick and heartfelt. "Of course, my

lord." She smiled slightly. "I have missed the caverns." She
looked from Kevla to Tahmu and pursed her lips shrewdly.
"Let me take—do you have a name, child?"

The girl shook her head shyly.

"I will name her Meli," Tahmu said, "if she likes it." Kevla's
throat closed up. The word meant "gift." "Does that please
you?" he asked the girl.

"Yes," Meli said in a whisper. She spoke with a strange accent; while the Dragon had taught the *kulis* to speak
Arukani, all of them had their own way of uttering the
words that made them unique.

"Come then, Meli," said Sahlik, "and I will tell you all
about life at the House of Four Waters."

Kevla watched them go, smiling. Her father touched her
arm. "Walk with me," he said.

Kevla knew she needed to go, but she couldn't tear herself away just yet. She walked and talked with her father for
a long time. He told her stories of Jashemi she had never
heard, some moving, some amusing, and when he had finished Kevla felt more connected to the man who had been
her brother.

He spoke also of her mother, and Kevla listened hungrily
as he described a woman of passion, beauty, and intelli-
gence. He explained his reasons for marrying Yeshi in
Keishla's stead, and even as he spoke them she realized he
thought them foolish.

Hesitantly Kevla asked, "Where is she? Yeshi?"

"I banished her," Tahmu said. "I couldn't bring myself to
order her death. And now, I am glad I didn't. That is one
less thing to blame myself for." He frowned. "Though there
are so many others."

Kevla chewed on her lip, weighing her words. "Have you
seen my mother since the day you took me with you to the
House?"

Sorrow settled over his fine features. "No," he said. "I thought it best not to. I tried to be a good husband to Yeshi."

She slipped an arm through his as they sat next to each other and laid her head on his shoulder. As they regarded the stars just beginning to appear in the sky, she said, "The world has changed, Father. You have changed with it. Would you want to see Keishla again?"

He closed his eyes. "Yes, I would."

"Then find her."

He looked at her with unspeakable sadness. "It's too late for that," he said heavily. "Far too late. Too late for so many things."

His eyes fell upon Meli. Sahlik was teaching her how to play *Shamizan*. Kevla's own heart ached at the sight.

You like the game, then?

Oh, yes, very much.

I am so glad. I hoped you would.

Her mind returned to the present as Tahmu continued. "I did not have the courage to claim you before, though now I do so with a pride you cannot imagine. I hid you in my house, and I let Yeshi dictate your future. I let you be abused and beaten. When you used your powers to save my life, I ordained your death. I have no excuse but that I thought I was obeying the laws of my people."

"Great lord, there is no need—"

But Tahmu continued. "A caste system that elevates some and condemns more, that exiles its own children, that walks with hushed step and head bowed in shame does not serve Arukan. It serves Arukan's enemies. I have seen the future in the eyes of my three children. One of them, I will never see again, and the pain of that—"

His flowing speech came to an abrupt halt as he bit his lip. In a rough voice, he continued.

"The pain of that can only be equaled by the joy I take

in having my two daughters returned to me. If you will, if I have not made you ashamed to own me as your father, Kevla Bai-sha will henceforth be known as Kevla-sha-Tahmu, the beautiful daughter of a very proud father."

Kevla was shocked. Mixed emotions flooded her. Evading the question, she replied, "I cannot stay. I want to. I want to get to know you, to know my little sister. But I have to leave. Arukan may have been able to stand against the Emperor, but the world is still in jeopardy. I must leave and find the other Dancers."

He sighed, and she knew he had understood her unspoken refusal. "I feared you would say that." He continued watching Meli play with Sahlik. "There's my chance for redemption, Kevla. Sweet and innocent and perfect. I sacrificed her to the Great Dragon, and beyond all hope, he has given her back to me. I used to believe that the Dragon had cursed me, but now I know it was only my own folly." His voice trembled slightly. "I no longer believe in curses, but by all that is good in this world, I believe in blessings."

Kevla was deeply moved. She regarded her father steadily, taking in the strong features that so reminded her of Jashemi.

She squeezed his arm and he turned to look at her. "Tahmu-kha-Rakyn," she said evenly, "I will take your name."

Slowly, his lips curved in a smile. "It was Jashemi's name," he said.

"May his name forever be spoken," Kevla said, as she leaned over and kissed her father's cheek.

The dawn was crisp and bright, a good omen. The clans were preparing for departure, breaking down the encampments. She had assisted them in a solemn duty before she had slept that night; lighting the funeral pyres for the honored dead. There had not been as many as she had feared, but enough so that the task was heartbreaking.

She was walking toward the Dragon, carrying a small bundle of provisions Sahlik had packed for her, when a woman approached her and said, "Kevla-sha-Tahmu?"

The name still sounded so strange, but also very sweet. Kevla turned to see who had addressed her and saw tears in the woman's eyes.

"My name is Shali-sha-Terku." Kevla hoped her face did not register the sudden shock she felt. This was Jashemi's wife, the one he said he did not love, who deserved better.

She found her voice. "I know your name," Kevla said. "You are...you are my brother's widow."

Shali nodded and placed one hand on her belly. She seemed to be a naturally thin woman, yet her stomach was starting to grow round—

"Can you tell me how he died?"

Guilt weighed Kevla down. To confess to this woman that she had lain with her husband, Kevla's own kin, would heal nothing and harm much. And though she had once burned with jealousy for Shali, now that she saw the woman and her pain, the only feeling Kevla had for her sister-in-law was compassion. Yet she could not lie. Gently, Kevla took Shali's hand in her own.

"Jashemi was my Lorekeeper, though neither of us knew it for too long," she said. "He helped me to discover who I truly am. In so doing, I lost control of my powers and...I killed him."

It still hurt her so badly she had difficulty breathing. Shali's hands tightened painfully on hers, squeezing so hard that Kevla wondered if the bones would break.

"You...?"

Kevla nodded. She kept her eyes glued to Shali's. "I have known no greater pain in this life than having to live with this. I didn't *want* to live with it. But I have to, because

Arukan needed me. Other people elsewhere need me, need the Dancers, or else we are all doomed."

"I should hate you," Shali whispered. "You killed my husband, the father of my baby. But I don't. I see your suffering. To have bought your power at such a cost—I do not envy you, Kevla-sha-Tahmu, no matter that you ride the Great Dragon."

Kevla smiled sadly. "Then you are wise indeed, Shali-sha-Terku. The basest beggar on the streets is happier than I."

"Did...did Jashemi speak of me?"

"He did," Kevla said. "He said you deserved better than him."

Shali laughed, though she was starting to cry. "Then Jashemi-kha-Tahmu was a liar. I could have had no better man for my husband in this world."

Shali began to weep in earnest. Her heart breaking for the girl, for both of them, Kevla took her in her arms and hugged her gently. Shali was smaller than she, and Kevla felt the wetness of tears on her shoulder.

"Be easy, sister," Kevla said. "I will tell you this and you may know that it is true: His body is gone, but his soul is free. He would want you to be happy, to raise your child in love and peace."

Your child. Any chance that Kevla had conceived during their single union had been shattered that same night. The fire that had claimed Jashemi had surely also destroyed any seed he might have planted in her womb. If there were to be any heritage from Jashemi, it would come from this woman.

"That is a comfort," said Shali, pulling back and wiping her wet face. "To know that his soul is free."

I'm glad you find it so, Kevla thought. *If only I could take comfort in it.*

"Will you return? To see your niece or nephew?"

"I hope to, but I cannot tell," Kevla said. She bent and kissed Shali on the forehead. "Stay well, my sister. Blessings on the child you carry."

Slowly Kevla walked to where the Dragon waited for her. He looked at her with compassionate eyes and lowered himself to facilitate her climbing atop his back.

Kevla looked around and despite her pain smiled at what she saw. Everywhere, the former *kulis* had found parents or siblings or even strangers to welcome them. Women mixed freely with the men. On the hard-packed, yellow earth were colorful veils some of the women had discarded. Others kept their veils.

Good, Kevla thought. *A woman should be the one who gets to choose to reveal her face or not. At least there is no Great Dragon dictating to her.*

Time would tell if this would last. Old habits were hard to break, and it might take a while before some of the older clansmen learned to accept former demons as children, wives as true partners, and the lower-born among them as equals.

But it was a good start.

"Are you ready, my dear?" said the Dragon, craning his neck to look at her with infinite affection.

She nodded. "I am ready," she said.

Her people cheered her as she rose into the sky, waving goodbye. Kevla saw her father holding Meli's hand in his own large, strong one. He placed his other hand on his heart as their eyes met. And she saw Sahlik, and Shali, rubbing the round belly that was filled with Jashemi's son or daughter.

They would be all right without her. Life would go on here. It was up to her and the other Dancers she was setting out to find to ensure that life went on everywhere in this and other worlds.

She lifted her gaze from the rapidly dwindling images of her people and fixed her eyes on the horizon, her heart lifting with every beat of the Dragon's powerful wings.

* * * * *

Will the Shadow be defeated? Don't miss
IN STONES CLASP,
coming from LUNA Books
in summer 2005!

GLOSSARY

Akana: rider of the Hawk Clan
Arukan: the name of the country
Arukani: native to Arukan
Asha: apprentice to Maluuk, a healer

Bahrim: obsequious *uhlal*
Bai: generic term for Bai-khas and Bai-shas
Bai-kha: "male without father," derogatory term for
  illegitimate boy or man
Bai-sha: "female without father," derogatory term for
  illegitimate girl or woman
Balaan: root, served raw or cooked, particularly
  in stews
Baram: member of the *Sa' abah* Clan

Clan, Cattle
Clan, Horserider
Clan of the Four Waters
Clan, River
Clan, *Sa' abah*
Clan, Sheep
Clan, Star
Clan, Warcry

Dragon, Great: see Great Dragon
Dumah: servant, member of the Clan of the
  Four Waters

eusho: a hot, bitter drink that takes time to prepare

five-score: slave/servants captured in battle. For each
  year they serve, they are "scored" on the arm. At
  the last score, they are freed.

Great Dragon: the keeper of the morals of the people of Arukan

halaan: slang for "prostitute"

Jalik: Second of the Star Clan
Jashemi-kha-Tahmu: Tahmu's son, Kevla's half brother

Keishla: Kevla's mother, a prostitute, Tahmu's great love
Kevla Bai-Sha: illegitimate daughter of Tahmu and Keishla
kha: unit of money, gold
-kha-: "son of"
khashim: Lord of a clan; plural *khashims*
khashima: Lady of a clan
khashimu: the young heir, prince
kurjah: Arukani term for the male organ
kuli: demon

liah: gazelle-like creature

Maluuk: Healer of the Clan of the Four Waters
Melaan: Second of the *Sa' abah* Clan
Mirya: *Sa' abah* tender

Naram: Jashemi's uncle, Yeshi's brother

paraah: sweet, thick-skinned fruit, usually peeled
Pela: Jashemi's aunt, Yeshi's sister-in-law

Raka: young lord of *Sa' abah* Clan
Rakyn: Tahmu's father
Ranna: young handmaiden to Yeshi
rhia: a flowing garment worn by both sexes. Men's rhias are shorter and worn with loose breeches
Rusan: Yeshi's father

sa' abah: desert animals with long, fluffy tails, long legs with broad feet, small "hands" and long ears

Sahlik: head servant of the Clan of the Four waters, five-score

sandcattle: cattle that survive well in the desert

Sammis: Jashemi's cousin

-sha-: "daughter of"

shakaal: long horns, blown at moments of high ceremony or great import

Shamizan: board game with colored glass stones

Sharu: five-score

simmar: big cat of the desert

skuura: female dog; used as an epithet

sulim: Arukani term for female genitalia

Swift-Over-Sand: Tahmu's horse

Tahmu-kha-Rakyn: Kevla's father, *khashim* of the Clan of the Four Waters

Terku: leader of the *Sa' abah* Clan

Tiah: voluptuous handmaiden of Yeshi

uhlal: term of respect; "gentleman" or "sir"

uhlala: female term; "lady" or "ma'am"

Yeshi: wife of Tahmu, mother of Jashemi

Yuma: Jalik's friend

Manhattan's nightlife just got weirder...

Wren Valere has a simple job. She uses her magical powers as a Retriever to find things that are missing and bring them back. But can any job be that simple, especially when magic is involved? Wren's current job, retrieving a missing cornerstone that contains a protective spell, is proving that it can't.

Sometimes what a woman has to do to get the job done is enough to give even Wren nightmares....

On sale July 27.
Visit your local bookseller.

LUNA